THE GHOST DANCE JUDGEMENT

THE GHOST DANCE JUDGEMENT

A NOVEL OF GOLGOTHA

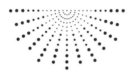

R.S. BELCHER

Charlotte, NC

FALSTAFF
BOOKS
WWW.FALSTAFFBOOKS.COM

This one is for my granddaughter, Torri Belcher.
Welcome to the world, beautiful girl. I can't wait to show you around.

PROLOGUE

THE ACE OF WANDS

August 23rd, 2020

W ill took the access road off of I-95 toward the town at the end of the world. A small sign posted beside the dirt road out into the desert said simply enough, "State maintenance ends here." It got bumpy past the sign. His SUV bucked and dipped as he lost sight of the highway, the only sign of progress, of civilization, out here.

He drove for a little less than an hour, following the dirt road the desert had done its damnedest to devour. A few times he thought he was lost and had to get out, get his bearings, and backtrack. GPS was useless out here.

Every time he tried to feed the coordinates into his phone, the app came back with a crazed voice that was not the calm, automated, female tone he was used to. It was the normal voice but in a frenzy, spitting and uttering words in some guttural language that made the reptile part of his brain twist and squirm and made his ears itch from the inside, like ants were crawling into his skull.

After several tries, and a notification from his phone that he had no service, and that his immortal soul was damned if he continued on, Will turned the phone off. A cut of a smile crossed his face. At least he knew he was headed in the right direction.

The road widened and the hills flattened out, and he saw her, saw the town. He slowed as he passed long-neglected fields and the collapsing shell of a farmhouse. This place was southeast of the Humboldt River, and it probably had gotten its irrigation from underground tributaries. The road was still unpaved, but it was clear. On either side of it he could see old, crumbling buildings, like the ribs of a starvation victim, jutting out.

At the edge of the town, there was a line of high, chain-link fence that had once encircled the town. It was crowned with tangles of rusty barbed wire. The fence was in disrepair, rusted, and falling in on itself. The gate that had once barred entrance to the town was long gone. Mounted on a section of the fence was a sun-faded sign that said, "WARNING: It is unlawful to enter this area without the permission of the United States government. USE OF DEADLY FORCE IS AUTHORIZED." Just beyond the fence and the ominous warning, on the other side, was a large rectangular sign that he suspected had seen its best days back in the 1920s. It said simply, "Welcome to Golgotha, Nevada: An oasis in the desert."

He drove past the fence. Golgotha welcomed him like a lonely old spinster, eager for any company. The buildings along what had been Main Street were a mishmash of simple clapboard shacks and businesses, many with sagging, dangerous-looking covered porches. They looked like they were probably a century and a half old. Other structures looked like they had been built later, probably in the twenties.

To his right, there was a fenced-in drive-in theater, its massive screen's canvas skin peeling off and hanging limply to the frame beneath. Islands of gravel held rows of speaker posts that reminded him of tombstones in a graveyard. The marquee, which looked like it had been very stylish in the space-age fifties, announced that the Mephisto Drive-in Theater was proud to present a double feature: *It, the Terror from Beyond Space,* and *The Thing that Couldn't Die.* Many of the red plastic letters had fallen off the sign.

He drove past a partially collapsed building that announced it had once been Shultz's General Store and Butcher Shop and spied ahead on his left a gas station convenience store that looked like it came from the seventies or eighties. There was a placard out front that announced gas prices that were appropriately usurious for a gas station in the middle of a desert wasteland. The neon sign in the window glowed a cherry red and announced the place was open. He pulled up and parked. Out front, there was an old military jeep and a scooter with an orange plastic milk crate bungee-corded onto the rear bumper. Both were covered with a thick coat of desert dust.

After the relative cool of the AC, the heat hit him like a baseball bat when he opened the car door. You had to be careful running your AC out here, but he had brought spare coolant and plenty of water. Even on low AC, the difference between the car and outside was stunning and immediate. He wondered how the hell folks in wagons had survived the crossing to California and Utah in this heat.

A little brass bell attached to the door tinkled as he opened it. The industrial AC was humming along inside the convenience store, and the claws of the desert's heat were forced to release him and wait outside to pounce on him again. The place looked like it served many purposes for the folks who still lived around here. There were rows of shelves, like a grocery store, with chips, laundry detergent, pet food, car repair products, and snake bite kits.

A prominent display of cheap southwest souvenirs included lots of turquoise and silver jewelry; t-shirts with wolves on a mesa, howling at the bright, full moon; lighters; string ties; plastic rattlesnake and cattle skulls; and black velvet prints featuring stoic Native Americans in completely the wrong headdresses and clothes for their tribe's ceremonies.

There were spinning racks of cheap toys, candy, beef jerky, trail mix. The coolers had every imaginable color, flavor, and type of alcohol. He paused at a wire spinner full of cheap old paperbacks, some

3

seventies-looking porno, pulp westerns, a smattering of audiobooks, and a hodgepodge of lurid titles designed to appeal to truckers like *The Brotherhood of the Wheel* and *King of the Road* penned by some obscure author.

"Afternoon," a voice said with a timbre as rich and smoky as good pipe tobacco. "What brings you out here?" He turned to see a man now behind the counter. He hadn't been there a moment ago. He was tall and slender. His black hair was long and tied back into a ponytail. He had a neatly trimmed, short, black beard. The man wore a pair of old jeans and a faded Led Zeppelin t-shirt with the band's logo above a faceless angel, back arched, arms raised toward heaven, either in pleading or defiance. His eyes were darker than night.

"Good afternoon," Will replied, slipping his badge off his belt and showing his credentials to the cashier. The cashier looked at him oddly, a sense of recognition, then a slight nod as if something suddenly made sense to him. He scanned the badge and the federal ID.

"Secret Service? We don't get too many of you folks out this way."

"I'm surprised," he said. "This is federal land. I didn't expect to find anyone out here still."

"Oh, that," the cashier said. "The military lost interest in this place back in the early seventies. They don't seem to mind us being out here still."

"No offense, Mr..."

"Bick," the cashier said, "Marcus Bick."

"No offense, Mr. Bick, but why would anyone want to be out here?"

"Everybody's got to be somewhere. My...family owned all this land until the government seized it in the late fifties. It's my home, has been for a long time. You could say I'm rather attached to the place. Golgotha tends to grow on you, Agent...?"

"Negrey," he said, "Will Negrey. Will's just fine. No, no, I do understand that. In fact, I guess, in a way, me being here in Golgotha is kind of a homecoming. I'm out here on a little bit of a family genealogy project."

"Do tell," Bick said.

"I understand a relative of mine, my great-great-grandfather, was a lawman in this town back in the late 1800s."

"That would be Jim Negrey," Bick said. "Yes, he was. Rather prominent, too, in his day."

"You know the town's history?"

"Intimately. Like I said, Agent Negrey, my family has been here for a very long time." Bick stepped out from behind the counter. "You might say I'm Golgotha's unofficial historian. Here, let me show you a few things that might interest you." Bick led Will farther back into the store.

They passed a small, carpeted room with a tinted glass wall and door. Inside, Will saw a scrawny old woman wearing a dirty shift dress with a faded floral pattern. Her skin was wrinkled and leathery, her hair, a tangled gray mop. She was playing one of the three electronic poker machines in the room. The wall opposite the poker games had three slot machines.

On one side of the store was a small café of sorts, with a cluster of chipped and stained Formica tables and vacuum-molded plastic chairs of orange and blue. One wall of the café had windows looking out on the parking lot, the gas tanks, and the decaying carcass of Main Street. Another wall was covered with framed pictures, all of them exceedingly old. Will scanned the photos of Golgotha's streets teeming with people and prosperous, thriving businesses. He placed the time period as the late 1800s. He spotted one photo of a group of men posing before a building whose window identified it as the Golgotha Bank and Trust. Will noticed one of the men, dressed head to toe in black finery, and looked over to Marcus.

"One of my relatives," Bick said. "Malachi Bick. He owned a saloon on this very spot."

"You're the spitting image," Will said. Bick smiled.

"There's a resemblance," he said. "Speaking of spitting images, I think this is what you're looking for." Bick walked a few feet over and showed Will a photo of a group of people posing in front of an ugly, brick, block building with a short, covered porch, a great iron door, and bars on the windows. Like all the photos of the time, the subjects had to stand still long enough for the image to be burned onto the photographic plate. The subjects posed, their faces, frozen. They each wore a lawman's star, proudly, and prominently.

The man at the fore was tall and handsome with a square jaw and a kerchief around his neck. To his right was a shorter man, a Native American with a weathered face and crooked beak of a nose. A sardonic smile played at the edges of his cruel mouth. There was something surreal about the Indian, Will thought, as if the man might wink at him and leap from the picture at any moment. To the tall man's left was a woman with brown hair, pulled back tightly. She wasn't plain, nor was she beautiful. She had the kind of face that would blend seamlessly into a crowd and slip out of memory. She wore dark pants and a short bolero jacket. Beside the native man was a tall teenager with a kind, open face and a natural smile. Will recognized the boy's face. He saw an older version of it in the mirror each morning.

"Sheriff Jon Highfather," Bick said, "and his deputies: The Washoe, We'lmeti outcast, Mutt; Kate Warne, the first female private detective in the United States; and your great-great-grandfather, Jim Negrey. They kept the peace in Golgotha during many tumultuous years."

"When...when was this taken?" Will asked, leaning closer to the photo, looking intently at his ancestor.

"Around...1871, 1872, as I recollect," Bick said. Will glanced at him. "At least, that was what I was told," the clerk added, almost as an afterthought. "Sometime shortly before the Ghost Dance incident."

"1870s?" Will said. "The Ghost Dance movement began in the 1890s." It was Bick's turn to give a stare of incredulity. "Everybody's read *Bury my Heart at Wounded Knee* in school, right?"

"There was an older movement, upon which the second Ghost Dance movement was born out of," Bick said, pulling out a plastic chair and gesturing to Will to sit. The federal agent did, and Bick joined him. "It started with a Paiute mystic, named Hawthorne

Wodziwob, and it began around these parts," Bick said. "As was so often the case in those days, Golgotha was smack dab in the middle of the trouble. You hungry, Mr. Negrey?"

"Pretty much always," Will said. Bick smiled.

"Let me buy you lunch and tell you a story."

EIGHT OF CUPS (REVERSED)

September 12, 1854

She ran as fast as she could, from the death at her back, but she couldn't escape the horror waiting behind her eyes. They had come before dawn, the hooves of their horses shaking the ground. It was their rumbling that woke her. It was late summer, so everyone was still sleeping in the cooler brush shelters.

They began to set fire to the rush-and-grass-covered huts as they rode by. Her father's strong hands scooped her up out of her bed. She heard many hushed and panicked voices in the darkness of the shelter. Outside was the crackle of mad fires, the blast of gunfire, and the screams of the dying.

"The damned federals," her uncle, Tooele, hissed, fumbling for his rifle. "They must think we're the damned Ute. Stupid *taipo!*"

Her father kissed her mother and then planted a gentle kiss on her forehead, too. He took up a rifle. He looked to her mother. "Take the children. Run as fast as you can and stay low. Go to old Cameahwait's hut out by the grazing patch. Warn them, and all of you ride as far away as fast as you can."

She smelled the acrid sting of smoke and snorted it out. There was another smell—sweet, greasy—like cooking meat. The child saw how her mother looked at her father, and she grew even more afraid. "I will meet you at the old man's place, with anyone we can free," Father said to Mother. She held him tight; the little girl clung to him, too. "*Ne en tepitsi tsaa suankanna,*" he said to them. He didn't have to; they knew how much he loved them. "Now, run!" he said, and they did.

It was the child, her cousins, her mother, and her aunts; they did as Father had said. They stayed low and hurried toward the edge of the village. Fire capered about like a drunken vandal, making the shadows shiver and jump. The most horrible noises and smells were everywhere, smearing the air. The whites' preachers spoke of a terrible place called Hell. The child wondered if she and her family had fallen into that evil place. Mother held her hand tight as they sped away from the only home the child had ever known.

"What did we do?" one of her cousins asked softly. They watched the mounted soldiers cut down their neighbors and family as they fled their burning homes. The child saw a man running. He was on fire. He staggered, crying out in pain, and then dropped and burned silently. "Why are they doing this to us? We've done nothing!"

"Because we were foolish," one of her aunts said, the anger tight and cold in her voice. "We treated them as neighbors, as equals, as human beings. They're animals. We should have wiped them out when we had the chance."

"Hush," her mother said to her sister. "The children do not need to hear such..." She never got to finish. The child felt the hot splash on her face. Her mother's hand gripped hers tightly, squeezing. Then the thunder of the gun arrived. Mother's hand slipped loose from hers as she fell to the grass. The child looked into what was left of her mother's face. All reason left the world.

"No!" her aunt screamed as the federal cavalryman fired again and again. Angry bees whined all around the little girl. Her aunt, her cousins, her mother all torn apart around her. She saw the soldier's face; the dancing flames made him look like a *co'a-ppiccih,* a monster, as he cocked the lever on his gun and fired again and again. The soldier, the white man, took aim on her, the last one standing.

The little girl did not even know the word for "hate," had no idea of its meaning, but she felt something rise up in her as she felt her mother's blood dripping down her face, tasted it on her lips. The feeling consumed her like the fire devouring the homes. She clenched her tiny fists, and she screamed at the soldier, at the world, at the heavens, with the purest form of hatred ever known. The soldier clutched his chest as his rifle fell from numb hands. His eyes rolled back in his head, and he fell from his horse, quite dead.

The child looked around. She felt like she was sunburned on the inside. She was glad the murderer, the thing that looked like a person but wasn't, was dead, and she was glad she had done it. She wished she could kill them all, kill all the whites, every last one. She felt ugly for a moment, thinking such a thing, hearing her mother's voice, like cool water, trying to quench the fire inside her. Then she hugged the dead meat that had been her mother, and she was no longer ashamed of what she was feeling. She ran toward the old man's house. She never saw her father again.

Outside Cameahwait's hut, she hid in the bushes as she watched the soldiers drag the old, crippled widower out of his hut and set it ablaze. When he cursed them and shook his fist at them, they shot him in the head without a word and rode back toward the false dawn that was the burning village. She ran, ran from the fires, ran from the whites, from the madness and death. She ran and never wanted to stop running.

The days across the basin were exquisite in their cruelty. The heat gnawed on the child, devouring her slowly. Her skin was red, swollen, and blistered. Her tongue was dry and dead in her mouth. Her stomach ached with hunger, and her feet were cut and burned as she staggered through the wasteland. The nights were equally a nightmare, frozen and full of dangerous predators. Even tears were denied to her in this awful place. The girl staggered along, no idea where she was going or why she was even going on.

Then, the memory of her parents, her family, and friends would swim into her dizzy, humming, pain-filled brain, and she would remember why she would live. She was the last, the only survivor of what the whites had done, the only one who could make them pay. The rage would balloon up in her and give her the fuel for another step, and then another. She summoned the anger to move forward, to refuse to die and give the *taipo* final victory.

"Hello, little one," a voice said as she stumbled on through the desert. She paused and looked around. "Over here, child," the voice said again. She looked and saw a snake coiled on a stone off to her left. The snake had the most beautiful scales she had ever seen. They refracted the light of the sun into a scintillating rainbow of brilliant colors.

"Hello," the little girl croaked. "How can you talk?"

"All things speak," the snake said, "but only the wise can hear. My name is Dogoa; some call me Snake. I am here to help you. I heard your scream across the worlds. You possess very strong medicine, did you know that?" The little girl shook her head. "In time, I will teach you some secrets, but first, I want you to study with some other teachers. Would you like that?" She nodded. It was so hard to talk. "Walk in the direction of that rock way over there on the horizon that looks like a man's head. When you reach there, you will meet your teachers." The girl smiled as best she could; it felt like her skin was splitting as she did.

"Thank you," she said.

"We will meet again, child," Snake said. "Study well."

The child struggled on, buoyed by the thought of arriving at the boulder she began to call the Giant's Head. It took another day, and by the time she arrived, night was falling. She was so weak, so sick, she thought she would die.

Just past the Giant's Head was the great face of a mountain. In the rock surface was the yawning maw of a large cave. She thought she heard voices in the impenetrable darkness inside. The girl climbed the sharp rocks, her feet leaving a trail of blood in her wake. Just outside the cavern, the voices stilled, shushing each other, as they heard her approach.

"Who's there?" a voice in the gloom asked.

"Snake sent me," she said. It was so hard to make her tongue and throat work. "He said you could help me, teach me?"

"Did he?" another voice asked. "Well, isn't he a clever one. He fears to come to our lodge, afraid we will not allow him to leave, so he sends a child to harvest our secrets for him. His wit is as sharp as his fangs."

"Please," the girl said. "I'm cold, hungry, and I'm so tired. I don't think I can go any farther."

"You are close to crossing over," the first voice said, "but then it would be too late to teach you. You would know our wisdom then, but never be able to return to the sunlight lands with it."

"Why do you want our medicine, want our wisdom, child?" the second voice asked, almost accusingly. The girl tried to think, to form words, but it was so hard.

"I...everything hurts," she said. "I hurt inside and out. My memories hurt me. My family were all killed...my mother...this is my mother's blood on my face." She wanted to cry, but the only place she could was inside herself. "There is no place that doesn't hurt. I just don't want to hurt anymore."

"Pain tells you that you are alive," the first voice said. "Pain is a gift."

"I don't want the stupid gift," she said. "I don't want to be alive anymore."

"Well, you are," the second voice said, "barely, but alive. You can't come in here alive, girl."

"Let us talk with the others," the first voice said. "Wait there, girl." So, she did. She heard many voices, soft like wind, cold and sharp like stone. They argued and debated and went around and around. At some point, she blacked out. A voice, the first voice, coaxed her back to awareness.

"Child, child, awake!" it said. "We have decided to welcome you into our lodge, even though you still live. We will teach you all our secrets, all our medicine." The moon was out, bloated and scraping on the desert floor. Its light held her as gently as her mother had.

"Just know, girl," the second voice said, "there is no food here. We do not eat, though hunger gnaws at us like a rat. There is no heat here, no warmth. Your bones, your blood, will be as ice."

"I understand," she said. "I...I have nowhere else to go. What brought me to you, what kept me moving across the desert, it will sustain me."

"Your hatred?" the second voice said. "Yes. It will keep you warm and fill your belly. There are many of us here that it sustains, many who suffered the same fate as your people."

"You will be our door into the warmth of the living world," the first voice said. "We will...help each other."

"Thank you," she said, her voice weak and nearly as soft as the voices in the cave.

"Enter, and we shall begin," the second voice said.

The child pulled herself up to stand, and on wobbly, burned legs she stepped into the cave. In a moment, the cold, yawning darkness had swallowed her whole, and even the moon could not find her.

THE THREE OF SWORDS

Nevada, March 9th, 1872
Eighteen Years Later

Dawn was an angry red scar on the back of the night as the Paiute hunters rode out of the village. They were organized into two parties; their silhouettes, mounted on their horses, were dark against the lightening sky. Amos Bagley and his brother, Braxton, remained still in the cold, damp grass, lying flat, looking down into the valley until the Indians had long vanished behind a ridge.

The sky brightened, and Amos and Braxton carefully slipped back down the hill from which they had observed the Paiute village and the hunters' departure. The other men were waiting on horseback behind the bottom of the hill. There were a dozen of them, all Mormons, all armed.

"They're gone," Amos said. "We wait about another twenty minutes or so to make sure. You sure this is the way you want to do it, Dal?"

Dallen Shumway was a raw-boned man with a wind-chafed face

from years of working the land. Shumway was about ten years Amos's senior. Dal gave Bagley a sour look. "You losing your sand, Amos?"

"No, no," Bagley said. "I just don't cotton to harming women, children, and elders. It seems wrong."

"Need I remind you," Dallen said, "how many times we've tried to minister to and live in peace with the Lamanites?" A hushed grumble of agreement drifted among the men. Dallen, spurred on by the encouragement, pointed in the direction of the village on the other side of the hill. "We've paid them for the land we settled, because they had some ridiculous notion that all this land is theirs! We've traded with them, extended them credit. Even tried to save their savage souls. And what did we receive in repayment? They've poached our grazing land, stolen our horses, our crops, our livestock. Their barbarous brothers have even attacked other settlements, killed our brothers and sisters."

"I heard those were other tribes," Braxton said, coming to his brother's aid, "Shoshone, maybe some of those damned Ute from across the border in Utah."

"They're all the same," Dal said. "Their souls are lost to their witchcraft and their animal passions. Why are we even debating this again, Amos, especially now?"

Amos wanted to say he was only trying to point out that they were about to do to these people the same thing Dal was accusing them of doing to their people. This all seemed wrong, sad, insane, and not in keeping with the teachings of the church. Instead, he said nothing and swallowed down his shame.

"No more, I say!" Elias Brookman, a rancher who had lost many horses and cattle to Indian theft, said. "We all agreed this was the only way they'll get the message and move along. Dallen's right. We've tried to make these people understand. All they understand is force."

"Let's teach these thieving Lamanites a lesson," Shumway said. He was speaking to everyone, but he was looking straight at Amos. A murmur of angry agreement passed through the men. "We chose you to lead us, Bagley. Now what say you?" Amos nodded and mounted his horse. Braxton mounted his as well.

"Aye," Amos said to all the men. "I'll do what I agreed to do." In his mind, a quiet voice that felt right and true whispered, *This is wrong.*

The party of men, many of them not much more than boys, had ridden out from Ezekiel. It was a small settlement with a handful of families. The people of Ezekiel carved out a living as best they could from what they could plant and by raising sheep and cattle. The past few years had been difficult ones, especially with the encroachments of the Lamanites, the Indians, on their land.

The Book of Mormon told that the Indians were descendants of the Israelites who came to America six hundred years before the birth of Christ. At first, the church saw it as its duty to bring redemption to the Indians. Mormons in Utah had gone so far as to lease the lands they settled from the Lamanites, but as disputes over the limited resources in this unforgiving land led to more and more conflicts, word came down from the church and its leader, Brigham Young. This land belonged to the Mormon people by divine right, and as holy land, it was worth defending.

Disputes that had been handled peaceably for years were being handled by the gun more and more often. Brigham Young, the leader of the Mormon faith, had sent out militia forces from Salt Lake City to deal with the Indian problem before. The people of Ezekiel were tired of the theft, tired of their hard lives being made harder by the Lamanites, and unwilling to wait any longer for an answer to their long-ago-sent pleas for help from Salt Lake City. They had even reached out to the Mormon mayor of the town of Golgotha for help with the problem. Golgotha's mayor, Harry Pratt, was said to be the living fulfillment of a Mormon prophecy—the One Mighty and Strong—and had fought many battles to protect the faithful in his charge. But their letters to Golgotha remained unanswered. Finally, the men of Ezekiel had taken it upon themselves to recruit a militia of their own.

"Enough time has passed. Their warriors are gone. Let's go," Amos Bagley said. He didn't feel right about this, but what could be done?

The raiders cleared the hill, came into view of the village, and saw the dancing flames of its morning cook fires in the gray-hued dawn. The horses thundered down across the fields, trampling the village's crops as they hit the flatland. The women of the village, seeing the riders coming, called out and began to hurry the children and the elderly into the wickiups, their huts made of sticks and covered with thick grasses. The riders from Ezekiel began to open fire on the fleeing villagers.

Braxton heard the cry first, carried on the cold morning wind. He glanced over to Amos, who nodded he was hearing the sound too. Soon, the whole raiding party was looking about, trying to find the source of the blood-curdling shrieks. Braxton saw them first. They were riding toward the Mormons, the ascending sun at their backs. "Dear Lord," Braxton called out, "what in heaven's name are they?" The riders turned their horses to face the new threat closing on them out of nowhere. Their horses screamed in maddening fear at what was coming.

"Open fire!" Amos shouted to his fellows. The riders opened up with pistols and rifles in a bellow of gunfire and drifting blue clouds of gun smoke. The volley of gunfire did nothing to slow or fell any of the approaching attackers. Their shouts and yips were like ice raking along the spines of the Mormon militiamen.

The spectral tide raced toward the men of Ezekiel. Layton Snow and his sons fired into them, panicking as the bullets did nothing. The rays of the morning sun passed through the attackers as if they were glass. Their war cries grew louder as they barreled down on the Mormon invaders. A young farmer named Oman Peterson was the first to die, ghostly arrows piercing his throat. Next was the shopkeeper, William Kimball, cut down by phantom bullets that left bloody, ragged holes in their wake. Snow and his boys were slaughtered in a flurry of axes and clubs.

Amos and the surviving raiders formed up a circle to try to defend themselves as their horses screamed and bucked, terrified by the attackers. They fired into their tormentors, but none fell; it was like shooting air. More shrieks smeared the wind as the two Paiute hunting parties who had ridden off at dawn now reappeared, charging in to join the ongoing attack on the Mormon raiders, flanking them. The Paiute fired toward Amos and his men, their bullets passing harmlessly through the seeming immaterial attackers, but striking true to wound and kill several of the white men.

"They're going to kill us all!" Shumway screamed a second before a tomahawk was buried in his skull.

"Run! Split up!" Amos shouted to the surviving men. "Head for home! We have to warn everyone!" They tried to break through the lines of the unexplainable, unearthly force circling them, a translucent, whirling barrier of blurred, angry faces, a wall made of rage. The Mormons suffered more injuries and death for their effort. Amos saw Braxton pulled from his terrified horse by non-existent hands. He lost sight of his brother.

Amos broke through the line, bleeding, wounded, but still alive. He wondered for a second what he'd tell Braxton's wife, his brother's children, their elderly mother.

He spurred his horse to a full gallop, not looking back to see if any other survivors were following him. He reached the top of the hill that had hidden them as they had prepared to lay waste to the Lamanites' village. What he saw today had to be reported to the church, to the army. He had to warn everyone back at the homestead. A thought struck him an instant before the bullet did. Were these shimmering, translucent opponents that had seemed to ride out of the sun itself, were they angels? Had they been sent by the Almighty to punish them for wishing to do harm to his children? He'd never receive an answer, at least not in this life.

A bullet ripped through Amos's spine, reducing his heart to pulp. He never knew if it was the living Indian warriors that ended his life or one of the dead. In the end, it made no difference; a bullet is a bullet, and dead is dead. Amos Bagley fell from his saddle and lay still, unmoving on the hillside.

An uneasy cheer came up from the Paiute villagers and the hunting parties as the last attacker died. The ghostly army rode past the village. Clothed in the dress of a dozen different tribes and nations, raising their weapons in a victory salute before they rode away, evaporating like the morning dew.

The spirits' victory cries hung on the cold morning air like the breath that plumed from the living and then faded. The flesh-and-blood hunting parties entered the village. They dismounted, hugging and kissing their loved ones, their wives, children, mothers, and fathers.

The Paiute made their decisions as a group with one usually selected to act as a speaker for the whole. A man named Kajika, the leader of the band's braves, was speaker. Kajika was tall and well-muscled with kind, thoughtful eyes. He had a little scar under his left eye from an accident when he was a boy. Kajika was well-known as a gentle soul, who often carried his young daughter around on his shoulders and sang to her. He was not one who was quick to anger or rash to act. He had not wanted to be the speaker, but several elders had told him that made him perfect for the job.

Kajika noticed the restrained cheer, an almost timid response of the village to the uncharacteristic carnage. They were afraid, afraid of the ghost warriors and their herald, and they feared what was to come next when the whites retaliated. Kajika understood the fear. He shared it to an extent.

The Paiute were nomads, usually camping near the banks of water, traveling a circuit of sorts, following the water and the game. It had been their way for as long as anyone could remember, but the world had changed, and they had been forced to change with it. The white men claimed those lands as theirs, now, used them for their animals, their farms. They didn't share and they didn't move on. Kajika's father, his grandfather and great grandfather, and further back than that had all had walked these lands and called them home. None of that seemed to matter to the relative newcomers.

Kajika slipped from his horse's back and dropped to the ground. He wore a buckskin shirt and pants with a coat of fringed hide. He carried a long, sharp blade at his belt that had been his father's and before that, his grandfather's, and he carried a rifle in his hand that he had traded from a Mormon for two bushels of pine nuts long ago.

For many years, the Paiute and the Mormons had lived peacefully. They had traded with one another. The Mormon teachers had shared their beliefs of their god and prophets, and many Paiute had accepted their faith, finding much good within it. In addition, like all good neighbors, they stayed out of each other's business. That had all changed. The Mormons and the other whites were pushing the Numu, the Paiute people, and all the other tribes off the land. They no longer bartered or traded; they gave orders, and they took what they wanted. The Paiute could fight, but they preferred not to. However, as they were pushed farther and farther from the lands they had always called home, more young braves bristled to address the injustice.

The celebration ended when the Goshute shaman stepped out from the darkness of one of the wickiups. She was tall, almost eye-to-eye with Kajika, the tallest of the braves. Her raven hair came to her knees. She wore a cloak of woven rabbit pelts and a rainbow-hued belt made of snake skins from which hung six black feathers and her medicine pouch. Her face and her naked skin were covered in dried mud into which she had drawn symbols of *buha*—power.

"See?" she said to the assembled village. Her voice was strong, beautiful, but it held a coldness. "The spirits speak the truth. They told you, through me, the *toha* were coming today, and now their bodies lay in the field, and your village still stands; your loved ones still breathe." The village murmured in agreement.

The Goshute woman, whose name was Izusa, had come to them a few weeks ago. She told them that the army had attacked her band many years ago when she was a child. She was one of the few not killed or captured by the federal soldiers. Izusa told Kajika and his people about the round dance. It was the same dance the Paiute elder, Wodziwob, had showed them years ago. Wodziwob was well-respected as a mystic, and there were many stories about his time on the mountaintops, communing with the spirits. They had showed him in visions the dance ritual that could bring about the departure of the whites. Wodziwob and his followers had been traveling around Nevada, California, and Utah for a long time, urging tribes to join in the dances.

"Listen to what Izusa says," Kajika said to his fellow villagers. "She's been right so far. The spirits of our friends and family, of all the tribes, have saved us; she has saved us."

"The dance has saved you," Izusa said, looking from face to face. "The dead hear it, and they rise to fight beside their people, all our people. The medicine of the dance will grow in power, as the medicine of the white man's god will grow weaker and weaker. We will drive the invaders out of this land, and it will be as it was before they came!"

Another cheer went up from the Paiute, this one more enthusiastic. While most didn't like the idea of slaughtering anyone, almost all of them dreamed of the whites getting chased back to the far-off lands they came from. Izusa looked toward the field, to the dead white men and their wandering horses.

"Take from the murderers all that they possess," she said. "Their horses, their guns, their bullets. You'll need them. Once you have taken your portion, skin them, and leave their bodies for Old Man Vulture and his family to eat. We will purify the land of the whites as Vulture purifies the world by eating the dead. Place the whites' skins on the plains, where they will flutter like flags, a warning to the white men, to their armies, that these lands are not theirs."

Another cheer and even Kajika felt the words move his spirit. The villagers went about the tasks set to them. Kajika watched as his family and friends looted the dead. They stripped their bodies and prepared to skin them like animals. *This is wrong*, he thought to himself. There were some in the village who had questioned Izusa and her talk of war, but they did so quietly in the deep of night in whispers around the fires. Izusa possessed much *buha*, and that was a good reason to respect and even fear her. Power gave the right to lead. Since her recent arrival, Izusa had shown many times the strength of her medicine. She had blessed the foraging and hunting parties and they had better than usual luck. She had healed one of the elders from one of the new sicknesses that had come to the land with the whites. One night, she made the stars in the sky move at her command. Izusa walked between worlds. The dead did as she commanded, and they whispered in her ear. The round dances she called for all the village to undertake were from the ancient times long, long before the white men had come. Wodziwob had said the dances possessed power to change the world, and Izusa had shown them exactly how much power that was.

"Have your men rested and ready to ride by sunset," Izusa said to Kajika. She was suddenly beside him. Had he simply been lost in his own thoughts and not heard her approach, or had she somehow magically appeared at his side? "We will take these assassins' homes and families from them as they would have done to you and yours." Kajika paused, a question on his lips. "Yes?" the medicine woman asked him, "*hainch ki-tum-ar-g?*"

"I'm...unsure killing more whites, especially those who are not warriors, is...wise," Kajika said. "They have many guns in that Mormon settlement, and they can summon aid from others of their faith, and the army."

The witch's face of mud cracked as she spoke. "The bullets will be as air to you and your braves," Izusa said. "You will be half in the spirit world, and they cannot harm you there with their lead, with anything. Trust in the spirits if you do not trust in me. They will guide your hand and stay the enemy's bullets. We have armies at our disposal as well. Let the whites come. It makes killing them easier when they deliver themselves to us."

"The Mormons' god has grown strong in these lands," the speaker said. "We hear stories of them building great, glittering domed fortresses in the lands of the Shoshone and the Ute. Are you sure..."

"Doubt will kill you," Izusa said. "You saw with your own eyes today the *buha* that now stands with us. They stand with us because we entreat them back to this world with the round dance. They return for justice and for revenge against the aliens."

"But Wodziwob said..." Kajika began.

"Wodziwob is an old man," Izusa said, a trickle of anger at the edge of her words. "He jumps at thunder and pisses himself in the rain. His way is not the way of the spirits. I speak for them, not him. We will fight with our fallen people to drive the *toha* away. The other tribes will join us. We will drive the whites into the distant sea in the lands of the Shawnee and the Cherokee. They will return to their own filthy, diseased lands and never come back. Put fear and doubt out of you, Kajika. The spirits will be with you tonight, and I swear you will not lose a single brave. We will be victorious. Who can stand against the spirits?"

Kajika nodded. "You are right, of course," he said. "You have saved my family, my people. Thank you. We will be ready to ride at sunset." He started to walk away.

"And Kajika," Izusa said. The eldest of the village braves turned back. "No survivors tonight," the witch said. "No women, no children. Slaughter even their dogs...but take their horses. Burn it all. The dead cry out for blood and vengeance."

Kajika felt his legs tremble at this. His inner voice told him that something was wrong with Izusa, that she was sick in her heart. Again came the doubt, the uncertainty that this was the best path for his band, for his people, to follow. This slaughter felt wrong to him. The medicine woman's eyes bore into his own. Kajika saw no pity there, only...excitement? Finally, he nodded. He didn't feel right about this, but what could he do?

"The dead...will have their blood," Kajika said, and then went on his way, preparing his braves for the ugly work ahead.

The shaman watched Kajika walk away. The speaker, for all his prowess as a brave, was full of questions and conflict, but he would carry out her will, the will of the spirits. She watched as the first of the vultures lighted down to claim their meat from the bodies of the dead Mormons. For a moment, the huge birds looked like women to Izusa. Women with long, beautiful, braided hair, gore-splattered golden mail, and bloody talons in place of hands and feet. They partly concealed their faces behind hunched, massive, angel-like wings, as they pecked and chewed, tore and feasted on the fallen men. The sounds they made as they fed thrilled her. Izusa blinked, and they were birds again.

Already, some of Kajika's men were moving out across the field to begin the process of skinning the dead Mormons. The vultures grudgingly gave up their feast. They flew a short distance away to wait patiently for the braves to depart.

Izusa thought of her vision of the vulture women as a good sign. More tribes would join them in the dance, and in the war. The dead would continue to grant them favor and rise to fight beside them. They had told her so. The land would be free of the white thieves. They would either leave on their own, or they would be forced off the lands they had taken. Either way, she knew there would be blood, enough blood for the spirits, for the dead, to become drunk upon it.

In her body, in her soul, Izusa felt the terrible *Uktena*, the great horned serpent, stir in its cave at the heart of the world, aroused by her dreams of slaughter, stirring to the song of war. Perhaps the *Uktena* could be roused to join their cause as well. Izusa smiled as the vultures patiently waited to resume their meal, the first of many they would enjoy.

THE HANGED MAN

Nevada, March 18th, 1872

She perched at the jagged fringes of death, of the 40-Mile Desert, her scarred arms always open, beckoning, for those who had traveled this brutal land. Some came seeking a better life for themselves or their children. Others followed the siren call of gold and silver, dreaming of wealth and power. Some were burying an old life, an old name, or running from their past, the stain of former sins, hoping to start again, clean. Many came chewed up by the war, seeking solace, a place where they could make peace with their demons, or at least let them run free. They all came west.

First, there was the 40-Mile; there was the hungry, pitiless desert. Every year, they came struggling to survive to reach the promised lands. Even with the new Transcontinental Railroad, many couldn't afford to travel by such fine means, such relative safety. So, they came in wagons; they came on horseback, in stagecoaches, on foot. They heard her midnight call; they struggled to reach her, to feel her embrace.

If she was hope, then she was a hope born in Hell, born of pilgrims full of promise and faith, greed and cynicism, the best and the worst. She called out to all of them, gave them all the same promises, that she would nurture them at her bosom, give them the same chances they'd have in a square card game, and to always, always keep their secrets. Her name was Golgotha, and she welcomed all comers, the blessed and the damned.

It was high noon when The Man Who Couldn't Die arrived at the house that had drawn blood. Sheriff Jon Highfather and his deputy, former secret service agent, Kate Warne, rode up to an audible sigh of relief from the crowd gathered near a section of sidewalk on Shultz Street, one of the newer sections of Golgotha south of Johnny Town to spring up since the silver boom of the last few years.

"Glad you're here, Jon," Mark Geary said. Geary rode shotgun for the Wells-Fargo Stagecoaches. A broad-shouldered man with gray hair and steel in his eyes, Geary made his living protecting lock boxes and passengers headed farther west or back east. "I've kept anyone else from going in there since the one fella made it out, but a few damn fools kept swearing that if you weren't going to show, they'd go in." He had his scatter gun in his hand, hanging low at his side. "I persuaded them not to."

"Much obliged, Mark," Jon said as he and Kate dismounted their horses. Golgotha's sheriff was tall, a lanky man with sandy hair and a scrub of a beard. Jon was handsome, but not for trying, and a feeling of calm, quiet strength came off of him. His silver star was pinned to his gray barn coat. His gray Stetson left his eyes in shadow.

"Glad to help," Geary said. "They were getting a might huffed about waiting to see what's going on in there, but it was crowd-courage. I don't think any of them really wanted to go in, especially when they saw the poor soul who did make it out. Not to mention, they got an unstoppable sheriff to do it for them." Geary chuckled.

As the law in Golgotha, Highfather had cultivated a reputation that often helped in his line of work; the local folks claimed that Jon was a dead man walking, that he couldn't be killed, more haint than human. The three distinct lines of looping rope scars on his neck, which he normally kept hidden behind a kerchief, added to the legend, so did the countless times he had cheated certain death. Most times the reputation kept the flies off him and kept the troublemakers polite. Sometimes, the reputation bit him, and he'd have to slap leather with some gunfighter looking to make a name for himself by killing the unkillable man.

"So what exactly *is* going on in there?" Deputy Kate Warne asked Geary.

Kate's face was one you would call neither beautiful nor plain; she could make herself look either way, though, as the situation demanded. Her brown eyes held a powerful, magnetic intelligence. Her long, brown hair, tied back and under a black bolero hat, fell to her shoulders. She wore a short bolero jacket with her deputy's star pinned to it, glinting in the noon sun.

Kate also wore pants, a curiosity bordering on scandal for a woman. Warne didn't appear armed, but Jon knew she wore twin short-barreled revolvers under her jacket in a curious leather holster rig, and she was damn good with them, too. Enough folks in town had seen Kate in action to keep their peace about a woman deputy and about her choice in clothing.

Kate was a former member of the Secret Service. She had come to Golgotha over a year ago to hunt down a killer. She'd decided to stay, and Jon had offered her a job.

"I'm not sure, ma'am," Geary said. "You might want to ask him, if he can still talk." Geary pointed to a man lying on the filthy boards of the sidewalk. He was covered by a horse blanket and thrashing about. A group of townsfolk were huddled around him, trying to keep him calm and still.

"Thanks, Mark," Highfather said.

"Give him some room, folks," Kate said in a loud voice. The crowd parted for the sheriff and deputy. A few townspeople stayed by the man's side, trying to minister to him as he convulsed and moaned. Jon knelt by the man. His face looked familiar, but Jon couldn't place it.

"It's going to be all right," Jon said, touching the man's shoulder.

The man was ice cold, his skin was waxy, and he was sweating. His eyes were like those of a horse mad with fear. He was trying to talk, seeming to mouth the word "please" over and over again. Jon glanced over to one of the townsfolk, Hugh Rafferty, the tanner. "Hugh, anybody called for the doc yet?"

Hugh shrugged. "I don't think so, Jon. This fella stumbled out of the door of that place with some kind of...rope or something sticking out of his back, shouting for help to wake the snakes. The rope popped loose and slid back inside, and he just dropped. He's bleeding pretty bad from some kind of big hole in his back."

"Okay, you go fetch Clay, and tell him we need him right now," Highfather said as he slid his hand under the trembling man and felt around his back. Rafferty was already running toward Main Street.

"Jon," Kate said quietly, "do you recognize this building?"

Jon regarded the narrow, little two-story, false-front structure, its shingles painted a pale green, its single, front window dark and curtained. "Can't say I do," Jon said. "But the rate people have been building over here, new places are popping up every day."

"You're right," Kate said, "but I walked Shultz Street yesterday, and I'd bet my badge this building wasn't here."

Highfather found the wound low on the man's back. It was a ragged hole about the size of a man's fist. The injured man moaned and shuddered when Jon touched the injury. The man sat up a little, hissed a whisper in Jon's ear, "Please...please. Let me go back...inside." The man convulsed, foam spilling from his mouth. He died in Jon's arms.

"Damn," Highfather muttered. Jon gently lowered the man's body to the ground and then covered him with the horse blanket. Kate thought the sheriff may have muttered a little prayer for the dead man, but she wasn't sure. Jon stood, looked at the narrow building wedged between two other larger buildings, rubbed his chin, then looked to Kate. "Wouldn't be the first time we've had buildings appear and disappear around here," he said. "That Austrian tailor, Hanser, he had a wandering house while he was living here. Folks said the devil

29

moved it about for him. Whole digs up and disappeared when he died. Then there was that British fella with his strange little blue shack with the light on top that came and went. I've heard tale, too, that Professor Mephisto claims his playhouse's smack dab in the center of the Axis Mundi, the crossroads between Heaven and Hell and everything in-between."

"So, this place could fade away into nowhere right in front of our eyes," Kate said, "and never show up anywhere again?" Jon nodded. "Sounds like fun," she said. "Let's go."

"You scared of anything?" Jon asked. Kate retrieved a coil of rope and a .44 Winchester rifle with a sawed-down barrel and stock from the saddle of her horse, a black and white patterned Appaloosa named Corinthian.

"Getting old," she said. "Getting bored." Kate tied one end of the rope to a hitching post next to the sidewalk. She tossed the remainder of the coil to Highfather. "Fortunately, with this job, I don't have to worry much about either happening."

Highfather looped the rope around his waist, tightened it, then gave several feet of slack. He looped it around Kate's waist. "Speak for yourself," he said as he tied the rope. "I intend to retire from this job an old coot with a pension." There was a moment as he made sure the rope was secure that they were both very aware of how close they were to one another. They both felt it; then they stepped back and tried to ignore it.

"Old men are all right," Kate said, a smile playing at the edges of her lips as she headed toward the door of the strange building, "especially ones with a pension." Highfather followed, shaking his head and drawing his gun. The front door was partly open, creaking a bit in the cold wind coming off the desert. There was a pool of the dead man's blood at the threshold.

"Mark," Highfather called out to Geary, "you keep a grip on that rope. Anything peculiar starts happening out here, you tug on it hard. You've lived 'round these parts long enough to know peculiar when you see it. If the building starts to vanish or collapse or, I don't know, turn into a giant scorpion or something, you grab that rope and pull us out as hard as you can." Geary nodded and moved over to the hitching post.

"Giant scorpion?" Kate said.

"Don't ask," Jon said. "Angry Scorpion God. Ruined the Independence Day parade."

Jon pushed the door open with his boot, and Kate covered him with her rifle. The two stepped inside the darkness of the house's maw.

Though it was midday, the gloom inside the narrow little building was thick, almost tangible. Highfather glanced to Warne, and they took up fields of cover, back to back with each other, the sheriff to the right of the door, the deputy to the left.

There was a steady, rhythmic creaking that had an association in Highfather's brain with a body swaying at the end of a rope; it made his neck ache. The sound was coming from the right. An old man lurched slowly in a rocking chair. His eyes were glassy and vacant. Tears streamed down his ashen, wrinkled face.

"Howdy, sheriff, deputy," the old man said. A joyless grin came to his face. "Come on in. Sit a spell. Everyone's welcome."

On Kate's side, she saw a small parlor to the left of the door. There was a table with four people seated around it. They were playing cards, but something was very wrong. The quartet was made up of two men who looked like cowboys, a woman who Kate thought she recognized as a working girl from the Dove's Roost, and a ten-year-old girl she had seen a few times around the town with her mother. All four held hands of playing cards, but many of the cards in their hands were facing the wrong way, as if they were merely going through the motions of the game. All four stopped playing and turned their heads to stare blankly at Kate and Highfather. They were all smiling the same emotionless grin that the old man had on his face; all of them had unfocused eyes.

"Yes, please," all four card players said in unison, "come join us." Kate felt something slither past her boot.

"Jon!" she shouted as she bumped into his back, lowering her rifle and firing a round at the floor at what she thought was a snake. "The floor!" The bullet pulped a long, rope-like tendril, like something from a plant. The tendril spattered across the wooden floor out of which it had seemingly grown. Highfather shifted, his six-gun suddenly in his hand, and fired at another of the sickly green strands that wriggled across the floor toward him. The vine was destroyed. Highfather and Warne circled one another, back to back. More of the tendrils sprouted out of the wooden floor and moved toward the pair. The seated card players and the old man in the rocking chair all stood and began to move jerkily toward the lawmen. As they stood, Kate now noticed each person had a thick, undulating vine running from their backs to the heaving, pulsating floorboards. The room was getting unnaturally warm, and the air seemed thicker, almost choking.

"It's so much easier if you don't fight," all the house dwellers said as one. Jon fired into a pair of the vines trying to attach to him and Kate. He hit one, which splattered. He managed to catch the other in his gloved hand. The end of the vine hissed at him and thrashed to be free of his grip. It had a sucker-like mouth, ringed in sharp, hooked fangs, dripping some mucusy-looking substance. Jon yanked it free of the floor, and it sprayed the green goo and went limp in his hand.

Kate cocked the Winchester and fired, repeating the action again and again as the vines hurtled toward them. The two cowboys, glassy-eyed and grinning, awkwardly drew their own guns, leveling them at Kate and Highfather. The little girl charged past Kate toward Highfather, a large kitchen knife in her hand.

"Jon!" Kate shouted as she fired on one of the cowboys. She hit him square in the chest. Dark green sludge gushed from the chest wound, and the cowboy staggered back but didn't fall. The other cowboy was about to fire on Kate when Jon's revolver boomed and severed the thick vine connected to the shooter's back. The cowboy had a look of pain at first, then relief, on his face as he fell to the floor.

The little girl was near—Jon knew that—but he'd had to take his eyes off her for a second to shoot the cowboy trying to kill Kate. He anticipated the knife blade plunging into his gut. There was another blast, this time Kate's rifle. Jon whipped his head around to see the little girl dropping to the floor, the vine leading up to her back severed and more of the greenish black ichor spurting out of it. Kate had cross drawn on the girl literally a split second after he had done the same thing to her cowboy. They spared a breath to lock eyes.

Highfather knelt by the little girl. He had been on enough battle-fields to see the life draining away behind her eyes. "Please, please," the girl whispered, "it's...using our bodies for...hands, for a voice. Bait...we were all bait to attract more people into it."

"Hang on," Highfather said to the child. "Doc's coming; he'll make you right as rain."

"It's eating us," the little girl said, her voice slipping away, foam flecked with red and green covering her lips, "and it's so...wonderful." The child died.

"If you relax, give in to it," the old man said, his gnarled hands clutching at Jon's throat, "you will know peace and pleasure like you have never experienced in your lives." Jon broke free of the old man's grip as Kate shot the tendril connected to his back. He fell with a wheeze and lay still beside the little girl's body.

The last of the victims, the woman from the Dove's Roost, was standing behind the table now. The air was so thick in the room it was hard to pull in a breath. It came to Highfather what was happening just as the headache began. The air inside the house was thick with pollen. Kate hacked, coughing fitfully, but she kept the gun on the woman.

"If you just breathe it in a little bit longer," the Dove said, her terror at some alien intelligence using her evident in her red-rimmed, drugged eyes. "You will get so warm and sleepy...then you can join me, help bring others in to experience the pleasure of being food for a superior being."

Jon's and Kate's heads were buzzing. The heat was like a thick mantle settling over them. It was getting hard to think, to remember what they should do next. The floor was alive with dozens of undulating tendrils, sliding toward them. Jon looked down at the floor, at the shoots growing up out of the boards.

Growing up out of.

"Kate," Jon said in a voice he hardly recognized, "the floor—shoot the floor." They both blasted away; the wooden boards exploded, splinters flying everywhere. Jon's pistol was out. He fumbled to reload it, bullets dropping from his numb, thick fingers. Kate kept firing, biting the inside of her cheek. The pain pulled her out of the stupor.

Beneath the broken boards, part of some massive, pulsating thing was visible; it had spongy flesh of purple, yellow, and green, covered in swollen, splitting nodules leaking the blackish-green ooze. Fleshy tentacles, like the ones that had grown through the floor, whipped about, seeking human skin to pierce. The thing made no sound, but now that it was exposed, the heat in the house was joined by the overpowering stench of blood and rotting orchids.

"Keep shooting!" Jon said, firing again on the thing as Kate reloaded her rifle. The prostitute, still attached to the thing by a tendril, launched herself at Kate, giving off a horrible wail as the bullets popped the creature's skin like balloons made of rotten meat. The deputy drove the short stock of the rifle into the woman's chin, sending her backward and down onto her backside. The tendrils on the floor writhed like snakes with broken backs.

Rows of symmetrical teeth began to erupt from every wall, every floor. The rooms began to lose their rigid shape, their corners, and both lawmen realized what they had actually stepped into. They looked to the front door, which was now a pulsating wound, lined with foot-long teeth and slick with the greenish-black slime. The opening was squeezing shut rapidly.

"Ladies first," he shouted to Kate, gesturing to the slowly closing portal as he emptied the last of his bullets into the shuddering thing under the rippling floor.

"Damn right!" Kate dropped her empty rifle and drew twin short-barreled .36 Colt revolvers from the shoulder holsters under her open jacket. Jon ran to the girl from the Dove's Roost, grabbing up the cowboys' guns off the floor as he did. The girl sat on the floor with a vacant, catatonic stare on her face. Jon hefted her up and noticed as he did the tendril in her back popped loose and fell with a splat. She was still alive.

Kate blasted the closing portal, and hunks of fleshly pulp and brackish ichor flew everywhere. The whole "house" shuddered. Kate leapt through the opening, back out into the bright light of Shultz Street. She hit the dusty ground, covered in slime, rolled, and came up with both pistols aimed at what had been, not too long ago, an innocuous house. It was now a two-story, shifting blob of green flesh, seeming to collapse like a disturbed souffle upon itself.

Kate scrambled to her feet, waving off the gawking crowd. "Everyone get back!" she shouted. "Jon! Jon!" There was no answer. The thing made a sound like a giant upset stomach, burbling and groaning. The opening had sealed itself. Mark Geary, shotgun at the ready, helped move the crowds back. Kate began to run toward the thing, ready to blow it open with dynamite if she had to.

"The sheriff?" some of the town folk in the crowd muttered and shook their heads.

"Jon...oh no, Jon," a few old timers whispered and said silent prayers.

In a hail of .44 bullets, Highfather, a pistol in either hand and the comatose girl in his arms, leapt through the gushing, smoking hole he had blasted in the thing's hide. He came through a rain of the creature's murky blood and moved to get clear of the thing.

"Everyone, back," the sheriff shouted. "It's going to collapse." He and Kate moved back to the center of the street with the crowd.

"Dang, Jon!" one of the townsfolk exclaimed. "Looks like a giant gizzard! It ain't like those gut-looking things that crawled up out of the old well, is it? One of them done went and dissolved my mother-in-law!"

"Could be worse, young'un," an old man said flatly. "I recall back in '49 when those damn Gila monster people invaded from their cave city. Sheriff Lansdale had to go and burn half the damn town down to git rid of the evil little bastards."

The creature that had been a building made a gurgling sound, and then the massive thing folded in upon itself and collapsed, knocking some of the siding off and breaking windows on the buildings on either side of where it had lain. What was left was a reeking pile of wet, formless flesh, more like a plant than an animal. The thing gave off one last thundering, flatulent sound as the last of the air escaped its bulk, and then it was still. Everyone was silent for a moment; then a cheer went up from the crowd. Highfather lowered the girl to the ground, her eyes open but vacant.

"Please," she muttered, not looking at anyone, just staring, "please, hook me back up." Jon wiped the ichor off his face and sighed. He looked to Kate, who was standing over the girl. Clay Turlough, the town's current physician, appeared through the crowd and knelt down by the girl.

Clay Turlough always had a weird smell about him, chemicals mixed with something organic and sour. He was skinny enough to be considered cadaverous, with wild wisps of white hair circling his liver-spotted pate. He had a prominent nose that made most folk think of a vulture's beak, and a drooping, thick brush of a mustache.

Clay still dressed as he had when he was a livery owner and taxidermist, a work shirt and baggy canvas work pants held up by suspenders. One thing Jon had noticed was that since becoming a doctor, Clay now wore cleaner clothes. He said it had something to do with some theory about germs.

"Jonathan," Clay said, almost blandly, "let me take a look at the child. Oh, by the way, if you'd like my fellas over at the stable to clean that mess up for you, we can. You don't mind if I give...whatever that is a good once over, do you?" Clay didn't act any more like a doctor than he had before he had grudgingly accepted the job after Golgotha's last doctor had turned out to be a mass-murdering fiend.

"She's got a wound at the base of her spine," Clay said. "Pretty bad one. I'm not going to do much more with her until I get her to the office. It's properly sterilized. Jamming a finger down in that wound is a sure-fire way to get it infected."

Clay was the first sawbones Highfather had ever heard of who talked all this business about germs and the infections caused by them. He'd seen too many men butchered on the battlefield and then again just as bad at the field hospitals. Clay was the most brilliant man Jon Highfather had ever met. He was odd, and could be off-putting, but he was a good man and always came through when you needed him.

The sheriff nodded to Clay and then called out to the crowd, "We need some men here to help lift her, carry her over to Clay's office!" Clay and his newly recruited retinue headed off. Jon looked over at Kate as they walked their horses away from the scene. They were both covered in slime and dirt. Several townsfolk wandered past the pair, offering thanks and congratulations but avoiding touching them.

"Jon, you look like a walking cow patty," she said.

"Well, you ain't exactly a little breath of spring yourself," he said with a chuckle. "Get washed up, and I'll meet you back at the jail in about half an hour."

"Mayor owes me a Winchester," she said as she headed back to Shultz's Boarding House where she rented a room. Highfather watched her depart for a moment too long. A pang of old, sore guilt poked him, but Jon let it be. He turned away from Kate and headed toward home.

When Jon and Kate arrived, there was a fancy, two-seat buggy with an awning and a pair of fine-looking horses parked to the side of Dry Well Road, in front of the simple cinder block cube that was the Golgotha jail.

"Queen Victoria paying us a visit?" Kate said. They ascended the covered porch at the front of the jail. A wooden board to the right of the iron door fluttered with nailed-on wanted posters and public notices, fighting against the strong, cold wind.

"If I'd known, I would have taken the time to shave," Jon said. The door opened with a hollow, metallic groan. "And make sure I got all that gunk out of hither and yon."

The office was dim, shafts of sunlight filtering through the bar-covered rear windows. A man leaned against Jon's desk, his face hidden by the shadow of the brim of his black derby. He wore a practical but well-made suit with a checked shirt, a narrow, knotted bow tie, and a vest. He was solidly built with broad shoulders, and what Jon could make out of his face was covered by a full, coal-black beard with a dusting of white hairs on his chin. "Nae, Sheriff Highfather, from one old lawman to another, you don't need to be putting on your Sunday suit for the likes of me." The burr was Scottish, and Jon felt Kate freeze in her tracks behind him. She gasped. The bearded man struck a match against Jon's desk and raised it to light the large cigar he placed to his lips. The blade of the match's flame illuminated a stern face and blue eyes that guarded what lay behind them.

"Allan?" Kate said, a quality in her voice Jon had never heard before. "What are you doing here?"

"Hello, Katie," Allan Pinkerton said. "It's good to see you. I've missed you." The legendary head of the Pinkerton Detective Agency turned to regard Highfather, offering his hand. "Sheriff, I've heard a lot about you." Jon shook Pinkerton's hand.

"Same goes for you, Mr. Pinkerton," he said. "What's a powerful man like yourself doing all the way out here?"

"We need to talk, you and I," Pinkerton said. "It's about your town, Sheriff. I'm afraid I need it."

THE KNIGHT OF WANDS

I t was close to sunup, and Jim Negrey could no longer keep hold
of sleep. Jim had grown since his coming to Golgotha almost
three years ago. When he had arrived in this town, he had been
a scrawny, sunburned, half-dead, fifteen-year-old boy rescued from
the heart of the 40-Mile Desert. Jim was seventeen now with hair the
color of sand and eyes the color of faraway oceans. He had grown a
good foot in the last few years, and his chest had broadened, his voice
deepened. He was still slender of build, but his work as a deputy
sheriff in Golgotha had assured him of some new muscle and new
scars.

Jim opened his eyes. The jade eye stared back at him from the
night table. The eye was a sphere of milky glass. The dark circle inlaid
within the eye looked back at Jim. Around the darkness was an iris of
flawless jade. Jim knew that if the light hit that ring of jade at the right
angle, a circle of tiny characters—Chinese, he had learned—would
make themselves evident. The eye was his legacy. It had been his
father's, and Jim had reclaimed it from the men who had killed his pa.
Somehow, the eye had freed itself from the small, leather drawstring
bag that Jim kept it in, and which he wore around his neck.

Jim began to sit up when an odd fluttering motion at the foot of
the bed caught his attention. There was a creature perched along the
iron bar at the foot of Jim's bed. It was nude. It had the sleek, pale
body of a woman but with talons like a bird's in place of human feet
and hands. Great wings of black, oily feathers shimmering with a
rainbow hue grew from the woman's back. The wings shuddered and
moved nervously. The face of the woman was slender, almost gaunt,
and delicate with long, raven-black hair that fell to cover her breasts.
The eyes that regarded Jim had the glaring, pitiless, golden gaze of a
bird.

"Death is circling in the 40-Mile," the woman said. Her voice
carried an odd accent that was familiar to Jim. He blinked and looked
at her face again. She cocked her head at an unusual angle and stared,
unblinking, into the young man's face. "My sisters are circling, waiting," she said. "If you hurry, you can save them, save her. You must
hurry, my sisters are hungry."

"Miss Shelly?" Jim asked. "Is that you?" The face, the voice,
belonged to Shelly Wollstonecraft, a local seamstress only arrived in
Golgotha a little over a year ago. Golgotha's resident taxidermist, and
now doctor, Clay Turlough, was sweet on her. Miss Shelly was a slender, quiet young woman who spoke with a German accent. She had
no claws, no wings or bird eyes, at least as far as he knew. In Golgotha, you could never be entirely sure.

"We come for everyone," she said. "We came for your father, we
came for your sister..."

"Lottie?" He said his little sister's name like a prayer. "You tellin'
me Lottie's dead?"

Shelly, or the bird-thing with Shelly's face, continued as if he
hadn't spoken. "And soon we come for him."

"For who?" Jim was panicked now, struggling to rise from his bed,
but he couldn't. Shelly cocked her head again and opened her mouth
wide, too wide for a human, and screeched, a chorus of dying doves.
Her merciless golden eyes burned into him.

Jim opened his eyes and sat up in bed, the weight of dream off of him. The sky was slate outside his window. A single black feather drifted slowly down to light on the foot of his bed. No bird woman crouched there now, and the jade eye was safely in its pouch as it should be. He lay back and exhaled loudly, started to relax, and then recalled what Miss Shelly had said in the dream. Jim clamored out of bed. "The 40-Mile!" he said.

Jim splashed some water from a basin onto his face and slicked his hair back as best he could. He pulled on his denim work pants and boots quickly, hopping around the room a bit as he did, almost falling over a few times. He slipped the cord with the pouch that held the eye around his neck and buttoned up a white biled work shirt he removed from the basket of fresh laundry Constance had brought him a few days ago. Jim buckled on his gun belt. He took his pa's old .44 Colt from the night table. He broke open the gun's breach and checked the loaded cylinder, just as he had before bed. Satisfied, he snapped the breach closed and holstered the gun.

Finally, he took the silver star from the bed table. He regarded his badge for a moment, polished it on his sleeve. It was real silver, an old Golgotha tradition, not some cheap tin badge like most lawmen wore. He recalled, as he did almost every time he put it on, the day Sheriff Jon Highfather had asked him to be a deputy. Every time he remembered, Jim smiled. He carefully pinned the star to his shirt and exited his room at Mrs. Shultz's boarding house.

Jim made his way quietly down the stairs to the first floor. Normally, he pulled feet down the stairs, his boots rapidly thudding to wake the snakes, but at this hour, he'd catch Jesse if he woke up the other boarders. He removed his heavy canvas coat and his hat from the pegs by the front door. He turned to unlock the door when a gravelly voice broke the silence.

"Where you sneaking off to ahead of the rooster, boy?" The voice came from the dining room. Jim walked in and found a lanky Indian sitting at the dinner table. The man's face was shadowed with scars and pockmarks as well as several fresh cuts and bruises. He had a pointed nose that was crooked from having been broken on more than one occasion. His nose was currently bleeding. His dark eyebrows were thick, unruly, and met over the bridge of his nose. His black hair was long and looked a bit greasy. His eyes were dark, and the devil's light danced in them. A silver star, twin to Jim's, was pinned to his mud and blood-covered coat.

He grinned at Jim with yellow, crooked teeth but straight, sharp, prominent incisors. "You trying to suck up to the boss?" His people had never given him a name—as was their custom—so he had claimed one for himself from the hateful slurs of "half-breed" the white and Indian worlds had thrown at him. He took the insult and made it a personal joke at their expense. He called himself Mutt, and he was Jim's best friend.

On the dinner table was a half-loaf of bread, a hunk of fresh cheese, and some of the scraps from the chicken Mrs. Shultz had prepared for dinner last night. Mutt was busily shoveling the food into his mouth. "'Cause I'll tell you right now," Mutt said, his mouth full, "no one likes a lick-finger."

"You jist getting in?" Jim asked. Mutt nodded as he swallowed half a glass of water. Mutt's blood was a drifting cloud in the water when he sat the glass down. "You okay?"

"Yep," he said. "Turns out it was Yule Hawker that was tearing those cattle and cowpunchers in half."

Jim sat at the table. "Well, cock my hat," he said. "Old Yule?" Mutt's grin grew, and he nodded. He started to cut himself hunks of bread and cheese with a huge Bowie knife he carried. He paused for a second and wiped the blade clean of bile-colored blood with his sleeve before he cut into the food.

"Sure 'nough," Mutt said. "Seems he got sold a talisman of some kind of critter called a Peluda by that French fella that had been passing through. Put a hex on him. When Yule'd get riled up enough, he'd get about as big as an ox, all hairy and ornery, and stronger than the stink on a shithouse in August."

Jim absently picked at a scrap of the chicken and popped it in his mouth. "Don't that beat the Dutch," he said, reaching over and grabbing the loaf and tearing off a hunk of the bread. "What happened?"

"I gentled him down with a scatter gun," Mutt said, "then we wrestled a spell. Turns out his tail was his weakness. I grabbed him by it, knotted it up, and broke that scatter gun over his head. Then I got the trinket off him, and everything was pretty quiet after that. He's taking a nap in a cell right now. Tomorrow I'll tell him he got a snootful, and I had to lock him up. He didn't mean to hurt nobody. It wasn't him; it was the thingamabob."

"Where is it?" Jim asked. "The thingamabob?"

"Locked up in the vault with all the other junk that wanders through," Mutt said and burped. "Remember that Green Ribbon Tong hatchet man that got his hands on those cloud-stepping sandals he stole from Ch'eng Huang?" Jim said as he wiped his mouth. Mutt snorted.

"I thought that ugly, damned flying Goatsucker thing was hard to catch."

Jim laughed and poured himself a glass of water from the pitcher. "Or that Necklace of Harmonica..."

"Harmonia," Mutt corrected him. Jim nodded around a long swallow of water.

"Right! That lady swindler, 'The Countess,' had it, and it made her young and beautiful forever, but it made everyone around her have awful accidents?"

"Yeah," Mutt said, "I seem to recall Bick courted her for a spell even after we took that thing away from her." Mutt burped again, stretched, and yawned. "So, I figure I earned my damn pay for the night. Kate was over at the jail when I dropped Yule off. Her and Jonathan dealt with some kind of living house over on Shultz Street today.

"Apparently some big shot from Washington D.C. showed up too. Probably means trouble brewing. Never met a politician that brought good news. Been a busy week. I told her I wouldn't be in 'till late next year." Jim chuckled. He picked off a corner of cheese and ate it. "So, that's why I'm still moving about," Mutt said. "What's your excuse?"

Jim's eyes suddenly got big as he remembered what he had been about. He jumped to his feet. "Aww darn it, Mutt, I plumb forgot! I think some people are in trouble out on the 40-Mile. I was going to check it out."

"What makes you think that?"

"A dream I had," Jim said. "Woke me up. I think it's the eye talking to me."

Most of the townsfolk of Golgotha worked very hard to ignore or explain away the strange things and forces that visited their town. Most would have given the young deputy a dubious look or a concerned pat on the shoulder and tried to forget what he said, what it meant. Mutt didn't blink at Jim's statement of oracle in a dream. He stood up and brushed crumbs off his bloody shirt, grabbed his battered leather Stetson, which had a black feather tucked in the band.

"Sounds square," Mutt said. "You get the horses saddled up over at Clay's. I'll clean all this up so Gillian doesn't skin us both for muckin' in the kitchen, change clothes, and meet you there in a few."

The deputies rode down Dry Well Road onto Prosperity, the drowsy sun's eye still closed. The town was waking up. The folks who made their living off the land, by hard work and sweat, by doing for the wealthy folk who were still sleeping, they were all on the move. Jim rode his brown mustang, Promise, and Mutt rode his silver-dappled Paint named Muha. They cut over onto Main Street by the town hall and the stagecoach station. The sun was clawing its way up behind them.

"Any reason we're heading out of town this way?" Mutt asked.

"It feels right," Jim said, "closer. That make any fool sense?"

"Dreams, instincts," Mutt said, "they're part of you, much as your eyes and ears...maybe more. You sharpen them up, listen to them, they can point you better than anything else you got. Hell, how do you think I found you out in the 40-Mile all those years ago?" Jim smiled. "That and the smell." The deputies laughed.

They turned right onto Old Stone Road, near the Baptist church. They picked up their pace, and, in a few moments, they were galloping past the old cemetery, which had been here before the town. The cemetery held an unmarked grave that the sheriff and his deputies encircled in salt, every day. Both Jim and Mutt sped past the boneyard and tried not to look back, even though they both felt something was watching them.

The desert swallowed them, and the sun stood now, bright and uncaring in the cloudless sky. There was a road through the 40-Mile, and if they kept to their current direction, they would eventually intersect with it.

"I told Clay if we weren't back by tonight to come looking for us," Jim said, "and to bring the wagon."

"It's close to a day's ride before we hit the road," Mutt said. "You got any more notions about where we should be headed?" Jim looked about, then shook his head. "Okay," Mutt said. "Most folks out here come in on the road and stick to it, so let's keep heading the way were headed."

They rode on. The desert grew warmer, but this time of year, the temperature wasn't that hot—it was actually a little chilly. Any travelers out in the desert now had to deal with keeping warm and getting water.

"Maude back from her business?" Jim asked. Mutt shook his head.

"Tonight, maybe tomorrow," he said.

"She's bringing Constance back with her this time, right?" Jim asked. Mutt turned his head to the young deputy and gave him a wide smile. Jim blushed. "Shut up."

"Miss Constance and Maude's pa are meeting her in San Francisco," Mutt said. "You'll be tickled pink, which is pretty easy for a boy as pink as you, to know she's getting a break from her schoolin' at Maude's school at Grande Folly. She's coming to visit for a spell."

"I was just curious..." Jim began.

"So, go hide all those other girls who are sweet on you," Mutt chuckled, "'cause you know Constance can whoop all of them put together and not muss her hair."

Jim got redder. "Just asking a simple question." Mutt chuckled.

After a time, the two deputies paused in their ride to give the horses some water and stretch their legs. Partly buried in the desert floor was an old spinning wheel, the wood salted silver from baking and freezing in the relentless sand. The wheel squeaked quietly as it turned in the bitter wind. Jim and Mutt both knew the wheel was a monument to another pioneer, another family, another life, that hadn't made it through the tribulation of the 40-Mile. They watched the wheel spin for a time and then rode on, Jim hoping they were not too late to keep the desert from claiming another soul.

After hours of silent riding, Jim looked over to Mutt. "You coming out to Auggie's for the do at the end of the month?" Jim asked. Mutt grunted and Jim laughed. "That's a 'Maude's going so I reckon I'm going too' grunt, ain't it?"

"Don't forget I got a gun, boy," Mutt said in a low voice. Jim grinned.

"See?" Jim said. "Don't feel so nice, does it?"

Auggie Shultz was a shopkeep in Golgotha. He was well-liked and respected by most of the town. The burly German had lost his beloved wife, Gerta, years ago. He had found love again with Gillian Proctor, herself a widow and proprietor of the boarding house Jim and Mutt lived in.

Auggie and Gillian had been married in late 1870 and had their first baby in September of last year, a beautiful, healthy boy Gillian had insisted on naming Augustus Clayton Shultz, Jr.—Auggie Jr. for short. The couple planned to have "Little Auggie" christened at Saint Cyprian's at the end of March. They had invited most of the town to their homestead for a celebration after to formally introduce him to the town.

"Don't get me wrong," Mutt said. "Auggie's a decent man. I'm happy for him and Gillian and the little *nana*..."

"But..."

"Since Auggie started working for Bick," Mutt said, shaking his head, "something's changed. Nothing I can put my finger on, just a..."

"Instinct?" Jim finished. Mutt nodded.

"Exactly," Mutt said. "Something unnatural."

Malachi Bick was the wealthiest, most powerful man in Golgotha. He owned a considerable amount of the town. His reputation was less than savory. He was supposedly one of the biggest crime bosses in the western United States and territories. It was all rumor, but it was the kind of rumor that Bick cultivated.

Auggie had begun working for Bick after a bad spot of trouble that ended up with large parts of the town wrecked, and Auggie shot. Fully recovered, Auggie now ran many of Bick's businesses in Golgotha and tried to run them much more humanely than Malachi Bick ever had.

"Bick's softened up a bit since his daughter, Emily, came to town," Jim said. "Maybe Auggie's a good influence on him." Mutt snorted.

"And maybe a rattlesnake will squirt sarsaparilla out of its fangs. Bick's trouble. Always has been, always will be. He courts it." Mutt paused, turning his head as if he'd heard something. He pulled back the reins on Muha and came to a quick stop. "Wait a sec. You...you feel that?" Jim looked around, shook his head. "Medicine, power," Mutt said. "Strong and old...very far from home. Truth be told, it feels kind of like what that," he pointed to the bag hanging from Jim's neck, "felt like when I sensed it on you out here, over three years ago."

Jim brought Promise to a halt. He slipped the eye out of its bag and held it tightly in his palm. The glass orb was ice-cold to the touch. Not the cold of the desert's basin floor, something more, almost a burning sensation.

The eye possessed powers Jim was still trying to get a handle on. Mysterious Chinamen had found Jim's father, Bill, convalescing in a Washington D.C. hospital after the battle that cost him his own eye. They implanted the Jade eye in his empty socket in the dead of night, apparently to hide and protect it. The eye caused Jim's pa great pain and suffering until the day he was murdered.

The eye was stolen by Billy Negrey's killer. Jim had revenged his pa and recovered the eye but at a terrible price. He killed some men—one of them a very powerful man, from a very powerful family—and he wounded his own sister, Lottie, in the gun fight. Jim had to run to avoid the noose for his crimes, and to this day he had no idea if Lottie was alive or dead. Jim suddenly remembered the words of the bird-woman with Miss Shelly's face. *We came for your sister…* He tried to shake off the last image he had of Lottie, bleeding and still.

During his years here in Golgotha, Jim had studied with the Chinese mystic, Ch'eng Huang, the undisputed lord of Johnny Town, to try to understand and harness the eye's abilities. Huang had told Jim the artifact he carried was known as the Eye of the Moon and was a source of great, almost divine, power. Huang had told Jim that the boy wasn't a very good *Wu*, a Chinese name for sorcerer. Jim liked the meditation he was introduced to, and he tried to do it as often as his chaotic life allowed. He had mastered a few abilities with the eye, but Huang told him that his mind flitted like a horse fly from one thought to the next. He had to learn focus and patience if he was ever to master the eye's secrets.

Now, in the desert, Jim began his breathing exercises as Ch'eng Huang had taught him.

"What you doing?" Mutt asked. Jim popped open one eye.

"I'm breathing," he said. He closed his eyes and began again.

"Why you breathing that way?" Mutt asked. "Usual way was fine." Jim sighed. He opened his eyes again.

"Dang it, Mutt," Jim said. "I got to breathe right if I'm going to get the eye to work for me! I got to do it the way Ch'eng Huang taught me, to help me focus." Mutt laughed.

"*Teaching* breathing," he said. "Crazy white men and picky China-men. Leave it to them to complicate something you were born doin'."

"Hush," Jim said. He closed his eyes and concentrated on his breathing.

Jim envisioned a door, as he had been instructed. He extended his perceptions through it. There was a howling, frigid wind shrieking at the fringes of the doorway. Past it, Jim felt a white-hot beacon of energy. It was like a geyser of burning, sputtering light reaching higher and higher into the sky. Whatever it was, it was reaching out from the deep desert ahead, and it had sensed them too, regarding them with guarded curiosity. "Yeah," Jim muttered. "Got it. It's got us too."

"Mmhm," Mutt said. "I got a whiff of that as well. It ain't nappin'. You've gotten a lot better using that shooter, Jim," Mutt said. Jim pulled his perceptions back to his body. He slipped the eye back into its pouch as he opened his eyes.

"No thanks to all that chin music you're making," he said, and Mutt shrugged. "Truth be told, sometimes it feels more like it's using me."

"Things with that kind of power usually do," Mutt said. "You keep at mastering it, like breaking a proud horse. You let it get out of control, it's going to trample you."

Jim knew Mutt was right, and his hand unconsciously went to clutch the rawhide bag at his neck. Jim looked to the north. "It's there up ahead, about fifteen or twenty miles, I reckon, and I think, whatever it is, it's alive, not a thing like the eye."

Mutt nodded. "I think you're right," he said. "Let's get a move on." The deputies urged their horses to a gallop.

It was early afternoon by the time Jim and Mutt saw the silhouette of a man moving slowly along the bleak horizon. They closed on the figure. He was a black man moving forward with a slow, steady gait. In his arms was a child, wrapped in a blood-stained blanket.

The deputies drew their horses to a stop within a few yards of the man. The man was a little over six feet tall and had some muscle to him. His hair was short-cropped close to his skull and shaved up on the sides and back. He wore a neatly trimmed beard. His eyes were brown and calm. There was something secret behind them, strong and old. He wore dusty, dark-blue cavalry pants with sky blue piping. His boots were army as well. He wore a tan poncho and a black bolero hat. Jim caught a flash of an odd, leaf-shaped blade tucked into his gun belt under the poncho.

"You here to help, or do we have ourselves a problem?" the man said. He spoke with no accent; his voice was strong, though it was a little rough after what Jim assumed was several days of walking in the desert with little or no water. It brought back Jim's own painful memories of his passage across the 40-Mile.

"What you doing out here with that kid?" Mutt asked, his hand moving to rest on his holstered six-gun. The man now had a sawed-off, double-barrel shotgun in his free hand. It came from beneath his poncho. The draw was so smooth that the child in the man's arms didn't even stir. He leveled the shotgun in Mutt's direction so fluidly, so fast, Jim didn't have time to act, but Mutt did, matching the draw. The two men scanned one another for any sign of weakness or hesitation across the steel barrels pointed at each other.

"You're a quick little fella," the man said, calmly.

"I'm a touch spry," Mutt replied. "I only know one man fast enough to take me in a draw. Two now. What we going to do about that?" The guns didn't waiver.

"You here to help us, or we going to dance?" the man asked.

"We're the law," Jim said. "Deputies from Golgotha."

"I'm afraid that doesn't answer my question, son." The man never took his eyes off Mutt. "I've known too many lawmen."

"Help," Mutt practically spat, holstering his pistol. "We're here to help, jackass. But if you would rather just keep doing the same all-fired great job you've been doing, keep walking."

"Mutt," Jim said softly. "That child needs help. We need to get her to Clay."

"Thank you," the man said to Jim, putting the shotgun away. "Name's Barabbas Hayes. You can call me Rabb."

"Girl your daughter?" Jim asked. Rabb shook his head.

"She's the only survivor of a massacre. Mormon town southeast of here near the Utah border called Ezekiel. I found her three days ago, wandering, sick from exposure and shock."

"Any idea who did it?" Mutt asked.

"Paiute, from the look of it," Rabb said. He glanced down at the little girl to make sure she was still slumbering. He lowered his voice. "They burned it to the ground, killed everyone. Skinned some of them —not scalped—skinned. Even killed the animals."

"That don't sound right," Mutt said. Rabb nodded.

"I agree," he said. "Paiute don't cotton to that kind of bloodshed."

"Know a little about Indians, do you?" Mutt said. It was more of a challenge than a question.

"More than some," Rabb replied, ignoring Mutt's accusatory stare. "I patched her up best I know how, but she needs a proper surgeon. We've been walking to Golgotha for a while."

"Why?" Mutt said. "There's plenty of towns that are closer, Elko, Eureka, Nightveil, Ely. Don't got to cross the 40-Mile, either."

"It had to be Golgotha," Hayes said as he lowered the shotgun and slid it back into a back sheath.

"Why?" Jim asked.

"Got business there. I've come across the country from back east to deliver a message to someone in Golgotha."

"And who'd that be?" Mutt asked.

"Not you," Rabb said.

"You are just growing on me by leaps and bounds," Mutt said.

"I promised I'd only give the message to the person it's meant for," Rabb said. Mutt gave Jim a skeptical look.

Jim lowered his voice and leaned into Mutt. "I'm pretty sure the power's coming off of him. I don't need to look at him with the eye to know that."

The Indian nodded in agreement. "Yep. Well, he don't exactly seem forthcoming. We need to git that kid to Clay. I'll ask him what's what when we get into Golgotha."

Jim climbed off Promise and walked toward Hayes. He moved back the blanket and took a closer look at the little girl. Mutt saw the instant of shock cross the young deputy's face.

"Lottie?" Jim almost whispered. It wasn't his little sister, but for a second she had looked just like Lottie. The little girl was about eight or nine, the age she had been when Jim had to flee West Virginia to avoid the gallows. Her cheeks were pink and wind-chafed, and her lips were cracked and dry. Lottie would be twelve now, Jim thought, if she was still alive. The child moved fitfully and moaned a little, a dry croak.

"She needs some water," Jim said, "and we got a first-class doc. You mind if I take her up on my horse, Mr. Hayes?" Rabb looked at Jim with mild surprise. He sized the young man up, and then nodded.

"That'd be fine..." Rabb said.

"Jim," he said, "Jim Negrey. Pleased to meet you."

"Likewise," Rabb said. They shook hands. "Thank you, Jim." Jim remounted Promise, and Hayes gently handed the girl to him.

"We've been drinking cactus water since ours ran out," he said. He looked over to Mutt. "Mind if I ride with you, smiley?"

"My friends can call me Mutt," he said, offering Rabb a hand. "You can call me deputy."

"Friends, huh?" Rabb said, pulling himself up onto Muha. He nodded toward Jim. "So, him?"

"Close," Jim said.

The horses turned and headed back toward Golgotha. Jim gave the little girl he was holding a small sip from his canteen. She coughed and sputtered a little but drank eagerly.

"Not too much too quick," Jim said. He wet her dry lips and pulled the blanket tighter around her. She whimpered for her mother and drifted back off into oblivion.

Mutt looked over his shoulder at Rabb. "So, this big, secret, highfalutin' message you got to deliver?"

"Yes?" Rabb said.

"Who gave it to you?"

"A dead man," Rabb said.

"Yep," Mutt said, "you're headed to the right place."

THE HERMIT

After decades of public service, Mayor Harry Pratt knew what usually brought out the crowds: free food and hooch, a hanging, well deserved or not, and a good old-fashioned juicy scandal. Since none of those were present currently, he decided to make his speech short and sweet. Harry snipped the red ribbon draped across the doorway to Shelly Wollstonecraft's newly opened boutique.

There was warm applause and a few hoots and whistles from the assembled crowd in the street in front of the small storefront on the newly named Canaan Street. "This is one of my favorite functions as Golgotha's mayor," Harry began. "It always gladdens my heart to see our town grow more prosperous and see new, fresh faces choosing to call Golgotha their home."

Pratt was a striking man, lean and long of limb with thick, wavy hair that fell below his collar, a handlebar mustache, and mutton-chops, all the color of rust. He had bright blue eyes and a melodic and powerful voice. He accentuated his charisma by often dressing well, as he was today, in a fine suit with a silk, brocaded vest and puff tie. An expensive wool long coat held the chill desert wind at bay.

Many would say Harry was born to be a politician. His father, Josiah Pratt, had been a close friend and adviser to the Mormon founder, Joseph Smith. His father had been the first mayor of Golgotha and Harry his successor.

The mayor scanned the crowd as they applauded and cheered. He spotted a few of Golgotha's Mormon elders among the onlookers. "And as we open our fair town to the miraculous wonders of this century, may we never grow so large, so populous, that we have not the time to welcome our new neighbors and celebrate with them their new-found prosperity."

Brodin Chaffin, a heavyset, well-dressed man in his thirties was one of the elders. He gave Harry a slight nod and cautious smile. Brodin thought the influx of non-Mormons to Golgotha would eventually lead to the wealthy Mormon families that had founded the town—like Harry's own—to lose control. Brodin was a savvy businessman, though. Harry could already see him doing the calculations in his head as to how his own businesses would benefit and grow from the influx of "unbelievers" and "aliens" like the German-born Shelly and the Chinese who were finding their way to Golgotha in greater number now that the Transcontinental Railroad project had come to an end. Rhetoric was fine for the tabernacle, but business was business.

Standing beside Brodin like a bleached, reptilian specter was elder Rony Bevalier. The old man seemed to drain the color from the very air around him. Harry had a theory that Rony's perpetual scowl and equally charming personality was the secret of his long life. Even the Grim Reaper had no desire to endure Bevalier's company.

It was an understatement to say that Rony hated Harry, and the feeling was mutual. The elder was a true believer in maintaining Mormon supremacy and Mormon values in Golgotha. He had long thought Harry was too progressive for his tastes. Rony had assembled a political machine to try to unseat Harry as mayor last year. Rony's son, Daaron, who stood next to his father now in the crowd, had run as a former military man, war hero, and devout Mormon opposing the "dandy and degenerate" Pratt. Daaron almost won the election four months ago, and Harry still hated what he had been forced to do to win.

The mayor handed the large shears to Shelly and doffed his hat to her. "I'll be patronizing your fine establishment for my first suit fitting next week, madame, if Golgotha's ladies don't monopolize all your time." He said it loudly for the crowd and was rewarded with laughter. Shelly smiled; she seldom laughed. She was a young woman of breathtaking appearance, with delicate features, flawless measurements, and raven hair she wore up today in a "la concierge" style. She wore a long-sleeved dress of black with a purple lace bib and a beautiful antique bone cameo Clay had given her.

Many in the town often wondered what such a beauty saw in old, disheveled Clay Turlough, the town's new doctor. Whatever it might be, it was clear the two were very much in love. Harry had to admit there was so much more to Shelly than her beauty. She had a sagacity and a bearing about her that reminded Harry of a much more mature woman. Shelly, it seemed had an old soul. Shelly gave the mayor a slight nod before turning toward the crowd to wave shyly. Harry stepped to the side to let the slender seamstress have her moment in the sun.

Clay, still dressed more like a liveryman than a doctor, was first in line to congratulate Shelly. There was an awkward moment where Clay first tried to shake Shelly's hand, then tried to hug her, and finally gave the seamstress a clumsy salute. Shelly tried first to keep up and then settled for returning Clay's salute, breaking into a beaming smile rarely seen on her face. She gave Clay a peck on the cheek. Everyone knew that the draggle-tailed, eccentric taxidermist and amateur-scientist-turned-physician had been sweet on Shelly since the day she came to town, over a year ago. Apparently, even peculiar old Clay had someone out there for him to love.

Behind Clay was Augustus Shultz and his wife, Gillian. Gillian was a lovely woman, tall with long coal and silver hair worn in a chignon bun. Her eyes were large and dark behind her wire-rimmed spectacles. Gillian held their six-month-old son, Auggie Jr., as he squirmed, trying to see everything and everyone at once.

Auggie Sr. waved to Harry through the encroaching crowd. Harry nodded back. Auggie was heavy and broad, built like a stevedore, with a sparse ring of hair along the edges of his bald scalp and a thick, red, handlebar mustache that was going gray. The German shopkeeper reminded Harry of a grizzly bear, with some good-natured walrus thrown in to boot. There was a twinkle in his eyes, and his chest was puffed out with pride at being with Gillian and their son. Good old Auggie.

The changes in Auggie since his ascension to being the right-hand man of Malachi Bick, Harry's most influential political ally, were not lost on the mayor. The once-struggling shopkeeper had traded his apron for fine gentleman's clothing. However, Auggie hadn't changed in all the ways that mattered to most folks. He still paused on the street to talk to his old customers, his neighbors, to pretty much anyone. He still cared about people, regardless of whether they could do anything for him or not. If Pratt was a natural-born politician, then Auggie Shultz was his opposite number, the real thing. Hell, if Auggie ever did run for mayor, he'd get Harry's vote.

The Shultzs and Clay surrounded Shelly, laughing and chatting with her. Harry was happy to see good people enjoying good fortune, but the cynical part of him whispered, wondering how long the town would allow that to last.

"Mayor Pratt!" A stern-faced woman was suddenly in Harry's face. She wore a dour black dress and bonnet, as if she were in mourning. "A word, if you will." It registered in his head who she was, Marjorie Lade—founder of the Ladies Temperance League. Harry often saw Marjorie's husband, Fredrick, at the Paradise Falls saloon, seeming to hide in the corner and drink like a man desperately trying to forget something.

"Of course, Mrs. Lade," Harry said.

"What do you intend to do about the plague of harlots and adventuresses spreading across our town?" Lade didn't really give Harry an opening to reply. "It was bad enough when they frequented the mining camps—you'd expect women of low morals in a cesspool like that—but now they are everywhere, Mr. Mayor, everywhere! I and my ladies supported you in the recent election, and we did so, because you made promises to bring decency and propriety to Golgotha...and that people would stop turning into wax and melting."

"To be fair," Harry said, "we have dealt with the melting problem, Mrs. Lade." Harry made eye contact with his assistant, Colton Higbee, and the young man worked his way through the crowd to the mayor.

"Ah, Colton," Harry said, "Mrs. Lade needs to schedule an appointment with me at my earliest availability. It's a matter of the utmost urgency. Can you see to that?"

"Of course, sir," Higbee said, sliding smoothly between Harry and Mrs. Lade and immediately engaging her. "Now then, Mrs. Lade, please tell me exactly what can the mayor do for you?" There were days Harry honestly didn't know how he survived without Higbee.

Harry stepped onto the wooden boards of the sidewalk and crossed the street. Most of the year, the sidewalk boards protected the traveler from stepping ankle-deep into filth; however, the road was relatively dry today, and Harry's shoes crunched over the mud and manure. He could feel Rony Bevalier's eyes burning into his back like a branding iron. He disappeared down a narrow alley on the other side of Canaan and crossed over into Johnny Town. He needed a moment to regroup his thoughts, and he wanted to find James and spend a little time with him. He needed that.

A massive shadow eclipsed the other end of the alley. Harry hadn't heard the man coming. "Mr. Mayor," a deep voice, smooth as pipe tobacco, said. The man blocking Harry's way towered over the mayor. "A word, sir." The man was hard, as if carved out of wood. He wore an odd but comfortable mix of clothing: the plain shirt, denim dungarees and boots of a working man but the dyed-brown waistcoat and the brocade vest of a man of means. The giant's face was rather unremarkable. His brown hair was parted from crown to nape, and he wore a bland expression behind his immaculately trimmed beard. Harry paused. "She needs to talk to you."

"Well, by all means," Harry said, the irritation seeping into his voice. "I'll stop by the Dove's Roost straight away. I'm sure my constituents will be happy to see the mayor ducking into a house of ill repute midday." The jab seemed to have no effect on the tall man, who was known about town as "the Scholar."

"She will call upon you in your office tonight after ten. Is that more to your liking, Mr. Mayor?" Harry nodded. "Fine, that's fine," he said, looking about.

"Then I bid you good day, sir," the Scholar said, stepping aside. "I'll let you be about...the people's business." Harry's complexion darkened, but he remained silent and still. The Scholar headed down the narrow, twisting street at the end of the alleyway, headed back toward Bick Street. Harry headed off in the opposite direction, toward the Celestial Palace.

Golgotha's growing population of Chinese immigrants resided for the most part within the insular community they had carved out in the southwestern section of the town. That area had come to be known as Johnny Town. Johnny Town was a maze of narrow streets, often with clotheslines swaying far overhead. To Harry, it seemed the streets constantly shifted and changed. He knew the general direction of the Palace, but the bustling, unmarked thoroughfares blurred into each other as he moved through the living, flowing corridors of people.

While he was usually accosted every few feet when he walked in the rest of Golgotha, in Johnny Town, Harry was blissfully ignored for the most part. The Chinese were not allowed to vote and cared little about his station. No one cared why he was here or where he was headed. The residents of Johnny Town kept their own counsel most of the time, a habit Harry admired greatly.

Ch'eng Huang controlled Johnny Town and presented himself as a "community leader." Huang was the undisputed master of the Green Ribbon Tong. He was a notorious and feared mastermind in every

Chinatown between here and San Francisco, with vast and subtle power.

Huang oversaw his far-reaching empire from the upper floors of the Celestial Palace, a popular saloon and brothel at the heart of Johnny Town, and Harry's present destination. Harry knew Huang well enough, and while the two may not be friends, they maintained a decent working relationship. As Harry was well aware—now more than ever—there was only a razor's edge that separated politicians from criminals.

Once he made his way past the Green Ribbon hatchet men at the Palace's front door, he heard the strains of the piano, a sweet, sad sound. Pain and experience drifting, darting like fish beneath the water, a soul laid bare across unforgiving wire. Harry could see the hands moving across the keyboard in his mind, could remember how those hands felt.

He pushed through a curtain of bamboo beads and saw James Ringo in the nearly empty barroom. Ringo hadn't seen him yet, and Harry took a moment to watch the piano player.

Ringo was beautiful by any definition of the word, breathtaking to Harry. The piano player was wiry and lean. His hair fell in long, dark curls, and he wore it long like many Indian men did. His skin was the color of dark cinnamon. His skin, his features announced he was a man born of many different worlds. He normally remained clean-shaven, but today he had a dark shadow of stubble. A rolled cigarette dangled, smoldering at the edge of his lips.

The wandering playing shifted into something new, directed—a new tune. Harry had heard Ringo work and fret on this one for years. He had told Harry once when they were in bed that the song was called "the Ballad of Golgotha." He joked he'd never get to finish it.

"I don't think the old bitch will let me," Ringo had said with a strange smile.

"The bitch?" Harry had asked.

"Golgotha," Ringo replied. "The town. She doesn't like anyone spilling her secrets...just like you, Harry. You were made for each other."

Harry shook the memory away. He walked toward the piano and sat at a table near it, where Ringo could see him. Harry noticed that when he took the seat that Ringo had a half-empty bottle of whiskey and a glass sitting on the ledge of the piano.

"Mr. Mayor," Ringo said loud enough for the bartender and the few other patrons could hear. "Come for a phlegm-cutter, have you?" Harry chuckled. They had played this game for so long. He wondered if anyone was fooled by it anymore or if they just played their roles as he and Ringo did.

"Ringo," Harry said, also loudly. "Indeed, a bit of refreshment and some lively music. Just the ticket." A scar-faced Green Ribbon Tong man named Quiáng, now too old to fight, and relegated to tending bar, approached Harry with a glass of Irish whiskey, his usual. Harry nodded and accepted it. The mayor never paid for his drinks at the Palace—Huang's rule.

Harry took a sip and sighed, feeling the chains of his public life slipping off his shoulders for a moment. He looked over at Ringo and said in a voice probably too loud for good judgment, "I've missed you."

Ringo glanced over to Harry, an unknowable expression on his face. He kept the music loud enough to mask their conversation pretty well. "You told me to stay away because of the election, so I did what I always do, waited for you to feel safe enough to come to me. I've missed you too, Harry."

"How was San Francisco?" Harry asked.

"A cesspool," Ringo said, "but a vibrant cesspool."

"You didn't need any money while you were out there?"

"No, Harry, I didn't. A relief, I'm sure, to your accountant."

Ringo kept playing with one hand and took the other from the keys. He plucked the cigarette out of his mouth and exhaled a stream of milky smoke. To Harry's surprise, he lifted the glass of whiskey, the cigarette between his fingers, and drained it. He never missed a note.

"So how drunk are you?" Harry asked.

Ringo slipped the cigarette back between his lips. He resumed playing with both hands. "The Ballad of Golgotha" changed and shifted into "Waste Not Want Not."

"Clearly, not drunk enough," Ringo said, never missing a beat. Harry sighed.

"You have every right to feel the way you do," Harry said. "I've been neglectful to you, but the election was so tight and I...had information that Bevalier's people were close to uncovering...us."

"'Us'?" Ringo said. His lips were turned up in a smile, but his eyes were dark and angry. "There was scarcely much of 'us' to begin with. Now, between your vicious, cutthroat obsession to hold onto a job you've bitched to me for years about hating and your efforts to be the Mormon equivalent of Achilles, or Hercules, or some other tragic hero...'us' only exists in the few spare minutes you have to attend to the needs of your cock."

Harry looked down at his glass. He emptied it and gestured to Quiáng for a refill. "That's fair," he said. The bartender brought him a fresh drink and retrieved the empty glass.

"You're goddamned right it's fair," Ringo replied, nodding for the bartender to bring him another as well.

A local silversmith whose name Harry couldn't recall drifted through the room, one of Huang's girls on his arm, headed for the private rooms upstairs. Harry caught himself, realizing he still thought of the prostitute as "Huang's girl," but that was no longer the case in this town. "I shouldn't have come. You're right. I'm sorry." Harry polished off his second drink in a single swallow.

He stood and walked toward the bamboo curtain and the front door. "Be seeing you then, Ringo," he said loud enough for the audience. His voice was flat and cold with pain. James didn't reply; he just kept playing. Harry was across the room when James finally spoke. There was a knife in his words. "Mr. Mayor," he said, still playing, "all my best to your wives, sir."

Harry nodded dully. He lost sight of Ringo on the other side of the curtain.

P ratt was well into finishing off a bottle of brandy in his office when his late-night appointment arrived. Harry had dismissed his secretary, Martha Poole, at five and then Higbee around nine. The young man's energy seemed endless, and Harry literally had to shoo him out of the office most nights upon threat of dismissal.

"Sir," Higbee had protested, "with everything we have going on with the railroad project, I think..."

"Go home, Colton," Harry slurred. "New work rule—when the drunken mayor says get out, you..."

"Get out," Higbee finished with a smile. "Yes, sir. Please be safe, sir, and if you need to summon me for anything..."

"Yes, yes," Harry laughed, shaking his head. "Good night, Colton."

A single gas lamp hissed on the wall, casting light. The rest of the room was shadow. Out his second-story window, Harry could hear the murmur of Main Street, even at this hour, a river of human sounds: laughter, bass and raucous, angry shouts, and calls to cama-raderie, the music of life. The day in Golgotha belonged mostly to the businessmen and tradesmen, the proper, prosperous folk of the town, but the night belonged to the cowboys, the outlaws, the streetwalkers, the dealers, schemers, and drunks. And often, in Golgotha, the mayor knew, other things moved in the darkness that simply could not abide the day.

It had long ago stopped surprising Harry how many of the good, pious, upstanding men of this town were down there right now, enjoying the pleasures only found in the night. He raised the brandy decanter.

"Here's to self-deception," he said and took a drink.

"One of my favorite toasts, Harry." The woman stepped out of the shadows. He had not heard the office door open, had not sensed her approach. She was small, barely five feet, and lithe with an almost elfin quality. Her skin was tawny; her hair was a black mane of curls that fell halfway down her back and covered her breasts. She looked at

Harry with hazel eyes flecked with emerald. Whenever Harry saw her, he was struck by a feeling of familiarity, but he had never figured out why.

She wore a loose, flowing poet shirt of green. Over the shirt was an unbuttoned black vest with a peacock pattern of green-and-black silk. Her blousing harem pants had the same emerald-and-black peacock pattern as her vest. She was barefoot, but now Harry could hear the faint ting of the bells on the toe rings she wore as she stepped forward.

"How do you move so quietly with those bells on your feet, Rowan?" Harry said, sitting up.

"Those bells taught me how to move so quietly," Black Rowan said, sliding down onto the couch beside the mayor. She smiled, and it made Harry think of a hungry kiss in the shadows. Rowan ran a hand covered in henna mandalas over Harry's tousled hair. "You look worn out, Harry. What's the matter?"

"Nothing," Pratt said. He looked at the now-empty decanter and walked over to the small bar to make himself a drink. He gestured with an empty glass to Rowan, but she shook her head in refusal.

"I think perhaps you've had too much to drink already," she said.

"An odd sentiment from a queen of vice," Harry said as he poured the rum. "Looking after your investment? A bought-and-paid for mayor is of little use to you if he's deep in his cups."

"Oh," Rowan said, sounding almost disappointed, "so you're still brooding over the election? You won it fair and square, you know. With my help."

"So, having your whores whisper in the ears of their clients who to vote for is fair and square?"

"Employees, and yes. It was simply aggressive campaigning," Rowan said. "Getting out the vote, so to speak."

"And the other...arrangement?"

"Harry," Rowan said, genuinely amused now, "such alliances date far back into history. You're not really so naive as to not see that, are you? And it's not like it was the first time you've ever done that for exactly the same reasons." Harry drained the rum and poured himself another. Rowan rose from the small couch and padded over to him. "Or would you prefer to have Daaron Bevalier occupying this office right now, running our town?"

"*Our* town." Harry looked down at Rowan. "How very magnanimous of you to include me in your conquest, Rowan. I'm touched."

"You made your choices, Harry," Rowan said. "I watched you make them. You're just as ruthless and just as driven as the Bevaliers, as me, maybe more so. I think booze makes you maudlin. It's an unattractive character trait."

"I have no desire to get into my personal issues with you, Rowan. Don't waste my time and yours pretending you give a damn."

"Then let's get down to business, shall we, Mr. Mayor?"

"Yes," Harry said, "by all means." Harry sat down behind his desk, and Black Rowan leaned on one of the edges.

"Our mutual friend in Virginia City is having some problems with land acquisition for the Golgotha dogleg of the railroad," she said. "He would like you to see if you can make those problems go away." Rowan slipped a folded scrap of paper out from under her vest and handed it to Harry. Harry unfolded it and looked at the map. "The holdouts are a group of Mormon families. They've been less than receptive to our friends' very generous offers. Hopefully, they'll be willing to listen to reason from a prominent hero of the faith, like yourself."

Harry stared across the desk. "I see," he said.

"Harry, you look like you want to kill me," she said.

"I do," he said. "But you are correct. I made this hell for myself. You merely opened the door for me. I'll see what I can do about the settlers. In return, I need you to have a bit more care in where your employees wander, at least in the daytime. I have the Ladies Temperance League about to make big trouble for you and me both." Rowan laughed.

"You know old withered-snatch Lade's husband is..."

"...is one of your best clients," Harry said and chuckled. "Yes. I think everyone knows but good lady Lade."

"I will reign the girls in, Harry," Rowan said. "For you."

Pratt shook his head and laughed. "I must say, Rowan, you are the most charming pirate I've ever done business with."

"Mr. Mayor, you certainly know how to make a lady feel grand." Rowan stood to depart. "Now, if you'll excuse me, I must see to breaking a gentleman's legs over mistreatment of an employee."

The ride home up Rose Hill to the Pratt family manor gave Harry enough time to slip back into his black mood. He felt like a boat cut from its moorings. He was aimless, nothing giving him joy or purpose. He felt he had betrayed himself and everything he had fought so hard to claim about his true self, sold it all for power—power he honestly didn't know why he even wanted.

Harry Pratt, who had worn the Mormon articles of the faith, the mystic sword and breastplate of Laban, who had battled madmen and monsters to defend his town, his people, the whole world, and the man he loved—that Harry Pratt seemed to have evaporated into memory, like a dream upon waking. Mayor Pratt was all that remained. Mayor Pratt, who greedily clung to his power, Mayor Pratt who had betrayed his lover, Ringo, his dead wife, Holly's, memory, and himself. Harry didn't know who he was anymore, and he was rapidly reaching a point where he didn't care to know anymore.

The gaslights were on in the front parlor as he approached the home that had once been his father's and mother's. He took his horse, a sorrel Morgan stallion named Knight, into the stables and helped their stable boy, thirteen-year-old Fredrick, remove Knight's saddle. Fredrick was the son of the Pratt family's servants, Lamarr and Judith. Harry entered the house from the kitchen door. Lamarr and Judith were both busying themselves with final chores before heading over to their cottage on the grounds of the manor.

"You missed your supper again, young man," Judith said, pointing a wooden spoon at him, narrowing her eyes, and wagging the spoon disapprovingly. It was the same name she had been calling him all his life. Lamarr and Judith had been runaway slaves from South Carolina who Harry's father and mother had helped through the Underground Railroad. They had worked for the Pratt family for two generations now, and they treated Harry more like a son than an employer.

"I picked up something in town," Harry said. "No need to fret." Judith sniffed the air as Harry walked by her.

"Supper doesn't come out of a bottle, young man," she said and swatted him on his ass with the spoon. "That's the devil's potion you're taking in, boy."

"Leave the man be," Lamarr said to his wife, laughing. "Heavy weighs the crown." Harry paused, nodded to Lamarr for his vote of support. He gestured to Judith hoping for leniency. Judith rolled her eyes and went back to her cleaning, shaking her head.

"You got company," Lamarr said to Harry at the door to the dining room. "Strange fella from Salt Lake City. Showed up around sundown. We told him you were indisposed. He insisted on waiting. He's in the parlor."

"Salt Lake City? You get his name?" Harry asked, sighing. Lamarr shook his head.

"No, but he's a squirrely one. Mrs. Pratt is entertaining him." Harry sighed again.

"Thank you," Harry said. "You're dismissed. See you in the morning." Harry walked through the empty dining room and made a left into the first floor's main hall. He already heard muted voices and laughter coming from the study to the left of the main foyer. One voice was a raspy bass, the other softer in tone. Harry slid the door to the parlor open.

"Good evening," he said, pushing away all his own sadness, his doubts and regrets, and projecting in his best, earnest politician voice. "I apologize for the lateness of the hour."

The two occupants of the parlor stood as he entered. The woman was a striking beauty by any standard. Her hair was blond, coiffed in a thick, high pompadour away from her lovely face, save for earlocks that fell on either side. She wore a formal evening dress of pale blue with a short bustle at the back. Her eyes were a deep green and penetrating. Her name was Ora Pratt.

"Not at all, sir," the man Ora had been entertaining said. "Your charming wife has been a superlative hostess." He looked to be in his sixties and gave off an aura of carefully restrained violence, as if the air was vibrating about him. His most immediate and off-putting feature was his eyes. They were a pale bluish-green, almost clear, and his gaze was intense and unwavering beneath a prominent brow. He had long salt-and-pepper hair that fell from a high widow's peak to well below his shoulders and a full, bushy beard the same color that grew to below his collar. He was lanky but carried some solid muscle in his arms and chest. He wore a frayed range coat that fell almost to his knees. A gray scarf with black checks was wrapped around his neck and hung to his coat's lapels.

Ora moved to Harry and gave him a hug and a peck on the cheek. "Mr. Rockwell, may I introduce you to my husband. Mayor Harry Pratt, Porter Rockwell."

Harry shook his hand and found his grip tested. Harry smiled. "The Destroying Angel of Mormondom," Harry said. "Mr. Rockwell, it's an honor. I've heard tales about you and your adventures all my life. You're a legend, sir."

"And I've been hearing quite a few tales about you of late, Mr. Pratt," Rockwell said, his fevered eyes never leaving Harry. "The One Mighty and Strong."

"A comparison I am unworthy of," Harry said.

Rockwell's eerie eyes stayed on the mayor as if they were burning into the core of his soul. "Indeed," he muttered. "We shall see, won't we?" He broke the grip of the handshake and stepped back to address Harry and Ora, like he was coming out of a trance. "I've been sent here by President Brigham Young, himself, to offer my assistance to you in a manner of great urgency to the church and our brothers and sisters." Harry noticed that Rockwell said Brigham Young's name the same way a member of the faith might say "God" or "Jesus Christ."

"How can we be of service?" Harry asked.

"The brothers and sisters of the faith are under attack," Rockwell said, "by the dark forces of the Great Adversary, and you, Mr. Pratt, you are going to save them."

THE KNIGHT OF PENTACLES

T he cramped office of Dr. Clay Turlough was in chaos. Clay's practice was located on Bick Street, across from the office of *The Golgotha Scribe*, the town's newspaper. As was usual whenever Clay's shingle was out, there was a steady line of people in and out the door, waiting to see the only doctor for many miles in all directions.

Shelly Wollstonecraft, one of Golgotha's finest seamstresses, and Clay's girl, often manned the counter in the office, bringing order and relative quiet to the place. However, with the opening of Shelly's own business, the counter was vacant. People were jammed into the front of the office, filling it with a buzzing wall of endless noise.

Clay was down the narrow hallway, past the counter in the examination room. He was finally getting the chance to examine the wounded woman that Jon Highfather and Kate Warne had rescued. Before Clay carefully examined the terrible wound in the woman's lower back, he had followed the procedures of the English physician, Joseph Lister. He cleaned his hands, his instruments, the wound, and the surrounding tissue with a solution of fresh water and carbolic acid.

Lister's theories of germ transmission and antiseptic procedures were being mocked and ridiculed by most of the medical profession in America and Europe. That just made Clay pay closer attention to them. He had long ago determined through independent observation and hypothesis testing that most learned "men of medicine" in this day and age were pompous jackasses.

During his time at the Medical College of Hampton-Sydney in Richmond before the war, and then later as a battlefield surgeon, Clay had seen first-hand that most doctors were dogmatic traditionalists. He'd seen the results to their patients of that intractability. The aftermath of most battles in the war were likened to slaughterhouses in his mind.

Clay saw the reason in Lister's theories and, more importantly, he saw the results. He studied how many of Lister's patients avoided infections—the most lethal being gangrene and sepsis—and survived. Clay made sure to clean his instruments and surgical theater with Lister's solution, and he didn't really give a damn that most other doctors thought it was all nonsense and a waste of time.

He began to probe the girl's back wound. She had lost a great deal of blood, and the clean, packed dressing he'd put in the wound was already wet and sticky with it. He didn't have the time to go in to try to clamp off the arteries that had been severed; he would have to use his bio-restorative formula if she were to have any chance.

"Hey, Clay!" a voice called out from the front room, "I got a fella out here that done fell off a ladder and hurt himself pretty bad! Shake a leg!"

Another voice, a woman's, immediately challenged the first. "Dr. Turlough! We had an appointment set with your girl last month at this appointed hour! I demand you see us first!"

Clay closed the voices, the noise, out. It was an old trick, one he learned as a child, to shut out the exterior world and live in his own head. He taught it to himself when his whole family died of yellow fever. Clay had been four when he had watched them die, one by one. It took over a week for the locals to find him. His time among the dead, in the silence, had taught him valuable lessons that had remained with him his whole life.

He opened a cabinet in the examination room and took out a small glass vial full of something that looked like black ink. Clay uncorked the vial, ignoring the pungent smell of the liquid, and poured it into the woman's mouth slowly, a few dribbles at a time. The woman swallowed it, coughing, and the color began to return to her face. Clay felt the base of her spine. The wound was closing, the blood loss slowing, stopping. Clay slipped a sheet up to the woman's neck, letting her sleep and rest.

He washed his blood-soaked hands and stepped out into the hallway, letting the noise of the world flood back in. He looked at the crowded room full of waiting, bickering people. "All of you, shut the hell up," he said. "I'll take whoever needs treating the worst first, and if you don't feel like waiting, you can git."

It was dark by the time the last of them were gone, and Clay was bone-weary. There had been a few final transactions to deal with at the end of the day. A man from West Virginia, an attorney, had come in and purchased a rather large quantity of the bio-restorative formula with arrangements to pick it up the next day. Clay had written instructions for Joe Williams, the man who ran his livery business for him these days, to fill the small wooden casks with the formula and deliver them to the attorney.

Black Rowan and some of her girls from the Dove's Roost had also come to claim their sister who Jon and Kate had saved. The young woman, whose name turned out to be Aubrey, was able to walk out on her own, though she had little memory of what happened to her inside the plant house.

"Much obliged, Doctor," Rowan said as they walked out the door. "You come on by the Roost sometime, and we'll show you our appreciation."

"The fiber samples of the strange plant life I retrieved from Audrey's wound are more than payment enough," Clay said. Rowan frowned. She and the other Doves looked at one another, a little confused.

Aubrey hugged Clay. "Thank you so much, Doctor." She kissed him on the cheek. He froze at the contact. The Doves departed, and Clay was finally alone. Being with so many people for so long was exhausting.

He flipped his shingle over to show he was closed. He touched his cheek as he sat, with a groan, on one of the benches in the waiting room by the windows. Clay leaned back in the chair and sighed.

"Physician, heal thyself," Gillian Shultz said. She stood in the doorway with a wicker basket on her arm.

"Nothing taking my boots off and getting some grub won't cure, Gillian," Clay said. "What are you doing out so late? Where's Big Auggie and Little Auggie?"

"Big is working late with Mr. Bick on the railroad business," Gillian said. "Little is with Mrs. Abernathy till I pick him up." Gillian pulled a chair in front of Clay and set the basket in its seat. "And this is why I'm still out," she said. She opened the basket, and the smell of hot fried chicken wafted out and enveloped Clay. Gillian pulled another chair over beside Clay and sat. She handed him a cloth napkin, which he looked at oddly, like he was unsure of its purpose. Gillian tucked it into the neck of his shirt and was briefly reminded of feeding her baby. "Gerta would skin me alive if I let you starve on one of the few days she can't look after you, Clayton." She lifted a dish out of the basket and handed it to Clay. He began to assault the food.

"Shelly," Clay corrected around a mouthful of chicken and mashed potatoes. "Not Gerta, not anymore."

Gillian carefully picked a small portion of chicken from the basket. She paused before eating it. "Shelly Wollstonecraft?" she said. "Clayton, you are very fortunate more folks in this town aren't terribly literate. That's an awful name to give poor Gerta. Just because you brought her back from the dead doesn't mean you can just remake her whole cloth. You saw how well that worked out for Mary Shelly's protagonist, didn't you?"

"Antagonist," Clay said as he gulped down some milk from a glass jug. "Doctor Frankenstein was clearly the villain of the piece, not the hero. I've never understood why folk get that wrong."

"How is...Shelly?" Gillian asked. "She seems happy, very content with her new life and prospects. Very much in love with you, I might add."

"She is," Clay said. "She's a rare woman, Gillian. I've never known anyone as kind or as full of life." He paused to wipe his drooping, milk-soaked mustache on his sleeve. "'Cept you, of course."

"Of course," Gillian said, stealing a forkful of Clay's mashed potatoes.

"I just wish I understood the dreams," he said.

"She still having those dreadful nightmares?" Gillian asked. Clay nodded.

"They started right after her resurrection," Clay said. "She predicted all that death and bloodshed in town just before Ray Zeal and his crew rode in. Since then, she's had nightmares predicting four people's deaths, all days before they passed."

"Oh no," Gillian said.

"I've been thinking that maybe because she was deceased herself, perhaps she has some kind of unconscious, sympathetic link with the dead," Clay said. "Some precognition of someone soon to die. It hints to a vast, connecting psychic ocean of sorts—a kind of necrotic telepathy. It would lend some credence to mediums, and spiritualists, table rappers and the like, at least more than they do now, despite the popularity of the fad."

"Clay," Gillian said, interrupting him, "Auggie has been having nightmares too ever since you...we brought him back. After he was shot...and killed."

"Really," Clay muttered, stroking his mustache. A few crumbs of food tumbled out. "That's fascinating. I wonder whether we could determine if Shelly and Auggie are having the same nightmares. If the content is similar or exactly the sa..."

"Clayton!" Gillian said, her eyes bright with fear and more than a little anger. "It's not fascinating! It's terrifying! We're not talking about test subjects in some experiment of yours; we're talking about people we love, people who by all rights should be dead!"

"By whose right, Gillian?" Clay asked, an edge of anger in his voice. "God? Which one? You tell me when the great cosmic grandfather in any of his guises has seen fit lately to intervene for his so-called 'children'? By the universe's natural laws, we've been given reason, and by reason I've found a cure for death. To think we should limit ourselves, what we can accomplish because it offends the powers that be. It's nonsense."

"This has nothing to do with God, Clay," Gillian said. "It has to do with you tampering with things that you claim yourself not to understand fully. You're performing an experiment without all the variables, isn't that so?"

"It's a scientist's job to pull at the threads, to trace them back to the skein, to see the whole picture, to endeavor to understand as much of it as we can."

"What if by pulling those threads you undo the pattern of the skein? Clay, did you ever consider that there is a reason why we can't see what lies past death?"

"No," Clay said. "I didn't. I don't. It's a puzzle to be solved, not some great inviolate boundary."

"No, of course you didn't," Gillian said. "This gunk of yours..."

"My bio-restorative formula," Clay corrected.

"It's made from the secretions of those worm things that took over people's bodies and attacked the town a few years back and vampire blood, for goodness sake. I heard today that you're selling it now, that people are coming from all over to buy it. Clay, you haven't told people it can bring back the dead, have you?"

"Of course not," Clay said. "But it does work. It heals and helps people. I saved lives with it today, as a matter of fact. The fact that its components are unorthodox is part of the reason it works."

"But you can't say for certain whether there are aftereffects, can you?"

"Over time and with continued application of use, I can make some safe projections about any potential side effects if they crop up, Gillian."

"But for now," Gillian said, "two people we love suffer every night, and the cause is most likely your 'cure.'"

"At least they're alive," Clay said. "Beats the alternative."

"Are you sure?" Gillian asked. "Never mind, of course you're sure."

Clay was silent for a few moments, pushing the food around his plate with his fork. "You made the choice to bring Auggie back, Gillian," Clay said. "Are you telling me you regret that?"

"I...no," Gillian said, wiping her hands with a cloth napkin. She absently brushed some food from Clay's cheek. "I don't, Clay. I just...something is happening, with Shelly, with Auggie, and I think now something is starting to happen with our baby, too."

"Little Auggie is fit as a fiddle," Clay said. "I think you're working yourself up for no good reason."

"Clayton, you remember me telling you my concerns," Gillian said. "That I couldn't be sure if we conceived the baby before or after you brought Auggie back. What if it was after? What if that...concoction somehow has affected Little Auggie?"

"Why would you say that, Gillian?"

"Something happened the other night," she began. Clay noticed the color leaving her cheeks as she spoke. "Auggie hadn't gotten home yet from the Businessman's Association meeting, and I had put Auggie Jr. down to bed. I was reading, waiting to have supper with Auggie when he got home, when I heard a noise in the nursery.

"I took the lantern and went to check on the baby." Gillian paused for a moment. "At the doorway...Clayton, I know it will sound mad, but I swear on the souls of my husband and my son, it's true...at the doorway I could feel cold, the kind of cold that sinks into your bones, that bites you deep. I...I could see my breath spilling out of my mouth. I tried to step into the room to get my baby out and..." Gillian was seeing something in her mind's eye, in that dark nursery, that she was struggling to believe herself.

"Gillian," Clay said, "what happened? Tell me."

"I couldn't step inside," she said, her eyes growing wet. "Some...force, some power, kept me out. There was a stench, Clayton, the same cloying stench as your potion, as those worm-things. I heard a voice, a horrible voice like a knife scraping on slate. It was whispering to my son. I couldn't understand what it was saying to him."

"What did you do?" Clay asked, and Gillian noticed that his eyes were fixed on her with no doubts, no suspicion. For all his shortcomings, all the gaps in his understanding of human behavior, Gillian recalled again why Clay Turlough was her best friend.

"I wanted to run," Gillian said. "My whole body was screaming to run, but I couldn't do that, couldn't leave Little Auggie in there alone with whatever that thing was. I pushed; I closed my eyes and kept pushing. I told it to leave my baby alone, and then, it was gone. The smell, the voice, the force keeping me out, all gone."

They both sat silently. Outside, there was an echoing shout from someone over on Main Street and distant, drunken laughter. Clay leaned forward in his chair, clasped his hands, and looked at the floor. "You know I don't believe in unknowable things, Gillian. I don't think there is anything that can't be unraveled with reason and time."

"You don't believe me?"

"No, I do. It just might take me a spell to figure out what's happening, but I will."

Gillian hugged Clay tight. "Thank you, Clayton," she said. "Thank you so much."

"Thank you for the supper," he said. Gillian laughed, but it was mixed a little with a sob. "Tell me, have you said anything to Auggie about any of this?" Gillian released Clay and wiped her eyes, shaking her head.

"No, no, of course not. He doesn't know. If I told him what happened, what my suspicions are, then he'd know...what happened to him, what we did to him. I can't do that to him, and to be honest, Clay, I'm afraid he might hate me for doing it."

"Auggie could never hate you," Clay said. "He was shot; he'd just died. You loved him, and you let me help you both."

"What if I was wrong? What if I damned him, Clay," Gillian said, "and our child, too?"

"The only damnation I've ever seen is what people do to each other in this world," Clay said, "what they do to themselves. Whatever's going on, Gillian, I promise you, we'll reason it out. If I've made a mistake, then by gum, I'll fix it."

The riders arrived in Golgotha well past midnight. There were four of them, all men, all wrapped in fluttering, bang-up coats and wide-brimmed Stetsons that hid their faces from the accusing moon. Anyone who knew horseflesh would sense that something was wrong with their horses. The beasts' eyes were glassy, and the horses slouched a bit as they carried their masters slowly down Main Street.

There were still folks out on the street near the Paradise Falls, laughing and carousing even at this late hour. The riders drifted past, staying to the shadows, seemingly immune to the frivolity. A bitter, icy wind rolled off the desert down Main in the riders' wake. At the intersection of Main and Prosperity, the party stopped. One of the men, gaunt, with dark rings under his bloodshot eyes, sniffed the cold air and pointed right, toward the dark homes that covered Rose Hill. "There," he said. "The vessel is up there."

"Where's the well, Lloyd?" another of the men asked. His voice had a thick British accent. He had a face that was blandly handsome and a perpetual smile that showed off rotten, yellow teeth. Lloyd sniffed the wind again and pointed to the left up Argent Mountain toward the mine and the lights of the camp above Golgotha.

"There, Rory," Lloyd said.

The dark, writhing maze that was Rory's mind quickly formulated a plan of action. He glanced over toward the cluster of dark houses and businesses off to the right near the foot of Rose Hill. "All right, lads," he said, "let's find some digs for the evening."

The small whitewashed clapboard house a few blocks over from Dry Well Road was dark at this late hour. The home's inhabitants, Zevon and Brighten Hamblin and their newborn, Joel, were all buried deep in sleep.

Zevon was a cooper by trade, but he and his wife had recently talked of him trying to get on with the railroad. All the talk recently about Golgotha getting a dogleg route off the Transcontinental Railroad had made it sound like a promising future for their young family. They didn't know at the time they no longer had a future.

The slumbering couple never heard the strangers enter their home, breaking through the lock on the door only a few dozen feet away from their bed. Little Joel began to cry, a nightly occurrence, and Brighten groaned as she fought to pull herself out of sleep to tend to him.

"Stay," Zevon muttered, "it's my turn. I'll bring him to you." She kissed him sleepily on the cheek and rolled over. The floor was cold on his bare feet, and he stumbled, his eyes half-closed, toward the baby's crib on the other side of the one-room house. He was halfway there when he felt a dry, scaly hand slap over his mouth and the hard barrel of a six-gun stick into his stomach. Zevon's felt fear pour into his stomach, like ice water.

The man in front of him was a shadow, but Zevon saw him raise a finger to his lips and make a quiet hushing sound as he cocked the gun.

Brighten felt the bed's simple wooden frame creak as her husband returned. "Thank you, my love," she whispered and rolled over to warm him. His chest felt wrong as he slipped his arms around her; it was too broad and almost lumpy. "Darling, are you all right?" Her fingers touched skin that felt like it was hard and calloused. She felt one of the lumps pulsate under her touch as if it were alive.

"Never better...darlin'," a man's voice close to Brighten's ear hissed. Brighten's eyes popped open in shock and horror. The man in hers and Zevon's bed had a wide face with a blond beard. His chest was misshapen and covered in throbbing, tumor-like lumps. Brighten began to scream, but the tumor-man grabbed her jaw and kissed her, muffling her cry.

Zevon pushed against the man with the gun as he heard his wife struggling. Zevon's eyes had adjusted to the darkness enough now to see that his captor had dark circles under his eyes. As he grabbed at the gunman's shirt, he was horrified to see that there was a raised ring of flesh that circled the base of the man's neck. The flesh was covered by little pairs of pits, like nostrils, in his skin that seemed to flair as if they were inhaling and exhaling. "What...*are* you?" the young husband gasped as he reared back to strike the man. "Let her go, damn you! I'm coming, Brighten!" A fist shot out of the darkness and struck Zevon from behind, his skull cracking like the sound of a log being split. Zevon fell to the floor, blood slowly leaking out of his ears and nose, dead.

Brighten heard the sounds of her husband's struggles suddenly stop, and she fought with all her might against the hideous thing pinning her to the bed, but he seemed impossibly strong. Little Joel began to cry again, and Brighten redoubled her efforts, driving a knee into her tormentor's groin. The tumor-man only responded with a grunt. She wrested a hand free of his iron grip and drove a fist into his chest. One of the quivering polyps on his skin erupted, and Brighten felt bitter, burning pus splash her eyes and mouth. She gagged and choked on the foul liquid, her eyesight leaving her in a wash of searing pain. The stuff that got into her mouth began to make her feel numb and dull. The tumor-man struck her in the face, hard, but she seemed far away from it. He struck her again, and Brighten fell into darkness, her beloved husband waiting for her there.

"Dead," the tumor-man said. His name was Kern. "I think she

broke. Don't make 'em like they used to." The men chuckled, except for Rory who was peering down into the crib at the red-faced, squalling baby. The fourth man, the one who had struck Zevon from behind, stepped over beside Rory. His arms were abnormally swollen with muscle, and his head was too small for the rest of his body. His small ears were pointed. His name was Tidbull.

"Want me to kill it?" Tidbull asked Rory in a voice that was a whisper. The smiling man shook his head.

"No, give it a bit of Laudanum to shut it up but no killing it. We'll need the snapper for later."

"These two?" Lloyd asked, pointing his gun down to Zevon's and Brighten's bodies.

"They're still warm," Rory said. "Seems a shame to waste them. Let's have a spot of fun before bed, lads."

The night was a willing accomplice in the horrors that followed. The little house was still again by the time the sun arrived and chased the darkness away.

THE KING OF SWORDS (REVERSED)

I appreciate you and Sheriff Highfather meeting with me on such short notice, Mayor Pratt," Allan Pinkerton said, slipping into one of the fine, high-backed chairs Harry had before his desk. Besides Harry and Pinkerton, Jon Highfather and Kate Warne were present, both seated. Colton Higbee stood near the door, his ledger and pen at the ready to make notes. Porter Rockwell stood off behind and to the right of Harry, his arms crossed, eyeing Pinkerton like he was a snake ready to strike.

"It's an honor to have such an august personage as yourself grace our fair town, Mr. Pinkerton," Harry said. "To what, exactly, do we owe this privilege?"

"Have you heard of a settlement southeast of here called Ezekiel?" Pinkerton asked.

"It's a Mormon settlement," Highfather said, "about two dozen families. Mostly ranchers and a few farms. Peaceful folk." Harry glanced over to Rockwell and then back to the detective and spymaster.

"I hadn't, until last night," Harry said, "when Mr. Rockwell enlightened me as to what had happened there."

Pinkerton's eyes flicked to Porter. "Ah, the infamous Mr. Rockwell. May I inquire as to your interest in these matters and your reason for being here?"

"You may inquire all you damn well please," Rockwell rumbled, his stare fixed on Pinkerton. For a moment, Highfather's hand reflexively dropped to his holstered pistol. Jon's instincts screamed to him that the Mormon gunslinger was a breath away from drawing and firing on Pinkerton. Instead, Rockwell said, "I'm very familiar with your detectives, Mr. Pinkerton. I've seen those brutes do your evil work upon the innocent brothers and sisters of the faith, all in your name."

Pinkerton held Rockwell's gaze. "In the years since you've been a trigger-man for Brigham Young…"

"Bodyguard," Rockwell corrected.

"…Bodyguard." Pinkerton allowed. "You've also been called a religious assassin, a killer of those who stood between the LDS Church and its goals. You've killed reporters that wrote stories casting your faith in an unfavorable light, and tried to kill the governor of Missouri for adopting anti-Mormon legislation. I've heard tell over a hundred men have fallen to your gun, Mr. Rockwell. Can you tell me that every one of them deserved that fate?"

The room was silent for a seemingly endless moment. Only the sounds of a bustling Main Street morning below drifted in past the windows, and Harry's grandfather clock. "Let's all stay focused on why we're here," Harry said, looking pointedly at the Mormon gunslinger. "Shall we?"

The tension left Rockwell, and Highfather's hand drifted away from his gun. Only Kate had noticed Jon's heightened awareness. She relaxed a bit now too.

"I never killed anybody who didn't need killing," Rockwell said, "and I ain't done yet. I'm here to see that the Mormon people are safe, their rights and faith respected, and the murdered saints avenged."

"Gentlemen," Highfather said, "perhaps we could put all this vinegar aside for a spell and get back to why Mr. Pinkerton and Mr. Rockwell are in Golgotha exactly."

"Heard of you too, Sheriff," Rockwell said. "You've killed quite a few in your time, too, haven't you?"

Jon looked down at his boots. "I don't count them," he said. He looked over to Pinkerton. "What happened in Ezekiel?"

"A slaughter," Pinkerton said. "Indians raided the settlement. They killed everyone, over a hundred men, women, and children. They burned it to the ground."

"Who was it?" Jon asked.

"They tried to make it hard for us to tell," Pinkerton said. "We found bodies with arrow wounds but no arrows and bullet wounds with no bullets to be found in the bodies."

"I've never heard of any war party doing that," Jon said, "digging their arrows and bullets out."

"There were no signs they were dug out," Pinkerton said, "just...not there. Our intelligence is reporting it was a Northern Paiute band, maybe some Ute renegades with them, stirring the pot."

"That the same grade of intelligence you gave General McClellan?" Highfather asked.

Pinkerton reddened at the jab. He turned back to face Harry. "Ezekiel wasn't the first place they've hit, and it won't be the last. We're seeing Indian uprisings popping up all over the territory. It's mostly the Paiute, but there's Ute and Shoshone activity as well. It's growing and threatens to get out of hand."

"This doesn't sound like the Paiute," Jon said. "How many settlements have they hit?"

"Seven," Pinkerton said, "over the last two months."

"Ten," Rockwell said. "You left out three Mormon towns and settlements over the Utah line that they decimated. Same thing with the arrows and the bullets. Holes, but no ammo."

"Mr. Rockwell has been sent here by President Young to investigate the massacres at Mormon settlements," the mayor said.

"And to put an end to this," Porter said. "If the federal army can't or won't protect our people, then I damn well will."

"You a one-man army, Mr. Rockwell?" Kate asked.

"I have the power and protection of the faith," Porter said, dead serious. "I need nothing more."

"Then we are here with the same goals, Mr. Rockwell," Pinkerton said, slipping two envelopes out of his coat pocket and placing them on Harry's desk. "Mr. Mayor, I have letters here from Governor Bradley and President Grant instructing you to provide me and my people complete and unfettered assistance in dealing with this uprising before this spreads to other parts of the republic and we have a full-fledged war on our hands."

Highfather glanced to Kate. The look on her face affirmed what he was already feeling: Pinkerton was holding something back, he wasn't giving the whole story. "Harry," Jon said, "I can have my people look into this."

"We appreciate any help you can provide the general and his men, Sheriff."

"General?" Highfather said.

"General Caxton," Pinkerton said. "His troop should be arriving in Golgotha by this evening. I want your half-breed deputy acting as a scout and translator for him when they ride out on patrol."

"Aries Caxton?" Jon said, an anger growing in his voice. "The Red General? He's got a terrible reputation with the Indians. The things he did during the war to keep the western territories pacified..."

"We don't need the savages to like him, Sheriff," Pinkerton said, remaining seated, his voice calm. "We want them to fear him and his reputation. I wonder if you've made peace with your own rebel sympathies. You did fight for the Confederacy, didn't you? Strange, considering your family were such staunch abolitionists."

"My family..." The words hit the sheriff like a sucker punch. Jon's fist began to clench. "You don't know a goddamned thing about my family, Pinkerton." Kate reached out and lightly touched Jon's arm.

"Jon..." she said softly. Highfather blinked and came back to himself. He sat back in his chair, and Kate squeezed his arm.

"My only sympathies, my only loyalty is to the people in this town," Jon said. "You march a bunch of federal troops in here and quarter them and then start hunting Indians, you make Golgotha a target for when they retaliate." He looked over to the mayor. "You really want that, Harry?"

"What I want, what you want, is irrelevant, Jon," Harry said, holding up the letters. "These say we have to give Mr. Pinkerton and General Caxton full cooperation."

"I see," Highfather said. He looked back to Pinkerton. "Just so you're clear, Mutt isn't 'my' anything, 'cept my friend. He's his own man, and I won't order him to do anything he doesn't care to. Same goes for all my deputies." Pinkerton remained silent. He glanced to Kate for a moment, and Jon was unsure what passed between them.

"Well, we have preparations to make," Harry said. "Higbee, see if Mr. Bick is agreeable to putting up General Caxton and his officers over at the Imperial."

"Very good, Mr. Mayor," Higbee said, writing down a few notes.

"I have a suite there already," Pinkerton said. "Fine accommodations."

"The troops can encamp in the field at the foot of Rose Hill," Harry said. "Should be ample room there."

"Very good, then," Pinkerton said, standing. "I'll telegraph President Grant and the governor that all is proceeding as planned. Thank you, Mayor Pratt, for your cooperation." Pinkerton walked past Highfather as he departed the office. "Sheriff."

Jon and Kate stood to leave as well, but Harry raised a hand. "Jon, can you give me a minute," he looked over to the unmoving Rockwell, "alone?"

The Mormon gunman drifted out of the room. As he passed Highfather at the door, Rockwell muttered, "See, you should've let me draw on him."

Kate lingered near the door."You good?" she asked Jon. "I know Allan can get on your last nerve, but he wouldn't be here if something serious wasn't brewing."

"I know," Jon said. "But we both know there's more to this than he's letting on."

"Yes," she said. "I'll see if he'll talk to me."

"I'll catch up to you," Jon said. "See if you can find Mutt, too. He needs to know what's about to happen with the Paiute." Kate gave Harry a cautious glance, and departed with Higbee. Jon closed the door, and the sheriff and mayor were alone.

Harry opened a wooden box of cigars on his desk, took one out, and offered it to Jon. The sheriff shook his head. "Good job dealing with that house-thing, yesterday," the mayor said. "Most folks are already saying the roof collapsed and the whole, dilapidated, old place came crashing down."

Harry snipped the tip off the end of the cigar. He saluted Jon with the stogie, "Denial is our chief export," and lit it. He puffed for a few moments before he spoke again. "I think that might be the first time I ever saw you get riled like that, Jon," he said.

"It won't be the last with Pinkerton in town," Jon said. "I'm sorry, Harry. I know you have to toe the line and do what the big muck-a-mucks in Carson City and the District say. I'm not trying to cause any trouble. I just know that Mutt, Kate, Jim, and I could handle this a lot better than a mess of federal troops and a blood-thirsty general."

Harry leaned back in his chair and puffed on the cigar. "Why are you so against Pinkerton? The man's practically a national hero."

"I thought that way about him, too," Highfather said, "until Kate told me more about the man, how he operates. Harry, Pinkerton secretly runs a division of the Secret Service called the Office of Special Intelligence Resources, Investigation, and Security."

"OSIRIS?" Harry said. Highfather shrugged.

"They were commissioned at the request of President Lincoln shortly before his death," Jon continued. "He signed them into law the night he was assassinated. They investigate supernatural occurrences —weird, unexplained things—that may be a threat to the nation. Kate used to work for Pinkerton. She was sent here undercover because Golgotha is...well, you know."

Harry nodded. "I do," he said. "Anyone who lives here a spell does.

You think there's something more to this Paiute uprising than he's letting on? Something 'Golgotha strange'?"

"I'd bet a steak dinner on it," Jon said.

"You sure this doesn't have anything to do with Deputy Warne having a previous...working relationship with Mr. Pinkerton?"

"Why would it?"

"Oh, come on, Jon!" Harry said with a smile. "You don't need to be a detective to see how you and Miss Warne are around each other."

"Harry!"

"No, no, don't get me wrong. I whole-heartedly approve. She makes you happy, Jon, happiest I've seen you since Eden passed. A man comes into town who has a previous association with her, and I've seen how she watches him, too—a father figure, a mentor, possibly more than that—of course you're going to not trust the man."

Highfather sighed and rubbed his face. "You'd make a good detective, there, Mr. Mayor." Harry opened one of his desk drawers and retrieved a bottle of whiskey and two glasses. He poured a shot for himself and the sheriff.

"A good politician has to be able to read people, read a room," Harry said. He raised the glass; Jon raised his as well. "To that little bastard, Cupid," he said. "May he get a cramp in his wing." They clinked glasses and drained them.

"You may be right about there being something bigger going on here. My glaring guardian Angel of Destruction, there, was sent to me personally by Brigham Young to look into the same thing that Pinkerton is here for, the Indian attacks. Of course, his only concern is the Mormon people and my protection."

"Of course," Jon said. "He seems very nurturing."

"Young sent him to check up on me," Harry refilled their glasses, "to see if I'm a threat to him politically."

"Well, Harry," Highfather said, "a lot of folks believe you're the One Mighty and Strong, the prophesied Mormon champion." Pratt groaned, and they raised their glasses again.

"You start that nonsense up, and I'll see you and raise you 'the Sheriff Who Can't Die, whose time has not yet come.'"

"Shut up and drink," Jon said. And they did.

Highfather wiped his mouth with the back of his calloused hand and set the glass on the mayor's desk. "I and my deputies will endeavor to provide a spirit of cooperation to the federal authorities," Jon said. Harry chuckled.

"You'd make a pretty good politician yourself, there, Jon."

"No need to get nasty about this, Harry," Jon said with a smile.

The Red Patrol rode into Golgotha ahead of the bloody, drowning sun. They were over a hundred riders strong, all dressed in the dust-coated blue of federal troops. At the head of them rode General Caxton and his senior officers.

Aries Harcourt Caxton was a squat, burly man with long, red hair and a fastidiously trimmed beard. He had a prominent, raised scar on his forehead that had come years earlier, during the war, from the knife of a Cheyenne brave. Caxton wore none of his medals, as many generals did. In fact, he wore no insignia whatsoever to distinguish him from a common trooper. The look in his mahogany eyes told anyone who saw him that he led these men.

Crowds gathered on the sides of the street to watch the procession move by. There were cheers and whistles but also many troubled looks and whispers. The people of Golgotha recalled all too well what had happened the last time an army had ridden into their town.

Jon and Kate rode up to meet the procession, and Caxton stopped the advance down Main Street with the raising of a gloved hand.

"General," Jon said, "I'm Sheriff Highfather. This is my deputy, Kate Warne. Welcome to Golgotha."

Caxton narrowed his gaze and frowned as he regarded Kate. "A woman deputy? That doesn't speak well to the safety of your town, Sheriff."

"Hopefully, we won't have any incidents to show you how wrong you are, General," Jon said. A prison wagon, with a single, narrow, barred window rumbled past, pulled by a pair of stout draft horses.

"What's that?" Kate asked.

"That, madame, is our secret weapon," Caxton said with a smirk. Jon and Kate exchanged glances.

"The mayor's arranged for you and your officers to bunk over at the Imperial," Jon said. "Take the left at Prosperity Road. You can't miss it. Rest of your men can make camp over at the field at the base of Rose Hill; take the right on Prosperity. Big tree in the middle of the field, can't miss that either."

"Thank you, Sheriff," Caxton said in a booming voice as if he had willed all that Jon had said into being. "This evening, please be my guest for supper. We have a great deal to discuss about the campaign we're about to embark on together, and I'm keen to meet this half-savage deputy of yours. I hear he's an excellent scout."

"I'll do my best to attend," Jon said, "as my duties allow."

"Well, if you can't make it, perhaps your lovely deputy will do me the pleasure of her company," Caxton said, his eyes fixing firmly on Kate's body. Kate's face lit up in her best undercover smile.

"Well, I'd be honored to spend the evening in such gallant company, General Caxton. Thank you!"

Caxton's barrel chest puffed out even more. "Very good. I'll expect you at six o'clock sharp. Sheriff. Deputy." The procession continued down Main, and Jon and Kate rode over to the side of the road near the Golgotha Bank and Trust.

"Kate, you don't have to..." Jon began. Kate laughed.

"Jon, I'll have that leering gasbag telling me everything he's planning before the first course shows up. He won't outflank me. Don't fret." She noticed the shadow still playing over Highfather's face. "Though frettin' suits you, I have to say." Highfather shook off his grim expression. He almost smiled.

"Okay," Jon said. "I know you can handle yourself. I...just don't care for it." Something crossed Kate's face for a moment.

"I know," she said softly, "and I really do appreciate that. A little frettin's nice."

Highfather spotted Mutt, riding Muha with another man sitting behind the deputy, as they turned onto Main at about the same time Caxton's troop reached the intersection. Jon and Kate rode up to meet them.

"Look what the cat dragged in," Kate said. "When you said you were taking the day off after that tussle with Yule, I figured you'd sleep in a little, but you were serious."

"Took a relaxing ride into the 40-Mile," he said. "Picked up some strays." Mutt glanced back as the last of the federal troops split into two groups, headed opposite ways on Prosperity Road. "What's with all the pretty blue bonnets on Main Street?" Mutt asked. "Is it time already for that Easter parade you white folks enjoy so much?"

"As usual," Jon said, "you blink and you miss a lot around here." Highfather extended his hand to the black man at Mutt's back. "So you were out in the 40-Mile. Been stuck out there myself. Not a pleasant place. Jon Highfather. Pleased to meet you, Mr...?"

"Hayes," Rabb said, "Barabbas Hayes. You can call me Rabb. I'm in debt to your deputies, Sheriff. They saved the child's life."

"Child?" Jon said.

"Little girl," Mutt said. "Only survivor of a massacre."

"Let me guess," Kate said, "Ezekiel, right?"

"Yeah," Mutt said. "Hayes here was passing through and found her, kept her alive. She's over at Clay's office now. Jim's with her."

"What happened at Ezekiel is part of the reason all the Billy-Yanks are here, now," Highfather said. Rabb looked over at the last of the troops.

"Looks like Red Patrol," Hayes said. "Caxton's men. If they're here, then there's going to be some bloodshed; I promise you that."

"You were in the army, Mr. Hayes?" Kate asked.

"The 10th Cavalry," Rabb said. "Under Colonel Grierson. I cashed out a few years back."

"Well, welcome to Golgotha," Jon said. "You're getting here on a pretty typical day."

"That bad, huh?" Mutt said.

"What you get for playing hooky," Jon said.

"Okay," Mutt said, "give me a sec. I'll meet you over at the jail, and you can catch me up." Rabb climbed down off Muha and looked over to Mutt.

"Much obliged, deputy," he said. Mutt nodded and rode off.

"I'll go check on Jim and the kid," Kate said, "before my big date." Highfather started to say something, but Kate winked and rode away.

"If you're looking for a decent place to bed down, Rabb," Highfather said, "you might try Shultz's Boarding House. All my deputies bunk there. Clean rooms, good spread, and fair price."

"Much obliged," Rabb said, still looking strangely at Jon. "They won't have a problem putting up a colored man?"

"Some places in this town, you'd find trouble," Jon said, "but not Gillian Shultz. She's good people, some of the best. Over off of Dry Well Road." Jon pointed in the direction of the boarding house.

"Thank you again," Rabb said and started to walk away. He paused and turned back to Highfather. "Sheriff?"

"Yes?"

"When you have the time, I have a message for you. I've traveled a long way to give it to you. I think you'll want to hear it."

THE CHARIOT

The stagecoach from Hazen to Golgotha jostled, shook, and rumbled over the rutted, nearly non-existent road. The interior of the coach was packed with as many people heading in the same direction as the stage company could pack in. At present, there were eight—six men and two women.

For most folks, a prolonged stagecoach trip was a preview of Hell. There were the sounds of coughing, throat clearing, snoring, groaning, and wheezing. Then there were the smells. Besides the reeking spittoon and chamber pot sloshing about on the floor, there were usually the scents of alcohol, sweat, body odor, flatulence, urine, vomit, feces, and often the stale smell of sex. The doors to the wooden box the passengers rode inside were sealed shut to keep passengers from opening the doors and falling out during the journey or jumping out when they simply couldn't stand it any longer.

The adult woman passenger had auburn hair with an occasional strand of gold or silver. Her hair fell below her shoulders, but she was wearing it up in a bun. The men on the coach would call her a "handsome" woman, perhaps a bit too mannish-looking—of course, not to her face. Her complexion was fair, but it was clear she had gotten some sun recently and had a healthy glow to her skin. Her build was slight, and her wrists slender. She was not a striking woman, at least by the estimation of most of the men on the coach. Normally, she would not receive a second glance in a crowd, but she carried herself with a power and dignity as well as a fluid grace. For the hours she had been in the coach, her posture never wavered from perfect. She wore a simple black dress with ankle boots and a butternut-dyed blouse with a high collar.

The younger girl to her right, apparently her teenaged daughter, was dressed in a sky-blue dress, stockings, and a shawl. The girl favored her mother a great deal, with fair skin and auburn hair held back by a blue ribbon. Her lips were fuller and her features a bit softer, but she was her mother's daughter.

The portly man in the too-tight, sweat-stained, tweed suit glanced up from his bible to give the woman a brief smile and to nod to her daughter. The woman, Maude Stapleton, regarded the man but did not return the smile. The man's gaze had only held Maude's eyes for a quarter of a second, as opposed to the half-second he scanned her chest, or the almost full second that his eyes had side-ways-lingered on Maude's sixteen-year-old daughter, Constance's, body. Looking at Constance, the man's pulse and a certain part of his anatomy had stirred a bit. The gesture of the polite glance, which would seem harmless, and actually neighborly, to the majority of the human race, made Maude want to get off the coach even more, or perhaps throw the man off—through the locked door. Oblivious, the lech delved back into the Good Book. Such minute observations were as natural to Maude as blinking. She had been trained in a crucible through much of her childhood—her senses, mind, and body honed to a level that for most on this planet would seem superhuman.

Constance's normally alabaster complexion was decidedly green at present. Maude's daughter wasn't as good yet at sorting through everything her heightened senses were throwing at her.

"Think of this as a real-life exercise," Maude whispered to her daughter. She had pitched her voice to a frequency only Constance's ears could comprehend and decode.

"It is already," the girl replied in the same inaudible whisper. "I've been keeping myself from getting ill for about two hours now."

It dawned on Maude that she had addressed Constance in a way very similar to how her own teacher—her great, great, great, great grandmother—Anne Bonny, would have. The old pirate queen would have cackled and told young Maude to endure the reeking olfactory assault and crude body language of her fellow passengers and to try to make it a game of it—figure out what you could about these men from the clues they were screaming at her with her heightened senses. Of course, Gran Bonny also would have run the portly man through with a cutlass for looking at Constance the way he did. That made Maude smile.

"All the gawking we're getting isn't helping," Constance added. "I wish we could have just sailed to Golgotha on *the Hecate*."

"There's not enough water near town to float her," Maude said. "It's a magic, teleporting, living ship, but it's still a boat, dear. I can't put her in a teacup."

Maude had a wonderful time in San Francisco, meeting up with her father, Martin, and reuniting with Constance again. Her father was headed for Canada now on business but had delayed his trip to escort Constance from school in Charleston to meet her mother. The three of them spent the last week enjoying all the wonders of the Golden City. They had taken the train inland and disembarked at Hazen, the closest dogleg of the Transcontinental line to Golgotha.

It wasn't just the man in the stained suit, either. Two other men were eyeing them with very bad intent. Two others were trying to act like gentlemen, and one man fancied one of the other men who had been eyeing Constance.

Constance, who was painfully aware of the unwanted attention, slipped one of Jim Negrey's letters out of her coat pocket and began to read it again, for what Maude estimated was the hundredth time, focusing on the paper as if it were the totality of the world.

Even given the circumstances of the unpleasant trip, it was good to be headed back to Golgotha. Compared to San Francisco, the little mining town wasn't much more than a dirty, flea-infested camp, but to Maude and Constance, it was home.

The coach bumped hard, and the men all flew into the air, groaning and cursing softly, and then came back down again, roughly, onto the wooden benches. Maude and Constance seemed to defy gravity somehow and remained perfectly still and seated. Maude could feel that the bump had placed a small crack in the coach's rear left wheel. The fissure would widen, and within a few weeks, the wheel would break. Maude would tell the driver when they reached Golgotha, but she knew, most likely, he would dismiss it as the mutterings of a hysterical woman. Still, she would try.

The coach lurched again, and the man sitting next to Maude, who apparently bathed in bay rum tonic, used the excuse to try to place a hand on Maude's breast. Instinctively, she analyzed the vectors of force at play and with a seemingly innocent bump of her elbow redirected the man's hand so he ended up hitting and groping his own genitals. The man let out a muffled grunt and looked toward the window, slumping. Maude glanced to her daughter and smiled.

"Just one long, smelly, bumpy, grabby training exercise," Maude subvocalized as she pretended to cough.

Constance was about to reply when they both sensed it, the subtle bloom in air pressure, the prescient hum a second before the Doppler wave, a gunshot. The bullet tore through the back of the coach, blasted its way through the back of the neck of the man reading his bible, blew out the front of his neck in a spray of meat and blood, and sped straight for Constance. Maude's hand shot out at a practiced angle and caught the slowed but still deadly lead slug. It hit her hand in a stinging wave of pain and heat, but its flight was ended.

No one had reacted yet. Even the dead man who had just been shot was frozen in place, in time. Maude opened her hand. Her palm was bleeding a little bit and bruised a lot, exactly as it had been every time in her life she had been forced to catch a bullet out of the air. What surprised her though was there was no bullet; it was as if the deadly projectile had simply ceased to be, had vanished.

The man with the tweed suit and no throat gurgled and slid to the floor, knocking over the spittoon and the chamber pot. More gunshots pealed across the desert outside, accompanied by the angry shouts of the drivers on top of the coach. Gunfire was returned by the strong box guard, and the whoops and howls of the attackers behind them could be heard closing rapidly.

"Oh, sweet Jesus!" the man who had tried to grope her wailed. "Injuns! They'll skin us alive and eat us for Sunday supper!"

"He's dead! He's dead!" another man barked, fumbling for a derringer he had in a vest pocket.

"How did you stop that bullet, girl?" one man asked, grabbing Maude by the shoulder. At least he thought he grabbed her by the shoulder. He ended up clutching the man next to Maude's shoulder.

Maude glanced to Constance. "You armed?" she asked her daughter, who had tucked Jim's letter away.

"Yes, ma'am," Constance said. "Three poisoned throwing pins, a smoke bomb, a strangle cord, and my nails are sharpened."

"Good girl," Maude said. "Keep them alive. I know it's a chore. I'll be back." Maude stood up, reached over the man who had tried to grope her, and reached out through the open window to grab the luggage rail on the roof of the coach.

"Sit down, you hysterical cow," the man with the parlor gun shouted out as more bullets tore through the cab. "You'll get us all kil..." Constance's hand shot out faster than anyone but Maude could see and tapped the man's chest. It sent him flying back against the bench and knocked the wind out of him, stealing his voice. Maude flipped herself out through the window to the top of the speeding stagecoach.

The driver was dead; half his head was gone. He was slumped forward on the box, the bench the driver and shotgun messenger sat upon. The shotgun messenger had the reins and was urging the team of horses on faster and faster, trying to stay low to avoid the bullets and arrows raining down on him. They didn't need much coaxing; the poor animals were terrified. Maude looked back at their approaching attackers, and she knew why.

An army of over a hundred Indians on horseback were closing on the stagecoach, shooting rifles, pistols, spears, and arrows as they advanced. Over half of the war party looked more like a desert mirage than flesh and blood. These Indians were transparent; their color was washed out, but they rode and cried and shot just as well as their material counterparts. Their weapons were just as effective, just as lethal, as their flesh-and-blood kin, splintering the wooden roof of the coach with each hit.

Maude felt a half-dozen pressure waves coming in toward her. She ducked and spun, and the bullets and arrows sailed inches-past where she had been an instant ago. She ended up in a crouch with the baggage of the passengers giving her a little cover. A stray bullet popped a hole in the corner of a leather valise.

The beleaguered driver looked back. His eyes popped when he saw Maude on the roof with him.

"Ma'am, you got to get back inside! It's dangerous out here!" An arrow flew straight for his back. Maude picked up one of the arrows that had clattered on the roof, aimed for her. She flicked her wrist, sending the arrow sailing, and the incoming arrow was split in two and missed the driver.

"Give me your shotgun," she shouted, and the still-stunned driver tossed the double-barrel to her without a word, as well as the bandoleer of shot shells. Maude felt the gun's weight and knew that it still had one chamber full. She didn't like guns, a trait she had inherited from Gran Bonnie, but Gran had given her as thorough an education in guns as she had everything else.

Maude had trained since the age of nine in the ways of the secret society known as the Daughters of Lilith. The Daughters were an ancient order of women that Gran had joined after her adventures in Africa in the 1700s. Each Daughter was trained to be the consummate warrior, assassin, counselor, and healer. They were charged with protecting humanity from its own shortsightedness, evil, and cruelty, to be mankind's secret protectors against the myriad inhuman forces of darkness that sought to prey on the innocent and unwitting.

The secret to the Daughters' power was the blood of the first woman—the Mother—Lilith. Both Maude and Constance had imbibed the supernatural blood during their training. The blood made them stronger, faster, and more resilient than any mortal upon the Earth. It gave them the ability to survive the inhuman rigors of the training. Maude was the caretaker of the Mother's blood. It resided in the Grail, an ancient, slender, iron vial that she wore on a chain around her neck. There was only a handful of the Daughters around the world in any given age. Last year, a terrible series of events had reduced their numbers even more. Young women, like Constance, were the key to the future and to the Daughters surviving this violent, rough-and-tumble age.

Maude brought the gun up and sighted, even as she dodged another hail of bullets and arrows. She fired, and three mortal braves dropped from the shot pellets sprayed. She angled the shot so that two of the tiny lead balls that spewed from the gun knocked a pair of incoming arrows out of the sky, too. Maude snapped the breach open, shucked the empty cartridges out, and loaded two fresh rounds in. She snapped the breach closed one-handed with a flick of her wrist and hurled the empty cartridges at two more advancing braves with her free hand, knocking another two off their mounts. Then she was sighting again, firing again. "Faster!" she shouted to the surviving but now wounded messenger.

"We can't get much faster unless we lose some weight!" the shotgun messenger said. He had pulled his six-gun and was blasting back at the braves while trying to keep the coach on the road. Maude fired, emptied the shotgun, reloaded, and fired again. She was maximizing the damaging effect of as many of the individual shot pellets as she could in each round. The living braves were falling back, trying to get out of her range, but the intangible braves kept advancing, ignoring the rounds.

One of the ghostly braves rode up beside the coach; his face was like stone. He and Maude locked eyes, and Maude could see the cold anger that simmered there. This was no parlor trick, no illusion or mindless phantasm; this had been a living, breathing man once, who now fought for his people and his land as zealously in death as he had in life.

The brave hurled a razor-sharp tomahawk at her, and Maude arced to avoid it, as she had been trained, as she had done hundreds of thousands of times. A white-hot pain tore through her arm, and she almost dropped the ammo belt. She had avoided a direct impact from the blade, but it had sliced deep into her arm and nicked a muscle on its way past. It occurred to Maude what she had done wrong; she was predicting speed and distance to dodge the tomahawk as if it weighed something, and apparently, it didn't.

The brave had his tomahawk back in his hand again as if he had never thrown it and was getting ready to hurl it at Maude again. The man with the derringer in the coach below stuck himself half-way out the window and fired on the spirit warrior. Maude heard the crack of the small gun and smelled the puff of gun smoke. If the bullet hit the brave or his horse, they showed no signs of it.

Maude felt something tug at her memory, as if someone were yelling for her attention. In the previous year, she had undertaken a new discipline of the Mother's blood. She discovered that Daughters of Lilith could share knowledge and experiences through the mystical link of the blood, accessing a vast archive of human knowledge, sometimes even across the ocean of time. Gran Bonnie was poking her with that hard, bony finger, reminding her of something Maude had forgotten long ago. *Remember the ghost stories I told you from the old country, girl? The ones about the ghosties and ghoulies. The one about the Bean Sidhe? Remember?*

The Indian lowered his gaze and arched his arm back to throw the tomahawk at the man in the coach. The axe sailed at the man's face when Constance's pale hand grabbed him and pulled him back inside, narrowly avoiding sure death.

Maude's hand slipped to the bandoleer and rapidly slid down the shells until she felt the ones she had hoped would be here, feeling the difference in the weight. The brave had his tomahawk again. He looked at Maude. Ignoring the pain in her arm, Maude slipped two new rounds into the shotgun, snapped it shut, and opened fire on the brave just as he was about to release the hatchet at her.

The shotgun boomed. A cloud of rock salt enveloped the spectral brave. The brave roared in pain and then seemed to dissolve in the scattering cloud, as if he and his horse were made of salt.

Blood was trickling down Maude's throbbing arm. A rain of bullets fell all around her. She managed to avoid them and looked down at the heavy lock box, wrapped in chains and chained down to the roof of the coach right behind the driver's box. Maude loaded a solid slug into the shotgun.

"Get ready to run for all you're worth," Maude shouted. She saw the living braves advancing again, seeing she had paused in her firing. They were getting close. Good. Maude froze for just an instant when she saw an immaterial figure on his equally translucent horse appear near the head of their ghostly pursuers. It was the brave she had shot with the rock salt, reformed and trying to close the gap between them once again.

Maude fired at the chains holding down the heavy iron box. They shattered and clattered onto the roof.

"What are you doing?" the driver shouted. "There's payroll in there for the mine, a bunch of legal papers! Company will have my hide if I don't get it to Golgotha!"

"These gentlemen have first claim to your hide if we don't lighten our load!" Maude called back.

"Good point there," the man said as an arrow landed and stuck in the bench beside him. "They can bill me."

Her arm screamed in pain, but Maude knew how to silence the sensation for a time, so she did. She lifted the safe box and hurled it off the back of the stage. It normally took two men to lift the strong box. Maude threw it far enough to land in the midst of a cluster of their mostly human attackers, scattering them and forcing them to plow into one another to avoid it. It crashed into the ground with the sound and force of a small bomb going off, raising a huge cloud of dust and grit. She could feel the coach moving quicker now.

"When I tell you, swerve a bit back and forth until I tell you to stop," she called over her shoulder to the shotgun messenger as she drew a sharp, slender dirk from a leg holster under her dress. Maude began slicing through the ropes that were holding down all the passengers' bags, steamer trunks, and other belongings. "Now!" The loose cargo tumbled free behind the stage and fell among the corporal braves blinded by the grit and dust of the cloud the strong box had raised. They banked hard to avoid the debris. Several didn't, and their horses stumbled over the obstacles and crashed to the desert floor, in turn tripping up and slowing even more of the raiding party.

One living brave swerved to avoid the obstacles and came close to the back of the stage. Maude selected a hair pin and pulled it free from her bun. She threw it at the man on the horse. The envenomed pin buried in his shoulder, and he began to slump and fall from his horse. The stage swerved in the drugged brave's direction, and Maude launched herself off the stage, hearing her skirt split as she did. She landed behind the now-unconscious brave, taking the reins of his horse and holding him upright. She urged the horse forward and came up beside the shotgun messenger.

"Go, go!" she said. The horse, terrified of the ghosts, struggled to focus and keep up with the now-speeding coach. Maude slid her injured arm down to the horse's neck and applied a gentle pressure to the knotted cluster of nerves. "It's all right," she whispered to the horse, feeling the anxiety and tension slip from the stallion's body. The horse began to gallop, freely, smoothly, keeping stride with the coach. The animal's breathing was loose and even, no longer panting. "Good boy," she whispered. "Nothing to be afraid of anymore."

The coach used the cover of the dust up to take the coach off the rutted road and put a few mountains between them and the Indians. Maude instructed the messenger to slow to give the horses a rest. She rode behind the coach, scanning the horizon for any signs of pursuit. There were a few tense moments before Maude felt confident that their attackers had moved on. The messenger brought the coach back onto the road after an hour.

They were less than two hours from Golgotha when they stopped to allow the passengers a brief rest. Maude stopped as well, setting the horse free and tying the insensate brave down to the rails on the roof with the ropes that had held the passenger's cargo.

"He dying?" the shotgun messenger, who Maude now knew was named Greg Steele, asked as Maude finished securing the prisoner.

"No," she said. Maude kept different poisons on each of her hairpins. The ends had different indentations on them so she could keep them straight. She seldom used the lethal variety.

"Well, then let's kill the damn red nigger," the man who tried to grope her said as he returned from relieving himself on the side of the road. Maude noted that he had piss stains on the front of his pants when he had climbed out of the coach.

"No," Maude said. "This man has information about whatever those...spirits were back there, and the rest of that raiding party. I'm sure the sheriff in Golgotha will want to..."

"You've caused enough trouble, you shit-house crazy bitch!" another passenger shouted. "I lost everything I own back there, thanks to you!"

Maude popped two shells of rock salt into the shotgun and snapped the breach shut as she looked square at the man who was white-faced with anger. "You haven't lost everything yet," she said, adjusting her voice to strum his nerves and send a shiver of fear down the man's spine. "Let's make a few things plain before we get back on the road. I don't want to hear any more about this man tied up here."

"Just like a stupid bint," the man who had called her crazy said. "That's a fucking Indian. They are savages. If he had his way, he'd be raping you and your daughter right now."

"That man is a prisoner of war, and he's my prisoner. You keep talking, I'll put rock salt in your knee and leave you out here for his friends." The man shut up, but a few of the other passengers grumbled.

"All of y'all shut the hell up," the man who had the derringer said. "We'd be dead if it wasn't for this lady. I don't have a hooter of a notion of how you did all that stuff you did back there, ma'am, but thank you." Maude glanced to Constance and saw she was smiling. A few of the others muttered a quiet "thank you." The other men remained sullen and glared at the shotgun in her hands, but did as they were told.

Maude patched up her arm as best she and Constance could. Her supply of medicinal herbs was lost with the rest of their luggage. She rode shotgun up top with Steele while they quickly made their way to Golgotha.

"I've been making the run to Golgotha for a long time," Steele said. "Seen some mighty strange things, but I never seen anything like that, especially in broad daylight. What was that, Miss Maude?"

Maude looked out to the horizon, saw the shadows stretching out their fingers, longer and longer, reaching to grasp the dwindling sun. Everything was bathed in blood-light. It was almost as if the sky itself had been wounded and was bleeding out, bleeding the empty void of the night. "I don't know," she said quietly, "but I'll lay odds on where it'll end up."

THE FIVE OF PENTACLES

The miners' camp on the eastern face of Argent Mountain overlooking Golgotha never slept, just like the work at the silver mine deep within the mountain never ended. Argent had developed a reputation for being one of the richest loads of silver in Nevada or California. The saying went that a drunk with nothing but his pecker in his hand to dig with could strike silver on Argent.

Prospector Gabe Reid was the first man to dig silver out of the mountain in 1856. In later years, before he mysteriously disappeared, Reid, then a wealthy man, claimed that while exploring Argent, a voice on the mountain wind had whispered to him. The "voice" had even plagued his dreams, as he camped alone on the slopes of the mountain, with visions of a vast room with a floor made of pure silver. Eventually, he claimed, the voice guided him to the spot on which he first dug. By the end of that first day, he'd struck silver and changed his fortune and his fate forever.

With the second boom in 1869, the mining camp had kept growing into a raucous town of its own. The camp had its own leadership, albeit entirely illegal. Malachi Bick, the wealthiest man in Golgotha, might own the mines, but the half-dozen crime bosses who'd staked their claims and fought wars to defend them over the years owned everything else. Of these, one man had crawled his way to the top of that heap. Niall Devlin, better known to friend and foe alike as "the Nail," held court at the Halla Damhsa, his saloon, dance hall, and brothel.

The Halla had begun as a tattered, canvas tent with a skeleton of cheap scrap wood, fitting in perfectly with the majority of ramshackle dwellings at the camp. Now, many years later, the Halla was a proper, two-story, wooden building, just as many other small, permanent cabins and businesses were popping up all over the still-raucous settlement.

The sounds of music, laughter, and drunken camaraderie spilled out the Halla's doors. Two aloof gunmen lounged on the rails of the dance hall's porch, checking that no troublemakers or enemies of the Nail made it inside.

The smiling man named Rory and his silent companion, the small-headed, huge-muscled Tidbull, stepped up onto the porch. The two gunmen stood and blocked them.

"You're two fresh faces," one of the guards said around a cigarette. "What's your story?"

"Oh, my mate here and I are killers," Rory said good-naturedly. The gunmen chuckled. "Actually, we're kind of holy men, too. We kill people for our god, who lives here in Golgotha." The guards laughed more loudly.

"They're crazy," one of the gunmen said to the other.

"Oh, yes," Rory said, "mad as fuckin' loons, both of us...and killers...and priests."

"Why should we let a couple of crazy fuckers like you inside, padre?"

"As you well know," Rory began, "wholesale slaughter is thirsty work, so we're here to drink a few pints and hopefully do some very lucrative business with your boss."

"Here to see Mr. Devlin, are you?" one of the gunmen said.

"Yeah," Rory said. "You catch on quick. I see why the Nail has you on the front door." The gunman seemed to tumble that around in his skull for a moment, trying to decide whether Rory had just insulted him or not.

"Okay, go on in, drink a spell. No stupid shit or we'll toss your asses out, hear?"

"Perfectly," Rory said, tapping both his ears.

"We'll tell the boss you want to talk. You talk funny. You from Ireland, like the boss?" Rory's smile widened, but something cold glinted behind his eyes.

"You know the difference between an Irish wedding and an Irish funeral?" The gunmen shook their heads. "One less drunk." The two guards laughed. Rory nodded slightly to the hulking Tidbull. The giant crushed both men's skulls, one in each massive hand. "English, actually," Rory said to the still-twitching dead men. Rory spit on the body of the one that had called him Irish, and they went inside the Halla.

Niall Devlin was in his office on the second floor of the Halla Damhsa, stacks of money laid out on his desk, going over account ledgers as he counted the day's take. The Nail was a lean man with reddish-brown hair, sharp features, and hazel eyes. He carried easily a half-dozen weapons on him at all times, and he was pretty obvious about it. His walking arsenal included the old carpentry hammer of his father's that was the source of his ominous nickname.

When the door to the office began to open without the proper coded knock, Devlin had a revolver in each hand pointed at the opening door. Rory paused and smiled wider when he saw the guns.

"I like a man who's always prepared, Mr. Devlin," Rory said, raising his hands and nodding for Tidbull to do the same. "Very good. May we come in? I have some very profitable business to discuss with you."

"What happened to Jack and Tanner on the door, and my lads inside?"

"Dead, I'm afraid," Rory said. "Nothing personal. One called me an Irishman and...well, I'd rather be called a hog fucker than that. I suppose that is rather personal, at that."

The Nail laughed, but the guns stayed on Rory's chest. "The way you mush your words together, like your mouth's full of spotted dick —Yorkshire, right?"

"Close enough," Rory said. "Leeds."

"Well, here we are," the Nail said, "two scions of the Isles, caught in the middle of a bunch of drunk American cowboys. Welcome. Shut the door behind you, if you please, Mr...?"

"Call me Rory," he said as they stepped inside and closed the door. "This is my associate, Mr. Tidbull." The Nail looked at the hulking man and now had a pistol covering each of them.

"If you're here to rob me, it ain't going to go very well for you, Rory," Devlin said.

"I'm actually here to give you a large sum of money," Rory said. "For the smallest of accommodations."

"Well that sounds rather foolish of you," the Nail said.

"Not really," Rory said with a shrug. "It's not my money. May I reach into my jacket and retrieve a packet?" Devlin nodded but kept the guns on their targets. Rory retrieved a large envelope from his coat and walked slowly toward Devlin's desk.

"May I?" Rory asked. He placed the envelope on the desk and stepped back. There was a knock at the door, the correct knock, and one of Devlin's men opened the door, pistol in hand.

"Boss," the man said, a little out of breath, "Jackie-boy, Tanner...the boys in the hall...they're all dead, someone crushed their skulls like crackin' a peanut."

"I know, Sax," Devlin said. "The fellas who did it are right here. Get a couple of boys in here to cover them." Sax departed quickly.

"Gosh, I hope you aren't going to kill us just yet," Rory said, casually. "It'd be a shame to piss away so much money."

"No, not yet," the Nail said. "I just want to give your proposal my undivided attention."

"Of course," Rory said. "Oh, and just so you know, that sum mentioned there, doesn't include the compensation for your dearly departed minions. I hardly knew 'em."

The guards returned with Sax, four of them with shotguns. They covered Rory and Tidbull from all sides. Devlin holstered his pistols and began to go over the letters in the envelope. He scribbled some note into the margin of the ledger he had been working on.

"Lady Alexandria Poole?" the Nail said, looking up from the letter of introduction. "The London Pooles? Practically royalty."

"Yeah, she does get around a bit," Rory said.

"You are agents of Lady Poole? These letters of credit and references of credit look clean as a new whore on her first day. This is quite a sum, Rory."

"Not for her," Rory said. "It is for blokes like you and me, though."

"What does Lady Alexandria want for her money?"

Rory stood up from the couch. He walked toward Devlin's desk, the ugly, oiled snouts of the shotguns following him. "Access to the mines," he said. "Passes, jobs as an excuse for us to be there, bribed supervisors to look the other way. Access...and no hindrance."

"You lads anarchists, or something?" Devlin asked. "Planning to blow up the mine?"

"I've always found anarchy rather tedious," Rory said. "No, Lady Alexandria wants something down in one of the old sealed-off sections of the mine, and we're here to retrieve it for her, no questions asked."

"I've heard all the ghost stories about the Argent Mine," the Nail said. "The men who died down there in the gas accidents and the cave-ins, the stories about the monsters down in the deep shafts." He held up the letters from Rory's mistress, acting as if he were weighing them and finding them wanting. "I think this might be a bit light for the amount of trouble helping you might get me into, Rory." Rory reached inside his jacket as he had before, and the guards prepared to fire. The Nail raised a hand quickly to stop them, and Rory's smile grew bigger at the gesture.

He produced a second envelope and tossed it into the Nail's lap. "Of course. That's why I've been instructed to provide you with this second letter of credit that is double the amount of the first."

Devlin opened the envelope and skimmed the documents. Rory paced the room, enjoying the nervousness of the guards. "You can keep them both, cash them both, if you provide the assistance we've requested. However, if that is not enough inducement to overcome your temerity, I will of course have to seek assistance from General Mitchell."

"Old Half-guts Mitchell?" The Nail chuckled.

"Yes, I understand you and he run similar businesses and that he could provide us with what we need if you cannot."

Devlin folded up the documents and laid them on his desk and patted them. "Aye, that he could. But I don't see any reason to include Half-guts in our dealings. This will be fine."

"Grand," Rory said, smiling. He reached across the desk, unafraid of the gunmen all around him. Devlin stood and shook his hand. "We have a deal."

"When do you need to get in the mines?" the Nail asked, noticing how cold and dry Rory's hands were, like snakeskin.

"We have a few days," Rory said. "Our associates in Golgotha need to...tie up...a few loose ends before we begin."

The knock on the door came well after dark. Jacob Winterton reached for his rifle, glanced to make sure his four children were still asleep in the loft, and then cautiously opened the door. Mayor Harry Pratt stood on his porch, his hat in his hand.

"Mayor Pratt?" Jacob said. "Sir?"

"Evening, Mr. Winterton," Harry said. "I apologize for the lateness of the hour. May I please come in?"

"Of, of course," Jacob said. The mayor entered, and Jacob led him to the table near the small iron stove that kept the night's chill off the house. Harry sat and looked about at the simple, one room home. There was a loft that ran along most of the roof with a ladder down to the main floor. Harry could hear the soft snoring and gentle breathing of children above him. "Coffee?" Jacob asked. Harry smiled.

"Yes, please," Harry said. "I had hoped to make it out here before sundown, but with all that has been going on in town, it didn't happen." The truth was that it had taken Harry a while to ditch his murderous new shadow, Porter Rockwell, so he could slip away and deal with this nasty bit of business unseen. Pratt sighed and rubbed his eyes. "Coffee would be a godsend." Jacob took the pot off the top of the wood stove, poured Harry a hot mug of Arbuckle, and handed it to him. He poured himself a mug and sat at the table opposite Harry.

"Sorry we don't have any milk," he said. "The children had the last of it at dinner." Harry gave a dismissive wave as he sipped his mug.

"I prefer it black," he said. It was a lie, but Jacob took it as truth. Harry needed to gauge this man's ability to sniff out deceit for everything that was to follow.

"What can I do for you, Mayor Pratt?" Jacob asked.

"It's actually what I can do for you," Harry said. "I understand you've been made a very generous offer for your land by the company that's building the railroad dogleg between the Continental railroad and Golgotha, Mr. Winterton. I hear that you refused that offer." Jacob looked at his table as he sipped his coffee. Harry frowned and cocked his head. "May I ask why?"

Jacob put his mug down and sighed. "I have reasons, sir. I'd rather not go into them, if you please."

"Normally, I'd say it was your own business, Jacob," Harry said, "but given the current situation, I have to think of what's best for the town, not just one family."

"Sir?"

"The railroad will bring jobs, new businesses, more people to Golgotha. Do you really think it's fair to hold up all that progress, Jacob?"

110

Winterton kept looking down at the table. Harry noticed his hand was clutching his mug tighter. "That all sounds real fine, Mr. Mayor, but I'm sorry. I just can't sell our land, our house."

"Winterton, you understand that if I talk to these people, I can probably get you more than they offered you, enough to buy some land up on Rose Hill, build a fine house."

Winterton looked up at Harry. His eyes were red and wet. His voice was trembling with anger. "No," he said. "I think it's time for you to leave, Mr. Pratt."

Harry stood, but he made no move toward the door. His stomach twisted, but he kept his discomfort far away from himself. "You heard the army has come to town, yes?" he said, his voice even and cold. "There is an Indian uprising brewing, and they are targeting Mormon settlements."

"That's terrible," Jacob said, wiping his eyes. "I hope the soldiers can corral those Lamanites before they hurt anyone else."

"I hope so, too," Harry said, wanting to rip his own tongue out of his mouth, "for you and your family's sake."

Winterton blinked. "What?" he said. "What do you mean?"

"Out here alone, this far from the town," Harry said. He let the implication hang, and he felt bile in the back of his throat as he did it, thinking of the small children above him. It was getting hard to keep his own feelings outside himself.

"You...you wouldn't do that. Would you?" Winterton slumped back in his chair. "You can't. We count on you, on the sheriff, to keep us safe. It's what you've promised us, took an oath to do."

"There's no guarantee you and yours will be safe out here, Mr. Winterton, especially since you seem uncooperative to do anything to help our community."

Winterton chuckled; it had a desperate, gallows sound to it. "We go to the same church. We pray to the same god." He was crying now, no longer able to hold back the wet sobs as he fought for words. "We...I, I've done my best to teach my children right from wrong, Pratt, and that people like you, Mr. Mayor, do what they do to make the world safer, better for everyone. But that's not true, is it?" He slumped forward and sobbed into his hands. Harry heard whispers in the loft. The children were waking up from their father's cries.

"Jacob, please," Harry whispered, looking up to see frightened little faces looking down at him. Their sleepy little eyes cut into Harry like knives. "You...you will be handsomely compensated for..."

"Do you even care why?" Jacob asked. "First time you've ever talked to me, acknowledged I exist, and it's because now you need something from me. You don't care. You want to know why I say no? Do you?"

"Tell me," Harry said.

"Four years ago, my wife, Hannah, we had our second child," Jacob said, sniffing. "He...died two weeks after he was born. We buried him a way back on our land. A tiny little grave. We've lost three children all told. They are buried here, on our land, our home."

Harry felt ice water pour into the core of him. *What the hell are you doing to these people?* He thought of his wife, Holly, of her death years ago, and he wondered if things were different would he be fighting as hard to protect her grave, her memory. Harry was the one to look down to the table now.

Jacob looked up at his children and spoke in a calm, strong voice, pushing back his inner storm. "Y'all go on back to bed. Everything's fine. Go to sleep, now."

The children's heads vanished back into the darkness of the loft. Tiny voices, sweet as angels, replied in a chorus of, "Yes, Daddy. 'Night, Daddy." Winterton sniffed, wiped his eyes and nose again, then cleared his throat.

"We lost Hannah last winter to cholera," Jacob said. "I dug her grave. I buried her with her babies, here, on our land, our home." He looked at Harry. "The One Mighty and Strong," he said. "The one who will protect us in the times of darkness. Tell me, Mr. Mayor, how much are you getting paid to chase us off so some rich folks can get richer? They're going to tear down our house, dig up my family? I'm thankful Hannah isn't here to see this. It would break her heart. Is that what you stand for? I've been lying to my children all these years about how the world works, how right and wrong work."

Harry stood. "No," he said, "you haven't, sir. I'm the one who has been lying."

"What?" Jacob asked.

"You're not going anywhere," Harry said. "This is your land. You've fought and bled for it. You deserve it. I give you my word, I won't let anyone take it away from you." Harry walked to the door.

"How can I..."

"Trust me?" Harry said. "Good question. I'd be asking that, too. I want you to come to town when you can. See my assistant, Mr. Higbee. I'm going to have some legal papers drafted that will make it very clear this land, that little graveyard, is yours in perpetuity." Jacob looked confused. "It means this land belongs to you and your children forever, Jacob."

"What about the railroad people?" Winterton said. "They won't like that. I've seen the plans; they sent me copies of them to show me how important it is I sell."

"I'll take care of them," Harry said. "They're my problem, not yours. Don't worry."

Jacob shook Harry's hand. "Thank you, Mr. Pratt," he said.

"For the hell I just put you through?" Harry said. "You never have to thank me for anything ever again, Jacob. I'm truly sorry." Harry stepped through the doorway into the bitter desert night. "Thank you, Mr. Winterton, for the coffee. It woke me up."

He mounted his horse, Knight, and began to head northeast toward the western face of Argent, looming above him, a huge shadow in a night lit by all the stars in Heaven. Unseen, wrapped in the deepest parts of the night, Porter Rockwell, on his horse, watched Harry Pratt depart the small farm.

So far, the Golgotha mayor hadn't shown Rockwell very much, certainly nothing that Brigham Young had to worry about. Young had sent him here since Pratt's name and his reputation as a legendary Mormon folk hero had grown in the last few years. Young had confided in his old friend and protector that he may have need of him for one more mission. If Pratt was a threat to the saints, to the church, then Harry Pratt had to die.

For now, Rockwell would remain at Harry's side and see if he was truly the One Mighty and Strong. If he was a danger to the order of all that Joseph Smith and Brigham Young had built, then Harry Pratt would die. It was God's, and Brigham Young's, will.

Unaware he was being watched, Harry paused briefly at the small cluster of graves with painted stone markers. He paid his respects, made his apologies, and swore an oath he'd long forgotten he had taken, once again.

THE MAGICIAN

S o, a crazy white man thinks the best way to gentle down a Paiute uprising is to ride in with mess of other crazy white men with guns?" Mutt said

Highfather propped his boots up on his old wooden desk in the jail. "Yep. I believe you have grasped the complexities of our current situation."

"Brilliant," Mutt said. "I am constantly amazed at the complexity of y'all's brains. How exactly did you people sail over here from wherever the hell you people come from and not get lost?"

"We did get lost, actually," Jon said. "An unerring sense of direction is but one of the tools in the superior white man's arsenal." Mutt chuckled and shook his head.

They were alone in the jail. It was the evening that Caxton and his troops had ridden into town. Across town, Jon knew that Kate was having dinner with the Red General, Pinkerton, and Golgotha's hoi oligoi. He tried to push the notion of Kate with Pinkerton out of his head, but it wasn't as easy as it should have been, especially after his talk with Rabb Hayes this afternoon. Work usually helped to keep his brain busy when he was troubled. Mutt always helped, too. He was trying to catch his deputy up on what he had missed while in the desert.

"Paiute slaughtering whole settlements?" Mutt said. "I ain't buying it. More likely Pinkerton is up to something."

"He is," Highfather said, "and given Caxton's history with the Indians, I wouldn't put it past either of them to be stirring the pot so they have an excuse to go after the tribes in the region." "Competition for good farmland and watering holes is getting pretty fierce here, in Utah, and in eastern California," Mutt said. He was sitting in his favorite wooden chair in front of Jon's desk, with his boots up on the side opposite from where the sheriff's were. Both men often joked that this particular arrangement was their "sleuthing pose."

"True," Jon said, "but then again, it looks like something is happening among the Paiute, the Ute, the Shoshone. That little girl you brought in from the desert, her family was murdered, her settlement destroyed by someone."

"We haven't been out there," Mutt said. "No telling who did that. No love between the federals and the Mormons either."

"Rabb Hayes has been there," Jon said. "He told me he was pretty certain it was an Indian war party."

Mutt made a sour face and grunted. "Hayes," he said.

"You don't trust him?" Jon asked.

"I do and I don't," Mutt said. "He seems a straight shooter. Anyone who hikes out of the 40-Mile with a dying child in his arms would have to be. He's hiding things, important things."

"Such as?"

"He's got power, Jonathan. Buha—medicine—whatever you want to call it. It's as strong as any I've ever felt—strong as Jim's jade eye—and he's hiding it under a bushel. He's also ex-cavalry—a buffalo soldier—those men have done some serious Indian fighting since the war. It seems too big a coincidence to me that he just happened to be here when all this Indian war business is starting up."

"He's here to deliver a message," Jon said.

"Oh, yeah his 'message from a dead man.' I'd nearly forgot. Even as wake-the-snakes-crazy as things get around here, I don't believe he's..."

"He's telling the truth," Jon said. "I'm the one that message was for." Mutt sensed something shifting inside Jon, retreating to his core. His friend was working hard to keep something to himself, not to let it distract him, pushing it out of his awareness. He knew Highfather had strong feelings for Kate Warne and that he'd not cottoned to Pinkerton coming to town, but this was something different, something that Jon was wrestling with that had nothing to do with Kate.

"Message from a dead man to a dead man," Mutt said.

"Something like that," Jon said, shifting.

"Anything I can help with, Jonathan?"

"You already do, and it can keep. Thanks." Jon could tell Mutt wasn't satisfied. His deputy hated half-answers and half-truths, but he also knew he'd give him his peace. Now wasn't the time for this nonsense. They had bigger things to deal with. "You trust me?"

"Stupid question," Mutt said.

"Then trust Rabb Hayes," he said.

"I'll try, but he's a thorny son of a bitch."

"Now who does that remind you of?" They both chuckled. Jon dropped his feet off his desk and leaned forward in his chair. "I want you and me to ride out first thing, before sun-up. Head out to Paiute country and see if we can shake loose a few answers to what's happening and why."

"Great idea," Mutt said, "but I'm going alone. I ride out there with you, no one is going to tell me a damn thing."

"I was a little more worried about you having someone to watch your back," Jon said.

"Yeah, me too, but I'll manage. You know how careful I am," the deputy said.

"I do. Hence, the wanting to ride along," Jon replied. "Okay, suit yourself. Head out before the general and Pinkerton stop snoring."

The iron door to the jail groaned open, and the cold came with it. Maude Stapleton, her arm wrapped in a blood-stained bandage, her clothing ripped and torn, entered the lantern-lit room. She had a tied, unmoving Indian brave slung over her narrow shoulder, and she was carrying the large man like a sack of potatoes. "Jon, Mutt," she said, "I have someone you need to have a chat with."

Both men stood when they saw Maude's condition, but Mutt was already across the room to her by the time Jon was out of his chair. "You okay?" Mutt asked. Maude smiled. Concern and protectiveness spilled out of Mutt's every syllable, every motion.

"I'm fine," she said. "Jon, can we get him into a cell?"

"Of course," Jon said, grabbing a ring of keys off the hook on the wall behind his desk. He unlocked the cell closest to the western wall. Maude placed the brave on the bunk and untied his hands and feet.

"Is Constance okay? What happened to your arm?" Mutt asked while Maude was about her work.

"She's gone on to the house. She was exhausted," Maude said. "As for this, I got sliced by a tomahawk thrown by a Shoshone ghost," she said, matter-of-factly. "He was in the company of Ute and Paiute ghosts and some tribes I'm afraid I couldn't identify."

"Ghosts?" Jon said. Maude checked the brave's slow, steady pulse.

"They attacked the stage from Hazen, killed the driver and a passenger, and wounded the lock box guard. I'm afraid I had to abandon the lock box and the passenger luggage to keep them from catching us."

The three retreated from the cell, and Jon locked the door behind him. "How big a war party we talking about?" Mutt asked, leading her to his chair by her uninjured arm. Maude touched his hand gently and sat, the exhaustion welling up out of her.

"I counted close to a hundred," she said. "About half living, breathing braves, mostly Paiute, and the other half these spirits." She looked up to Mutt and clutched his hand. "And they were not some trick, no illusion or soulless shades conjured up and directed by another. I saw into the eyes of one them. They are as aware, competent, and self-motivated as any living person."

Jon and Mutt looked at each other. "I think I know where to start asking those questions," Mutt said. He looked over to the brave in the cell. "How long is he going to be out, Maude?"

"At least twelve hours," she said, "longer than that before he'll be any good to talk to." Mutt looked over to Jon.

"I'll be back by tomorrow night," the deputy said. Highfather nodded.

"Where are you going?" Maude asked.

"To see a man about some ghosts," Mutt said.

Mutt escorted Maude out of the jail, intending to walk her home. Highfather was alone, and as the silence of the jail settled over him, so did the weight of his thoughts. He opened a drawer and looked at the bottle of bourbon inside, next to a pair of glasses. He stared at it for a long time and remembered how good it felt to feel nothing. How after Gettysburg sinking into madness and alcohol had become as comforting as slipping into a hot bath.

He closed the drawer and stood. Running away did nothing; it only made it harder on everyone you cared about. Jon Highfather walked out of the jail, into the cold Golgotha night to go do his job.

———

Ghost warriors," Maude said as she and Mutt walked slowly up the path on Rose Hill. "We never seem to catch a break, do we?"

"I'd end up chaffing you something awful if we did have all that free time," Mutt said.

"You're probably right," Maude said. "You chafe me now and I hardly ever see you."

The desert night was cold, the sky crystalline with brilliant stars. Mutt walked arm-in-arm with her, her head resting on his shoulder. Since her return from rescuing Constance and making peace with her father last year, Maude had been much less concerned about showing him affection, even in public.

"Ain't you afraid they might try to lynch me again, a savage with a white lady," Mutt joked as they walked up the starlit path. Maude shrugged.

"You can handle them," she said, and then smiled. "And if you can't, I will." Mutt laughed and pulled her a little closer.

"When we git this all settled down," he said, "and get those pointy-headed federals out of town, I'm going to take you out for a proper dinner over at Del's restaurant. What'd you say?"

"Delmonico Hauk's?" Maude said. "I'd love that. You know, though, we could eat hardtack on the back of a horse, as long as we get to do it together."

They branched off the main cobblestone walking path and headed onto a dirt one that led toward a cluster of homes part of the way up the hill. One of them was Maude's.

"Well, here we are," Mutt said as they reached her door. "You go have Clay take a look at that arm tomorrow for me? Please?" Maude smiled.

"I'll tend it now," she said. "Most likely, it will be healed by tomorrow, but if not, I'll go see Dr. Turlough."

"'Dr. Turlough,'" Mutt said. "There is no time in which that don't sound weird." Maude laughed and pulled him close.

"Be safe," she said, "as safe as you can be."

"I will," he said. "You too."

They were close, a breath apart. Their heightened senses luxuriated in each other's scents, touch. Even with all that they both could discern about the world around them, about other people, the fear, the uncertainty, the sweet tension remained. It hung in the air, vibrating, yearning.

They reached for one another when they could no longer bear the separation. The kiss felt like all the stars above were filling them with weightless, infinite, hurtling light. They both leaned in and let the kiss become their world, the only world that mattered.

Mutt rode Muha out of Golgotha and headed north, riding out on Old Stone Road under the cover of night. He rode toward the snow-covered rises of the Sierra Buttes. The trip and the solitude did him some good. He missed Maude, of course, and had even considered asking her to ride along, but the same reasons he couldn't bring Jonathan out with him applied to Maude as well. He'd get nothing but lip service out of any Indian he met out here with a white man or woman in tow.

He couldn't say as he blamed the tribal members for that. In the span of a few generations the traditional ways of life had all be shot to hell by the immigration of the whites, the blacks, and the Chinese. It was a new world, with new rules, and a lot of folks liked the old world better. It was always easier, less painful, to stick with an old, comfortable pair of shoes than to break in new ones. Like it or not, the world had changed, and it wasn't done changing yet, not by a long shot.

He arrived at the camp by late morning. It was set up in a wide, grassy plain, bordered on all sides by a forest of Lodgepole Pines. There was a shallow creek that dribbled between the rocks of the bed, bringing down clean, snow-melted water. The large, old canvas tent that had been here when Mutt had visited back last winter had been replaced by a central, permanent wikiup. Last year, there had been a few scattered tents clustered around the central one. Now, tents, wikiups, and shelters were scattered all across the vast field, a whole settlement, or a standing army.

A group of braves rode out to meet Mutt. He recognized the garb of his welcoming party, a few Shoshone, some grim-faced Modoc, a few Northern Paiute, and one Goshute. They all were armed with rifles and blades. All of them had a black feather in their headbands or hats, as Mutt did. Mutt slowed and then stopped as the party surrounded him.

Mutt recognized the man leading them, a Paiute named Mahkah, dressed in white man's clothing, a collarless work shirt and canvas jeans. He had first met Mahkah in Golgotha over a year ago.

"*Maiku*, Mahkah," Mutt said in Paiute.

"*Maiku*, Mutt," Mahkah said. "What brings you out here?"

"I have some news he needs to hear," Mutt said. He looked around at the sprawling settlement. "Place's grown quite a bit, pretty quick. What's going on?"

"Maybe if he spent more time with his own people and less whoring himself to the whites, he'd know," one of the Shoshone rumbled to his fellows in their own language. "The war's begun, little man, the war against the invaders." Mutt gave the big brave a sidelong glance.

"Oh, well, my," Mutt began. "If it's a war where you fight it by flapping that shithole you call a mouth, then you must be a mighty warrior indeed." The other braves laughed except for the Shoshone who had been insulted and Mahkah.

"Enough," Mahkah said. "Come with us, Mutt. I'll take you to him."

"Wait!" the Shoshone said. "I'm not done with this little piss-stain yet!"

"Yes, you are, Jolon," Mahkah said. "I'm saving your life."

They rode into the settlement, and Mutt left Muha near a water trough made of hide with several other horses, including Mahkah's.

"I'm impressed," Mutt said, petting Muha. "All these tribes, all the old blood, and everyone is getting along like a punch social, or at least trying to."

"Things are in motion, Mutt," the Paiute said. "Moving very quickly."

Mahkah led him into the large wikiup with a sole occupant. Mahkah turned and waited outside. Shafts of sunbeams crisscrossed the room like a web of light. At its center, sitting among a pile of cushions and blankets was an old Paiute man with long, silver hair that fell to his shoulders. His dark eyes were filmed with age, and he seemed to be looking far beyond the world in front of him. He dressed in modest clothing and had a single, black feather in his headband. The old man looked up from his musings and seemed to take a moment to reorient himself to this world. He saw Mutt and smiled.

"So, how deep are you buried in this cow flop?" Mutt asked.

"It's good to see you, too. I wondered when you'd turn up in all this," Hawthorne Wodziwob said with a chuckle. He gestured for Mutt to join him. Mutt sat down next to Wodziwob on the cushions.

Wodziwob was the leader of an ancient secret order among the tribes in the region, the Black Feathers. The Black Feathers were scholars of the hidden medicines, keepers of terrible secrets, and custodians of power that had mostly vanished from the land. They had long protected their peoples from the unnatural forces and predators that had walked the earth since the rise of man, since Shin-au-av-skaits had spilled all the people out of a sack onto the floor of the great deserts. The cabal had asked Mutt to join them after he had helped them deal with a dangerous renegade member and recovered a powerful and deadly artifact.

"What the hell do you think you're doing?" Mutt asked. "You've got an army out here?"

"A bleak way to see it. Tribes from all over are coming together, dancing the round dance. Standing up for themselves, for their rights," Wodziwob said.

"Jist to git themselves knocked right back down again, hard. You've been preaching for years, the dead are rising," Mutt said. "Apparently, they are, and they are pissed."

"Why shouldn't they be? Things are worse now than when many of them last drew breath. The outsiders wander our lands as if all of this was created just for them. It wasn't. They need to go back to where they came from."

"I don't think that's going to happen," Mutt said. "If you haven't noticed, lately, you're at a powerful disadvantage in this tussle."

"Not with the dead, with the spirits on our side. I know you thought I was some kind of a huckster," Wodziwob said, "but I've traveled to the mountains, spoken with the dead. I was told they would return if the people joined together and performed the dance. The dead are with us, and with their support, all who are not the *Numu* will be driven from the land."

Mutt shook his head. "I've dealt with the dead on occasion, too. They are one-minded, sneaky sumbitches—just like the living—maybe sneakier. It occur to you that they just wanted back in the bright lands, that they are willing to tell you what you want to hear?" The old mystic shook his head.

"The time's come, Mutt. It's time for a reformation."

"Yeah, well, your 'reformation' is killing people," he said. "I got a little girl back in Golgotha who's lost her whole family because of this. She's the last survivor of a place called Ezekiel. Ring a bell?" Mutt could tell Wodziwob recognized the name. He felt the elder pull something deep into himself and try to hide it. It reminded Mutt a bit of how Jonathan had reacted when he asked about Rabb's message.

"I'm sorry to hear about the child," Wodziwob said. "How many of our people have had their homes destroyed or stolen? I can walk you through this camp and you can meet scores of children orphaned by the federal soldiers, by the Mormon settlers. Where is your compassion for our people, for your people?"

"Don't play that game with me," Mutt practically snarled. "I told you when we first met, I don't give a damn about 'our people.' They never cared about my mother, or me. They humiliated her, reviled her, and hounded her. Those judgmental piles of pig shit drove her out of the only home she'd ever known. They broke her heart and wrecked her life. From where I stand, 'our people' ain't much better than the 'outsiders' you keep going on about. A bastard is a bastard, don't make no never mind where they come from."

"You were a child then," Wodziwob said. "You can't hold a grudge against all of the *numa* for the short-sighted actions of a few. They didn't know you were the son of Coyote. How could they know? Many of our people still believe it's only a story."

"You know one of the things 'our people' and the fucking white men have in common?" Mutt said, anger, hot and glowing in his suddenly yellow eyes. "You both hold up or ignore your gods whenever it's convenient to whatever you're trying to get accomplished. The same elders who you are defending claimed on a weekly basis to 'speak to the spirits' to 'do the spirits' will.' That's usually how the old *togus* got the maidens to kick up their heels."

"This is bigger than your bitterness," Wodziwob said, his own voice now rising with anger. "The *toha* are pushing us off our lands—land our people have called home since our ancestors came north from the great empire they founded there. They refuse to share the water, the grass, the very soil." The elder was angry now, as angry as Mutt. "We are made to feel like intruders in our own nations. They convert our children to their religions, try to silence the spirits, to eradicate our cultures, our way of life. They murder and rape our people like common criminals. They bring horrific diseases—like the typhoid that killed so many of us just a few years ago—with them like filthy animals. They want to erase us! How can you not see that?"

Mahkah, as well as Weneyuga and Tavibo, Wodziwob's disciples, appeared at the entrance, summoned by their teacher's angry, raised voice. Tavibo's teenaged son, Wavoka, stood by his father looking in with great concern. The old man shooed them off with a dismissive wave of his hand.

"It's fine," Wodziwob called out. "When you are having a conversation with a rock, you must often shout." They departed.

"You telling me you don't know who's responsible for what happened out at Ezekiel," Mutt said.

"So, you're going to ignore me, rock?" Wodziwob said. "Ignore my question?"

Mutt sighed. "If I'm able, I'm going to do all I can to keep everyone alive," he said, "most of all, the ones on either side who don't deserve to be dead, but I'll even try to keep the stupid fucking zealots alive, so they can keep on doing stupid fucking things, like this. Now, who else is mixed up in all this? Who hit Ezekiel?"

The old man was silent for a moment. "Her name is Izusa," he finally said. "She's Goshute, and she is the one who speaks for the rising ghosts, the one who has led the dead back to the land of the living."

"How's that?" Mutt asked. "You mean after all your preachin' and huffin' and puffin' about making the whites disappear, the stiffs are following her lead? How'd she win that contest?"

It was obvious Mutt's taunt had gotten under the elder's skin, but Wodziwob ignored. "Her whole family, her whole village, was murdered by the cavalry," Wodziwob said. "The legend goes that she was taken in by the dead and raised among them, taught all their secrets. She is the most powerful shaman I have ever seen. Her *buha* is tied to the spirits of our dead, to the powers of their land. Braves, living and dead, loyal to her, destroyed Ezekiel and several other settlements."

"So what are *you* doing about that, exactly?" Mutt asked.

"My part," Wodziwob said, opening a crumbling, old, stone box in front of him. "Teaching, encouraging more of the tribes to perform the circle dances, to be proud of who we are, and to resist." He gently removed a single, perfect black feather from the box, holding it as if it were fragile as glass. "Marshaling and controlling the medicine at my command."

Mutt chuckled as if he had just gotten a joke. "But she's not here with the rest of the gang, is she?" Mutt said with a smile. "You can't 'marshal or control' her, can you?"

"She's killed six of your fellow Black Feathers that I sent to bring her back," Wodziwob said. "I taught her for a time, years ago. I would have inducted her into the Black Feathers if she were not a woman."

"Well, there's another enlightened point of view that splits y'all so much from the whites," Mutt interjected. Wodziwob frowned.

"Her passions are only governed by her loss, and her time among the dead," the elder said. "I had hoped to show her the wisdom of my path, but I was not a strong enough influence. She and Snake-Man met one another through me."

"Well, this jist got more awful," Mutt muttered. "You have really lousy tastes in who you bring into your confidence, Hawthorne."

"Present company included." The old man smiled. Mutt shrugged.

"No argument there. At least Snake-Man is locked up in a federal pokey for his last spree of murder and insurrection. If I'm lucky, he'll be fitted for a rope presently."

"The son of Snake and Izusa shared much in common. They inflamed each other's hatreds, strengthened each other's ideology. I fear she is sick in her spirit, but the dead do her bidding.

"I tried to convince her that this path—attacking non-military targets, civilians, like the federals do—would only lead to greater harm for our people. I tried to explain that we needed to make our people's spirits stronger, get more of us to do the circle dances, to trust in the spirits to free the land of darkness. Then, when we were strong and united, then we could challenge the federals. She called me a timid old man, afraid to act. For better or worse, Izusa is taking the war to the whites, *all* the whites. I think it unwise, but I do understand the emotions that drive it. We all do."

"What neither of you seem to have ciphered out, or give a damn about," Mutt said, "is that the federal army has been called out to use your little war as an excuse. I'm pretty sure the general in charge of this operation and the blowhard from Washington pulling his strings, plan to use the occasion to settle accounts with all the tribes—all the people, regardless of if they are taking part in your 'reformation' or not. You just gave them what they need to speed up the process of doing what you've been bitchin' about them doing. Congratulations."

Wodziwob looked over at Mutt. "Do you recall when I told you that you couldn't straddle the line between worlds forever?" he asked. "Your time's up, Son of Coyote. You have to choose a side."

"And you remember when you told me that you'd need someone of two worlds to piss you off and make you think about what you were doing? Well, guess what? It's raining." Mutt stood. "This isn't the way anything gets better. It's how everyone ends up losing. Do you know where I can find Izusa? Yes or no? No more dancin'."

"Last I heard, she was camped near the Great Basin," Wodziwob said. "You can't stop the arisen dead, Mutt. Izusa has given them a path into our world. Vulture and his maidens have given Izusa his blessing, his protection."

"Vulture, huh?" Mutt said. "Figures. 'Bout the only one who comes out ahead in a war is the eaters of the dead."

"Izusa is going to destroy the invading aliens, and Vulture's going to clean the land of the foreign carrion," Wodziwob said. "There is no way you can stop them, Mutt. It's the spirits' will; it's the will of the dead."

"I think you've done forgotten about *my* family tree, old man," Mutt said as he walked outside without looking back. "Our hobby is fucking up other people's good times."

THE KING OF PENTACLES

Augustus Shultz fought his way out of the nightmare and back to the waking world. He found his beautiful wife, Gillian, there to greet him. "Auggie?" she whispered, her lips near his ear, the smooth warmth of her body against his.

"Are they here?" Auggie sat up, blinking. "The birds? We have to save Little Auggie." Gillian ran her hand over his bare, hairy chest and unconsciously noted the place there should be a scar from a bullet wound, but there was none. She kissed him gently, trying to calm him.

"No birds," she said. "Our boy is fine. He's sleeping. Shhhhh, my love." Auggie kissed Gillian and held her tight.

"*Mein schatz*," Auggie said, fully awake now. "I'm sorry. I'm sorry I woke you."

"Hush," Gillian said, kissing him again. "We need to be up soon, anyway. Was it the same dream again?" Auggie nodded. He had been having the nightmares almost every night, always about large predatory birds with black wings and golden, alien eyes.

"Talking birds," he said, "feeding on the corpses of...of people..." He stopped there. Gillian knew he was keeping part of the dream away from her, but whatever it was, it was haunting Auggie. Pain and fear rimmed those kind eyes. Gillian pulled her bear of a husband to her as if he were as weak as a kitten. Gillian kissed him and did not let him go.

"We're all here. We're all fine," she said after the kiss. "Between your work on all this railroad business Mayor Pratt has cooked up and Bick's involvement in it, this is the first quiet moment we've had lately where neither of us is asleep."

"*Ja*," Auggie said. "I'm sorry, I..." Gillian stopped him with another kiss, a long one.

"I'm not complaining," she said with a smile. "I'm saying stop talking and let's enjoy the time we have before the rooster or the baby starts crowing." Auggie beamed, and he pulled her to him, this time with his massive arms. They kissed and explored like it was their first time again. He broke the kiss and looked down at her.

"Auggie?" she asked, her eyes, dark like opals, sparkled.

"How...did I ever get so lucky, so blessed, to have the love of someone so beautiful in every way?"

"I ask myself that same question, every day," Gillian said. "I love you, Augustus."

"I love you," he said. They lost themselves in one another for as long as the world would allow.

G illian prepared breakfast while Auggie got dressed. Auggie Jr., now awake, sat in a wooden highchair in the kitchen. Auggie had built the chair himself shortly after Gillian had told him the news that she was expecting. She heard Auggie's booming base singing in their bedroom as he shaved. It was one of the songs from *The Songs of the Wrens*, by Sir Sullivan and Lord Tennyson. Gillian and Auggie had heard the whole cycle performed beautifully at Mephisto's Playhouse just before Auggie Jr. was born. Auggie was singing his favorite of the bunch, "The Lights and Shadows Fly," or simply, "On the Hill." Gillian loved to hear Auggie sing, and it had been a while since he had. She glanced over to Little Auggie, who was looking in fixated amazement in the direction of the sounds of his father's voice. He looked over at Gillian and laughed. Gillian did too.

Gillian had gotten pregnant with her late husband, Will, many years before Will's death. Gillian had miscarried, and Doctor Francis Tumblety had told her it was unlikely she would ever to be able to have a child. He placed the blame squarely on her "advanced age" of her late twenties. There had been no pity in his voice as he pontificated that this was the very reason why it was ill-advised for women to delay their wifely commission and why the suffrage movement may very well doom the educated white Anglo-Saxon race to extinction. Gillian endured his presence as she had endured the pain and fear the night before when she knew something was wrong. She didn't give the bastard the validation of her tears, waiting until he departed to finally cry. Will had gone off to get drunk in town to assuage his loss.

Her first months of being pregnant with hers and Auggie's child were stressful. She kept waiting for the pain in the dark of night, the blood, the loss, but it didn't happen. Maude Stapleton, Gillian's best friend, had arrived back in Golgotha shortly before she delivered and had midwifed for her in their new home. Maude was amazing. She told Gillian she had never overseen a birth with as few complications. It was a miracle. She hoped it was, anyway. Lately, she thought that Clay's potion, its effect on her baby, perhaps had been the cause of the ease of Little Auggie's birth.

"*Ach!* I'm going to be late," Auggie said, fumbling with his bow tie. "Mr. Bick wanted me there early to go over a few things."

"No time to eat?" Gillian said. She poured him a cup of coffee from the pot off the stove and removed the small glass vial from its hiding place in the cupboard, behind the container that held the flour. She dribbled a few oily drops of Clay's bio-restorative solution into the coffee and then added some fresh milk. She placed the cup on the table next to him, kissed him, and began to work on his tie.

"You are a wonder," he rumbled as he held his head back for her to work the little bow tie around his massive bull neck squeezed into the shirt's collar.

"At least drink your cup of coffee, please," she said, finishing the tie. Auggie lowered his head. "It will at least make up for that sleep I robbed you of this morning." When Auggie smiled deeply, his eyes all but disappeared behind his apple-like cheeks.

"You stole nothing," he said, kissing her. "You gave me a wonderful gift." He picked up his coffee and took a sip. "Perfect, as always," he said, and took another. She knew he was lying. The face he made the first day he had drunk her coffee with the formula in it told her that. It was just one more testament to how much he loved her. He was willing to put up with her lousy coffee for the rest of his life, to make her happy. *His life.*

She had asked Clay when she could stop having to give him the formula covertly altogether. Clay said he didn't know, that since it had brought them back from death, their bodies might need the formula forever. Clay still had to give it to Shelly, though she was aware of what she was taking, unlike Auggie. She hated keeping it from him; she hated lying to him about it every morning.

"Goodbye, my little man!" Auggie said to Little Auggie. The huge man puckered his lips in an exaggerated manner and made loud kissing sounds. His little boy giggled. The baby puckered his own tiny lips as well and tried to make the same sounds as his father. Auggie laughed, knelt down next to the chair, and kissed his son, who grabbed at Auggie's whiskers and pulled him forward to hug him as well.

"You keep showing him to kiss that way, and he'll have a rough time getting himself a girl," Gillian said.

"It worked on you, *ja?*" he said, making the puckering lips and kissing noises again and beckoning to her. Auggie Jr. joined in and Gillian grinned and walked over to her two men.

"That is true," she said hugging and kissing them both. "That is true."

A uggie walked down the stone path on Rose Hill and headed into the already hectic swarm of morning in Golgotha. He took another sip of Gillian's coffee as he did every morning after he left and then poured the rest onto a bush. He stuck the empty mug in his leather folio. The bush seemed to be thriving, getting bigger every week. He loved his wife with all his heart, but she made the worst coffee he had ever tasted, not that he'd ever tell her.

Auggie reached the end of the path at the bottom of the hill and saw the large army encampment that now covered the grassy field at the hill's foot. Well over a hundred men busied themselves with duties, including caring for the string of horses stabled with the camp. A pair of soldiers standing watch tipped their caps to Auggie, and he returned the gesture.

Since the terrible ordeal the town had faced at the hands of the outlaw Ray Zeal, a few years ago, Auggie had to admit he did not care for soldiers in his town. If the stories already filtering across Golgotha were true, then these men would be needed to defend the town and many other nearby settlements. His mind drifted back to his looping nightmare. Zeal was in it, pulling the trigger, sending the white-hot sledgehammer of a bullet into his chest, hearing his heartbeat slow, stop.

He hadn't wanted to tell Gillian that part of it, nor that not all the birds were just birds; sometimes they were part-bird and part-woman. Occasionally, they would look up from their morbid feast of Auggie's friends and loved ones and shriek out one hideous word, *Valkyrie.* One of them was Shelly, Clay's Shelly, Shelly who once upon a time had been his first wife, Gerta.

It seemed like some fever dream, some madness, but after Gerta had died from illness, Clay had brought her back to Auggie. All he could save of her was her head. She had lived a nightmare, twilight existence for years like that, because Auggie had been too afraid, too selfish to let her go.

Gillian had saved them both, had showed him that he could live and love again and released Gertie from her endless hell. But Clay had secretly loved Gerta since he met her, and while Auggie had learned to let her go, Clay had not. He created his bio-restorative formula out of the remains of horrible creatures that had attacked the town long ago. He fashioned Gertie a new body from the remains of dead women like something from the scientific fiction of Clay's favorite author, Mary Shelly. Clay rejuvenated her into a much younger incarnation of herself and gave her a new identity—Shelly Wollstonecraft—and a new life with him, the man she had fallen in love with as well.

There were parts of the whole situation that still troubled and confused Auggie. He had no idea how to reconcile any of this with his, and Gerta's, Catholic faith.

Auggie's thoughts went back to his dreams, to Gerta as one of these hellish bird-valkyrie- creatures. Perhaps Gerta's resurrection had in some way given her a connection to death, to what lies beyond it. But then why would he be having these dreams? He thought he should discuss all this with Clay and with "Shelly," but they were so happy. He hated the thought of bringing any chaos or trouble into their lives when they were finally in a place to know love and peace.

Auggie had lived in Golgotha long enough to know this town did not grant many happy endings. He was fortunate enough to be one of them. He prayed that Clay and Shelly would have the same luck as he and his family. He pushed the dreams aside, as he did every morning, and got on with his work.

A s usual, Mr. Shultz, you have done an exemplary job," Malachi Bick said, closing the ledger laying on his desk. They were in Bick's office on the second floor of the Paradise Falls, Bick's saloon.

"Thank you, sir," Auggie said.

Bick was a slender man, with hair, eyes, and a neatly trimmed goatee the color of coal. Bick owned most of Golgotha. His wealth and influence were vast, and if they had limits, Auggie had never seen them. Bick's family had been on this land as long back as anyone could recall, further back than the Pratt family and the first wave of Mormons who decided to settle here and who named the town Golgotha.

Bick was dressed in a tailored burgundy shirt with a black vest and trousers. His hair fell to his collar. He seemed to enjoy cultivating a sinister mien. There were so many tales about Malachi Bick, the criminal overlord, the respected and influential businessman, the power broker, the saloon owner, the gambler, the murderer. The stories persisted but were always thin on facts.

Bick seldom seemed to mind the dubious reputation he owned. He had once told Auggie, "Fear and uncertainty from an opponent give you an edge, Mr. Shultz, and in this world, you need every advantage you can summon to overcome."

"But what about fairness, friendship?" Auggie had asked. "Can't those, too, give one an advantage, perhaps turn an opponent into an ally?" Bick had smiled.

"Yes, they can," he said, "but only if you're not a son of a bitch, and I, Mr. Shultz, most assuredly am. Luckily for me, that is exactly why I hired you to be my knight."

There was truth in that. Auggie had been the only man in town to defend Malachi Bick when all of Golgotha turned on him. When it was over and Auggie had nearly died for his stand, Bick had hired him on as the public face of his businesses. He gave the shopkeeper *carte blanche* to run his affairs as he saw fit, which, in Auggie's case, was much more gently and more forgiving of the townsfolk than Bick had ever been.

"I thought with the concern over Indian raids," Auggie said, "perhaps we should pay for some private security to ride along with the coaches for the time being."

"An excellent idea," Bick said, standing as Auggie did. "We have the stage coming in this evening with the mine's payroll. I agree we should either hire on guards ourselves or see if you and I can convince

Caxton and Pinkerton tonight to use some of their rather expansive resources to guard the stages for us. Public safety and all." Auggie put his papers away, then paused.

"Tonight, sir?"

"Yes, the general has invited us, and your wife, of course, along with several others to dine with him at the Imperial. Six o'clock. That won't be a problem, will it?"

"Oh, no sir," Auggie said, almost absentmindedly. They'd need to find someone to watch the baby, and Gillian didn't care much for Malachi Bick, but Auggie knew she'd put that aside for his job.

"Excellent, I'll see you..." Bick paused as if he had caught a scent on the wind. "Mr. Shultz, is something wrong?"

"Wrong, oh no, sir, not at all."

"You seem...off, a bit. Feeling out of sorts?" Bick asked. He was looking intently at Auggie. The burly shopkeep shook his head.

"*Nein*," Auggie said, shaking his head. "I'm fine, Mr. Bick. Thank you for your concern, though."

Bick looked at Auggie for a long moment. "Very good. We will see you and Gillian tonight." Auggie departed, shutting the office door behind him. Auggie paused for a moment outside the door. "We?" he said.

Malachi Bick, the angel Biqa, felt Auggie move away from the door. He had sensed the "wrongness" in Auggie a few times over the past year. He opened his perceptions wider, deeper.

Far below the mines in Argent Mountain, Biqa sensed the Darkling, the timeless, deathless entity that he had guarded since the beginning of the world, was churning, thrashing in its troubled, eternal sleep. For countless eons Biqa had stood watch, protecting the vast stage known as the Earth. Many times, he had almost failed in his task, and the Darkling, last and most dangerous of its kind—an entity older than death, more powerful than the Almighty—had almost been loosed upon creation.

Forces were gathering in Bick's town right now, he could feel them, agencies working in concert with the monster at the heart of the world to bring ruin and destruction to all life, everywhere. The part that puzzled the angel, worried him the most, was that somehow, in some way Biqa could not yet fathom, Augustus Shultz was at the heart of their horrific plan.

W ell, ain't this cozy," Clay Turlough said as he bounced Augustus Clayton Shultz Junior on his knee. "The little tyke's hand-eye coordination is coming along just fine. I was thinking of working up a contraption to change his diapers without anybody having to actually..."

"You will do no such thing, Clayton Turlough," Shelly said. "If you start using their child as a test subject, Augustus and Gillian will never ask us to tend him again. Is that why you brought that big box with you? Give him to me before you turn him into a lizard or something."

"Don't fret," Clay said, standing up and carrying the baby to Shelly, who happily received him. "This is the reason Gillian asked me to come tonight when they had to go to that dinner with Bick. Something's been happening in the little fella's bedroom. She wants me to check it out, but she doesn't want to fret Auggie."

"Something?" Shelly asked. Clay opened the case and began to remove some odd-looking apparatus.

"Whatever it is, it's got her spooked something terrible," Clay said. "I'm hoping this will give us some answers."

"Is Gillian saying the house is haunted?" Shelly said, holding Little Auggie and rocking him gently. The baby squirmed, fighting sleep. Clay started connecting the parts of his device.

"Some invisible force," he said, sliding a large metallic coil into a steel cylinder.

"Clay, I didn't think you believed in ghosts," she said. The baby was losing his fight to stay awake. Shelly walked slowly around the dinner table, rocking and humming a tune softly that she had known when she was Gerta Shultz. Clay paused in his labors and looked over at the woman he loved.

"I don't believe in fakes, phonies, or charlatans," he said. "I don't believe that 'the Almighty' or any other mythological folk made a universe full of things man wasn't supposed to cipher out."

"So, is that a 'yes'?" Shelly asked softly, looking down at the sleeping baby. He looked so much like Augustus. He had his ears and those sweet, kind eyes.

"We live in an age of wonders, Shelly," Clay said. "Man is mastering the fundamental forces of the universe. You're proof that death is not immutable. If that's the case, then perhaps non-corporeal entities may be possible, some kind of electrical-magneto footprint that lives on past the flesh. Perhaps certain constructions and material can sustain and even amplify that. Who knows, perhaps there are even non-physical entities that exist completely separate from human origins."

"Why, Clay, that's the closest I've ever heard you say that you might believe in angels."

"From what Gillian described," Clay said, "I don't think we're talking about angels here."

Shelly put Little Auggie down in his crib while Clay made final adjustments to the dials and switches on the metallic cylinder on the floor of the nursery. The device crackled as a blue arc of electricity jumped between a fork-like antenna on the cylinder. The baby's deep breathing stalled for a second, and he snorted, almost waking. Shelly put a finger to her lips.

"You wake this child up, then you can get him back to sleep," Shelly whispered.

"Sorry. He's sawin' wood, don't worry," Clay said standing with a groan.

"Clay, you sure that's safe? It won't start a fire or anything, will it?"

"No darlin'," Clay said. "That little spark was just the magnetos rotating inside the cylinder starting up the device."

"What does that thing do?" she asked as she took Clay's hand and they walked back down the hall.

"It generates magnetic auras," Clay said. "If non-corporeal entities exist, they still have to operate within the known laws of the universe. So that should mean that they will interact with the magnetic curtain I just set up in the little fella's room, and we'll know."

They sat at the dining table, side by side. Shelly kept Clay's hand.

"What exactly did Gillian say she saw or didn't see?" Shelly asked.

"A darkness," Clay said. "It kept her from coming into the room. There was a disembodied voice whispering to the boy." Shelly's hand clutched Clay's tighter. He saw the change pass over her, the same shadow of concern that came whenever she awoke from the dreams.

"That sounds like the kinds of things you hear about in an exorcism," she said.

"I don't see how reading prayers to a non-corporeal being would have any effect at all," Clay said. She knew he wasn't trying to be insulting; it was just his way, but it did sting a bit.

"I saw one when I was a girl in Germany," she said. "An exorcism. It took days." She turned to face Clay. "Darling, I had a dream, one of those dreams, not too long ago. I was in this house and you...you were there. So were Augustus and Gillian. You were all dead. There was blood everywhere. It was so cold...ice was forming on your bodies. The whole house reeked of blood and the ichor that came from those worms that possessed people, the same thing you made your formula from.

"There was a voice...a terrible voice down that hall. It was chanting, speaking in some language that seemed familiar to me...very, very old, but I couldn't understand it. I ran down the hall to the nursery...and the baby, the baby was coiled inside a huge black snake, no, not a snake—it...it went on forever, like the death between stars, like yawning, endless, dreamless sleep—a dragon, cold, and immutable, and hungry. The voice was coming from the dragon."

Shelly's face was bloodless, her eyes wide and dark. She was looking past Clay, past this place. "The snake began to slide into the baby's mouth. I tried to stop it, but something wouldn't let me. I just had to watch and scream as it went...inside...the baby. The voice became Little Auggie's voice." Shelly shivered, and pulled Clay to her. Clay held her tight. "There was a man suddenly in the room with me. He said this was only a dream, a window. He was there to help me. I knew him, I knew him from town..."

The insistent dinging of a bell began down the hallway an instant before the baby began to scream. Clay was up and running, but Shelly was already halfway to the nursery. She had a knife from the kitchen in her hand. The shadows in the hallway seemed to swirl around Shelly like great black wings.

She reached the door and screeched like a bird of prey. Shelly launched herself forward into the room, her wings of tattered shadow trailing behind her. To Clay, it looked as if something he couldn't see was pushing her back, but she fought her way through. When Clay reached the door, he saw a giant, ink-black serpent coiled around Little Auggie, beginning to lift him up out of the crib. Shelly's knife flashed out at the thing's coils, but the blade passed through them as if they were smoke.

Clay fought his way into the room, feeling as if an invisible slab of granite was pushing him back. He kept his eyes on Shelly, her hair torn loose from her bun, whipping about as if there were a hurricane within the room, and the terrified, wailing baby. He reached his cylinder, the origin of the alarm bell, and kept his eyes on Shelly, still battling the shadowy creature futilely with the knife. "You will not take him!" she screeched, flashing out in desperate instinct, with her fingernails, like a great cat might slash at prey. She was rewarded with the coil she shredded seeming to unravel and disperse, bleeding darkness. Even as the tiny victory registered with Shelly and she began to slash again with her nails, a second shadow-snake began to uncoil behind her.

"Shelly!" Clay shouted. He looked down at his device, and he flipped two switches and turned a dial all the way up. The casing of the machine was ice-cold. He felt the static electricity run over and through him as a bright blue arc jumped between the forks of the antenna. The arc threw Clay back against the wall as the shadow creatures melted into nothing more than harmless night.

Little Auggie wailed as he dropped back into the crib. Shelly, stunned, lifted him up and held him tight. "It's alright," she whispered to the frightened child. "The bad old serpent is gone." Shelly looked over at Clay. "Are you all right, darling? Are you hurt?"

Clay looked at his device. The steel cylinder had been crushed as if by an invisible hand, the antenna mangled. "I'm okay," he said. "Shelly?"

"Yes, love?"

"That fella in your dream?"

"Yes?"

"The one you said wanted to help stop this, whatever it is?"

"Yes?"

"You catch his name?"

THE QUEEN OF WANDS

Jim Negrey sat in a chair he'd brought into the jail cell and placed beside the bunk. The door to the cell was open. The occupant wasn't a prisoner but a child who no longer had a home. Her name was Leeza Turley, and she was the sole survivor of her family and of her town. Jim had brought her with him to the jail after Clay had seen her. She didn't want to be alone, and Jim didn't want her to be.

Jim was reading to her. "'Every few weeks, she would shut herself up in her room,'" Jim read aloud, "'put on her scribbling suit'"—the little girl giggled at the words "scribbling suit," and Jim chuckled as well—"'and fall into a vortex, as she expressed it, writing away at her novel...'"

"Jim," the child said, her voice lilting with sleepiness, "what's a vortex?"

"Kind of like a storm, a big tornado, spinning around. They're saying she got sucked into the world the she was writing about, sucked into her own imagination."

"Oh," Leeza said. "I don't like storms, but I like pretend."

"Me too," Jim said. The iron door to the jail groaned as it opened, and Leeza jumped at the sound. Jim placed a hand on her shoulder. "It's okay," he said. Rabb Hayes walked in and shut the door behind him. "See? It's just Mr. Hayes."

"Rabb!" The little girl sat up in bed and held her arms out. Hayes and Jim laughed. Rabb hugged the little girl, and she wrapped her arms around his neck.

"You look better," Rabb said. "You don't look like a sugar beet anymore from all that sun." Leeza laughed.

"Dr. Clay gave me some yucky medicine. It smelled funnier than he did, but it took all the red and the sore out of my skin!" Rabb looked over to Jim and raised an eyebrow.

"It's Clay's bio-restorative formula," Jim said. "Whatever's in the gunk, it works faster than a greased rooster. Folks from all over have been coming to buy it from him. They say it can cure anything."

"I've never known a medicine that could do that," Rabb said. He looked down at Leeza, who was smiling at him. "But as long as it helps my little desert cactus here, then Dr. Clay's all right with me."

"Jim was reading me this book about these sisters," Leeza said. "You want to listen with me?"

Rabb looked at the book on Jim's lap. "I would love to," he said and sat on the edge of her bed while Jim picked up where he had left off.

In a short time, Leeza was asleep. Rabb watched her for a while. Jim got up quietly and walked out of the cell. "Coffee?" he asked. Rabb nodded and followed him out.

"How is she?" Rabb asked as he sipped his coffee and leaned on the half-rail that separated the office proper from the corridor of cells. Jim sat at the sheriff's desk and put the book back in one of the drawers.

"Clay said she's a tough little knot. She's doing as well as she can. She's trying not to think about it."

"Children are amazingly resilient," Rabb said. "What she's seen, in time she will have to make her peace with it."

"Not now," Jim said. "She's been through enough."

"Agreed, not now. Who's he?" the ex-soldier pointed to the Paiute brave still slumbering on a cot in another cell.

"Part of a war party that attacked the Hazen stage," Jim said. "Mrs. Stapleton brought him in this evening."

"Mrs. Stapleton?" Rabb said.

"Yeah, she owns the local laundry."

"This is a tough town if a laundress can wrestle down a Paiute warrior."

"I wouldn't mess with her," Jim said sipping his Arbuckle.

"Has the sheriff or Caxton decided what they intend to do about the Indian raids?" Rabb asked. Jim shook his head.

"They're all jawin' tonight over at the Imperial," Jim said. He glanced over to Leeza's cell and walked over to stand by the open door, checking on her.

"She reminds you of someone," Rabb said.

"My sister, Lottie," Jim said. For a moment, Rabb thought he was going to say more, but he held his tongue. "She's so young to have the world do her this dirty. She's never hurt anyone. I know the way the Indians get done is wrong, too. I didn't used to. Back when I was in West Virginia with my family, I read those dime novels, gobbled them up as fast as I could git them." Rabb smiled. "The Indians in those stories were always scary and dangerous, wanting to kill and eat people. When I got out here, met real Indians, I realized how wrong I'd been. They've got a right to be angry. They got a right to do something about it." He looked across Leeza to the slumbering brave. "They ain't got the right to make children into orphans."

Rabb sighed. "I've seen too many wars to even recall, but they all have one thing in common. People get so caught up in their own cause, their own loss, their own hatred of whoever is on the other side, they can't see past it, can't see the innocents who always pay the price."

"I understand that," Jim said, a sadness in his voice and eyes. "I've been that way, too. I was so all fired up to see justice done for my pa, to see a sumbitch get what he deserved...I didn't think about...who else might get hurt. I don't know if my sister is alive or not, 'cause of me. I can't do spit about it now, but I am going to keep Leeza safe and try to keep as many other Leezas on both sides safe as I can."

Rabb pointed to the silver badge pinned to his shirt. "The five-pointed star, it's a very old symbol," he said. "It stands for protection. I know you will do all you can, Jim. I just hope other folks follow your lead." Rabb glanced over at the cell, at the slumbering girl. "Some men got a taste for blood, for hate. They make a career out of it."

T he suites of the Imperial hotel were designed to be the envy of hotels as far away as Carson City, the young state's capitol. The Imperial's owner, Malachi Bick, had made sure that General Caxton and Mr. Pinkerton were given the finest of accommodations. The suite where the two Washington dignitaries hosted their dinner guests had an awe-inspiring view of the setting sun, a cauldron of boiling colors at the cool indigo terminator of the night.

General Caxton sat at the head of the table, in his finest uniform, all his medals of rank and recognition polished by his aide and arrayed across his barrel chest. To his left was Mayor Pratt and his lovely new wife, Ora. Next to them was Mayor Pratt's assistant, Colton Higbee, and his fiancée, Elise Whittimore, a woman who was seemingly as reserved as Higbee himself, with straight, blond hair and wire glasses. Porter Rockwell, Harry's new "bodyguard," courtesy of the LDS Church, sat laconically, his tilted chair resting against the wall behind the Pratts. On Caxton's right was Allan Pinkerton. Pinkerton's agents and a few of his aides stood silently by the doors to the suite, servile shadows. Next to Pinkerton sat Deputy Warne.

Kate was dressed in a black, strapless gown with a gossamer silk shawl of pale gray held in place by an onyx-and-diamond clasp. The detective's brown hair was loose, parted to one side, and fell just short of the base of her neck. Next to Kate was Malachi Bick and his beautiful, young daughter, Emily Rose Bright.

Emily was in her twenties. She kept her long, brown hair, which flashed golden in the gaslight of the suite, pulled back and up in an elaborate braided chignon. Emily had arrived in Golgotha a few years ago, around the time Ray Zeal and his killers had ridden into town. After a rocky start to their relationship, Bick's artist daughter from San Francisco had decided to stand by her father come what may. Now, she was one of Bick's closest business confidantes and ambassadors. Emily took an active role in trying to promote and cultivate culture in the booming mining town, often working with Professor Mephisto, the owner of the local playhouse and theater, to bring performers to Golgotha.

"I must say, Bick," Caxton said, dabbing a napkin to his lips, "you provide an excellent table. I didn't eat this well in Virginia City or San Francisco! Who is your chef?"

"Delmonico Hauk," Bick said. "Though, he's not technically mine, General. Hauk comes to us from New York where he was personal chef to John Rockefeller. I tried to woo him to be the Imperial's full-time chef, but he prefers to own his own restaurant. He comes to us on special occasions when we want truly to impress." There was soft murmur of laughter around the table.

"If I had a cook like that out in the field, I fear my poor horse couldn't hold me in short order," Caxton said. More polite chuckles. "Well, now that we have broken bread, perhaps we should discuss the undertaking ahead of us." Caxton glanced briefly at the women at the table, his eyes lingering the longest on Kate. "My apologies, dear ladies. I know such matters are far too substantive and crass for your fair sensibilities." The women around the table were gracious. They smiled, but the general's insult was clear to all of them. Sadly, they were all used to it.

"We'll suffer along, sir," Kate said with just the right amount of sincerity. "Thank you so much for your care. You are truly a gentleman, a rarity on the frontier, sadly." Emily pretended to wipe her lips with her napkin to hide her smile. Gillian looked down, but the corner of her lips curled. Kate felt Allan's foot softly tap her own. Kate looked over at Pinkerton and gave him a smile of the proper dim demeanor. Pinkerton raised an eyebrow but buried his smile.

Caxton's plan was pretty straight-forward: send out scouting parties with Indian guides, including, he blandly assumed, "Sheriff Highfather's Indian." Auggie almost choked on his port when he heard that but remained silent. Then, once they had located some of the Indian forces, summon Caxton's Red Troop to eradicate them.

"Isn't 'eradicate' a harsh word to use, General?" Auggie asked, puffing on his after-dinner cigar.

"Not at all, Mr. Shultz," the general replied. "I know the Indian mind in all its childlike savagery. They will learn nothing from half-measures. When they see their brothers, their sons, their fathers dead upon the plains, only then will they understand the extent of our resolve. Spare the rod and spoil the child, Mr. Shultz."

"But they're not children," Gillian said, squeezing Auggie's hand under the table. "They're not savages. They have a way of life, that stretches far back. Far longer than we've been here." Caxton chuckled and addressed Auggie.

"Well, *Herr* Shultz," the general said, "I see where you get your ideas from. Mrs. Shultz, dear lady, forgive me for being so indelicate, but you, madam, have no idea of what you speak." Caxton's fever-bright eyes became unfocused, but his voice remained authoritative, unwavering, and strangely calm. "The Indians are not like the slaves..."

"*Former* slaves, sir," Gillian corrected. Auggie squeezed her hand. It was not to stop; it was his "I love you" squeeze.

"The negro," Caxton allowed with a dismissive wave of his cigar. "They were broken over a century—domesticated, if you will. What do you think would have happened if the most savage negros had not been weeded out of the herd?"

"I think perhaps we would have reached the changes that have benefited our society in the last few years much, much sooner," Emily, interjected. "Many men of color fought in the war—Powhatan Beaty, William Carney, and Robert Smalls, for example. I'm sure their names have never graced your ears before. None of them have the reputation of being 'tame,' sirrah. Perhaps if you had fought in the war instead of being here, cowing natives in the west, you'd be able to speak with a bit more authority." Bick let the ghost of a smile haunt his lips but said nothing.

Caxton swallowed but remained calm; at least, his voice did. "I have seen good men, decent, god-fearing men—many with the same misguided ideals as you and Mrs. Shultz, young lady—murdered, their bodies savagely desecrated by the creatures you would give human sensibilities to." Miss Whittimore, Higbee's fiancée, paled visibly at the general's descriptions. Higbee patted her hand and tried to give her some comfort. "These Indians are like wild animals. We can't begin the long and odious but vitally necessary task of domesticating them until the untamable ones, the rebellious ones, have been put down."

"I must say," Ora Pratt began, "I, for one, am very thankful you are here, General Caxton. I've heard stories about the savages destroying railroad tracks, attacking trains, and cutting telegraph lines from my father my entire life. Whatever their grievances may be, they have no right to flout the laws of this land, destroy private property, and murder innocents."

"Thank you, dear lady," Caxton said. "I am happy to see not everyone in this town is hobbled with unrealistic notions of how the savages behave."

"I like to think of myself as a realist," Ora said. Harry noted that Ora and the general held each other's gaze a second too long for propriety.

"Mrs. Shultz and my daughter are correct, General," Bick said, his voice like honeyed smoke. While he was not as bombastic as Caxton, his voice reverberated smoothly in every ear. "The tribes in this region are made up of human beings, not animals. They are not immune to reason. It seems much more profitable and much less disruptive for all parties involved to try to negotiate with their leaders."

Caxton shook his head; he looked to Pinkerton for support, but the spymaster's face was inscrutable. "Did you fight in the war, Mr. Bick?"

"I fought in *the* Civil War," Bick said, somewhat cryptically. "The bloodiest conflict of all the ages. Brother slaughtering brother." The door to the suite opened, and a soldier entered. He quietly conversed with one of Pinkerton's agent who had been standing guard by the doors to the suite.

"Then you should have learned the lesson that it is always easier to dictate terms to the enemy from a posture of superiority, sir. First we crush them, then we help them."

"What war has taught me, General," Bick said, "is that when you fight against yourself—your kin—there is no victory, no term, that does not taste of ash."

"The Indians are not my kin, Mr. Bick," Caxton said, obviously disgusted by the notion, "nor yours."

"You have a reputation for using that position of superiority you spoke of not to accept surrender, not to dictate terms, but to utterly annihilate your opponents."

"Which is why Mr. Pinkerton and President Grant saw fit to summon me to help you people resolve your Indian problem once and for all, Mr. Bick," Caxton said, raising a glass of port in salute to Bick before he took a sip. Bick nodded but did not bring his glass to his lips.

The aide leaned in between Caxton and Pinkerton and whispered to them briefly, then retreated. Caxton dried his lips with the back of his hand and smiled broadly. "Ladies and gentlemen," the general said, "I have received excellent news. It appears as if your good sheriff has captured one of the Indian raiders." Kate gave Pinkerton a sharp look, but, as usual, Pinkerton's face was unreadable. "Once we squeeze the location of his accomplices from him, we can move with utmost haste and crush this uprising."

"How do you plan to 'squeeze' this man, General?" Harry asked. "Indians are notoriously resistant to torture."

"I have a secret weapon," Caxton said, smiling at Pinkerton.

K ate!" Pinkerton called out to Warne just as she was about to join the Pratts and the Shultzs on the Imperial's passenger elevator, heading down to the lobby. "A moment, please." Kate and Pinkerton went around the corner from the elevator lobby.

"You look lovely in the dress," Pinkerton said. "I'm glad you received it."

"It's beautiful," she said. "Thank you. Allan. Did you know Jon had captured a prisoner?" Kate asked.

"No, I didn't know 'Jon' had," Pinkerton said, "but it's an excellent opportunity to get ahead of this. I need to debrief you about everything going on here. I need to know the local players and their backgrounds."

Kate looked at Pinkerton. For the briefest of seconds, just the tone of his voice, his manner, had almost immediately made her comply. She stopped herself. "No, Allan. These are my friends. They are not investigative subjects. I don't do that anymore. I don't do that for you."

"I agreed to this extended assignment," Pinkerton said, "because you convinced me we needed a permanent presence here."

"And six months here, six months after we took down Vellas, took down the D.C. prostitute killer, I tenured my resignation to OSIRIS," Kate said. "I like being a deputy, Allan. I like helping people and not lying to them all the time."

"To save people, to stop evil men," Pinkerton said, "we must sometimes use the tools and methods of evil men; you know that. Kate, you've saved lives, you saved a president's life, saved a nation. You are the best detective I've ever known...and...I have missed you, terribly."

He began to reach for her, to pull her to him, and it was as natural a feeling as breathing to Kate. Then she saw the quick, furtive glance about. "Let's go to my suite," he said. "I brought you some of that Greek liquor you fancy so much. I figured you couldn't get it out here." He took her hand and began to walk her down the hall. Kate stopped and pulled her hand away.

"No, Allan," she said. Pinkerton turned and stopped. "I can't do that anymore, either."

"I see," Pinkerton said. It was his professional voice, his give-them-nothing voice. "Perhaps I underestimated your square-jawed, clear-eyed Sheriff 'Jon,' or perhaps I gave you too much credit."

"Perhaps you did," she said and began to walk back to the elevator.

"Kate," Pinkerton said. She paused. The tone still had power, even now. He stood in the hallway. "Do you know him? Really know him?" Kate turned and disappeared around the corner, headed to the elevator lobby. Pinkerton stood still for a long time, his eyes on the spot where she had stood. "You will," he said.

The knock came at his door just as he was sitting down to supper. He had forgotten to eat all day, and his stomach had finally reminded him. He walked to the door and opened it. Kate Warne stood there in a dress like a faerie princess, like a dream.

"Jon," she said, "may I come in?"

"Of course, Kate," Highfather said. "You look...I've never seen you look so pretty."

"Thank you," she said. Jon closed the door. Kate looked over at the table and frowned. "Beans and bread? You forgot to eat again, didn't you?"

"Been a hell of a day," Jon said. "I figure I'm entitled. How'd the dinner go?"

"Caxton is a fanatic," she said. "He's not even going to try to settle it peacefully. He's just going out there to wipe the tribes out, clear the land. They know you have a prisoner. They plan to interrogate him to find out where the renegades are hiding out."

Highfather shook his head. "Mutt's out there somewhere, trying to find out too, but without killing everyone. Damn it. Maude brought the Indian in. She said something about ghost braves, an army of them. That ring any bells with you?" Kate shook her head and put her hand on his shoulder.

"There was a company of ghost rebels during the war that kept popping up, so ghost braves aren't that far a stretch. Caxton says he has some secret weapon to get the brave to talk. He's bringing it to the jail with him tomorrow. Allan's coming too."

"Did your date go good?" Highfather asked. He tried to keep the emotion out of his voice, but he was pretty sure he failed. "I may not be Allan Pinkerton, but I'm enough of a detective to know you wouldn't think to buy yourself a dress like that. Even if you wanted to, you'd have to leave town to get it or mail-order it in a catalog." The wicked, playful smile came to Kate's face. The one he'd seen many times when he, Kate, Mutt, and Jim sat around his desk and played cards, joking, and laughing. That smile was her tell; she had a winning hand.

"It didn't go as well as he would have liked," she said, stepping toward Highfather. She pulled him close. "You owe me a bottle of ouzo," she said, and kissed him. Jon enveloped her in his arms, and he felt her hands on either side of his face, holding him. One of his hands coiled around her waist. There was a crash, and it took a moment for him to realize that they had knocked his plate off the table, knocked the coffee pot off the stove, and knocked over a few chairs. They both laughed at the ruckus they were making, and kept kissing, breathing each other in, devouring each other. Kate spun him, and they began to back toward the bed.

A cold thought sliced through the warmth, and Jon paused, his whole body froze as he remembered. He broke the kiss. It was the hardest thing he'd ever done.

"What, what's wrong, Jon?" Kate asked, breathless. Jon was fighting to get his breath, his body, back under control.

"I got...someone told me...Kate, it ain't right for me to drag you into my messes, especially right now."

"Your messes?" Kate said. "Jon, we almost got eaten by an evil plant house the other day. We've fought monsters, crazy cowboys...demon cows, you remember the demon cows?"

"I do," he said, smiling. Even when he felt like shutting down, felt like becoming safe, numb ice, she found the cracks, found her way inside.

"Your messes are my messes," she said.

"He wants you back, doesn't he?"

"He does," she said, "but I'm not that damaged girl anymore. You treat me like an equal, you respect me, and you trust me..."

"With my life," Jon said, the words, a cold rock in his stomach suddenly.

"...And you have, never, never let me down." She lightly grazed his lips with her own.

Jon swallowed hard. "I'm afraid, Kate. For the first time in a long, long time since the war, I'm really afraid of what comes next. Since I became sheriff here, I've always known what I needed to do, never doubted, never hesitated. Now, I feel like I'm falling into...something I don't understand, and I don't know where that takes me, don't know what I become when I finally hit bottom."

"I know who you are, Jon. I know all I need to know about you, about who you'll always be. Come on," she said, "I trust you. We'll fall together."

He pulled her to him again and kissed her, burned for her, in her, and she did the same with him, kissing him as if he were life itself. They found the bed, bumped into it. Clothes were torn and tossed. They laughed and moaned, whispered and gasped, then there were no words, no world, just two tattered souls clinging to each other in the crucible of the night.

THE KNIGHT OF SWORDS

T he dawn had chased away the damp chill of the night by the time Maude entered her laundry, located on the corner of Dry Well and Prosperity. "Anyone here know how to get bloodstains out of a perfectly good blouse?" she called out in the Yue dialect of Chinese.

"Maude!" Jiao and Ron, the two Chinese women who had worked at Maude's laundry since she had opened it a few years ago, called out. The two women stopped their labors and ran to embrace Maude.

"How was San Francisco?" Jiao asked in her native language.

"Lovely," Maude replied in the same as she handed Jiao a small bundle of letters. "I got those letters to your cousin like you asked. She sends her love and the love of your aunt and uncle. Here's their replies."

"Come tell us everything," Ron said. She walked over to a small table near the wood stove and poured Maude a cup of tea.

"Where's Chuan?" Maude asked, taking the cup and saucer and sitting at the table along with the other two women.

"Delivering the diapers that Mrs. Hamblin hadn't picked up," Jiao said. "It's unlike her to not come by, especially when it's something she needs so desperately with the baby."

Maude's reply was drowned out by Chuan's screams. The young woman ran into the laundry as if the Devil were at her heels.

"Dead!" Chuan gasped "They're all dead!"

The once-cozy little cottage of Zevon and Brighten Hamblin now resembled an abattoir more than a home. The place stank of death. Even the biting wind whistling through the open door couldn't clear the stench of slaughter off the room. Kate Warne squatted back on her haunches at the threshold and took in all of the details of the crime scene. "Well," the detective muttered to herself, "this is certainly the way to dash a good morning."

The couple had been found by a laundress who had knocked on the partially open door to deliver a bundle of diapers they had dropped off at Maude Stapleton's laundry. The couple's corpses were propped up against the bed's headboard, naked, their bodies covered in scratches, bites, and semen.

The flesh and skull-bone of their faces had been cut out off of them, leaving bloody holes where their visage should be. The killers, and it was more than one—Kate had already spotted at least two distinct, smudged, bloody boot prints—had taken the time and effort to saw, cut, and then scoop the brains out of the skulls. *Who the hell carries a bone saw around with them?* Kate thought. *Someone sick enough to do this, that's who.* The deputy stepped into the room, careful to avoid the tributaries of blood. Her work with Allan Pinkerton had long ago taught Kate that no detail could afford to be overlooked. She hadn't found any brains, and that troubled her even more.

The flesh of the couple's faces had been nailed to the wall over the empty baby crib, stretched and fixed to approximate a grisly replica of the famed "Comedy and Tragedy" masks. "No brains, no baby," Kate sighed. "This couldn't get any worse."

"I sent Chuan home," Maude said, suddenly standing at the door. "You or Jon can call on her there if you need any more information. She was understandably overwrought."

Kate closed her eyes at the sound of Maude's voice, as if it caused her physical pain. "I was wrong. It could get worse." She turned to Maude. "Stay there by the door; I don't need any help on this."

"So, I suppose you already spotted those hairs on the blanket that clearly don't belong to either victim?" Maude asked. Kate sighed.

"All right," she said, "get your freakish senses in here. Any idea what they did with the baby, or why they'd take him?"

"Not yet," Maude said. "Let me poke around a bit."

"Looks like they got about a day's lead on us," Kate said, "from the condition of the bodies. No blood in the crib, so if we're lucky, the kid's still breathing. They may have been passing through, which means we might still be able to track them, if we can figure which direction they went in and what they're after."

A crowd was milling near the door and out into the street, trying to get a look inside the murder house. The gawkers were being especially bold.

"Worse than damn vultures," Kate said as she examined the bloody, shredded bedclothes of the Hamblins. "Get the hell back, all of you!" Kate called out to the crowd. "Have a little respect for the dead!"

"Shut up!" a man's voice from the crowd called out. "You ain't the real law!"

"Yeah," another man's voice sneered. "Sheriff Dead Man ain't here, girlie. We ain't got to do a blamed thing you say!"

Maude was focused on the bodies. The was a strange scent she was catching at the edge of her perception. It was so faint and yet familiar, she couldn't tell if it was coming from the bodies or the bed. She closed her eyes, blocked out the banal murmur of the crowd, and coaxed her sense of smell to a fantastic degree.

Many of the crowd backed away from the door when Kate emerged from the small house. "You move along and keep a civil tongue, boys," Kate said to the troublemakers, "or I'll blow your kneecaps off and drag your whining asses to the pokey." Kate spotted Mayor Pratt's new best friend, Porter Rockwell, at the fringes of the crowd, munching on a grease-stained paper bag full of roasted peanuts. The killer laughed out loud at her pronouncement and gave Kate a nod of approval. He made a silent sign with his fingers like he was cocking and shooting a gun, his eyes on the rabble-rousers. He mouthed "pop-pop" in time to the finger-gun shooting. Kate shook her head no. Rockwell shrugged and moved along.

Another familiar face appeared near the back of the crowd and began to work his way through. "All of you, go on, now," Barabbas Hayes called out. "Let the deputy do her job, and let those folk rest in peace." His deep voice was powerful, and it seemed to hang in the air almost like thunder. Most of the crowd scurried off. Others grumbled but began to disperse. Only a handful stood their ground. Rabb could smell the liquid courage on them from ten feet away.

"Well, don't this just beat the Dutch?" one of the remaining men said. "Some uppity nig-nog taking up for a strumpet wearing a tin star. What's this country comin' to?" The man next to him began to laugh, and the remaining instigators joined in. They all stopped when Rabb was standing directly in front of the ringleader.

"I'm sorry," Hayes said, "I couldn't hear what you boys were saying. Some jackasses were braying in my ear. Come again?"

The few remaining onlookers grew quiet. Rabb didn't seem to mind the attention on him, he seemed to ignore it, focusing on the two hecklers. "You gonna let him talk to you like that?" the heckler's companion blurted out.

Hayes's eyes narrowed. As if on cue, the bright morning sun fled, cowering behind looming clouds that had come out of nowhere.

"Yes," Rabb said, "he is."

For a moment, Kate thought the men might draw on Rabb, but then the whole mood of the drunks shifted to an uneasy dread. Kate felt it too. The blood drained from the heckler's face; his lips moved, but no sound emerged. There was a look on the man's eyes as if he had just seen Death itself. The same pall of fear encompassed the others as well. Rabb stared squarely at them, almost through them.

"I'm...I'm sorry..." the heckler said, his voice quavering in fear. He glanced over to Kate. "Ma'am."

"Move along," Kate said. The men did, as fast as they could. Hayes walked up to Kate. "Much appreciated, Mr. Hayes," Kate said.

"Hope you don't mind," Rabb said. "It looked like you had it under control. I'm just allergic to idiots."

Kate shrugged. "You saved me some bullets, and their kneecaps. It's one of those days where we're a little short-handed. How *did* you do that, exactly?"

"I can be very persuasive when the mood strikes," Rabb said. The sky was clearing again; the dark clouds fled as quickly as the troublemakers.

Inside, Maude had chased down the scent, a musky, organic smell. She had snorted it out of her nostrils before, and the sense association that accompanied it was one of death and madness. The connection came to her in an instant, and she immediately wished she was wrong.

"Rory," she whispered. *The Sons of Typhon. Here, in Golgotha.* She stood and regarded what had once been a loving husband and wife, and she knew she was right.

Maude stepped outside to join Kate and Rabb. "I know who did this," she said to Kate. "I need to talk to Jon."

"Anne?" Rabb said to Maude, a startled look crossing the unflappable ex-soldier's face.

"Excuse me?" Maude said.

"Mr. Hayes," Kate said, "this is Maude Stapleton, the local laundress...and civic busybody. Maude, this is Rabb Hayes; he's the one Mutt and Jim brought out from the desert. He rescued that little girl, Leeza."

"Maude Stapleton," Hayes said, "she who overpowers Paiute warriors. Very impressive work, ma'am. I'm sorry I didn't make the connection until now."

An odd sense of deja vu came over Maude as she looked at Hayes.

"You head on down to the jail," Kate said to Maude. "Jon's there. He'll want to know who the bastards were who did this."

"Deputy," Rabb began.

"Kate," she said.

"Kate, do you need any further assistance here, or do you mind if I accompany Maude down to the jail?"

"Go ahead," Kate said. "I'll be along as soon as I get everything sealed up here. And thank you, Mr. Hayes."

"Rabb," he said with a smile.

Kate gave Maude a curt nod. "Thanks," Kate said, "for mucking about in my investigation."

"I know that was painful," Maude said as she and Hayes began to head down Dry Well Road. "Should I fetch Doctor Turlough?" Kate nodded and reentered the cottage without another word.

"Are you two at odds?" Rabb asked, glancing back in the direction of Kate.

"A bit of...professional rivalry," Maude said. "We get along well enough, I suppose." The two were getting looks walking together on the sidewalk, but no one said anything to their faces. Maude noted that Rabb seemed just as uncaring about the disapproval tossed at them as she was. "May I ask you a question?"

"Certainly," he said.

"Why did you call me 'Anne' back there? Have we met?"

"I called you Anne because you are the spitting image of your great, great, great, great grandmother when she was young. It's remarkable, really. And yes, we have met. Once, back when you were a little girl," Rabb said, with a smile. "You were Maude Cormac Anderton then. It was not too long after you first came to live with Anne at Grande Folly."

"You knew Gran Bonny?" Maude asked.

"Yes, we sailed together for a time, had many adventures," Rabb said. His voice became wistful as he pulled at memories from long ago. "She was my very dear friend. She was very proud of you."

"Forgive me for saying," Maude interjected, "but I hazard you and I are fairly close in age to one another. You seem far too young to have been running about with Gran during her adventuring days. She never mentioned a 'Mr. Hayes' to me."

"She wouldn't have," Rabb said. "Back in those days, I traveled under one of the many names I was known by before I came to America—Adu, Adu Ogyinae."

———

Highfather and Jim looked on as the military prison wagon clattered to a halt in front of the jail. A dozen of Caxton's soldiers, rifles at the ready, had escorted the wagon down from the military camp at the foot of Rose Hill. Pinkerton and Caxton disembarked from a carriage that had taken them from the Imperial. They were surrounded by a contingent of Pinkerton's finest and most formidable private detectives—the legendary, and oft-times infamous, "Pinkerton men."

"Sheriff," Pinkerton said. "Good work on capturing a prisoner. How'd you do that exactly?"

"Not my doing," Highfather said. "Citizen arrest. Folks around here are pretty scrappy." Pinkerton and Caxton glanced at each other and looked a bit confused. The soldiers had folded down the small block of stairs in front of the locked and barred door at the back of the prison wagon. While a soldier busied himself with unlocking the door, the other troops leveled dozens of rifles on the door.

"What you got in there," Jim asked, "a tiger from the circus?"

"Worse," Pinkerton said, flatly.

"This your secret weapon, General?" Jon asked. "Never cared much for weapons you don't seem to be able to control."

"Trust me," Caxton said as the door on the wagon swung open. "This one is completely under my control."

An Indian man, dressed as a Northern Paiute, stepped out of the darkness of the wagon. He was of average height and a little on the slender side, with a fluid, muscular grace to each movement. His hair was in the style of a black crest shaved bald on either side, not normally favored by the Paiute but popular among the Mohawk, the Pawnee, and the Seneca. He wore a simple leather vest and pants with no shoes or sandals. Steel manacles were fitted to his wrists, neck, and ankles, connected by thick chains. Despite lacking his multicolored war paint, Jim and Highfather recognized him immediately. The Indian looked at all the men leveling guns at him and seemed bemused. Highfather had thought the gesture of so many guards to merely be military overkill. Now he wished there were more of them.

"Sheriff, deputy," the Indian said with a nod as he walked slowly down the steps to the street. He spoke excellent English, with no hint of an accent. "So good to see you both again."

"Snake-Man." Jim said the name as if it would summon the Devil.

"This is your secret weapon?" Highfather turned to Caxton. "That man is a maniac. He rode into town a few years back with a cult of murderers and worse. He nearly killed my deputy, Mutt, twice. We turned him over to the military at the end of all that mess, and now you've let him go, Caxton?"

"I've done no such thing, Sheriff," Caxton said. "Snake-Man is still a federal prisoner. He agreed to provide us with intelligence about the growing insurrection among the tribes that he was part of, and he's acted as a scout for my troop, under scrutiny of course, for the better part of a year. He's a tool, Sheriff, a valuable weapon, and he's mine. Now if you'll lead the way, he's going to get the information we need out of your prisoner to lead us to the Indian forces."

"You may trust him; I don't," Highfather said.

"You don't have to trust him," Pinkerton said, stepping in front of Jon. "You just have to follow orders, Sheriff." Jon's eyes narrowed, and he and the spymaster held each other's gaze for a very long second.

"What do you intend to do?" Jon asked.

"I want you and you alone to accompany the guards inside. The general and I will remain out here. It is to appear as a simple transfer of a prisoner. Lock him in the cell next to your Indian brave and leave them alone for a time. Do you understand your orders? Do I need to repeat them?"

"No," Highfather said, his eyes burning into Pinkerton.

There was a pause while Pinkerton and Caxton conferred with Snake-Man quietly. Jim sidled up next to Jon. "Mutt's going blow his stack when he sees him," Jim muttered to Highfather. Jon looked past the armed cadre circling Snake-Man and saw Maude and Rabb approaching on the sidewalk. He saw Maude's face when she recognized Snake-Man.

"I'm not sure Mutt's who we need to be worrying about," Highfather said, moving to cut off Maude as she began to bolt ahead, her eyes hard like diamonds. "I don't think they got enough troops!"

"What is he doing here!" Maude snarled. Jon held up his hand but didn't try to restrain or halt Maude, only put himself in her way. "He nearly killed Mutt!"

"Twice. Caxton says he's working with them against the Indian raiders," Jon said.

"Caxton's an idiot!" Maude said loudly enough for several of the soldiers to turn and look.

"Yes, he is," Jon said, "but unless you are planning to wage war against the federal government, we have to stay cool."

Maude looked at Jon, then to the contingent of soldiers. "Okay," she said to the sheriff, her eyes never looking away from Snake-Man, who was now looking at her. The Indian licked his lips and smiled at Maude as he was led to the jail's door. "You need to know, Jon, we have other problems in town beside the federals and Snake-Man. Big problems."

"I told you not to get me anything for my birthday," Jon said glumly. "Well, once we get this circus resolved, you can tell me all about it."

"Sheriff," Pinkerton commanded, snapping a finger in Jon's direction. Highfather looked again to Maude.

"If I can't kill mine, you can't kill yours," Jon said and walked over to join the procession of soldiers. They entered, with Jon and the commanding officer of the soldiers of the detachment in the lead. The party disappeared inside the jail, and the door shut behind them with a loud thump.

"Isn't Leeza in there?" Rabb asked Jim. The young deputy shook his head.

"No," Jim said. "I took her to stay with Reverend Rourke and his wife. Jail's no place for a little girl, especially with all this mess going on."

"Good," Rabb said. Kate, grim-faced and pale, walked up to join the three.

"Scene's locked up," she said to Maude. "Clay's fetching the bodies as soon as he can. Had some kind of appointment this morning. What's all this?"

"Caxton's 'secret weapon' is Snake-Man," Maude said.

"You mean one of Zeal's crazy crew?"

"Can't be that many Snake-Men around," Maude said, "can there?"

"Allan's on-board with this?" Kate asked.

"Up to his shifty little eyes, apparently," Maude said.

Twenty minutes later, Jon and the soldiers exited the jail. Highfather went to Kate, walking around and past the General and Pinkerton. Maude noticed a strange current of interaction shift back and forth between Highfather and Kate and tangentially to Pinkerton. Kate caught her staring, and Maude looked away.

"You okay?" Jon asked. Kate nodded. "How bad was it?"

"Pretty bad," she said, "even for around here. They took the Hamblin's baby, Joel. About three months old. Not sure if he's dead or alive, but he wasn't in there."

"Let's assume he's alive," Highfather said. He glanced over at the soldiers and Pinkerton's men. "We need to start looking fast if he's going to stay that way."

"It could be worse than just a kidnapping, Jon," Maude said. "I've run into at least one of these creatures before. He calls himself Rory. The little boy's in grave danger. The whole town is. This is the beginning of whatever they are up to."

"They?" Jim asked. They all grew silent as the general and Pinkerton approached them.

"Now, we let our secret weapon do its job," Caxton said, chuckling. He slapped Highfather on the back as he walked by. The general and Pinkerton headed back to their buggy, speaking in hushed tones to one another, while the soldiers milled about, pulling out their fixing bags to roll cigarettes.

"Come on," Jon said to Kate, Jim, Maude, and Rabb. "Lunch is on the mayor."

The most popular brothel in Golgotha was the Dove's Roost on Bick Street. Most of the "doves" left their old names behind them when they became "public girls," and now went by handles like "Hambone Jane," "Molly b'Damn," and "Cimarron Rose." Most of the women had never intended ending up out on the frontier alone and in this line of work. Someone—their husbands, fathers, or lovers—had abandoned them out here or died, leaving them in debt with no way to get back east. It was this work or dying.

It was a life punctuated by violence, rape, disease, and pregnancy. A few years back, the pirate, Black Rowan, had come to town from San Francisco and taken control of all the prostitution trade in Golgotha. She had made things better for public girls. Men who hurt the girls now faced the wrath of Rowan and the Scholar, her right-hand man. They got a bigger cut of the money they earned now, but it was still a hard, ugly life.

Many of the doves spent the daylight hours dozing, but others, like Becky and Ample Alice, did their assigned chores, while other Doves wrote letters to their families full of wishes and lies about how well they were doing and when they would be coming home. One of the girls, called Aspasia, played the piano in the parlor.

The last few days had been busier than usual with the influx of soldiers to Golgotha. The Scholar was busying himself with a few minor repairs to the house before the night and the men arrived. He'd had to eject a drunken trooper the night before, and the man had taken part of the back door with him when he was tossed out. There was then the unpleasant business of having to deal with the trooper's drunken comrades. In all, the Scholar and his faithful cudgel had to beat and expel a half-dozen men. He had ripped one of his favorite shirts in the process, and he intended to mend it once he had attended to the door.

Black Rowan was surprised when she entered her office and found Harry sitting in a chair. The mayor looked tired. He stood when Rowan entered.

"Harry, what a pleasant surprise," she said. "I thought you didn't want to be seen coming in here in daylight?"

"It doesn't matter," Harry said. "I wanted to give you these." He removed a packet of papers from his coat pocket, and Rowan noticed he was carrying the mystic Sword of Laban in a scabbard under his long coat. He also appeared to be wearing the weightless, indestructible magical breastplate of his Mormon faith under a loose linen tunic. "I've signed a special mayoral proclamation ceding the Winterton's lands to Jacob Winterton and his posterity in perpetuity. It's all filed in the town courthouse."

"You're joking," she said, opening the envelope and scanning the documents. "Harry, what are you doing?"

"For the first time in a while, the right thing," he said. "You heard what happened to those people in Ezekiel?"

"The Paiute raided it," Rowan said. "It's all over town. It's why the federal troops are here."

"They asked for my help," he said, his voice full of a pain Rowan had never heard from Harry before. "They wrote me. Higbee found the letters. They begged for my help, for the help of 'the one mighty and strong.' What a joke."

"Harry," Rowan said, trying to reach out to the mayor, but he stepped back, shaking his head.

"No," he said. "No. They're dead, Rowan, all of them. Because I was too busy playing at politics, trying to win a job I hate most days. Tell my new father-in-law he's going to need to find a new path for the Golgotha dogleg of the railroad."

"He's not going to do that, Harry," Rowan said. "He's going to find himself a new mayor."

"He can try," Harry said walking to the door.

"Harry, I've seen that look on the faces of plenty of men in my life. You're not thinking this through. People die all the time. It's always someone's fault; most times it's their own fault. Please, reconsider. You're a decent man, I've fought beside you. I don't want to ruin you."

"That's up to you. It's your choice. Good night, Rowan," Harry said. The door closed behind the mayor with a soft click. The mistress of the Dove's Roost sat behind her desk and watched the shaft of afternoon sunlight sneak in under her blind and slowly stretch across her desktop. Finally, she withdrew a piece of paper and pen from her desk and began to compose a very grim telegram to Virginia City.

THE DEVIL

By late morning, word had already spread about the terrible murder of the Hamblin family. A current of unspoken fear passed through the town. If you lived in Golgotha for any length of time, you knew about the strangeness of the town, the deaths, the disappearances, the fantastic and horrific creatures, the madness, and the magic. Most folks did what people were wired to do: ignore it or explain it away. They tried to go about their day and not think too much about it.

Denial was an art form in Golgotha. Giant, living, plant-houses melting turned into a simple house collapse. A brutally murdered young couple and their missing child became an ugly rumor of Indian cutthroats sneaking into the town in the dead of night, killing people, and stealing babies. Those who knew the truth, who couldn't hide from it or lie to themselves well enough, envied the ones who could. The world was a much easier place to navigate with blinders on.

Professor Mephisto's Playhouse and Showcase was at the edge of Main Street. It was one of the first buildings visitors to Golgotha saw as they rode in on the northern road from the 40-Mile Desert that eventually became Main Street. The playhouse was hard to miss. It was a two-story structure done up in gray and mauve with a wide marquee that stretched across the front of the building. The marquee currently announced the ongoing nightly production of *Titus Andronicus.*

Clay, Gillian, Little Auggie, and Shelly entered the theater's lobby. "You sure this is the place?" Clay asked Shelly. The seamstress nodded.

"You've asked me that six times now, Clayton," Shelly said. "This is the right place."

"And this all came to you in a dream?" Gillian said. She held her son in her arms. The baby was very clingy today, but given what Clay and Shelly had reported about the events of the night before, it was perfectly understandable. She kissed Auggie Junior's forehead, and the baby sighed in contentment.

"My dreams have been very strange since my resurrection," Shelly said, a strange, wistful quality entering her voice. "Very...graphic, very violent. And I remember everything."

The lobby was empty. They walked across the marble-tiled floor and past large potted ferns and floor-to-ceiling Greek columns to one of the sets of double doors that led into the theater. There was the sound of a single voice reverberating through the doors. Clay opened the doors for Shelly and Gillian, and they entered the performance space.

A man stood alone on the stage in front of the closed red velvet curtains. His voice was a booming bass-baritone, rumbling across the sea of empty seats like a crashing ocean wave, as he sang, acapella, "*Me voici d'ou Vient ta surprise,*" from the opening act of *Faust*. They walked down the carpeted aisle toward the man.

Walking toward the stage, Gillian looked about. She had been to the theater a few times with Auggie, and once even with Will before his death. It was always packed on a performance night. She had never noticed before that the gargoyles in their parapets at the edge of the balcony and in alcoves along the walls were not the traditional grotesques. They had knobby octopus heads with faces full of tentacles and clusters of insect eyes, bat-like wings folded around ape-like bodies, and curved stone claws clutched at the edges of their eternal perches.

At capacity, the theater's ground level and balcony could hold close to two hundred people. At present, only a young woman sat on the front row, center, listening with rapt attention to the man's performance. It was Emily Bright, Malachi Bick's daughter.

The man acknowledged Gillian and the others with a nod but continued to sing. He was close to seven feet tall, fit, especially for his age, which looked to be mid-sixties, but he could have been younger. He had a mop of curly salt and pepper hair that fell below his collar. His eyebrows and immaculate goatee were black. He wore a mauve velvet smoking jacket over a white poet's shirt. Numerous necklaces and amulets hung about his neck, and he had rings on most of his fingers. Black velvet pants and ankle boots completed his somewhat foppish attire.

The man held the final note, sustaining it for what seemed an eternity, before finally allowing it to end. The theater was silent for a breath, then Emily, Gillian, and Shelly clapped loudly. The man crossed his legs and took a deep bow.

"Bravo!" Emily called out. "*Magnifico*," she continued, "*la tua voce è un uccello che sale verso il cielo, professore.*"

"You are very kind to an old man, my dear," the singer said. Then he smiled at the others. "As are all of you, Mrs. Shultz, Dr. Turlough, and Mrs. Wollstonecraft. I hope you are all well."

"I thought you said you hadn't met," Clay said to Shelly.

"Only in the dream," Shelly replied. The man retrieved a silk handkerchief from his jacket pocket and dabbed his face and lips with it as he descended the stage by the stairs on one side of the orchestra pit.

"Professor Mephisto," Gillian said. "It's so good to see you again."

"You as well, my dear," Mephisto said. He looked down at Little Auggie. "Is this the fair fellow causing so much concern? Are you, lad?" The baby made a gurgling sound and tried to reach for Mephisto's goatee.

"How did you...how could you know?" Gillian asked. Emily came to join the others as Mephisto gently touched the top of the baby's head.

"'Lovers and madmen have such seething brains,' Mephisto almost whispered, "such shaping fantasies, that apprehend, more than cool reason ever comprehends.'" He looked over to Shelly. "I take it your dream came true?"

"Yes," Shelly said.

"I hate to intrude on what's obviously private business," Emily said. "Professor, you and I can discuss the Faust production next..."

"No, Miss Bright," Mephisto said with a smile. "Some places act like a magnet, drawing forces, people together. Golgotha is such a place. These people need my help, and I need yours. Please stay." He looked over to Gillian. "If that is all right with you, Mrs. Shultz?" Gillian smiled at Emily.

"I remember how bravely Miss Bright fought during the business with Ray Zeal. I trust her judgment and her discretion."

"I admired what you said to General Caxton last night," Emily said to Gillian.

"And I you," Gillian replied. "That man is a menace. I don't care what his standing is."

Mephisto looked over to Clay. "Dr. Turlough, you are very quiet. That usually means you're thinking. What is it, my friend?"

Clay scratched his head. "Shelly said you were in her dreams, Professor, said that you offered to help her against whatever this non-corporeal thingamabob is. I just don't understand how that can be."

"I respect your intellect, Clay, and your open mind," Mephisto said. "Dogma, any dogma, is the enemy as much as ignorance is. A rarity in a scientist. Regarding this particular phenomenon, I can tell you that Shelly was broadcasting, if you will, with an unnatural clarity and power." Gillian, Clay, and Shelly traded furtive looks at one another. "I'm rather curious to know why that is. Tell me, Miss Woll-stonecraft..." He paused. "Perhaps you could just tell me your real name. I'm afraid your literary *nom de guerre* is showing."

Shelly looked to Clay and then back to the professor. "I'm Gerta," she said, "Gerta Shultz, or at least I used to be." Emily looked confused.

"Wasn't that Auggie's first wife?" Emily asked. "I thought she died?"

"She did," Mephisto said. The professor looked over to Clay. "Remarkable," he said. "Your much-vaunted bio-restorative formula?" Clay nodded. "Interesting. It regenerates the body, but what of the soul?"

"I don't truck much in souls," Clay said.

"Of course, Clay," Mephisto said. "That's more my specialty." He looked back to Shelly. "Still quite a few mysteries tangled up with you, Shelly. Those mysteries may be tied to the entity coming after the baby and your apparent sensitivity to it." Gillian's mind went to Auggie's nightmares, and she wondered again if he too was connected to this faceless presence that was terrifying their son.

"Professor," Gillian asked, "the thing that Clay and Shelly and I have all encountered, what is it? Why does it want Auggie Junior?"

"Let's retire to my study," the professor said, "and see if we can get you some answers." Mephisto led them up the stairs to the stage and behind the closed velvet curtains. They crossed the darkened stage—covered in stacked scenery flats and smelling of sawdust and grease-paint—and passed through another door into a narrow room with an iron spiral staircase going up. They ascended the staircase and found themselves in a spacious and luxuriously furnished maze of rooms. "Welcome to my humble abode," Mephisto said, leading them past a beautiful mahogany piano. A silver candelabra with the leering faces of demons set into the capitols of each arm rested on the piano. Partly melted red candles had dripped down onto the faces.

"How lovely," Gillian remarked, pausing for a moment to touch the keyboard's cover.

"I'd let you play if it wouldn't be so detrimental to you, my dear," Mephisto said. "I know what an accomplished pianist you are."

"Well, that is very generous of you to... How could you possibly know that?" Gillian said, blushing in surprise.

"However, this particular instrument has wires within it that were used to strangle and decapitate innocent victims in horrific rituals and then were used in the construction of the piano. Each note played is a supplication and a sacrifice to a very old dark god. It never ends very well for those who play it." Gillian quickly took her hand away from the piano.

"How did he know I play?" Gillian whispered to Shelly. Shelly shook her head.

The party passed into a room with high, narrow windows on the eastern wall. Natural light from outside fell down into the room in shafts. The room was filled with fine Persian rugs, medieval and oriental tapestries, bookcases spilling over with books, stone tablets, scrolls, and various artifacts. A quilted fencing practice dummy with a bright red heart target lurked near a rack of antique guns and swords. Shelly noted the dummy also had black heart markings on its torso in several places that did not align with the placement of the human heart.

In one corner of the room, the rugs had been pulled back, and elaborate chalk symbols and formulae were drawn upon the bare floor. Several hand-drawn wall scrolls with tables of numbers and symbols on them hung on the walls. A sword, seemingly made of gold and encrusted with gems, had been lain carefully on one of the chalk symbols, its blade pointing east. Something seemed to move silently in the shadows of the dark corner within one of the symbols, but it was impossible to make out what it was, only that it was pacing about like a wild, caged animal.

"Please," Mephisto said to his guests, "take your rest." A comfortable circle of cushions was arranged in the room, and a beautiful, Indian hookah of silver, adorned with elephant-headed gods and the winding coils of the dragon, Vritra, towered at the center of the circle. "Anyone care for a bit of refreshment?" the professor asked as his guests seated themselves among the cushions. Clay seemed to be having difficulty with the concept of no chairs and kept trying to stuff more pillows behind himself. "Tea? Hashish? Opium, perhaps?"

"Uh, no thank you, Professor," Gillian said, gently rocking Auggie Junior. Mephisto sat and scanned the faces of the others.

"It is very rare, almost unheard of, for an entity to attach itself to a human being without a reason or at least a way in," Mephisto said.

"What could a six-month-old baby possibly have done to deserve this?" Gillian asked.

"Nothing," the professor said. "However, this could be transmigratic baggage from a previous life, unresolved and haunting him in this one."

"A previous life?" Emily said.

"If you don't mind me saying so, Professor," Clay said, "but that sounds an awful lot like the claptrap they rattle on about in the pews in the churches and temples. I have no use for theirs, and I don't see how yours is going to help the boy out of this spot."

"Clay, if I were to jump off a cliff, I would fall to the ground below, correct?" Mephisto asked. "Well...yes, of course," the scientist said.

"If I were to sink under the waves, I would drown, correct?"

"Yes."

"Could you explain to me in detail the whys of that, if someone were to ask you? 'Why do I fall to earth?' 'Why do I drown?'"

"Those are physical laws of nature—gravity, density, states of matter, biology," Clay said.

"If you explained them in full detail, leaving out nothing, would this baby be able to understand you? Would a person not schooled in the sciences be able to follow you? How about someone from a different culture, with different explanations for the same phenomena?"

"Child's too young," Clay said. "Lacks language, development, lacks references for understanding. A grown person or someone from another background...it would be tough, but perhaps if you simplified the concepts, used examples, went back to the math of it all...I might be able to give them the gist of it."

"Forgive me," Mephisto said, "but from my perspective, the things I'm trying to explain and discuss with you, you have no frame of reference for. The universe has laws and energies that our science has simply not caught up to yet. It would be the same if you tried to talk me through the creation of a motor, of how they work and why. I'd be equally lost. There are celestial mechanics, as certain and as complex as any other laws of nature."

"I don't much care for things I can't cipher out," Clay said. Mephisto smiled.

"Nor do I. You and Shelly saw with your own eyes the physical manifestation of this entity. If such entities had the ability to interact with our world unfettered, don't you think they would? But they don't; therefore, to have the ability to do what it's been doing, it must have a point of entrance, an invitation, a link. Does that seem logical to you?"

"Very," Clay said.

"You wouldn't think of such things, Clay," Mephisto continued, "why would you? It is possible that the same process that you used to bring Shelly back to life may interfere or disrupt certain metaphysical processes, like reincarnation, transmission of karmic debt, or lines of fate. Tell me, Gillian, have you had any of this bio-restorative formula?"

"No," Gillian said.

"Auggie, perhaps?" the professor asked. "I know he had that close call with the gunshot wound a while back."

Gillian looked over to Clay. Shelly looked at both of them.

"You need to tell him," Shelly said. Mephisto looked from the scientist to the mother.

"You treated him with the formula for the gunshot?" the professor said. They were both silent. Awareness spread across Mephisto's face. "You...brought him back...like you did to Gerta, Shelly, didn't you?"

Gillian couldn't look at anyone. She focused on the twisting scales of the silver serpent on the hookah. She wanted to cry, but there were no tears, and they wouldn't help Auggie or her son, anyway. She felt sick and guilty inside. "I...it was *my* decision. I asked Clay to do it." She finally summoned the strength to look at Mephisto. "I loved him so much...I didn't want to lose him."

"We may have found our access for this entity," the professor said, standing. "But I need more information to be sure what we are dealing with." He excused himself from the room, and they could hear him rummaging, looking for something.

"Does...does Auggie...know?" Shelly asked.

"No," Gillian said.

"Gillian," Shelly said, taking her oldest, and dearest friend's hand, "you must tell him. He must know."

"I know," Gillian said. "I'm just afraid what it will do to him, to us."

"Nothing built on a lie ever lasts," Emily said.

"I wish the world worked that way," Gillian said to the young girl, "but in my experience, the lie tends to outlive the liar. Sometimes that's not a bad thing."

"But in this case," Shelly said.

"In this case, he deserves to know," Gillian said. Shelly hugged her old friend with her new arms. The professor returned with a small leather case in one hand and small glass jar in the other.

"I'll need a bit of the lad's blood," he said. "Just a few drops. Clay, if you'd be so kind to assist, please?" The doctor stood and made his way over to Gillian and the baby. Clay opened his bag and removed a small scalpel he had previously sterilized and kept wrapped in a cloth soaked in the water and carbolic acid mixture.

Gillian held her baby close as Clay carefully took the baby's tiny hand and chose one chubby finger. "Shhh," Gillian said. "It's going to be fine. Uncle Clay is going to be so gentle." Clay's eyes looked sad, Gillian thought. She knew in the furnace of his immense intellect, he was feeling lost with all this talk of souls and ineffable bonds and consequences. Clay had the eyes of a nervous child as he looked at her.

"Only hurt for sec," he said softly. The baby squealed at the pain a second after the knife had done its work. Mephisto opened the small jar. It held red paint. Clay mixed a few dark drops of the baby's blood in with the pigment. Mephisto sealed the jar. Gillian kissed her baby's little red fingertip and let him fuss and cry for a moment. Mephisto handed the jar to Emily.

"What do I do with this, Professor?" she asked.

"Emily, I know you are an accomplished painter, and I also know of your gift," he said. "You possess a wonderful talent to paint someone and capture their inner essence, their soul, if you will, on the canvas. I would like you to do that for the child, if you please, and use this pigment in your work."

"I've never told anyone about that but my father," Emily said. "Did he tell you? I know you two are close."

"He did not betray your confidence to me, my dear," Mephisto said. "I know things about you all because it is one of my gifts, my talents, to see pieces of the lives of those with whom I interact, whom I find in dreams. And yes, your father is my friend. I am indebted to him in a way I will never be able to repay. He gave me sanctuary here when there was, literally, nowhere else on this earth I could run. I need your help, your talents, Emily, to help this child."

Emily looked down at the jar and then to little Auggie's red, chubby face. "Of course," she said. "I'll do all I can. You should know, though, sir, that Dr. Turlough did use his formula to help me get over being shot around the same time as Auggie was."

"Was it a life-threatening wound?" Mephisto asked Clay.

"No, but it did regenerate the damage to her spine," Clay said. "Without it, she'd have been in a wheelchair for the rest of her life."

"I am guessing that as long as the formula did not return someone to life," Mephisto said, stroking his goatee, "it should not be a concern, other than a bit of fate divergence, which the normal turning of the cosmic wheel should regulate in time." He looked to Emily. "In other words, it shouldn't be an issue. Paint away, my dear."

"It will take me a few days," Emily said. "If you don't mind, I'm going to discuss all this with my father. He may be able to help as well."

"At this point," Gillian said, "any help is appreciated. Thank you, Emily."

"The magneto-etheric scattering field I deployed seemed to chase the thing off," Clay said. "Didn't seem to care for it much either. I'm going to get to work on another one."

"An excellent idea, Clay," Mephisto said. He removed a small metal amulet from the case in his hands. He carefully placed it against the baby's blankets. "This is a cold iron amulet," he said to Gillian. "Keep it close to the baby. It should help deter the entity as well."

"Thank you so much," Gillian said. "I can't even begin to thank you."

"Thank me when this business is at an end," Mephisto said. "We will meet again in a few days and see if we can find where we stand."

The guests departed, Gillian intent on explaining it all to Auggie, Clay and Emily off to their separate labors. Shelly lingered in the professor's quarters, promising to catch up with Clay quickly.

"Ask your question, Gerta," Mephisto said.

"What's become of my soul?" she asked softly. "Clay may not believe, but I do. What am I? Why am I having these dreams? Am I somehow in the thrall of the thing that wants Little Auggie?"

"No," Mephisto said. "From the dream, I would guess that some other power has claimed your soul, something old and tied to your bloodline."

"What?" Shelly said, her voice desperate.

"You hear the wings fluttering in your dreams, feel the ice and the snow in your blood, the ache to soar, to protect the weak, to dance in glorious battle. You smell death on others, and the reeking, earthen stench of it intoxicates you."

"Yes," Shelly said, her voice distant, dreamlike. The fear and the concern had melted away. Her dark eyes were damp with desire. She shook off the trance and looked at Mephisto with pleading eyes. "What's become of me?"

"You, my dear," Mephisto said, "are a Valkyrie."

177

From the porch of Shultz's General Store the two killers known as Lloyd and Kern watched Emily, Clay, Gillian, and the baby leave Mephisto's Playhouse and walk past them, never giving the two men a second glance.

"I'll tell Rory we're ready," Kern said. "Time for the little fella to meet his real father."

THE PAGE OF CUPS

They call themselves The Sons of Typhon," Maude said. "They have existed since the dawn of mankind. They worship and serve the creature that is buried under Argent Mountain. They call it 'the Greate Olde Wurm.'"

They were in one of the private dining rooms at Delmonico Hauk's restaurant down the street from the jail. The food was excellent. Hauk had just kept bringing it in, course after course. Rabb, Maude, Jon, and Kate were all stuffed, but not Jim, who seemed incapable of ever getting too much food.

"And you tumbled with this cult while you were away last year?" Jon asked Maude.

"Yes, their leader, Typhon, was some kind of projection of the imprisoned creature's will. We managed to get him locked away, but his followers are still alive and spread out across the world."

"Could they be here to kill you for taking out their leader?" Kate asked.

"It's possible," Maude said, "but I don't understand why they'd take the baby."

"I might know," Jon said, "but I pray I'm wrong. You recall the first

Wurm-worshiping cult we tangled with? Reverend Ambrose and his Deacon, Phillips, back when Jim first came to town? Me and Mutt crashed some ritual they were doing at the old Reid place up on Argent. They had...murdered a baby...and were using the blood for, I don't know, crazy, evil stuff.

"Ambrose called the baby's blood, the 'Blood of the Wurm.' It was, among other things, a deadly poison, the same stuff the cult used to murder Arthur. Sorry to bring that up, Maude."

Maude felt an old bruise of sadness at the memory of her dead husband, Arthur, over three years ago, but it was a distant pain, an echo from another life. She had loved Arthur for a time, before the drinking and the abuse, and she owed him for the gift of their daughter. But Maude was so far away from that incarnation of herself now, if felt like Jon was talking about another person. "We brought them to justice, Jon," she said. "No need to apologize."

"We know anyone who might be able to throw some light on this ritual?" Kate asked.

"Professor Mephisto?" Jim offered around a mouthful of chicken-fried steak.

"I...have some understanding of the Darkling cult," Rabb said. Everyone at the table looked at him, surprised. Jim's knife and fork actually paused for a second.

"Of course you do. You pick that up in the U.S. Cavalry?" Kate asked. "In the 10th?"

"Not exactly," Rabb said. "I've studied the occult for most of my life. It's...a hobby of mine."

"I reckon it beats looking for four-leaf clovers or joining a glee club," Jim said. He recalled the power he and Mutt had sensed off Rabb when they had found him in the desert with Leeza.

"Well then, please tell us what you can," Jon said.

"I think you're right, Jon," Rabb said. "The cult keeps most of its rites hidden away from non-believers; however, some occultists, myself included, have heard of this ritual. It's normally used to create a direct spiritual connection to the thing this generation of cultists calls 'the Wurm.' The Sons of Typhon use the Blood of the Wurm in their induction rituals."

"That," Jim said, "doesn't sound good."

"The Blood transforms the Sons," Rabb continued. "It changes, deforms them physically and mentally."

"It makes them super-humanly strong," Maude said, "resistant to harm, and often gives them some kind of power or ability."

"So, they took the baby to kill in this ritual and create more cultists?" Jon said.

"That's the part that still puzzles me," Rabb said. "There are years of tests and training involved before a cultist is given the Blood of the Wurm. So, why are they doing this?"

"Well, we best figure it out," Jon said. "We're running out of time, and so is that baby."

Jon, Jim, Kate, and Rabb returned to the jail mid-afternoon. Snake-Man and the brave were gone from the cells. Pinkerton sat at Jon's desk and was sorting through papers when they came in. "Well, I'm glad to see you run such a tight ship, Highfather. You and your people have nothing better to do than fritter the day away at some cafe?"

"I figured with so many Pinkerton men all over the place," Jon shot back, "they could handle anything that popped up. Or at least write a report about it. Where's my prisoner?"

"We know where the Indians are attacking next," the spymaster said. "Caxton and his troop are headed out in the morning to stop them before they have a chance to slaughter another settlement. The general has his men out rounding up any of your townsfolk who care to ride along. Where's that Indian deputy of yours? Getting his hair done?"

"Took some leave," Jon said. "Had it coming." Pinkerton shook his head.

"Sheriff, if I didn't know better, I'd swear you're undermining our mission and disrespecting direct orders of the President of the United States."

"No, Mr. Pinkerton," Jon said, "I'm only disrespecting you. Now, one more time, where is my prisoner? Where's the Paiute brave?"

"Allan," Kate said, "this is Jon's town. He knows his people. You need to understand..."

Pinkerton stood and interrupted Kate. "I understand that if I have to, I will place the sheriff and his entire department under arrest for endangering a federal military operation."

"You're being played. Snake-Man is giving you exactly what he thinks you want," Highfather said. "You know that, right?"

"The general has had him the field, and he's been reliable," Pinkerton said. "That's more than I can say for you, Sheriff. Caxton rides at dawn. He expects some of your people with him. He best not be disappointed." Pinkerton paused in front of Kate for a moment. "Make sure you're on the right side of this, Kate." He looked over to Highfather. "Make sure." The iron door creaked as it closed behind him.

"You still want the job?" Jon asked Rabb.

"I think I want it more, now," Hayes said. "He's a bitter fellow."

"What?" Jim said. Highfather walked over to his desk and opened the drawer, rummaging about.

"I've asked Rabb if he'd like a job," Jon said. "He's got experience soldiering, and he's got his...hobby. We could use the help, especially right now." Something strange passed between Jon and Rabb. Kate and Jim were uncertain what it was. Jon held up a silver star. "You sure? It's a world of trouble you're entering into, but there are good people in this town, some of the best you'll ever meet, and they make it worth it." He looked over to Jim and Kate. "That, and the people you work with."

"I'd be honored," Rabb said.

"Then raise your right hand," Jon said, "and repeat after me."

W hat's his name again?" Leeza asked Jim.

"Billy," Jim said as he watched her feed the goat out of her hand. "He's kind of the unofficial mascot of the sheriff's department. He helped us with a case a while back."

"Really?" the little girl asked.

"Yep, he's a brave one. We used to keep him at the jail, but he got too big for that, so Clay let us keep him out here on his land."

They were at Clay's livery, outside of the town proper, down on Duffer Road. Mutt had made it back to town, and Jon had asked him to ride out with Jim and Leeza to visit the scientist. Jon had spent a while talking to Clay about their problem with the ghost warriors, and Clay had said he might have just the thing. Jon could tell something was troubling Clay and Shelly, but they held their peace, and Jon didn't want to pry.

It was growing dark, but the sun was still a smoldering smear of oranges and marigolds, spreading at the edge of the sky. Jon watched Jim and Leeza play with the goat as he and Mutt leaned on a fence post. "So, Wodziwob isn't behind what's happening," Jon said.

"He's stirring the pot," Mutt said, "been doing that for years, but he ain't calling the dance. It's this Goshute woman, Izusa, that's directing the attacks and the spirits of the dead warriors. She's got an ax to grind."

"I'd bet a month's pay Snake-Man is in this, too," Jon said. "It's no coincidence he's back and pulling Caxton's chain." Mutt shook his head, spat, and swore in Numu, the Paiute language.

"Well, I can sneak on over to that army camp and end his part in this grand tale with a slice or two, Jonathan," he said. "I should have killed that *loda* when I had the chance."

"That might have been helpful," Jon said, "but you kicked his ass...twice, and for a guy like that, that's worse than killing him." Mutt laughed.

"Yeah, got me there," the deputy said. They were quiet for a while.

Jon watched Jim talking to Leeza while Billy nuzzled the little girl. She laughed, and it carried on the night air.

"I think the boy's sprouted up more than that goat has," Jon said. "Time plays tricks on you, doesn't it? Stretches some things out and hurries others up. He's grown into a good man, hasn't he?"

"One of the best," Mutt said. "He's got grit...and a good heart."

"That he does. I think he sees his little sister in that girl," Jon said. "You need to see to it he doesn't let his ghosts eat him up." Mutt looked to Highfather, taking his measure.

"Jonathan, you all right?" he asked. The sheriff smiled.

"I'm good," he said. He looked at Mutt in the gathering darkness. Then went back to watching the light die. "Remember when it was just you and me running around with badges on our chests in this asylum, both crazy enough to wake the snakes?" Mutt's chuckle was a dry rasp. "Trying to keep this town from getting gobbled up?"

"I think we tussled as much in those days as we did with all the monsters and lunatics. You ever regret giving that drunken, half-breed that kicked your ass a badge?"

"Nope, never," Jon said. "And I kicked *your* ass, as I recall."

"How would you recall shit? You were falling down drunk," Mutt said.

"So were you." Both men laughed.

"I figure you and me ride out with that jackass Caxton," Mutt said. "You know they're riding straight into a trap, right?"

"Oh yeah. I want you and Rabb to go find Izusa," Jon said. "I'm going to have Jim and Kate work with Maude and find these Sons of Typhon and that baby." He saw the look on Mutt's face. "You coming with Caxton's army would do the same thing as me riding out with you to see Wodziwob. Besides, you going along would make Caxton and Pinkerton happy."

"And we can't have that," Mutt said.

"Oh, no," both said in unison.

"All right, Jonathan," Mutt said. "If you're sure. I hate it when you make sense. You watch yourself and be careful. Caxton's mad. You get in his way, he'll gun you down. And don't stick your neck out for these idiots following Izusa, either. They're a bunch of bloodthirsty fools on either side. Just cause you're a dead man don't mean you can take on ghosts." A strange look passed Jon's face for just a second.

"That's why we're here," Jon said, shaking off whatever was troubling him. "Clay said he could help me with that."

"Maude said rock salt scattered the ghosts for a spell," Mutt added. "We've had luck with that with spirits before. Remember when Gil Lesbye was haunting the assayer's office? A few rounds of rock salt sent his disagreeable ass packing to the hereafter." They both chuckled.

"I don't know what I'd have done without you by my side all these years," Jon said. "You've rode into hell beside me with a bucket of water more times than I can count."

"I knew you couldn't count," Mutt said. "There are a lot things in this life a man don't get no say-so over. Who he calls friend, he chooses." They both stood and watched the stars unfurl from behind the cloudy gauze of the scattering day.

"It's a beautiful world," Jon said.

"Yeah. Let's keep the assholes from fucking it up."

"Agreed," Jon said. "If you track her, don't pick a fight you can't win. Find out all you can. We need to stop Caxton and Izusa, before they both drag us into a full-fledged war."

"You sure seem to have put a lot of trust in Rabb Hayes," Mutt said. Jon nodded.

"He came here to see me," Jon said. "Maude knows him somehow, too. We need all the help we can get right now. Give him a chance, Mutt."

"You were the one his message was for?" Jon nodded. "The message from a dead man?" Jon nodded again. "Well, spit it out." Jon hesitated.

"I'll tell you when we get back," Jon said. "It's not important right now."

"Bullshit," Mutt said. "You be careful, Jonathan."

"You too," Jon said.

———————

"J im," Leeza said as they led Billy back to his paddock, "the reverend and his wife that you had me stay with..."

"Yeah?"

"They're real nice people and all, but said they were going to try to find a family back east to take me in."

"That's good, Leeza," Jim said. "Back east there ain't all this craziness going on all the time. You can grow up safe." The little girl stopped and took Jim's hand.

"Jim, I want to stay with you. Can I? Please?"

"Aw, you don't want to stay with me," Jim said with a chuckle. "I can't cook worth a hoot. I work weird hours, so you'd always have to be with other folks, like the reverend, or Mrs. Shultz—you'd get tired of it. I don't know how to put fancy ribbons in your hair or teach you lady-stuff."

"I know," Leeza said. "I don't care, Jim. You remind me of my brother, Timothy. He...he got...with Mother and Father..." Jim squeezed her hand tight.

"It's only been a little while since everything happened to you, Leeza," Jim said. "In time, you'll feel different. This...this ain't no place for a kid to grow up."

"You did," she replied, a little desperation in her voice, "and you turned out great! Please, Jim! The only place now that feels safe, that feels like home, is with you, here. Please, can I stay? Don't send me off alone. Please."

The sensible thing was to bite the bullet and send her back east, away from wars and danger—give her a proper home for a young lady —away from the madness that permeated this town. Jim looked across the field at the two men who had become his fathers over the last few years, Highfather and Mutt. They were talking, leaning against the fence. He thought of what they would do, remembered what they did for a half-starved boy when he came across the desert, lost and alone. Jim looked down at the little girl, thought of his mother, of Lottie.

He knelt, looked into Leeza's face. "Okay," he said, "we'll give it a go." Her face lit up like a tiny sunrise. "We'll figure it all out. You're not alone, okay. You never will be. That's a promise." Leeza hugged him tight, and the young deputy found himself hugging her back just as tight.

———

So, you met Anne Bonny in Africa in 1721," Maude said as she and Rabb Hayes made their way down Bick Street, walking toward the Dove's Roost. "A hundred and fifty-one years ago?"

"Yes," Rabb said. "In Badagry. It was the beginning of an association that would last for close to a century."

"You hold up very well for your age," Maude said.

"Thank you. Anne did as well, as you'll recall," he said. They were getting surly looks, a white woman unaccompanied with a black man, side-by-side as equals. Maude felt the malice swirling about them in the air, with each disapproving look. "I am one of the first men," Rabb said. "I and my companions walked out of a cave at the dawn of time. We knew nothing of where we came from or why we existed."

"Given the things I've seen," Maude said, "who am I to doubt?"

"We don't age," Rabb said, "but we can die by violence. A few of us have, but only a few. We've had a long time to learn how to fend for ourselves."

"You may have to do that again soon," Maude said. "We have some very unwise people following us." They continued down the street. "How long have you been living in America?" Maude asked.

"About seventy years," Rabb said. "I saw what was coming before the war. I worked with a man named John Rock. He was a lawyer, mathematician, teacher. He felt, as I did, that it was important that black men, like he and I, be counted and fight for our independence, for our rights, when the time came and the war began.

"We started the Loyal League—a secret society—to spread the word that our people must stand for themselves and gather men ready to fight and die for the cause of freedom in the war." Several soldiers wandered by in the opposite direction and gave Maude and Rabb a long and confrontational look before moving on. Hushed, tense words and cruel laughter were at Maude's and Rabb's back. "What did we fight for again?" Rabb said, shaking his head and glancing back at the soldiers.

"It runs deeper than north and south, black and white," Maude said. "So much fear and hatred—Protestants and Catholics, the immigrants, the Indians, women—in a land that is as close to paradise as you can imagine. I had to fight last year to prove my faculties were not those of a child, that I was enough of a person to control my own destiny, have guardianship over my own child. It was maddening. As much as I worry about who's going to get hurt in what's happening now, I do understand why the native people are fed up with being treated the way they have been...and so do you."

"It's human nature," Rabb said, "as old as our blood. Tribes fight tribes. Those in power want more of it at the cost of those who have none. The powerless rise up and enslave their former masters. This was all around long before America, and it will be around when this country is an echo in history."

"That's a bleak thought," Maude said. Rabb laughed.

"It is. We fight for decency, for humanity, where we can. It's usually a brawl, more than a war. The victory is not becoming the thing you hate. Some days, victory is fleeting."

They arrived at the Dove's Roost. On the porch of the Roost, several of the doves were leaning on the rail or sitting in rocking chairs, engaging and coaxing numerous potential customers. Music spilled out of the Roost's parlor, as did raucous laughter and raised voices. Maude led Rabb to a dirt-floored alleyway beside the brothel that was bordered on one side by a high wooden fence.

Someone had laid a bouquet of flowers against the wall. It was clear they had been there for a long time. The flowers were wilted and

faded, but still lovely. "I'm going to duck inside," Maude said. "I won't
be long."

"Go," Rabb said. "I'll keep our admirers company." Maude took a
few steps into the alley and seemed to vanish. Rabb turned as four
men approached him.

"You lost, boy?" one of them said.

"No," Rabb said. "You?"

"What you doing creeping around out here?" another asked. "You
can't be with those white girls, y'know."

"I think he's looking to sneak in and ravish one of them whores,"
the third man said, with an ugly smile that wasn't a smile.

"I think you have a very sick imagination," Rabb said. "You all need
to move along. Now."

The men laughed. Rabb took a few steps deeper into the alley.
They followed him back.

"You steal that star on your chest, boy? I think we need to teach
you a lesson," one of the men said. "You can't walk through this town,
pretending to be the law, accosting white women, skulking about
trying to break into a whorehouse."

"Are you going to teach me?" Rabb asked, almost smiling. "'Cause
you four don't seem the educating type." One of the men drew his
pistol, covering Hayes.

"Take off that star," the big one, the leader, said.

"Come and get it," Rabb said.

The other three drew blades, big hunting knives, and began to
advance. They were almost on top of him when he drew his own leaf-
shaped short sword, an *ida*, from under his poncho. In the drawing
arc, Rabb slashed one of the knife men's forearm, making him drop
his blade. Rabb made sure to nick the proper nerves in the arm to
make the pain of the cut bloom. The wounded man doubled over,
clutching his bleeding wrist. The other two lunged in. Rabb pivoted
sideways, and both men missed him, slashing at his poncho instead.

Rabb cross-drew his Colt, jammed it against the side of one of the
knife wielders, and pulled the trigger. The man's side stomach fat—his

handle—muffled the blast. Rabb raised his elbow and shifted his stance just as he pulled the trigger. The force of the gunshot drove his elbow back and square into the face of the other knife attacker who had been trying to flank him. The force of the blow broke the man's nose, knocked him out, and sent him sprawling to the ground.

The gunman covering him was shaking a little by this time. He raised his pistol to fire. Rabb leveled his own still-smoking gun at the man. "You sure you want to do that?" Rabb said. "At this point, it's just some fellas scuffling a bit in an alley by a whorehouse; everyone goes home, everyone keeps breathing. You don't drop that gun, you are going to die. Sure as water's wet." The pistol thudded to the ground near the man's feet.

* * *

Inside the Roost, Rowan was navigating the hallway to the front parlor when Maude stepped out of the shadows in front of her. Rowan slipped into a defensive posture that Maude recognized.

"I'm not here to fight you," Maude said. "You remember me?"

"How could I forget?" Rowan said.

"You owe me," Maude said. "You have some training in the ways of the Daughters of Lilith. I need to know how."

"And why would I give you any of my secrets?" Rowan asked.

"The first time we fought, I trounced you," Maude said. "I'm better at this than you are, and because I'm here to pay you to do something for me. But first, I want the how."

Rowan smiled. "Counteroffer," she said. "Keep the money. You teach me."

"We'll see," Maude said. "How do you know about the Daughters?"

"I grew up on the Barbary Coast," she said. "When I was a young girl, something happened to my father, my mum, and my little brother. To save them, I was given an opportunity. I joined...a religion, if you will, among the pirate clans that frequented the docks there. They call themselves the Sirens. They worship the goddesses of the sea, the *rada*, the *loa*, the ancient African spirits. They also revere and worship the pirate queen, herself, Anne Bonny. She is the embodiment of Mami Wata, Mother Ocean. They taught me to fight, taught me the secrets of observation and response, improvisation, the ways to move unseen. They said Bonny, the goddess herself, taught them these secrets long ago."

"A goddess, huh?" Maude said. "It would be hard for her to pass that up. Is this cult still about?" Rowan smiled.

"Of course not," she said. "Cult? What cult? Merely a drunken tall tale told by old salts."

"Of course. I'm looking for some men, new to town, at least two, maybe more, that your girls may have seen. They will seem...wrong, disturbed."

"Well, that narrows it down considerably," Rowan said with a snort. "Do they have distinguishing features like arms and legs, too?"

"Disturbed enough to register with your people. They are dangerous. Any news, any leads. They might have a baby with them."

"A baby? Is this about that couple that got murdered?"

"If you hear anything, get any information, you let me know."

"So that's a 'yes.' What's in it for me?" Rowan asked. Maude sighed.

"They killed two people that did no one any harm and stole their child," she said. Rowan's face was impassive. "People like that have to be bad for your business."

"They are. All right," Rowan said. "I'll find your disturbed men and your missing kid, but you owe me a lesson for it, deal?"

"I'm going to enjoy that," Maude said, and then the shadows devoured her, and she was gone.

"Show-off," Rowan muttered.

○ utside, Maude found Rabb leaning against the wooden alley wall, near a fresh bloodstain. "Our friends?" she asked.

"Made their way to Dr. Clay with a new-found understanding of emancipation," he said. "They'll be by the jail tomorrow to turn them-selves in. You get what you needed?"

"Yes," Maude said. "The net is cast."

Mutt awoke knowing someone else was in his room with him. He reached for his gun on the night table, and a soft but powerful hand covered his. "You won't need that," a voice said as she climbed on top of him and kissed him.

"Maude?" he said as if he were in a dream and desperately didn't want to wake up. She kissed him again, and they were locked together, silent for a long time. Finally, she broke the kiss. "Well this is...unexpected," he managed to croak. He felt her smile in the dark-ness, not needing to see it.

"I heard you were back," she said, "and in the same breath that you were leaving again in a few hours. Rabb told me."

"Yeah," Mutt said, running his hands through her hair. She smelled faintly of honeysuckle. It was one of the many sense-memories of her that remained with him, sustained him when he was alone, apart from her. "We never seem to get a break, do we?"

"No," she whispered and kissed his forehead, his crooked nose, his cheek—so many scars. She knew the worst ones weren't tied to flesh. "We do not. It's the price we pay for being so damn indispensable."

Mutt chuckled and pulled her head down toward him. She allowed it, but a momentary thrill of surprise ran through her—he might actu-ally be strong enough to pull her down anyway. He didn't force, only coax. He found her lips, felt her melt against him and he into her.

The kiss became more insistent, unspoken need building behind it. He growled against her lips and was pleasantly surprised when she snarled back. The pressure of their bodies built, the tumbling, rolling wave of something that bypassed thought, overrode logic—the language of love, of undeniable hunger. The dance to get closer grew in tempo, to become a single breath, a single heartbeat.

For Maude, it was the release of discipline, of control, to allow herself to simply feel, to enjoy feeling, with no thought for caution, or direction. In a life where every breath, every motion was calculated, monitored, and examined. It was a battle to simply be after a lifetime of focus and carefully crafted instincts. He made her feel safe, though, and free to let go of her defenses, free to let go of everything.

For Mutt, his instincts burned to claim her, to run wild, violent, to have her with no thought, no delay. He fought to keep his mind, keep control. He fought to love her like a man, not an animal. She deserved that respect, that care. She deserved protection from the cruel, careless thing inside him. Mutt wanted something denied him by the blood of Coyote, something his brethren could never understand, never comprehend—a sacred thing they had no words for.

They both stopped, gasping, warm flesh freed from clothing, their bodies damp against each other, silhouettes against the silver predawn light. "I...I don't want to rush with you, Maude," he said, almost growling the words, fighting his body. His blood screamed to continue. His mind, his heart told them to shut up. "When we...do...I want all the time in the world with you, and I don't want to have to leave you ever again."

Her eyes were huge in the darkness; her hair had tumbled down around her shoulders. She carried as many scars along her flesh as he did, and in this moment, their scars flowed into one another. Mutt had never seen Maude look more beautiful. Maude's heart, a heart that she could control, speed or slow as her will decreed, beat wildly of its own accord. She kissed him tenderly, slowly, like savoring the last of a sweet, perfect wine. Her body knew the clock of the spinning world, of the stars and planets, and she knew exactly how long they had. "We have less than an hour," she said. "Hold me." And he did.

193

Over a hundred mounted soldiers made their way down Main Street in the gray light that heralded the dawn. The icy winds that had blustered through the streets all night had finally gentled down. Wagons with supplies and Gatling guns rolled along with the troopers. General Caxton, once again in his nondescript uniform, led the troop. Jon Highfather on his horse, Bright, was at his left side; Snake-Man on an army horse was on his right.

Jon had seen Mutt and Rabb away on their mission an hour earlier. The troubling thought he had been wrestling with for days came to the fore for a moment, but then he banished it and focused on his job.

There was a lone rider waiting by the side of the road as the troop rode past the fringes of Golgotha. Kate Warne watched Jon pass. Her eyes kissed him, and he kissed her back. With a curt nod, she turned and headed back into the town, their town, and the job there that needed doing. Jon girded himself for whatever was about to come, watched the sun struggle to free itself from the cold desert floor, and rode off to war once again.

THE LOVERS (REVERSED)

James Ringo lived in a tar-paper-roofed shack he had built in the mining camp up on Argent. The wind tonight was bitter. Winter was not going to depart without a fight, and it howled and moaned down the tent-and-shack-lined streets of the camp. Ringo watched the flame from his oil lamp jump and flutter, even behind a chimney of glass. He sat on the edge of his bed and smoked the day's final cigarette, sipping a glass of rye.

He wondered for the millionth time what was holding him here. Harry? Rowan? Golgotha was an outhouse. It had pretensions of becoming some oasis of culture and wealth in the desert. Its fate was so clear to him, clear to anyone not invested too much in the place. Golgotha was doomed. Maybe not today or tomorrow, but at some point, the silver would play itself out. The people only here for that or to make money off the parasites would dry up and blow away. This town wouldn't be here in a hundred years, probably not in fifty, maybe twenty-five. It would be a memory, an echo. He raised his glass to the roaring wind, a harbinger of oblivion, and drained his drink.

There was a rap on the flimsy door that was already shuddering in the wind. Ringo crushed out his cigarette and drew his parlor gun, a double-barrel derringer, from his vest pocket.

"Come," he called out. The door jumped open, caught by the wind. Harry Pratt stood there, another harbinger of oblivion, Ringo thought with a smirk. "Come on in, Harry," he said. "Shut the door."

Harry looked rough—dark shadows under his eyes, rumpled clothing. Ringo no longer cared. "I'm sorry to intrude so late," Harry began.

"No, you're not, Harry," Ringo said. He still held the pistol, absently pointed at Harry's chest. "It's a polite thing people say when they shove their way into your life for their own selfish purposes. It sounds very civilized, but at its core you're telling me what I already know. You are important, and I'm an accessory."

"You have every right to be angry," Harry said. "Everything you said before, it's true. I left you alone, I abandoned you, hid you like a dirty secret. I don't deserve to have someone love me the way you did."

"You can wallow in your pain at home with your new wife," Ringo said, putting the gun on the table. He poured a glass of whiskey and handed it to Harry and then took a long draw off the bottle. Harry sipped the drink and leaned closer to the piano player.

"I'm going to tell you something," he said. "I don't expect it to make a lot of difference, but I wanted you to understand why I did what I did."

"You enjoy saying 'I' a lot, did you know that, Harry?" Ringo said, taking another drink. Harry tossed back the rye and then looked into the empty glass.

"Just before the election, I was approached by a woman. She's a very powerful criminal who came to Golgotha from San Francisco a few years back to take over all the town's prostitution trade. I'm sure you've heard of her; Huang has done business with her. She's called Black Rowan." Ringo said nothing, just took another sip from the bottle. Harry continued. "She knew about you and me," he said. "She said that if I wanted her to keep quiet about it and not pass the information along to Rony and Daaron Bevalier, I was going to do what she said. I told her I'd think on it."

Harry held out the empty glass to Ringo, and he refilled it. "So, you're now in the pocket of this woman because you couldn't bear the thought of giving up the mayor's job? Congratulations, Harry, you graduated from a small-time politician to a full-fledged whore." Ringo took a drink. "So, keeping me under lock and key won you the election?"

"No," Harry said. He was angry now, but Ringo knew that Harry's anger was cold and under control, at least most of the time. "No, I told her I wasn't going to play along. That was when she said she had gone to the Bevaliers with what she knew. She hadn't given it up yet, but they were licking their chops to know the dirt on me."

"She did what?" Ringo said, pausing. Harry tossed back his drink.

"You will fucking laugh at this," he said, "but I did part of it for you. I did. Sure, I hated the idea of what that bitter old mummy and his idiot son would do to this town, and I *like* the power this job gives me. I like being able to make things good for some people and try to keep the bad away as much as I can. It wasn't the damn job; it was you I was really worried about.

"I had a lover in college; his name was Thomas. He was from an excellent family back east, had wonderful prospects. He was like me though, like us. He denied it, the same way I had for so long, but eventually we discovered each other, and it was...wonderful. You know that feeling, that you can finally, fully breathe, that you don't have to pretend, don't have to hide. You get to have the same portion of life as everyone else. We should have known it wouldn't last. Word got out that Thomas was a 'nancy,' a 'sodomite,' and the fellows all decided one night after lights out to beat the perversion out of him." Harry pulled the bottle violently from Ringo, who gave it with no struggle. Harry tipped the bottle back and let the whiskey burn him on its way down. "He never gave me up," Harry said, "even when I joined in the beating."

"Harry..." Ringo whispered.

"The schoolmasters, the deans, they knew about the beating we gave Thomas. They all approved, quietly, of course, but they approved. The attack left him lame the rest of his life. He resigned from the college soon after he healed up. He went home to New York, married a fine woman from a fine family. Began a legal practice that was very successful. Had some children, I'm led to understand. I wrote him while I was still in college, then a few times after, when I was finding any excuse to not come back here. He never answered me."

Harry put his head down but kept talking, clearly and coolly. "If a bunch of well-educated, well-bred college fops would do that," he looked up at Ringo, "what do you think the sterling, frontier clientele of the Celestial Palace would do to you, James?"

"I've taken a beating for being a faggot, Harry," Ringo said. "I can hold my own. You didn't have to..."

"But I did," Harry said. "Because I love you, and I didn't want you to suffer for the 'crime' of loving me. So, I said I'd go along with whatever she needed me to do to secure the election, and that was when I was introduced to Ora and her father, Howard Cooper."

"Rowan set up your marriage?" Ringo said, a strange look crossing his face. "She did that?"

"It was a marriage made of convenience. Cooper planned to go after Malachi and take control of the Argent Mine. With the mine and the Golgotha dogleg both belonging to his interests out of Virginia City, he'd own the town and make a tidy profit, too. Owning me was just an added bonus."

"I didn't know," Ringo said. "I thought you had set up the marriage yourself to secure the dogleg, so you could win the election, that it was cover for the rumors that popped up."

Harry shook his head. "No, but I went along with it, just like I did nearly beating the life out of Thomas. I am a weak, frightened son of a bitch, James. I'm sorry." The bottle was empty. Harry placed it on the floor next to his camp chair. Ringo came off his bed and knelt next to Harry's chair.

"I didn't know," he said. He kissed Harry's hand. "I'm sorry. I didn't know."

"How could you?" Harry asked, and again, a strange looked crossed Ringo's face. "Well, I've finally managed to do something to get me loose of all this," he said. "I refused to chase off a Mormon family that is refusing to sell their land for the dogleg. Cooper and Rowan wanted me to do it, and I refused. I'm sure I won't be mayor very much longer, and I won't be very welcome in this town."

"Harry, you can't do that," Ringo said. "Rowan and Ora's father will ruin you."

"Come with me," Harry said. "We've been talking about this for years. Let's just go."

"What about the town?" Ringo said. "You're right—Rony and his son will hound every non-Mormon, non-white out of Golgotha. What about the Mormon artifacts you're been entrusted to protect?"

"I don't care," Harry said. "Let Rony and Howard Cooper fight over the town. Let goddamn Porter Rockwell and Brigham Young have the treasures of Heaven. What's God done for me, exactly, that I should want to be part of his fucking plans?"

"Harry, what about 'the One Mighty and Strong?'" Ringo asked. Harry paused. He recalled the pleading letters from the good people of Ezekiel, all dead now.

"Whoever that is," Harry said, standing up, "I don't know him." He pulled Ringo to his feet and kissed him. When their lips finally parted, Harry said, softly, "Come with me. I know I've let you down, but I love you. I always will. Think about it." He opened the door. The cold wind slapped him hard. "Thanks for the drink." Harry closed the door behind him. Ringo tasted him on his lips, and even the cold wind couldn't dispel that warmth.

Malachi Bick's office on the second floor of his Paradise Falls Saloon gave a wonderful view of Main Street. His daughter, Emily, had joined him for tea and had been regaling the most powerful man in Golgotha with what she had been privy to at Professor Mephisto's Theater involving Gillian's and Auggie Shultz's baby. Her father's dark, half-lidded eyes, took in every detail.

"Have you begun painting the child, as the good professor asked you?" Bick asked. Emily sipped her tea and set the cup and saucer back on the table in front of the sofa she was sitting on.

"Yes," she said. "I have to say, the feelings I'm getting are very disturbing."

"You are sensing a malevolent force working to get access to the child," Bick said.

"Yes," Emily said, nodding. "You've sensed it, too?"

"When I was meeting with Augustus Shultz the other day," Bick said. "I could feel his connection to the Darkling below Argent and to its agents here in town."

"What are we going to do?" Emily asked. "Should we let the sheriff know?"

Bick shook his head. "No, Sheriff Highfather has enough to deal with right now with General Caxton and his ill-thought-out crusade...and other things. I hope this does not end poorly for Auggie. He is one of the finest human beings I've ever encountered. He holds malice for none in his heart, and he genuinely cares for everyone. I wish I could do more in the matter. You'll have to deal with this, Emily."

"Me?" she said. "But I thought you'd want to deal with this. You were given your commission to guard the Darkling and keep it from ever escaping. I just assumed you'd want to step in."

"What I want is irrelevant," Bick said. "I am being prevented from acting, at present."

"Prevented?" Emily said. "But, Father, you're an angel. You're older than the Earth. Your power is virtually infinite! No one could prevent..." Emily paused as the thought came to her. "Is God prohibiting you?"

"No," Bick said. "He's silent, at least in the way most things in the universe communicate. No, this is a problem of my own making. You'll discover that the more powerful you become, the more you tend to become the source of most of your own problems. I'd hazard a guess that God is so still out of the fear of what he would set in motion if he were to move." He leaned closer to his daughter.

"You remember I told you about the feathers my kind will often give to those we trust, and how the feather is a token of our respect and love because it gives the possessor control over us?"

"Yes," Emily said. "You gave me one shortly after I arrived in Golgotha."

"Long ago, before white men lived in this land, I lived here as Be'kiwa-ah, a medicine man who guarded these lands. I gathered mortals around me to help me defend this place from the unnatural forces drawn here by the Darkling. These mortals helped me guard the Darkling, just as the sheriff, his deputies, and a few others here in Golgotha do now.

"I gave one of my feathers to the leader of a loyal and powerful band of Indian mystics from many tribes. The secret society they founded, the Black Feathers, aided me then and they still exist to this day. They still protect the lands from supernatural threats. Their current leader, Wodziwob, possesses my feather. It was passed down to him from one leader of the Black Feathers to the next. He commands me now to do nothing, to wait. So, I wait."

"Why is he doing that?" Emily asked.

"Because, my dear," Bick said, "he hates what the European settlers have done to his people's land, to them. He thinks I would move to stop him."

"Wouldn't you?" she asked her father.

"I'm...unsure. Emily, I have been here since the planet cooled. I watched the little primates develop that eventually became humans, and I watched them fight over hunting grounds, over mates, over water and shelter. One thing that has never changed about humans is they will always find something to fight over and someone to blame for it.

"Perhaps it is time for the Europeans to depart. It's not for me to decide. God doesn't play favorites, a fact both sides in this conflict seem to be ignoring."

"I could use my feather," Emily said, "order you to help the Shultz's protect their baby."

"It might work," Bick said. "It might also bring Wodziwob's ghostly allies down on Golgotha to stop you, possibly kill you. I almost lost you once, my dear child. I never want to stand by helpless and watch you suffer again."

"So," Emily said, "what do I do?"

"To start, finish your picture," Bick said. "Remember, you are Nephilim, blood of my blood. You are more powerful than you know. I believe in you, Emily. I trust Professor Mephisto. Paint the portrait and see what it uncovers."

There was a knock at the door. Black Rowan, dressed in a black satin corset with a black damask bustle skirt, stood in the doorway. She had not waited to be invited in. The front slit in the dress gave a flash of knee-high boots and stockings as she entered the office. "I'm sorry," the pirate queen said, smiling at Emily, "am I interrupting?"

"Yes," Emily said.

"No," Bick said at the same time. "Not at all. You're a bit early for our meeting, but please, come in." Rowan walked past Emily on her way to the chair before Malachi's desk. "Emily, keep me informed on what's happening with your...art project," he said as he walked over to his daughter and kissed her on the forehead. She kissed him on the cheek.

"I'll deal with my unspeakable evil," she whispered and gave Rowan a withering look. "Just be careful that yours doesn't give you something you have to see Dr. Clay about." Emily departed, and Bick shut the door behind her.

"Your daughter despises me," Rowan said, sitting down.

"Yes, she does," Bick said. "She was fine with you until it became clear that you and I were more than business associates."

"She'll get over it," Rowan said. "I have a quandary, Malachi. I wanted your advice before I act."

"Of course," Bick said. "It must be grave. You normally trust your own council."

"Harry Pratt," Rowan said. "I'm afraid I'm going to have to remove him from his position and destroy him in the process."

"I'm sorry to hear that," Bick said. "Harry is a very good man, and he's been an effective mayor during some very difficult times."

"He's also your friend and crony," Rowan added. "However, we had an understanding. I helped him get re-elected, and he owed me his allegiance. He has decided to balk at a service I requested of him. That's causing me a lot of trouble with another very powerful and influential business partner."

"Who are you planning to put in his place?" Malachi asked.

"The most obvious choice is Daaron Bevalier," she said. "He made a good showing in the election, and once Harry is humiliated and run out of town, there will be a backlash by the Mormons for a more 'traditional candidate.'"

"You realize that Daaron is basically a puppet for his father, Rony," Bick said, "and that Rony Bevalier will make business very difficult for a great many 'non-traditional' people in Golgotha. People like Ch'eng Huang, the Nail, you, and me, just to name a few."

"Yes," Rowan sighed. "I know. Damn Harry! If he'd just do what needs to be done, everything would be fine."

"Is there any chance you could find another way to work with Harry?"

"I'm afraid not," Rowan said. "There is no room in this negotiation for variance." Bick paused for moment. His eyes, dark as sin, seemed to look through Rowan, and the pirate queen almost blushed but caught herself. Rowan had survived on the dangerous streets of the Barbary Coast by her wits and her instincts. Her instincts told her Malachi Bick was a cobra, was death, and yet she found herself playing these games with him, drawing him close, tempting death to take her.

"It's always best to get yourself into deals that you can get yourself out of," Bick said, freeing Rowan of his gaze. "In our line of work, few things, and even fewer people, are sure bets."

"You're right, of course," Rowan said, rising from her chair and siting on the edge of Bick's desk. The slit of her dress fell open, revealing a scandalous amount of leg and thigh. "I knew it before I came to see you. I guess I was hoping there was some angle that I had overlooked. There isn't. I'll miss Harry."

"As will I," Bick said, walking around his desk and standing close to Rowan. He reached out to her and cupped her chin, bringing her gaze up to meet his own. "Now I have a question for you."

"Yes?"

"Do you always dress this way when you simply want to ask for advice?"

"Yes," Rowan said, drawing closer to Bick. "When I want to make absolutely sure I have your undivided attention." Bick took her by her hair and pulled her to him; his lips were fire on the juncture of her throat and shoulder. His kiss became a bite. Rowan wrapped her legs around his waist, holding herself aloft as she grabbed the back of his hair and clutched it tightly.

"You do," Bick said, "you most assuredly do."

The Red Troop had made camp not too far from Round Mountain. The sentries had been posted, and most of the company, exhausted from a long day's ride through harsh country, slept. Snake-Man was locked up in his prison wagon for the night. Jon Highfather made sure he was there to see the renegade put under lock and key before he headed off to catch some sleep himself.

In his prison, Snake-Man sat cross-legged on the floor of the wagon, closed his eyes, and waited. Something moved in the shadows of the wagon's interior. Snake-Man opened his eyes and smiled.

"Come out, shadow-weaver. I've been expecting you." Izusa, the Goshute medicine woman, slipped from the darkness, her face and body cloaked in dried mud. She made no sound as she crossed the wagon floor to stand before the renegade.

"I've missed you, Awan, son of *Dogoa*," she said. "*Tukku Kammanka.*" Snake-Man stood and pulled her to him.

"You've gotten very good at moving through dream," he said. "I can touch you, feel you as if you are here."

"I wish I were," she said, "or, better yet, you here with me. The guards outside hear nothing. To their weak eyes and ears, you slumber, alone. Is the trap set?"

"Yes," he said. "They captured one of Kajika's braves. He recognized me. I told him what location to feed them, the canyon you and I had already selected as the perfect spot. They are riding toward their end."

"Good. Caxton believes you?" Izusa asked. Snake-man laughed.

"A fool believes what he wants to believe. A year spent leading him to 'hostile tribes'— any tribe too timid to join us in revolt—has paid off. He's helped eliminate the moderates and stoked the anger of those tribes who needed encouragement to join our war. Caxton wants what we want, the eradication of the other race. By the time he understands how badly he's been used, it will be too late for him to do anything about it. The spirits of the dead, they are still with us?"

"Their number grow daily, Awan," Izusa said. "They scream for vengeance, for justice. As long as the dances continue, as long as the people believe, they will stand with us. Many of them await you and the Red Patrol when we close the box on the trap. Something does trouble me, though. The spirits say there is a white man with you. They say he walks in two worlds. He is very powerful in the lands of the dead. He bears a star and the marks of death upon him."

"Highfather," Snake-Man said. "He is here. I will make sure when the trap is sprung he is the first one to die. He is the friend of *Dobo'it-sapeh's* son. His death will bring Mutt pain."

"I know he hurt you terribly," Izusa said. "It took everything in me to not ride to Golgotha when you were turned over to the army and kill him myself."

"The plan you created," Snake-Man said, "to go into the spirit land, to rally our fallen peoples, it is much better than just killing Mutt. When his town, his adopted family, are ash, when he has nothing left, then we will kill him together."

"He deserves no less for walking away from his people," she said. "The son of a god has an obligation."

They kissed again, forgetting themselves in it. Moonlight drifted through the barred window on the wagon's door and passed through Izusa as if she were spun of glass. "I love you," Snake-Man said.

"I love you," she replied. Their lips brushed again. It occurred to Izusa that in another world, another life, they could be happy together, live a normal life with no fear, no death, and no hatred. It made her loathe the invaders even more for all the joy and peace they had stolen from her and so many others.

"You're powerful," he said. "Someone like you—someone with as much *buha* as you wield—comes once in a generation, in a dozen generations. You will change the face of this world, restore the *numa* to their rightful place. Things will again be as they were in days when it was only us in our land, before they came like thieves in the night."

"Your father, *Dogoa*, came to me after I left the cave of the Dead," Izusa said. "I met him when I was a frightened child. He taught me his medicine. He opened my eyes to the hidden powers, made me stronger. I can feel the pain of the world. The *Uktena* thrashes in the bonds the whites' gods have snared it in," she said. "It grows closer and closer to waking. The earth will shake from its rage. Once Golgotha is gone, the *Uktena* will be free, and the world will be remade."

Even Snake-Man hesitated at the mention of the great horned serpent locked away under Argent Mountain. It gave him pause that Izusa not only seemed not to fear freeing such an ancient and powerful being, it was clear the prospect excited her. Even Snake-Man's father feared his distant relative, the *Uktena*.

"I have a secret to share with you when we are truly together," she said, playfully.

He looked around at his cage. "I could use some," he laughed.

"Soon," she said. "We will hold one another again. Our people will stand united, fierce, and strong. Mutt will be dead, the whites will be a bad dream, forgotten in the dawn." She kissed him, and he felt her begin to evaporate against his embrace like morning dew.

"Soon, *Tukku Kammanka*," he whispered to the now-empty wagon.

TEMPERANCE (REVERSED)

Auggie arrived home to the cottage on Rose Hill after dark. He found Gillian waiting for him and supper on the dining table. "You are wonderful," the big German said. "I intended to get something in town, but I..."

"But you never had the time," Gillian said, smiling, rising to meet him as he removed his coat and set down his folio. "I'm onto your ways, Mr. Shultz. Remember, I was the one who used to bring you baskets after the store was closed, because even then, you'd forget to take care of yourself."

Auggie chuckled. "*Ja*, you've always been better than I deserved, my love." Auggie sat down and poured himself a glass of water from the pitcher. "How is our future legal scholar today?"

"He debated me soundly on why he should eat his hand instead of his carrots, but I won in the end. How was your day?"

"Mr. Bick is concerned because a businessman in Virginia City is positioning himself to try a take-over of the mines," Auggie said. He continued, but Gillian was fighting to focus on his words. Gillian tensed a bit. This was all perfect, and wonderful, and the way things were supposed to be, and she was on the cusp of destroying it all. She tried to summon her courage and her calm. She looked up to see Auggie looking at her.

"Where did you go?" Auggie asked, a twinkle in his eye. "You got lost. Is everything all right, *meine geliebte?*"

"Yes," Gillian said, smiling, but then the smile slid from her face. "No, no Augustus, it isn't. I need to tell you something. I don't want to, I've never wanted to, but now..."

Auggie turned and took her hands. "What is wrong, Gillian? I know you have been talking with Clay a great deal recently. Are you ill? Is the baby all right? Talk to me." Gillian clutched his big, warm, calloused hands in her own and looked into his kind, pleading eyes.

"When you were shot by that madman, Zeal," she began, "you...didn't survive the gunshot, my love. You died, Auggie."

"What?" Auggie said, his normally strong voice almost a whisper.

"You died." Her voice was cracking; her eyes were hot and wet. She fought not to blink and lost. "And I begged Clay to...bring you back to me."

"Gillian," Auggie said, "this isn't some horrible prank? You're serious?" Tears were rolling down her beautiful face.

"I wish it were," she said. "I wish it had never happened, but I love you so much, Auggie. I love you, and I couldn't lose you. I couldn't." Gillian broke. "I'm sorry, I'm so sorry!" Her whole body was wracked by her sobs.

Auggie reached forward and held her. He was numb, but he couldn't bear watching her in so much pain, even through his own shock and churning fear. Perhaps this was what being dead was like: you were fine, you felt alive, and then in an instant, you weren't, and you were the last one to know the news.

"It will be fine, darling," Auggie said. Gillian made a sound that was a kind of groaning laugh mixed with a soul-deep moan.

"Oh, my sweet man," she whispered. "I tell you this and you try to console me. I'm sorry, Auggie. I thought you'd hate me for lying to you." Auggie took her by the shoulders and held her gaze.

"I've lied to you before, hidden awful things when I helped Clay bring Gerta back," Auggie said. "You forgave me, tried to understand why I had done it."

"Auggie," she said, "you really are the finest man I've ever known, the finest father, the finest husband."

"I love you," he said. "I could never hate you. You and Little Auggie, you're my life." He kissed her, tasted the tears on his lips, and tried to wipe them away. She kissed him the same way she had the very first time, the way she had the last time, when the life had slipped away from his dying body. It was a sweet urgency, the knowledge that these times were not meant to last, or to come again.

"Auggie," she said, wiping her eyes, "something, something not human wants our child. It's been tormenting him at night. Clay and Shelly have been trying to help. We've even asked Professor Mephisto..."

"Mephisto?" Auggie asked. "The table rapper? Gillian, are you sure this isn't some kind of a swindle?"

"No, darling," she said. "It isn't. You know how Clay is, he'd sniff out a fraud. He's convinced it's some kind of 'non-corporeal entity.' So's the professor."

"Why is it after our boy?" Auggie said. They were both quiet for a moment. "It has something to do with me, doesn't it? With me being...dead."

"The professor said he's not sure, yet," she said. "It was hard to follow all he was talking about, but he seemed to think there had to be some kind of a way, a connection, for it to get to him. It may have something to do with Clay's formula."

"I...can't be the cause, can I?" Auggie sounded so lost. "How?" Gillian swallowed hard and held his hands tighter. A stone was in her stomach, aching.

"Auggie," she said, "I'm not sure if we conceived Little Auggie before or after you died."

Auggie's hands slipped from hers. The color drained from his face. "What am I?" he asked. "What have I done?" He sounded more lost than Gillian had ever heard.

The door to the cottage exploded. The splintered and cracked remains of the door bounced and crashed across the room. Four men entered the cottage, the leader grinning with yellow, rotting teeth. He glanced over to the shocked Gillian and Auggie. "Evening, folks," Rory said as the other Sons of Typhon spread out about the small house. "We're just here for the little nipper. Where is he?" The baby, startled awake by the door being kicked in, wailed in terror. "Ah, there he is," the smiling man said. "Kern, Tidbull, if you'll be so kind as to gather up the little scamp."

Auggie stood and charged toward the men. "Leave our son alone!" Lloyd leveled a shotgun at the charging shopkeeper.

"Eager to die a second time, are you?" Lloyd said, about to fire. Gillian came from out of nowhere, shrieking in anger, a large butcher knife in her hand. She crashed into Lloyd as the shotgun went off. She drove the knife into the slight man's shoulder as she took him to the ground.

"Get her off me!" Lloyd shouted as Gillian stabbed him again and again.

"Leave them alone!" Gillian screamed. "I'll kill you!" She didn't see Rory leveling the pistol at her head. Auggie, sounding like a bear, drove a ham-sized fist into the side of the grinning man's head. It felt to Auggie like hitting a stone wall. Rory staggered back, the gun unfired.

"Off me, bitch!" Lloyd backhanded Gillian, and she flew across the room as if she were made of straw. Auggie winced as she hit the wooden floor, bounced, and didn't move. Bleeding and angry, the Son of Typhon brought up the shotgun, a single shell remaining in one of the barrels, and aimed it at Gillian's prone form.

"No!" Auggie roared.

Kate Warne and Jim Negrey launched through the doorway, guns blazing. Lloyd was hit three times by Kate's duel .32 short-barreled revolvers, one in each hand. Jim put a .44 round through Rory's chest, sending the Son's leader stumbling back. Kate took cover behind a kitchen counter.

"Kern, fetch the brat," Rory croaked, standing and returning fire on Jim as the young deputy dove behind an overstuffed chair. "Tidbull, break them, but mind daddy, we need him intact." The Son with the deformed mass of muscles and the tiny head hefted up a four-hundred-pound dish cupboard to hurl across the room. Auggie rushed the giant, trying to get past him to stop Kern from running down the hall and reaching his son, but Tidbull held the massive cabinet up with one hand and shoved the big German back. Auggie crashed back into a bookcase. It tipped over, and he was buried under a rain of books and the heavy wooden case.

Jim and Kate opened fire on Tidbull, then ducked behind cover as Lloyd and Rory returned fire. Bullets ripped into Tidbull's chest. Jim swore he saw a few of them bounce off, flattened. Tidbull chucked up his grip on the cabinet and hurled it across the room.

Maude Stapleton, dressed in the dark clothing of a man, caught it mid-air, twisted, and hurled it back to Tidbull, smashing it into the surprised giant like a speeding freight car. It drove him through a wall and crashed on top of him. "Remember me?" Maude said to Rory.

"You," Rory said. The smile fell from his face. He fired at her. The remaining few bullets in his pistol missed the Daughter of Lilith, who was moving toward the hallway, toward the baby's howl.

Lloyd shucked the empty shells from the shotgun and loaded two fresh ones in. He came up ready to fire on Kate behind the crumbling counter. She wasn't there.

"Hi, cowboy," the detective said, her voice close to his ear. Lloyd began to spin. Kate emptied the remaining rounds from both pistols into him at nearly point-blank range. The bloody meat that had been Lloyd jerked, shuddered, and kept moving, kept trying to make his fingers squeeze the trigger. Jim emptied his dad's Colt, loaded with silver bullets, into Lloyd, and finally, the Son of Typhon dropped, rattled, and died.

"Jesus," Kate muttered.

"Reload," Jim gasped, shucking empty shells from the smoking .44, "in case he gets back up."

Rory stumbled out of the open doorway, reloading his gun as he ran. "Tidbull!" he called out.

Maude was halfway down the hall toward the nursery. Gillian's baby had stopped crying. She saw a shadow fluttering in the nursery. Before she could take another step forward, a muscled arm the size of a small tree trunk ripped through one of the walls of the hallway, grabbed her, and pulled her through the crumbling rubble of the wall. Before the hand grabbing her by the skull could crush her, Maude's hand shot out. Normally, she'd strike a cluster of nerves near the armpit that should paralyze the arm. However, Maude had fought the Sons before, and she knew that blows that would kill a normal man would hardly phase them. Maude twisted her arm up and used her nails to sever the nerves. The giant's arm stiffened, and the grip on her head loosened. Maude rotated and launched herself into the air, driving both of her legs into Tidbull's side in a sacrifice kick that would send her to the ground. The lumbering Son flailed through the air, destroying another wall in his wake. A support beam cracked, and a section of the house fell on top of Maude.

Jim and Kate moved up the debris-littered hallway, guns sweeping every shadow. They cleared the doorway to the nursery only to find the room empty, part of the wall demolished. Auggie and Gillian, both bloodied, cut, and disheveled, joined them by the side of the crib.

"Where's Auggie Junior?" Gillian asked.

"Those monsters, they took him," Auggie said. He looked over to Jim and Kate. "The others? The one with the shotgun, that man with the terrible grin?"

"Skedaddled," Jim said. "Cut and ran when the section of roof collapsed."

"How did you know we were in trouble?" Gillian asked. "Who were those terrible men?"

"Professor Mephisto told us," Jim said. "He came to us, said we had to get here quick, that you were in trouble."

"We've been tracking these 'Sons of Typhon,'" Kate said. "They kidnapped one baby already, and now they've taken yours too."

"Please," Gillian said. "Please, we have to find our son."

"We will," Maude said to her old friend. She appeared at the doorway, covered in dust, bruises, and blood. She placed a hand on Gillian's shoulder. The Daughter of Lilith's eyes burned with tightly controlled anger. "I promise you, we will."

***

F ollowing Rose Road to its end, you come to a rise, a small hill northeast of the town. It was the final resting place for Golgotha's outcasts, its outlaws, its whores, those too poor to have a name, a memory in eternity. Ringo had walked out to Boot Hill in the darkness. It gave him time to smoke and to decide exactly what he was going to do. He stood and watched the stars burn and rolled another cigarette, smoked it, and then made another. The cold filled him, made him feel like a part of the beautiful cosmic boneyard, the cemetery sky full of glittering tombstones to long-dead light.

Since Ringo had been a young boy, he had learned to live in the present moment, to not look too far ahead and to never look back. He held up his cigarette and watched it eaten by fire, by entropy, then took a long drag on it, speeding its demise. To survive in prison, living now, moment-to-moment, was a necessity. You lived in that present, crowded it with attention. To run in either direction, past or future, when your body was in a cage was to court madness. The luxury of reflection was for people with money, power, and freedom.

That way of living had served him pretty well until he met Harry Pratt. Harry-goddamn-Pratt. Ringo chuckled. The man fucked up everything he touched, and he had touched Ringo. Touched him in a way he had been taught couldn't possibly be real.

He met Mayor Harry Pratt one night not too long after he had arrived in Golgotha, about five years ago. He had worked for Ch'eng Huang at one of his watering holes in San Francisco. Raised as a dock rat, he spoke decent Chinese, among other languages, and he had learned to play the piano sitting on his father's knee in every dive and pirate haven in the Barbary Coast. Ringo had been planning to leave town after an unfortunate affair with a pirate captain had turned into something destructive and dangerous. Huang had been more than happy to acquire him as his piano player for the Celestial Palace, and as always, the Chinese crime lord asked no questions.

Ringo remembered the first time he saw Harry, sitting at a table in the back of the crowded barroom with Malachi Bick and Ch'eng Huang. Harry was so beautiful, he made Ringo catch his breath. Harry had sensed his eyes on him, and when they met each other's gaze, they knew.

At first, it was just sex, not an unusual parameter for a relationship like theirs, hell—not unusual for a lot of relationships. Harry was powerful and married. It had to be discrete. Ringo was fine with that. Somewhere along the way, though, Harry had begun to linger longer in Ringo's bed. They talked more, learned the other's histories, or at least the parts they felt secure enough to open up about. One night, Harry began to leave. The goodnight-goodbye kiss lasted for a very long time. The kiss became passion, then something stronger, deeper. Love.

That night was the first time they said they loved one another. It had terrified Ringo, and had shaken Harry even more so, but it was the truth. In time the fear departed and made way for something far stronger, far more powerful and more dangerous.

The clopping thud of a horse's hooves echoed across the graveyard. A small buggy pulled by a single horse made its way up the road from town. The lone occupant of the buggy, wrapped in a heavy, black, hooded cloak brought it to a stop on the road before the simple wooden gate of the weathered fence around the boneyard. Black Rowan climbed down from the buggy seat. "Could you have picked a more ominous place to talk, Jimmy?" she said.

"Where's that hulking thesaurus you call a manager?"

He offered Rowan a cigarette. "The Scholar's running things at the Roost," she said. "I don't need a bodyguard with you." She took the cigarette, and he lit it for her with a match. Rowan let the smoke settle in her lungs. She sighed as it streamed from her nostrils and lips. "You always rolled the best of these," she said. "It was worth the whipping to sneak them. I could have just come by the Palace instead of this gruesome place."

"I don't work at the Palace anymore," Ringo said.

"What, why?" she said.

"I'm leaving Golgotha," he said. "I'm sick of this shit, Ro."

"Look, I know this has been hard on you," Rowan said, "and I know Harry has hurt you terribly."

"He has," Ringo said, "and he had some help doing it, didn't he, big sister?"

"He told you," she said.

"He did," he said. "Of course, he doesn't know I was fucking in on it, and he doesn't know I'm your brother. I'm done with this, Rowan."

"You remember you came to me in San Francisco," Rowan said. "You were angry, and you were tired of being taken for granted. You spent his money in revenge, and you confided in me about your tryst."

"It is *not* a tryst," Ringo said. "I told you I didn't want to hurt him. You remember that part too, don't you?"

"Jimmy, I got him elected," she said. "The dogleg of the railroad would have made him a power in the entire state. All I needed him to do was move a few people out of the way, and he balked." Ringo shook his head.

"For someone who makes such a fuss about being able to read people, Ro, you really don't know the first thing about Harry Pratt. Now, you ruin him, right?"

"Not because I want to," Rowan said. "I like Harry, but this is business, little brother. Don't act like you don't know that side of this too. Remember Timbers Cotton? You shot him dead because he had the opium and he didn't care to share. Don't stand there and pretend to be some knight of moral authority, Jimmy. You and me, we grew up in the same air."

"What are you going to do?" Ringo asked.

"It's already done," she said. "I spoke with Rony Bevalier today. He was willing to agree that his son will make sure he frees up that land once he's declared mayor."

"The railroad," Ringo said. "It's worth chasing a family off their land and destroying a good man? You arranged Harry's marriage to Ora Cooper to insure he got the goddamned railroad built."

"Howard Cooper is going to have that land," Rowan said. "I tell him no, and he will roll over me just like Harry. Like him or not, I'm not going make Cooper into an enemy for Harry Pratt. He's got enough reach to damage me, maybe end me. Cooper, the railroad, that's the future, Jimmy. You can't fight the future. It rolls over you."

"Bevalier already knows," Ringo said. Rowan nodded.

"He's making it public tomorrow afternoon," she said, "demanding Harry be removed from office for 'moral turpitude' and his boy, Daaron, as the second-biggest vote-getter be installed as mayor." Rowan looked at her brother. "Maybe you *should* go away for a while. It will get bad for you."

"Yes," he said. "Harry wants me to leave with him."

"Good," Rowan said. "The Pratts are wealthier than King Midas. He doesn't need the job; he never did. He hasn't wanted to be here for a long time."

"Harry stays for a reason," Ringo said. "One I don't think someone like you or me could ever really understand."

Ringo knew that if he told Rowan how Harry had been commissioned, like his father before him, to protect the magical relics of the Mormon faith, relics that resided in a secret cave beneath the Pratt household, she would either think him delusional, or start to scheme about how best to steal them. When Harry had told him, he'd thought it was some Mormon claptrap, but then he saw Harry in action during some of the town's worst hours and he knew there was something to it. He figured he'd never truly understand it. He knew that Harry abandoning that cosmic responsibility, abandoning the innocent members of the faith who looked to him as their hero, their protector, would eat him alive. It would be a slow death and one Ringo simply couldn't bear to watch. He could not see a way out of this nightmare, except through it.

"Maybe this is the best thing for both of you," his sister said, as she caressed his cheek.

"Yes," Ringo said flatly. "Perhaps it is."

"Give you a ride back to town, up to your place?" she asked. "I'll arrange tickets for two of you on the train out of Hazen tomorrow," she said. "You and Harry can go wherever you want." They began to walk back to the buggy. Ringo stopped her for a moment and took her by the shoulders. His voice cracked a little as he spoke.

"There are only two people I ever really loved in this life," he said. "You and Harry. I hope you know, I'd do anything for you, Rowan. I love you."

"I love you too, little brother," she said and hugged and kissed him on the cheek. "Please trust me for just a little bit longer, and it will all be all right."

THE TOWER

Caxton's army was over two hundred strong with the civilian volunteers he had recruited in Golgotha. They were two days from the location the Paiute brave had given Snake-Man as the site of the renegades' camp. After bedding down the first night in the wilderness, they rode for Armageddon before the sunrise. The troop wound its way into the foothills of the Cherry Creek Mountains, seeing the dawn sky chewed up on either side by teeth of jagged stone.

"It's going to get mighty tight in here, General," Highfather said to Caxton as they rode deeper into the maze of rock.

"It's perfect," the Red General said. "They have no idea we're coming. We can set up along these ridges. The only way in or out of Armageddon is this road. It will be a turkey shoot, Sheriff." Jon glanced over to Snake-Man. The renegade's eyes were dead, giving Jon nothing.

"A turkey shoot," Jon said. He pulled back on the reins of his horse, Bright, gently, dropped back from Caxton, and scanned the canyon walls. "That's what I'm afraid of."

The Paiute prisoner had confided in Snake-Man that the renegades were planning to attack the Mormon settlement of Armageddon. Armageddon got its ominous name from the original meaning of the word, translated from the Hebrew to the Greek, meaning "a range of hills or a mountain." The settlement had thrived with its close proximity to the Utah border and the Mormon control of key resources in the region, including water and grazing lands for animals.

These mountains, however, were the ancestral home of several Goshute tribes that had been pushed back by the expansion of settlers. Highfather had heard plenty of rumors about the extensive network of caves in this range and how the Goshute used them.

"You look troubled, Sheriff," Snake-Man said. He and his mount had dropped back as well and now kept pace with Highfather. "I take it you see a flaw in the general's plan?"

"I'm looking at the flaw right now," Highfather said. Snake-Man laughed.

"You know, it's refreshing to find a white man who actually hates me for me, not just for the color of my skin."

"You tried to kill my friend," Highfather said. "I don't believe for one second that you aren't up to your mohawk in whatever's going on."

"Where did your parents come from, Sheriff?"

"Sweden," Jon said. "A long way across the sea. They came here about ten years before I was born."

"I see, and did they teach you these most kind and genteel habits, or did they hate and fear the blacks, the Chinese, my people, even the poor old Mormons, as much as most do in this great land of freedom?"

"They were abolitionists. They taught me to judge men on what they do, not what they look like," Jon said.

"My," Snake-Man laughed, "what noble nonsense. Only someone who's never been spit upon, never been beaten for just walking into the wrong place looking the wrong way, could afford that kind of philosophy."

"Your people have been lied to, cheated, murdered, and robbed," Highfather said. "You deserve redress, but this...killing, destroying...it only encourages more of the same."

"Redress? In a white court, from white judges, white lawyers, white politicians? You're either naive or stupid, Sheriff. I'll pay you the compliment of assuming naive. So, be patient and see whether the well-meaning fools, like you, get to the finish line before the ill-meaning fools, like Caxton, complete their work. No, thank you." He looked around him. The canyon walls grew higher, and the patch of sky grew narrower. "We'll seek our 'redress' the good old-fashioned way."

"Two wrongs don't make a right," Jon said.

"No," Snake-Man said, "but it does make things even. And when you've been denied 'fair' all your life, had to settle for less than that, 'even' begins to look very good, indeed."

B y midday, the troop had spread out, due to the narrowing of the road. The troopers and the civilian volunteers from Golgotha were down to riding two abreast. The supply wagons, including the wagon Highfather had insisted on bringing, trailed near the rear of the winding, living snake that twisted as it moved forward, deeper into mountains.

Caxton paused the troop to confer with Snake-Man. Jon thought he saw a few slender tendrils of black smoke in the direction of Armageddon. He rode up beside Caxton and his scout. "Smoke from the settlement," Jon said.

"Probably cook fires or maybe a blacksmith shop," Caxton said.

"Or we're too late," Highfather said, "and we're riding into an ambush."

"General," Snake-Man said, "the sheriff may be right. Let me ride ahead and reconnoiter."

Caxton stared at the back of his horse's head for a bit, then nodded. "Ride and see what's what."

"I'll go with him," Highfather said. Snake-Man's eyes darkened with anger.

"No offense, Sheriff," the renegade said, "but I'll have a better chance of not getting noticed or shot if I ride out alone."

"Agreed," the general said. "Snake-Man knows what he's doing, Sheriff."

"That's my concern, General," Jon said, never taking his eyes off Snake-Man.

"He goes alone," Caxton said, sounding more than a little irritated. Snake-Man rode out shortly after. Caxton also sent out a scout to check their rear and make sure that the renegade force wasn't approaching yet. Jon noticed the smoke from the direction of the settlement stopped about an hour later. The troop held for about two hours. By then, Snake-Man returned. The sun was well past its zenith, and the shadows in the canyon grew.

"All clear," Snake-Man reported. "From where I was at, it looked like maybe a small building had caught fire, but the settlement's fine, and I saw no hostiles on my approach."

"Excellent," Caxton said. "Our rear guard also reports clear. I hope that makes you feel safer, Sheriff Highfather. Let's proceed. I want us in place before sundown."

They rode along another hour. Jon felt something inside of him tighten like a vice. He fought the rising dread in him and tried to relax. He breathed and stroked Bright's mane. He noticed many of Caxton's men looked nervous, too. The only ones who seemed oblivious to the ever-tightening constraints of the canyon trail were the civilians—all eager to volunteer for what they thought was going to be a grand adventure, a chance to garner some Indian-fighting stories. Caxton and the majority of his high-ranking officers seemed calm, almost arrogant in their refusal to acknowledge the precarious spot they were all riding deeper into. Even Snake-Man was preparing for something, but Jon wasn't sure what.

On the cliffs above, the Paiute brave, Kajika, watched the line of the federal soldiers and their allies slowly wind their way along the canyon floor. He looked down his line of warriors, Ute, Shoshone, and Paiute, standing side by side with their Goshute brothers. He looked across the canyon to the rest of the braves waiting for his signal to open fire. They had raided a small military camp a few days earlier when this attack was being planned. They had plenty of arms and ammo and a very special surprise for the Red General when the time came.

Kajika knew General Caxton by reputation. Last year, Caxton had attacked a Washoe settlement. The people there had no heart for fighting; they were simple farmers and gatherers. Caxton lay waste to their whole settlement, dozens massacred. Kajika had kin among the casualties.

Fighting against another warrior, that was honorable, reasonable. You and your opponent entered into a contract of sorts to battle. There was no *buha* to be had by killing women and children, old people, gentle souls. That was the part of Izusa's strategy that Kajika struggled with daily. He was more than willing to fight and to join his ancestors in battle against the likes of Caxton and his men. He had no desire to slaughter innocents, even if the soldiers had done the same. It was clear that the whites were sick in their souls, and this fighting was making many of his own people sick as well. He had no desire to become as they were—as Izusa was—hollowed out with hate.

Kajika tried to shake the doubt from his mind and focus on the enemy below. Here, in this narrow passage, the murderer Caxton would finally face justice. Each brave was silent as death. They all waited for Kajika's sign, waited to nail the soldiers' coffin shut.

Jon felt it before he heard it. He glanced over to one of Caxton's junior officers, a wide-shouldered, heavy-bearded sergeant by the name of Justin Curtis. Curtis was one of the few officers who didn't seem thrilled with this adventure. He had sensed it, too. A loose rock clattered down from high up on the right side of the canyon wall. Jon saw the glint of sunlight on gunmetal and knew what was only a second away.

"Ambush!" Jon shouted. Curtis took up the call, as they both drew their weapons. A rain of bullets poured down on the patrol followed by cordite thunder.

Jon twisted Bright's reins hard to the left. Bright snorted and turned sharply, giving himself and Jon the cover of a narrow, rocky ledge. Curtis was firing his rife up the ridge wall without aiming, his horse pivoting to take him back along the congested patrol lines. The rest of the patrol was returning the fire now, but the braves were well-obscured by the high, jagged cliffs. However, the sheer mass of gunfire blasting back up was hitting some Indian targets, but only a few. Dead and wounded braves plummeted to earth to join the soldiers and horses that were dying on the ground.

"Goddamn the treacherous savages!" Caxton shouted. He glanced angrily over to Snake-Man, but the renegade had vanished. The general aimed and fired again and again, and Indians fell. "Lieutenant," he called out calmly to one of his subordinates who was already bleeding from a nasty neck wound. "Sound the retreat. Have the men stick to the canyon walls as much as possible."

"Yes, sir."

"When I find that red-skinned Paiute son-of-a bitch," Caxton said, shooting another brave when he popped up from behind his cover, "I'm going to skin him alive." A bullet whined past the general; he hardly noticed. He glanced over to his lieutenant again. The man was dead, slumped in his saddle. "Damn it. You, Corporal!"

From above, the patrol looked like a snake with a broken back, turning on itself. They were trying to flee. Kajika ordered his men to keep up the relentless fire. Izusa had been true to her word, and the ghost shirts, the leather tunics she had blessed, seemingly gave his men lucky enough to wear one proof against the bullets of the troopers. Kajika had seen it with his own eyes—the bullets would bounce off the thin leather—another miracle. He'd let Caxton's men fall back to the crooked bend, thinking they had evaded their death, that they were lucky.

Kajika summoned one of the young braves, little more than a boy to him. The youths were acting as messengers, fetching ammo, pulling the wounded off the line, and reloading guns. The boy sprinted up to the war chief. "I want you to run down the line," Kajika said. "Tell the braves stationed past the crooked turn to be ready and to wait until most of the patrol clears the bend before they begin." The boy nodded and took off at a mad clip across the uneven, rocky floor of the cliffs.

Jon shouted for men to retreat, to make for the canyon's mouth. He led a group of them around the bend in the canyon wall and out of the withering line of fire. The dead and dying were everywhere. For one terrible second, he wasn't sure which battlefield he was on. He looked about frantically for his brother, Larson. He blinked, and his mind reset itself to cold reality. Larson was dead. The war was over, and this—this was not a war, it was an execution. Jon had his wits back about him, which saved his life in the next instant.

Snake-Man launched himself from the shadows of a boulder and knocked Jon off Bright. Jon twisted even as he fired a round at point blank range into the renegade. The curved thumb blade "fangs" Snake-Man wielded on each hand missed the carotid artery in Jon's throat by less than an inch. The blade left an ugly, looping cut on the sheriff's already-scarred neck. They both rolled up into a crouch, Jon bleeding from his neck, Snake-Man with an ugly gunshot wound in his gut.

"I should have known better," the renegade said. "Anyone that's sheriff in a *gudisiipeh* place like that town of yours would have to be tough. The way you gave in to Zeal, I underestimated you, Highfather."

"I get that lot," Jon said, his gun remaining on the renegade. "You're lucky I found you before Caxton did."

"I'm sure he enjoyed being used as a Judas goat as much as I did," Snake-Man said. He winced in pain. "You intend to kill me."

"Thought's crossed my mind," Jon said, "but I think I'll just bring you in and let the army do the killing."

"I thought we discussed how those noble intentions would be the death of you, Sheriff." There was a whirring sound to the left of Jon's ear. A rattlesnake, a big one, was on a rock ledge near Highfather. "My father lends his children, my brothers and sisters, to our struggle," Snake-Man said.

Jon fell back on his ass as he spun, taking the gun off Snake-Man and blasting the angry rattler. When Jon looked back around, the renegade had vanished. He heard terrified shrieks echoing all around him and sprinted across the canyon floor, grabbing Bright's reins as he did.

Rattlesnakes were everywhere, coming out of the canyon walls, from under rocks, dropping from ledges above. They were biting horses, biting men, even biting the wounded and the dying. It was a scene straight out of Hell. The survivors fell back to the relative cover of the bend. That was when the Indians on the other side of the bend cranked up the Gatling gun they had taken from the raided army camp.

Men cried out, cut into a bloody rain of mutilated flesh all around Jon. He took a bead on the gun emplacement and fired, but it was too far up and too far away. He swung up into Bright's saddle and replaced his empty six-gun with his rifle even as he urged his loyal horse on, dodging bullets and snakes as she got up to a full gallop. The patrol had Gatling guns too, back on one of the wagons in the rear, but it would take too long to get it up here and set up.

Jon saw Caxton and a few of his men, all bloody, their faces red with rage, thunder past him as they fired up at the gun emplacement to no seeming effect. One of his officer's horses whinnied and bucked its rider as it was struck multiple times by rattlesnakes. The man dropped and cried out as a nest of snakes fell upon him, too. He lay dying next to his horse.

Jon saw a rattler about to strike at Bright's flashing legs. He fired, and the snake's head flew off. He patted his horse's neck and stayed low in the saddle as a wall of death showered the canyon floor. There weren't many survivors to make it past the kill zone of the Gatling gun. Those who did, huddled bloodied together, en masse, catching their breath, praying, or weeping. The mouth of the canyon yawned before them, the sun's ruddy, bloated eye smearing everything in hues of ocher-red. The desert beckoned, an escape from so much horrific death.

That was when the army of ghostly Indian braves rode out of the sun. They flooded into the canyon, filling the mouth and blocking the patrol's escape.

"Sweet Jesus!" one trooper to Jon's right gasped as he saw the transparent warriors and heard their blood-chilling war cries. "We're all dead. We're all dead, and this is the Devil's pit!" A spectral tomahawk buried itself in his face, and he fell among the snakes before Jon could even try to calm him. A bullet ripped into Highfather's shoulder, and he nearly passed out from the pain. He spun Bright about and headed back, deeper into the canyon. He passed Caxton and his handful of surviving officers. The rage drained from Caxton's face as he saw the ghostly army. "Demons," Jon heard Caxton mutter on his way by, "demons from Hell itself."

"Rock salt!" Jon shouted to the stunned officers. "Use rock salt shotgun rounds!"

The wagons had been abandoned in the retreat. Jon climbed from Bright to the buckboard of the wagon he had brought from Golgotha. A rattlesnake coiled near him on the bench. It lunged and struck him in the side. Jon blasted it with the shotgun a second too late, blowing it off the wagon. He whistled for his horse to follow the wagon and slapped the reins to get the horses moving. He came closer to the canyon mouth and saw the ghostly braves tearing through the survivors, who were pinned down near the entrance. A few soldiers, like the wounded Curtis, were blasting back at the ghosts with shotguns. The rock salt dispersed the spirits it struck, but there were so many of them. Second after second, they were killing and wounding the remaining soldiers.

Jon pulled the cart to a stop. He was dizzy and wanted to vomit. He bit the inside of his cheek, hard, and the pain held him in the present. He climbed into the back and untied the ropes, pulling the canvas off the machine Clay had built. When Jon had explained the problem to Clay, the eccentric inventor had said he had already developed a device for a very similar purpose. The machine was a large metal cylinder about five feet long, lying flat on the bed of the wagon. Arrows and bullets smashed the wooden side boards of the wagon as Highfather knelt down and looked at the panel of switches and knobs. He blinked, cold sweat was dripping off his face. Acid was in his blood, his lungs. His shoulder and arm throbbed from the gunshots. He ignored it all, fought it down. "Okay, Clay, I hope I remembered this right," the sheriff muttered.

A ghostly brave garbed in the clothing of a Shoshone galloped up to Highfather, pistol in hand. The red light of the sun filtered through the brave's translucent body. The gun came up, less than a foot from Jon's face. Highfather gave the warrior the remaining barrel of his shotgun. The rock salt scattered the spirit on the wind, the ghost bellowing in pain and frustration.

Jon dropped the empty shotgun. He flipped the switches in the sequence Clay had instructed him. The machine began to hum and vibrate. He heard more riders approaching; the yips and howls of the ghost braves grew louder. A ghost bullet tore through Jon's arm, and he felt the world tilt and turn as his blood sprayed across Clay's machine. He grunted, focused, and turned the machine's dial. The approaching ghosts evaporated, blown apart as if they were made of fog. The wave of magnetic force spread outward, enveloping the mouth of the canyon. The ghostly war party vaporized, fading away to glittering motes that were devoured in the glare of the sinking sun.

There were still the sounds of war cries and gunfire behind them, farther back in the canyon. The living Indian renegades were working their way down from their position on the ridge of the canyon walls. In no time, they'd have that force to engage once again. In their current state, they would be slaughtered to a man...

Highfather blacked out for a moment but clawed his way back to awareness. There was something important he had just been thinking, something urgent. *Out! They had to get out of the canyon now*! He half-climbed, half-fell onto the driver's bench and slapped the reins. The wagon jerked forward. The wagon clattered out into the sun along with the ragged bands of survivors, Clay's machine still humming behind him.

"Let's get the hell out of here," Caxton's voice boomed out. "Retreat!"

"Thank you," Sergeant Curtis said as he rode by the wagon. "Whatever you did back there saved us."

"Not everyone," Highfather muttered, fighting to stay awake, "not everyone."

"What are we doing here, wasting time?" Gillian asked. Her voice echoed through the empty theater, tight with fear and anxiety. "We have to find little Auggie." It was the dead of night, less than an hour since the Sons of Typhon had come calling. Jim, Kate, Maude, Auggie, Gillian, Clay, and Shelly had gathered at Professor Mephisto's theater in the wake of the abduction at the Shultz's home. Many of them were tending wounds with the aid of the professor's medical supplies and Clay's ministering. Jim and Kate were taking stock of the extra items they had liberated from the jail, including more silver bullets, shotguns, and rock salt shells. They grimly loaded the weapons.

"I understand, Gillian," Mephisto said, "but we need clarity. We must find where they took your child and why. We can't afford to run off wildly. It only wastes time and puts Little Auggie in greater danger."

"We found their trail," Kate said. "It led down the back side of Rose Hill out toward the 40-Mile. We lost it from there. Even Maude couldn't pick it up. If Mutt was here, maybe he could."

"Please," Auggie said, "Professor, those...creatures. They have our child now, maybe out in the wild. What are we waiting for?" The doors from the lobby to the theater opened, and Emily Bright walked down the aisle, a covered canvas under her arm.

"Ah, Emily," Mephisto said. "Thank you for coming. You've completed your painting?"

"Yes," Emily said. She set the covered canvas on one of the seats in the front row and then rushed over to Gillian. "I'm so sorry," she said, hugging her. "We will get him back."

"Let's take a look at your work," Mephisto said, lifting the canvas. Everyone in the room caught their breath. The work radiated a life of its own without actually moving. It was more like looking at a window than a painting. The colors seemed to bleed off the edges of the frame. Little Auggie hung in the upper part of the canvas; warm, pure light came off the baby in waves, like sunlight reflecting on water. The lower part of the canvas was churning, thrashing darkness, the ocean on a moonless night. Something reflected in the black mirror of ink, something bright, distorted. Above the darkness was a figure, a man, his arm outstretched skyward, toward the child. His face was obscured in the light coming from the baby. The lower half of the man, his wrists, his waist, were bound in ropes of fluid shadow. While the face was washed out, there was hint of a handlebar mustache, and the man was burly and broad. The darkness crawled up the man like ivy, struggling, reaching for the baby, for the light.

"Oh, no," Auggie whispered. "No, no. Please don't let it be me." He looked to his wife, his love. "Gillian, I'd never... You know I'd never..." Gillian embraced her husband, tightly.

"I know, my love, oh, I know! We'll figure this out, make it right." She looked to Professor Mephisto. "Won't we?"

Mephisto paused before he answered. Only Maude saw the knife-flicker of pain in his unfathomable eyes for the barest of instants. "Of course we will. There is a kind of blood tie, Auggie. Something that is giving this dark agency access to your boy through the connection of your blood. Has Gillian and Clay explained what happened to you after you were shot?"

Auggie looked to Clay, then to his wife. His eyes were red and damp with tears. "*Ja*," he said softly.

"I may have an idea where they're taking the baby," Maude said. She was studying Emily's painting closely. She knelt and pointed to the seething darkness at the base of the canvas, to the faint reflection. "This," she said. "It took me a bit to make it out, but I think it's a reflection of the silver floor." She stood and looked at the assembled group.

"The silver floor?" Kate asked.

"What?" Jim said, looking up. "Oh no!"

"What is the silver floor?" Auggie asked.

"The floor in the well room," Maude said. "It's a sealed chamber deep in the Argent mine. The floor is pure silver, etched with rings of alien script. Years ago, it was where they took Constance and a group of locals who had all succumbed to the control of the cult by exposure to these worm-like creatures and the oily, black substance they exuded."

"The same substance I used as the primary ingredient in my bio-restorative formula," Clay said. He looked down at his shoes, his eyes unable to meet anyone's gaze.

"Clay," Jim said, shock in his voice, "you've been selling that worm poison to people as medicine? How could you do that?" Clay was silent.

"The cult was sacrificing people under the creature's control," Maude said, "walking them into the well. Jon, Mutt, Harry, and I fought them and barely managed to stop them. They worshiped the thing imprisoned under Argent Mountain, down in the mines. They called it 'the Great Olde Wurm.'"

"There's a thing under the mines?" Gillian looked from face to face in confusion and growing apprehension. Auggie held her as tightly as she held him.

"It's not widely known," Mephisto said. "It's actually one of the great occult secrets in the history of the world. The Wurm must never awaken, never be set free." Silence filled the theater, and perhaps something else, something ancient, wordless, terrible, and cold, slithered into to fill that stillness.

Maude looked to Mephisto and then to the others. "Over three years ago, they tried to do a ritual in that room to wake up the creature. I think they are trying again."

"Agreed," Mephisto said. "The cult of the Sons of Typhon have grown very bold and very active in the last few years worldwide. Freeing their god would be a high priority for them."

"What happens if these Sons of Typhon succeed?" Kate asked. "What happens if it wakes up?"

"The whole world," Mephisto said, his voice deep, echoing seemingly beyond the confines of the material world, "the universe, the very walls of Heaven and Hell, and countless other realms, would shatter like broken glass. It would be as the darkness that existed before all things once again."

"The world dies," Maude said. "Everything, everywhere dies."

THE MAGICIAN (REVERSED)

Mutt and Rabb Hayes rode less than a day toward the arid wasteland of the Great Basin where Wodziwob had said they'd find Izusa and her forces. They stopped at a small Northern Paiute camp of about six families who were staying out of the fighting as much as they could. They told the two deputies to keep heading north toward the Battle Mountains to find the Goshute medicine woman.

"I'd go the other way, if I were you," one of the Paiute, a man named Guyapi, said. "Angry spirits, bad magic, witches... I just want to be able to fish again," he said.

"You're a ways off from that," Mutt said. Guyapi nodded.

"We had a good place, plenty of pinyon, the lake, and clean water, good for fishing. We had to move."

"The Mormons?" Guyapi shrugged and threw up his hands.

"The Mormons, the army, Izusa's renegades. We've been pushed all over the damn place by everyone, and all of them got a drum to beat. We're just trying to live and be left the hell alone. I got children to feed."

"Things have gotten tight in these parts," Mutt said.

"No shit. We're headed south," Guyapi said, "a lot of the *numa* are. Crescent Valley. Trying to stay together, stay out of the way of the bullets and the arrows." Guyapi threw up his arms encompassing everything around him. "Assholes, the whole bunch...even the dead ones."

Mutt slipped the former fisherman a little money when they shook hands and wished them luck. They rode on. It was getting dark.

"All this land," Rabb said, "and it's still not enough."

"Some folks think they deserve better," Mutt said, "and they don't give a damn if better belongs to someone else already. The *Cui Ui Ticutta*'s right; they are all assholes." They rode for a time in silence. Mutt looked over to the former soldier. "You knew Maude's Gran Bonnie?"

"She told you?" Rabb asked. Mutt nodded. "I did. She was a hell of a woman."

"Runs in the family," Mutt said. "So, you came out here to give a message from a dead man to Jonathan?"

"Yes," Rabb said.

"Well, that's a damn fine coincidence. Run into an old family friend in the same town you're just happening to pop into to drop off a message from the hereafter."

"Is this jaw music going somewhere, *pua'a*, or do you just like the sound your voice makes?" Rabb said. Mutt chuckled and pulled Muha to a stop. Rabb stopped his horse as well. "I've seen you winding up to this for a few days now. Let's get to it."

"Fair enough," Mutt said. "I don't buy it. I don't think you 'just happen' to do a damn thing. You've been hiding and lying since the moment I laid eyes on you. I want to know why. Jon may trust you, Maude too, but me, I got a feeling about you. I think you show up when things are bad and they get worse."

"That is not an inaccurate estimation," Rabb said. "I'm sure the fact that the man who's like your brother and the woman you love are both being taken in by my flimflam doesn't help either. Am I correct?"

"Come again?" Mutt said. His eyes narrowed, and his grip on the reins tightened.

"Some of the only folks you respect can't see what you see," Rabb said. "Is that it?"

"Maude and Jon don't see the world the way I do," Mutt said. "The way *we* do. They can't see what's all around you, like black wings. You walk in power, in different worlds. Me, I was born into it, no choice."

"You may not believe it," Rabb said, "but so was I."

"You reek of death," Mutt said. "You've brought it with you."

"I give you my word, my word by my true name, Adu Ogyinae, I mean you and your friends no harm."

"Never heard of you," Mutt said, flatly.

"That's the general idea," Rabb said and spread his arms, "but if that's still not good enough for you, then by all means, let's waste time while this shaman we're seeking kills more people, and you and I can beat the living hell out of each other."

Mutt was silent for a moment. "Scuffle wouldn't take that long," he said.

"No," Rabb said, "it wouldn't."

The desert's twilight sky seethed. Mutt finally turned Muha around. "Come on, let's go," he said. "I'll whoop you on my day off."

An hour after dark, they reached Izusa's camp. They left their horses about a mile back and came in on foot. There were about thirty shelters and tents huddled up against the wall of the mountains. Dozens of campfires dotted the rocky hills that led up to a yawning cave entrance.

"What do you make?" Rabb asked Mutt.

"About fifty," he said. "Braves, no civilians."

"Could be more in that cave," Rabb said. He cocked his head. A dry, cold wind brushed his mind. "You feel that?"

"That cave," Mutt said, "something about it ain't right." He looked over to the former soldier. "Go check it out? Providing of course you can get past those warriors without making a ruckus."

"I'll endeavor to keep up," Rabb said. Mutt led the way down the ridge, sticking to the shadows and the sparse cover of the brush. Watches had been posted, more than in most federal military camps. The posted sentries were close enough to create a line of observation between their small fires. Mutt paused near the edges of the line. He gestured for Rabb to hold. Hayes nodded and crouched low to the ground.

Mutt appeared out of a shadow near one of the guards, a Shoshone brave. Mutt put the man in a headlock, squeezing his neck and depriving him of oxygen. The man fought against Mutt's silent attack and managed to squirm enough to get his mouth free. Before he could scream a warning to his fellow sentries, the desert's breath, the wind, picked up in a long, sustained howl, drowning out his struggle. The sudden gust nearly extinguished several of the guards' fires, forcing them to crowd the fires, their backs turned to block the wind, to keep them burning.

Mutt took the seconds he needed to finish knocking out the brave and propped him against a large rock. The unconscious brave's fire had guttered out, leaving a small pool of darkness in the line. In the diminished light and jumping shadows of the guttering fires, he looked like he was merely resting his back against the rock. Mutt stepped back into the pool of darkness and found Rabb standing there. "That wind," Mutt whispered, "that was you?"

"No," Rabb said. "It was the wind. I merely encouraged it."

"You magic guys are all the same," Mutt said. "Cryptic assholes."

Rabb looked over toward the rock face of the mountain. "If we hurry, the shifting light will mask us well enough to make it past the rest of the sentry line along here, right behind them." The two men made their way, their invisible accomplice whistling and roaring to mask their approach.

Near the cave entrance, Mutt paused, as did Rabb a second later. They looked up to see translucent braves, dozens of them, looking down on them, silently, from the rocks above, the night sky visible through them. "Jig's up," Mutt said. "They know we're here."

"They're not raising the alarm," Rabb said. "That means she wants a private conversation with you and me. Let's not disappoint her." He gestured toward the void of the cave's massive maw. "Shall we?" Rabb paused near the cave's mouth at a squat, hardy Ephedra bush. A tiny spider had woven a fragile web between the branches of the shrub. Rabb knelt and whispered something to the insect.

"What're you doing?" Mutt asked.

"We don't know how big these caves are," Rabb said. The little spider sat on the tip of his index finger. "It doesn't hurt to have a guide."

The cave was cold and dry. There was no light, save the struggling, stolen illumination of the night sky filtering through the cave's mouth. It was devoured a few feet in by absolute tenebrosity. The feeble light gave Mutt and Rabb a general idea of the size and layout of the cave. The place was like a cathedral of stone, vast, with multiple levels of rock formations. The "sky" far above them was fanged with stalactites. A carpet of shuddering, chattering bats, thousands of them, hung from the ceiling. Mutt glanced over to the cave wall near the entrance. Hourglass-shaped pictograph people hung upside down among symbols of horned circles and spirals within diamonds.

"'Dead people and strong medicine,'" Mutt said. "I think we're in the right place."

Rabb and Mutt paused at the terminator of faint light and unrelenting darkness and then stepped forward. A few steps in, Mutt felt the familiar corners of creation peel away and realized too late what was happening. "Shit," he said, his voice echoing in the thick, Stygian air.

"Yes," Rabb said. Both men stopped, scanning the fathomless depths, instinctively shifting to stand back-to-back. They both had felt the shift. They were no longer on Earth, no longer in the world of sunlight, and mortals, and natural laws. They had stepped over into another's domain.

"*Maiku*," a woman's voice said somewhere above them. "Welcome to the home of the dead." There were sounds in the darkness, dry bone scraping against dry bone, the rustling of worm-eaten cloth.

Mutt could sense the sounds shifting all around them as things that reeked of decay surrounded them.

"Show yourself," Rabb called out. The woman whispered something unintelligible, and there was a hissing noise. Sickly green light began to fill the cavern. It came from a glowing gas that emanated from now-moaning, skeletal corpses, partly fused within the stone walls and columns of the vast cavern.

Now that they could see, Mutt and Rabb saw they were being circled by a group of braves, spears and axes at the ready. They didn't look transparent, but they also were not breathing, Mutt's ears told him. The woman stood on an elevated ledge of rock, roughly thirty feet above them. More warriors, with bows and arrows nocked, stood with her, as did a group of older men dressed in the regalia of chiefs from many different tribes and nations. She was dressed in a long, rabbit-fur coat, and her bare skin and face were covered in dried mud with various symbols of power and protection drawn into the mud. In the dim light of the cave, her eyes were hidden by shadow.

"The whites send their champions to challenge me for control of these lands," Izusa said, "so, naturally, they send a half-breed and a black to do their dirty work."

"Well, damn," Mutt said, looking around at the weapons arrayed against them. "The irony of my situation had eluded me. I'm powerful inclined to join up with you, now. Which ass-cheek you want me to kiss?"

"We're here, Izusa," Rabb said, "to come to an understanding that doesn't lead to more innocent people on either side dying anymore."

She pointed down at Rabb. "You are the one coaxing the wind?" Rabb said nothing. "It was subtle. I hardly noticed your hand in it."

"I've courted enlightenment for a long time," Rabb said, "as obviously have you. I sensed your power far off, and I've felt it moving through the land for some time now, like a wildfire with a will behind it. Tell me, why are you pursuing this path when you could do so much to help the native peoples of these lands?"

"Like make it rain, so their crops would prosper? Talk to the earth so that she would accept their seeds and help them to grow even in this harsh land," Izusa asked. "Bless their hunts so the game would be plentiful, bless their children to grow up strong and healthy and wise?"

"Something like that," Rabb said.

"Even if I did," Izusa said, "if their crops prospered, the whites would steal them; if the land accepted their seeds, if the game was plentiful, the whites would claim the land as their own and chase them off it. If I blessed their children, the whites would curse them with sickness and steal them away to 'educate' them, to teach them to grovel to their god and to 'the Great White Father' in Washington. No thank you. I'll do all those things when this land is pure again, great again."

"Pure?" Mutt said. "That's a joke, right? This land wasn't exactly a paradise before the whites came along, and we sure as hell weren't standing around holding hands and singing songs together. Tribes and nations fought one another, killed one another, stole from one another, and enslaved one another. I ain't saying the whites haven't rolled in here and outdone all of us at being sons of bitches, but don't pretend they're the first or the last to play this game."

"I'm impressed," Izusa said. "I thought it was impossible to find someone more cynical than me. I stand corrected. I'm aware of the problems of the past, but with the invaders unifying us and their armies slaughtering those of our people too timid to choose to fight, that leaves us to create a great nation of strong tribes, resolute tribes, from sea to sea."

"When you say 'us,'" Mutt said, "I think I hear 'me.' So, if the Sioux and the Cherokee back east don't cotton to becoming part of your grand nation, what you plan to do about it?"

"I spent most of my life here, among the dead," Izusa said, gesturing around her to the cavern. "I came here when I was a child, running from the murderers of my family. Even then, I had *buha* growing inside me. I was born with power, with sight. It took me losing everything I loved to discover it...that, and my hate. Snake led me to the lodge of the dead. They taught me to hone my gifts.

"Here, I never needed food or water, never had to sleep or to fear the soldiers. The greatest of the shamans of old taught me their medicine. The greatest of chiefs gave me their wisdom. The dead gave up their secrets to me, taught me to cover my skin in mud to deaden the feeling, the warmth. They told me what they wanted, what now burned in their veins instead of blood, the desire to fight once more, to finish their battles, to save their kin.

"I came here a child, but now, the dead follow me. They will lay low anyone who seeks to stop us, anyone. Be it the foreign occupiers, our those of our own people too proud, or too frightened, or short-sighted to join us."

"Well, that clears things up," Mutt said.

"It's all irrelevant," she said. "In the whites, we have a common enemy, a common goal. That's all I need to rally and unify the people."

"The dead can be very single-minded," Rabb said, looking around at the braves. "If they died at the hands of an enemy, revenge can be all they crave, literally, all they are. The living can change; the dead cannot. This isn't a healthy place for a child to grow up, with vengeful spirits whispering in your ear."

"What you claim is a weakness is actually great strength," Izusa said. "The living know fear, seek forgiveness, understanding, mercy. To fight an enemy that considers you less than human, you must be more than human."

"What about your soul?" Rabb said. "Don't discard something so precious, so fragile, so quickly, Izusa. I saw Frederick Douglass speak once in Philadelphia. He was born into slavery, made an unthinking brute by it. But he freed his body and his mind, and in doing so, freed his soul. He hated the institution of slavery, fought it savagely with every tool at his disposal. He saw the need to work across lines of race, lines of division, for the betterment of his people, for all people. You could be that for your people. You can change the world without killing, without fostering hatred. You can save them."

"I'm familiar with Douglass, too," Izusa said. "I saw him speak once as well. I recall him saying, 'Power concedes nothing without a struggle. It never has and it never will.'"

"That's true, he did. He also said that it is 'easier to raise strong children than it is to repair broken men.'"

"I don't need repair," she said. "Unlike you, my purpose is clear."

"You understand the army is not going to go away," Rabb said. He glanced over to Mutt, who caught the look in his eye. "Caxton is as committed to destroying your people as you are to destroying his. The federal government will send as many troops, as many weapons, as they need to..."

"General Caxton is most likely dead right now," Izusa said. She looked over to Mutt. "As is his patrol, and Jon Highfather. They were led into an ambush by Snake-Man. If Grant wants to send more men to die, so be it."

Rabb saw Mutt's eyes darken, felt his every muscle tighten from a few feet away.

"The federals have some knowledge of the dead's power," Rabb said. "They will find ways to stop them. There is no way this ends the way you wish it to."

"Ah, but no one can stop the *Uktena*," Izusa said, smiling.

"*Uktena?*" Rabb said, glancing at Mutt.

"The great horned serpent," Mutt said, "the thing imprisoned under Argent Mountain." He glared up the medicine woman. "If you're so damn 'enlightened,' you know that if the *Uktena* gets free, it will destroy everything, everyone, white or not. It doesn't give a damn."

"Not free it," she said. "I draw power from the dead, from death. The *Uktena* existed before death, but its stirring, shaking the earth, the destruction that it will cause, *that* much death, will give me the power I need to reshape the world, make it a world for the *numa*, for us, and us alone."

"You're all kinds of crazy, all on one stick," Mutt said. "You think you can just poke it a little and then put it back to sleep? How you plan to do all that exactly?"

"Once I have the *Ulun'suti,* it will all be easy," she said. "The jewel that rested in the *Uktena's* skull, once I have it, the *Uktena* will do as I command. I understand a boy—a deputy in Golgotha—is in possession of it now."

"What?" Mutt said.

"Wodziwob told me all about it, when the old fool tried to court me back to his cause," she said. "He used the secrets you gave him to try to reconcile with me. He still has traces of mercy, of understanding for the whites for all his talk of chasing them off. I scared him with my vision. He also told me that the jewel gives great power over the dead. With it, I can raise all our fallen, all across the land. I'll no longer need this cave."

"That son of a bitch," Mutt said.

"You want to kill me so badly, don't you?" she asked Mutt, looking down on him.

"Oh, I'm going to kill you," Mutt said. "I'll bury you next to Snake-Man. You two deserve each other."

"You are so lost," she said. "It's pathetic, really. I'm taking an army of the dead to Golgotha," she said, "to claim the *Ulun'suti,* to wake the *Uktena.* Another army of flesh and blood is on its way to Carson City with Snake-Man at its head, now. He will burn the white's capitol to the ground, slay everyone. I have one final army, as well. A secret army that will ensure that this war never ends by their actions, and you will never guess who leads that army."

Izusa stepped to the edge and raised her arm. The archers prepared to fire. "Once you die here," she said, "you will join the dead, and in time, you'll serve me, gladly."

"You honestly think you can keep one of Coyote's kin locked up?" Mutt said. He glanced over to Rabb. "You ready?"

"Just been hoping she could be reasoned with," Hayes said. "She can't. Let's go."

"Kill them both!" Izusa barked. The archers fired, and the circle of warriors around them closed.

Rabb dropped to one knee and touched the stone floor. The cavern shook, and Mutt saw the strain on Hayes's face as he literately shook another world. Great stalactites and hunks of stone tumbled down around them, blocking most of the rain of arrows. The agitated bats swarming everywhere stopped many more, a living curtain. Rabb grunted as one arrow got through and embedded itself deeply in his upper back, near his shoulder blade.

Mutt tore into the braves around them, slicing and cutting, parrying and dodging with his big, thirteen-inch Bowie knife, flashing, ducking, lunging everywhere. He sidestepped a brave's tomahawk and sliced the dead man's throat open, almost decapitating him. The brave's face turned from cold focus to horrified surprise as frigid blood spilled from the gaping wound.

"Yeah," Mutt said, "ain't that gist a kick in the pants?" The bleeding brave fell backward and faded away before hitting the cave floor.

"The knife!" Izusa shouted over the rumble of the stone rain. "It has the power of Coyote's blood within it! Take it from him!"

Another brave fell to Mutt's knife. "Here it is." He sneered as he drove it into the chest of a brave that had sliced Mutt's side with a spear. Mutt ripped it clear of the man's chest and used the force of that to spin and kill another brave closing on him from behind. "Come get it."

He glanced over at Rabb, who was up again and engaged with three warriors, all at very close range. The former soldier was bleeding from several wounds and was fighting with his Ida blade, striking the braves with his knee and elbow, even head-butting one to give him a momentary advantage to sink his sword into him. His blade seemed to have the same effect as Mutt's. In a few seconds, all three braves had faded to nothingness, "slain" by Rabb.

"Nice sharp you got there," Mutt said, as he killed a brave and suffered a slashing wound inflicted by another spirit across his chest. Rabb killed another brave coming up on his left with a short spear, twisting into and aside the blade. He took the man's head off with a single powerful stroke.

"It was a gift from Ògún," he said. "Orisha of iron and war for the Yoruba. I take it yours was a gift from your father?"

"Shit," Mutt said, dropping low at the final second and opening up the guts of a brave trying to hit him with a tomahawk in either hand. "*Never* accept a gift from my old man. Only thing he ever gave me was his blood, and that wasn't his intent." Mutt slashed at two more braves, keeping them at bay. "I mixed a bit of my blood into the steel to make this. It kills things from a lot of different worlds now. Magic knives or no, if we don't get out of here, we are going to get dead sooner or later."

"Agreed," Rabb said, backing toward Mutt as he parried and slashed at two new warriors advancing on him.

"If I had a hot minute, I could probably find a crawlspace or something to lead us back to the living world." Mutt twisted at the last second to avoid a knife in his kidneys. The blade scraped his side like a razor made of fire, and he felt more blood spill from him. "Fuck!" He killed the brave, burying his blade in the dead man's skull. "I don't think these gents are going to give me the time to do that."

Rabb glanced up and saw that Izusa was no longer on the ledge. The archers were continuing to rain down arrows, but the fallen rocks were providing them some cover. "Fortunately, we have a lifeline." He held up his free hand and blew upon it. A tiny thread of spider silk, hanging between his fingers, flared to life, blazing a brilliant silver. "We have a friend on the outside, provided he hasn't been eaten or squashed or something. Grab on!" Mutt fought his way over to Rabb, who was holding off three more braves himself. Mutt grabbed Rabb by the shoulder and felt him wince from his wound there.

"Quit your bellyaching," Mutt said with a grin.

"Jackass," Rabb muttered through clenched teeth. He closed his hand about the fragile, glowing thread and tugged on it. They were in the light and the moving air once again. The morning sun was rising high in the sky. It looked close to ten o'clock. The two deputies were standing beside the spider's home in the bush, next to the cave entrance. Both men were bleeding and exhausted. They both greedily drank in the sunlight and the cool, clean air.

"Well, that wasn't so bad," Mutt said, sheathing his knife. "Been in worse scraps."

"Uh," Rabb said and pointed down the rocky slope toward the camp of over fifty braves, who were now all staring at the two lawmen. Rifles, bows, and pistols all came up and were all aimed at them in cacophony of clicks and snicks. "You still are."

"Well...that's...disappointing," Mutt said and drew his six-gun, opening fire. Rabb's shotgun appeared in his hands in a blur of a draw, and the two men sprinted for a rock outcropping to get some cover, Rabb firing buckshot to cover their run. Clouds of dust erupted around their stony cover as an endless stream of bullets poured down on them a second after reaching it.

"After some consideration," Rabb said hastily reloading his shot-gun, "I'm of a mind to give this badge back. I've decided to pursue other interests. Poetry, perhaps." He popped up from behind the rock and returned fire with the shotgun, then ducked back again.

"No take-backs," Mutt said. "Believe me, I've tried." He came out from the side of the boulder and fired at the small army. "That cave back there," Mutt said, "that's how the dead are coming back into this world."

"Yes," he said, reloading. "Her long time among them has made it a bridge of sorts for her and for them."

"Where's some dynamite when you need it?" Mutt said. He spotted something that gave him an idea just as he popped back behind cover. "Okay, there's a group of horses about twenty-five yards off to the left. They are tied up to that stand of Pinyon Pines. Let's make a run for them. Any chance you can scare up a little dust storm?"

"That 'making the ceiling of the land of the dead fall down' thing took a bit out of me," Rabb said as Mutt reloaded his pistol. "I got nothing."

"Fair enough," Mutt said as more bullets cracked and whined off the other side of the bolder. "We do it the hard way. Ready?"

"I was born ready," Rabb said. "At least I think I was. It's all pretty hazy, that far back."

"Never mind," Mutt said. "Let's go." The two men stood and fired as they sprinted toward the nervous, shuffling horses. As the gunfire got closer to them, the animals began to spook. Rabb made a shushing sound, and all the horses seemed to calm down immediately. A bullet ripped a chunk of meat out of Mutt's shin, and the deputy almost fell. Rabb grabbed him and kept him up, firing both barrels of the shotgun at the braves firing on them, forcing them under cover themselves. It gave the deputies the seconds they needed to mount the horses and take off at a full gallop.

Bullets buzzed and hissed all around them as they threaded the needle of the rocking landscape. There was no plan, no thought, just ride and run as fast as they could. A few moments after the last sound of gunfire had died away, they slowed and stopped. It took an effort for both of them to stay upright in the saddle. "Let's get to our horses," Mutt said, catching his breath, wiping desert dust off his face and spitting it out of his mouth. "We don't have long before they're on our trail."

Back with their well-rested mounts, Mutt and Rabb took a few moments to address the most serious of their wounds. The places where arrows had pierced them in the land of the dead still bled, but the arrows had evaporated in the morning sun. They mounted their original horses and set the other two off to confuse the trail they both knew Izusa's braves would be following.

"Okay," Mutt said. "We've got to split up. You ride like the devil for Golgotha and warn them what's coming. Tell Jim to use the eye. It's the best weapon we got to deal with the dead. If the telegraphs haven't been cut, you warn Carson City, too."

"If they have," Rabb said, "I'll get word there somehow. Where are you going?"

"After Jonathan," Mutt said.

"Mutt, he's probably dead. She sounded fairly certain of that."

"You haven't been around here that long," Mutt said. "Jon cheats death on a weekly basis. He's the luckiest man I ever seen." There was something in Rabb's face, again. Mutt felt him holding something back.

"There's a limit to luck," Rabb said, "for any man."

"If there's a chance, I owe it to him to find him," Mutt said. "Besides, I'm gathering up a few reinforcements of our own on the way. Snake-Man, Pinkerton, Wodziwob, Caxton, Izusa—we've been letting them all call the tune in this damn war. That's about to change. I'm of a mind to end the dance."

THE STAR (REVERSED)

S arah Pratt and her farm hands were already up before the sun
tending to the farm. Sarah was in her early fifties with gray
hair she wore up to keep it out of her way while she worked.
She was skinny, like a broom, and her hands and face showed a lifetime of hard work in the unforgiving desert sun. Her smile, however,
was warm and genuine, her eyes fiery and shining. Sarah may not
have been a beauty, but she was as strong as a team of horses and had
worked the land with her first husband, Gabe, from the time she was
seventeen. Looking back, she was glad the good Lord had gifted her
with a sharp mind and a strong body instead of a pretty demeanor.
Beauty faded, especially in the desert, but with her strengths, the
harsh wilderness only made her stronger. She waved to her son and
daughter, Elias and Molly, as they headed down the dirt road from the
farm to Golgotha and the schoolhouse on the far side of the town.
"Have a good day!" she called out. "Mind your lessons and home
straight after!"

"Yes, Mamma," both children intoned and waved back before they
began to race each other to the end of the road.

She had married Harry Pratt years ago, after Gabe, the father of

248

her two children, had died. She had been alone out here, drowning in the debts she and Gabe had amassed. She worked the farm alone, her children too young to be of much help. She couldn't afford hands to help her, and no one wanted to court her, wanted her as a wife, until Harry Pratt, beautiful, sad, Harry, had come into her life.

She knew, and he had admitted to her, that he had married her in part because his father and the town elders were hounding him to take a bride, and he chose her out of defiance. But Harry had also done it to help her and her children. In time, they had become best friends, and Sarah knew all of Harry's secrets and kept them well. Harry also knew all of hers. She loved Harry Pratt, and she knew, as sure as the scent of the soil could tell her rain was coming or that a planting would take, that Harry loved her too. She was his counsel and had tried her best to help him with everything from what to do about his stormy relationship with Ringo, to the nature of the seemingly "magical" treasures of the Mormon faith he guarded as his father had done before him, to advising him not to marry that manipulative bitch, Ora Cooper, no matter how it affected the election's outcome. Sometimes he listened to her, and sometimes he didn't, but she always liked the fact that he trusted her judgment and respected her opinion.

The hands were about the chores, and Sarah had carried two heavy pails of milk from the cows in the barn up onto the porch when she saw the lone rider coming down the road, a cloud of dust in his wake. It was Harry and Knight. She sat the pails down. Harry rode up to the hitching post near the horse trough and climbed off Knight. "Well, Mr. Mayor, congratulations on your victory!"

"Oh, stop it," Harry said, tying Knight to the post. "I've been by since the election...haven't I?" Sarah crossed her arms and shook her head. "I'm sorry. It's been so busy..."

"All is forgiven," Sarah said, "if you lug these buckets into the kitchen for me. Pot of Arbuckle's on the stove."

"Now you're talking," Harry said, ascending the porch steps.

They sat at the dining room table next door to the kitchen. Harry breathed in the aroma of the hot mug of coffee and sighed. "It's a toss-up between you and Higbee as to who makes the better coffee. They both could revive the dead."

"You best say it's mine," Sarah said, sipping her Irish tea, "or I'll cut you off." Harry laughed. He took several deep sips of his coffee. "You been up all night, Harry?"

"Several. Things have been complicated."

"I saw the soldiers riding in and out of town," Sarah said. "Looked like an army rode out two days ago. I saw Jon Highfather with them. The hands were talking about Indians raiding the settlements around here."

"Yes," Harry said. "Washington sent us an addled general to deal with it, and, of course, it's not just Indian raiders, it's...Golgotha complicated."

"Oh," Sarah said. "That is never good."

"It's not just that," Harry said.

"Tell me," Sarah said. He told her about refusing to intimidate the Winterton family off their land, how Black Rowan was going to use Rony Bevalier, and his puppet son Daaron, to replace him as mayor by threatening to give the Bevaliers the information about his relationship with Ringo. Sarah listened. She didn't interrupt or attempt the fill the silences left several times by Harry's weary voice trailing off into silence. She took his hands in hers and listened.

"I was planning to leave Golgotha," Harry said. "Once the truth is out, neither James nor I will be safe to stay. I asked him to come with me. I think he might. He's still pretty hurt and angry at me about everything with Ora."

"Can't blame him for that," she said. "What about the relics, Harry? The divine treasures Joe Smith sent your father out here to find and guard. They are very important. They're historical articles of the faith with powers—well, the stories you've told me. Who will protect them if you're gone?"

"You will," Harry said. "I've drafted several legal documents and filed them with Higbee. You now own the Pratt Family mansion and this farm. They are legally yours now, with Higbee acting as your advocate and sponsor in case it comes down to any legal issues you can't directly attend to."

"Yes, yes, being a woman and all," Sarah said shaking her head, "such rubbish. Harry, what are you doing?"

"I'm making you my primary beneficiary," Harry said. "I...I don't have anyone else I can trust, and I can't think of anyone better qualified to look after my holdings and to protect the treasures."

"What about the new Mrs. Pratt? I'm sure she's going to have a few choice words for you in this."

"I ensured that Ora is very well provided for," Harry said, "and she's already beyond wealthy. She hates this town; she hates living here. She's only here as an agent of her father's interests. She'll be fine with it, and she'll leave you alone."

Sarah looked down at the remains of the tea in the bottom of her cup and tried to see some wisdom, some outcome in it as her grandmother had been able to do. She knew it was considered witchcraft by the LDS Church, but in this moment, and in this town, a little witchcraft seemed a paltry sin. "I'm an old woman," she said. "You really want me to guard Heaven's treasures? You expect me to take up a magic sword and a breastplate and battle the forces of evil, like you have?"

"I'm damn sure you could take on the forces of evil with a meat cleaver and a cook pot," Harry said with a weary smile. "I've seen you with your dander up."

"I'm serious," she said. "The people around here, they think you're the One Mighty and Strong, a defender of the faith. A lot of hopes are going to be dashed if you just up and leave."

"Once Rony tells the town that the One Mighty and Strong is a philandering sodomite," Harry said, "those dashed hopes will turn into anger. Sarah, they'll kill me; they'll kill Ringo. Let's both be honest, I've never been a hero. It was just a lie, like most of my life has been."

"What you just said is the lie," Sarah said. "You are a hero. You've stood for the helpless and weak. You've saved lives and saved the world. You saved me and the children, Harry. When it would be so easy to push that poor family off their land and save yourself a world of trouble, you did the right thing. I'm proud of you, Harry. I hope one day you'll be proud of you too."

They sat for a time quietly. Sarah fixed herself another cup of tea. Harry refused more coffee. Outside was the sound of the hands singing "the night herding song" as they worked.

"The arrangements I've made ensure that Judith, Lamarr, and their family will remain on, at full salary, for as long as they wish to."

"Of course," Sarah said.

"Thank you," Harry said. "You are the only one who knows how to get down into the cave with the artifacts. There's an old, cracked skull down in there, in a locked iron box with some loose teeth. Don't *ever* touch the skull or the teeth, Sarah. I've left a sealed letter with Higbee for the sheriff about the treasures, but only if anything should happen to you." He removed a packet of documents from his coat pocket and set them on the table as he stood. "There is no one in this whole world who'll do this better than you. I love you." Sarah stood and wrapped her arms around Harry's shoulders.

"I love you too," she said. Her voice was cracking as she said it. "Thank you for everything."

"Thank you for being my best friend," he said.

"Try, Harry, try to be happy," she said, the tears hot on her face.

"I'll miss you," he said.

O ra was waiting for Harry at his office. His new wife was beautiful, as always, dressed in a very expensive, imported Worth gown of violet and cream. The skin the gown revealed was

THE GHOST DANCE JUDGEMENT

flawless and milky. She wore her blond hair as she usually did, in a high pompadour with earlocks falling on both sides of her face. Harry had seen enough covert looks aimed at Ora to know he was envied by many of the town's men to be sharing her bed, though in reality, they seldom did.

"Shut the door on your way out," Ora said in a terse tone to Higbee as he followed Harry in. The young assistant looked to the mayor and then turned on his heel. After the door was closed, Ora's green eyes darkened with anger. "Why?" she asked. "Why couldn't you just do this one thing?"

"I assume you're talking about the Wintertons' lands?"

"You know damn well what I'm talking about," she said, walking to Harry's small cart bar and preparing herself a glass of gin. "One simple task. But instead of doing it, you've decided to act the fool."

Harry sat behind his desk. "It certainly wouldn't be the first or last time I've played that part," he said. Ora spun and hurled her glass at him. It exploded on the wall to the right of his desk.

"God damn you," she shouted. "I *chose* you, Harry. I knew all about the dirty little skeletons in your closet, your...proclivities. I didn't care, because I saw your potential. You could be governor of Nevada; hell, you have Brigham Young running scared. With the right woman at your side, you could have gone all the way. Wealth, power. You could screw any ass you cared to, as long as you did it away from the public. But no, you had to...do you even *know* why you decided to destroy yourself?"

"Because," Harry said, "I'm not going to chase a man away from his wife's grave so your fucking father can make a few extra million dollars." Ora gasped. Her face reddened.

"You son of a bitch," she almost whispered. "Obviously, we backed the wrong horse in this election."

"I am proud to say yes," Harry said, "you did." There was commotion outside, down on the street in front of city hall. Harry walked to the window, moved aside the curtain, and looked down at the crowd gathering.

"That's a mistake about to be rectified," she said as she walked to the door. "And as for the Wintertons, with all these Indian raids going on, who knows what might happen?" Harry snapped his head around.

"I knew you were a mercurial bitch when I met you, Ora," he said, "but I didn't think you'd commit murder over a parcel of land."

"That's your problem, Harry," Ora said, opening the office door, "you lack vision...and will." The door clicked shut behind her.

Harry and Higbee made their way outside. A crowd close to a hundred were gathering around the part of Main Street in front of city hall. Harry's growing dread increased as he looked over and saw Rony Bevalier in his most somber black coat and hat standing on the flatbed of a wagon, Daaron and some of the "Bevalier machine" people next to him. Rony and Harry locked gazes as Harry walked past the wagon that was acting as a makeshift stage. A scar of a smile cut Rony's face. Harry had never seen Rony smile before, and it was a horrifying thing.

"Sir," Higbee said, "should I fetch the sheriff? Have them disperse this...whatever it is?"

"No," Harry said with a sigh. "They've got the right to speak their peace."

The crowd was a sea of curious faces. Harry drifted to the edges. He knew what was coming, and he should run, but part of him didn't want to. Part of him wanted to fight, even though he knew it was a fight he could never win. Rony stepped forward. Daaron was a few steps behind him and to his right. There was a little cheering and applause, mostly coaxed by his supporters planted in the crowd. He raised his hands for silence, and the crowd settled down.

"Good people of Golgotha," Rony began, "attend to my words!" Harry winced a little. You could always count on Rony to sound like he just fell out of the Old Testament. "Like yourselves, I and my family have too long watched our town fall under the sway of decadence and immorality as we have been inundated by those who are not our brothers and sisters in the faith."

The crowd murmured, as Rony's people stirred up a response. Most of the crowd at this time of day were Mormons, shop owners on Main Street and their patrons. Bevalier continued. "Yes, you've seen it, too. Seen our streets filled with unbelievers, aliens, drunkards, those of low moral hygiene, and degenerates." When he said the last word, he let his eyes settle on Harry at the back of the crowd for a moment. No one noticed it but Harry, or at least he thought that was the case. He felt other eyes on him and looked about. Porter Rockwell regarded him over the heads of many in the crowd. His gaze was cool and relentless. Harry went back to watching Rony, ignoring the gunslinger.

"My son, Daaron, who distinguished himself in numerous battles in the war, ran for office last year, as you may recall, to try to bring our town back to a place of godliness, safety, and morality. Unfortunately, he was narrowly defeated." This brought about a mixed reaction in the crowd, and those closest to Harry glanced at him to see his reaction. Harry kept his face as stone. All of this yammering had been boiler plate, the kind of stuff Daaron had gone on about during the election, Rony's words coming out of his son's mouth. This was just Rony setting the table for the main course, and Harry knew it was coming any second now. He glanced over and saw a flash of color in the crowd. It was Ringo! He was moving through the crowd, a cigarette dangled between his lips. Harry's heart punched his chest. He had to get him out of here. He started to shift through the flesh maze of the crowd. He lost sight of him as Rony droned on.

"My fellow citizens of Golgotha, today, my son and I come before you to reveal to you the source of our town's sickness."

Harry was deep in the crowd now. He couldn't find Ringo, and he was starting to panic. When Rony exposed them, this crowd would become a mob. He kept looking.

"This impurity, this degradation eats at the cloth of our community, and it must be addressed, must be dragged into the light and exposed, expunged, driven out!" Harry was near the front of the crowd now and still no sign of James. He looked up at Rony and saw the elder glaring down at him, a grim, pitiless god casting judgment. "Of what I speak today is..." Ringo stepped out of the crowd in front of the wagon, a pistol in his hand.

"No!" Harry screamed and lunged toward him, a wall of bodies blocking his way. Ringo fired, and the bullet tore through Rony's skull. A second and third bullet blew through his chest. Daaron Bevalier rushed forward, in defense of his father. Ringo shot him twice, once through in the neck, once through the heart.

It was as if the gunshots somehow had broken time. In this frozen second, Ringo looked across the sea of faces slowly blooming into realization and saw Harry. The piano player's eyes spoke, screamed, the things his lips were not allowed to say in this immutable age, *I love you, Harry. I always have. You'll be safe now.* Harry pushed through the crowd, knocking larger men aside, rushing toward Ringo. Later, eyewitnesses would comment on how Mayor Pratt had fought with such vigor to reach the assassin, with no regard for his own wellbeing. Ringo raised his pistol and placed it under his chin, cocked it. "I love you," he whispered to Harry's pleading face, and pulled the trigger.

THE EIGHT OF SWORDS

The streets of Golgotha were empty in the dregs of the night as Rabb Hayes rode into town. All the excitement of the day, the shootings at town hall, were over, and the town slept unaware of what was coming for them out of the desert. Rabb was cold and past exhausted. He'd had to engage two different bands of Izusa's warriors to make it home, and he'd suffered another gunshot wound for his trouble. He turned his horse onto Dry Well and stopped before the jail. A group of horses and a wagon were already gathered by the hitching post. Rabb groaned as he climbed off his horse and looped her reins around the post.

Inside, he found a grim group gathered. Jim and Kate were busy pulling weapons from the gun cage behind Jon's desk. They already had piles of silver bullets stacked upon it. Besides the two deputies, Gillian and Auggie Shultz, both looking bruised and battered, sat in a pair of chairs, their wounds being tended by Emily Bright and Clay Turlough. Shelly, Professor Mephisto, and Maude were pouring over a map of the Argent mines.

"You might want to break out the rock salt rounds too," Rabb said. "Company's coming."

"You're hurt," Maude said. "Where's Mutt?"

"He's alive," Rabb said. Maude walked him over to a bench, and Clay began to check Hayes's wounds. "He went off looking for High-father and to hopefully call up some reinforcements."

"Reinforcements," Kate said, "for what?"

"That army of ghost braves is on its way here," Rabb said. "I'd guess they'll be here by dawn at the latest."

"That's about two hours," Mephisto said, checking his pocket watch, "maybe less."

"Lovely," Maude said. "We're on our way up to Argent to recover Gillian's and Auggie's baby and stop some crazed cultists."

"Y'know, some bank robbers or cattle rustlers would be really refreshing," Jim said, loading another rifle with silver rounds.

"So how do we play this?" Kate asked the group. Everyone looked around from face to face.

"Well," Jim said with a sigh, "Kate, you, me, and Rabb, we got a job to do. If the town is in trouble, we're all they got standing between them and it. That's what the sheriff would say."

"He's right," Kate said. "We'll have to deal with the raiders coming in."

"We'll take care of the Sons of Typhon," Maude said. She looked over to Gillian. "Why don't you and Auggie go home? I'll bring Little Auggie back to you. I promise."

Gillian shook her head. "No, Maude. We're going."

"It's going to be dangerous," Maude said. "Neither of you is really used to this sort of thing."

"He's our son," Auggie said. "We'll go into Hell if we have to bring him home. Besides," he paused, looking a little sheepish, "our house...it's demolished, ja. We...don't have any place to go."

Shelly knelt beside Clay as he stitched up one of Rabb's wounds. "Clay, I'm going to stay and fight the spirits that are coming," she said. "I know I can help protect the town. I've dreamed it."

"Shelly," Clay said, "I don't want to lose you again. It's going to be..."

"Dangerous," she said. "Unlike where you're headed?" She kissed Clay on the cheek. "We both need to help our friends, love, and trust we will find our way back to each other."

"As much as I hate to admit it," Kate said to Maude, "it would be nice to have you helping out on the streets."

"I think I know someone who can help out with that," Maude said.

"I think I do too," Kate said.

Less than an hour later, the two parties were gathered outside the jail, mounting horses, going over final preparations. Clay climbed on to his wagon, and Auggie and Gillian joined him on the driver's bench. Rabb had taken Jim aside briefly while everyone was packing up weapons and ammunition and preparing to go.

"Mutt told me to let you know they are coming for the eye," Rabb said. "He also told me to urge you to use it against the dead. He said it was our best chance."

"I'll try," Jim said.

"May I see it?" Rabb asked. Jim pulled the bag on the cord around his neck out of his shirt and opened it. He lifted the jade eye out and held it up to Rabb. Hayes eyes widened as he saw the invisible nexus of forces swirling around the orb.

"*Yemoja*," Rabb whispered. He looked to the face of the young man in front of him. "Jim, you have been given something of extraordinary power and value. Izusa *can't* be allowed to get this. Do you understand?"

"I've kept it safe for a long time," Jim said grimly. "It's one of the only things I have left from my pa. Someone's going have to kill me to get it."

"I understand. I hope it doesn't come to that."

"Me too," Jim said.

"Where's our girl?" Rabb asked. "She safe?" Jim nodded.

"I went looking for Mayor Pratt," he said. "The sheriff and Mutt told me he helped them against the Greate Olde Wurm cultists a few years back, when I first came to town. I thought he could help us now, but no one has seen him since Elder Bevalier and his son were killed this afternoon. I asked Mr. Higbee, his assistant, to take Leeza in until this mess is over. She'll be safe."

Jim glanced over and saw that Maude had returned, dressed in her "working clothes," a man's loose-fitting work shirt, trousers, and boots. Her daughter, Constance, was with her and dressed similarly.

"Excuse me," Jim said to Rabb and walked over to Constance. "Hey," he said. "What are you doing here?"

"Keeping your hide safe," she said with a smile. "Mother wanted me to give you and the others some help." A grin spread across Jim's face. "What?" she asked.

"I figure our chances of living through this just got a sight better," he said. Constance smiled back.

Kate rode up with a group of mounted, black-suited Pinkerton men and the remainder of Caxton's cavalry he had kept in town. Many of Pinkerton's men were armed with large, strange, rifle-looking devices connected by cables and coils to bulky apparatus carried on their backs. Allan Pinkerton rode with his agents. Pinkerton himself carried one of the odd rifles on his back.

"This is everybody I could scare up," Kate said. "I hope it's enough."

"You get a message through to Carson City?" Rabb asked her.

"Yes," Kate said, "just before the telegraph line went dead. I also reached out to Ch'eng Huang, since his hatchet men helped us when Zeal's crew came to town. He said, and I quote, 'The dead will not enter Johnny Town, and as for the rest of Golgotha, these spirits have a right to their vengeance.'"

"That sounds like Huang," Rabb said.

"You know him?" Kate asked.

"We've had a few run-ins from time to time in other places," he said. "I would call us...acquaintances."

"Oh, Jim, Huang did say that if you wanted to come sit this one out

260

at the Celestial Palace, you were welcome to," Kate added. Jim chuckled.

"Nice to have options," Jim said, "but I'm staying put."

"I also went looking for Black Rowan to see if she could lend a hand," Kate said. "The Scholar said he had no idea where she had gotten to. Hadn't seen her since all the craziness this afternoon in front of City Hall. He's staying at the Roost to look after the Doves." Kate looked over to Maude. "He did report some of their girls up in the camp caught sight of a peculiar looking group of men that fit the description of our 'Sons of Typhon' this evening. They headed for the mines. They're pretty sure they had children with them. At least they don't have much of a head start on you."

"Good," Maude said. "Everyone loaded up with rock salt and silver?" she asked the assembled. A mumble of affirmation drifted through the small army. "The rock salt disperses them for a bit and causes them pain, but it doesn't take them out permanently."

"Leave that to us, madame," Pinkerton said to Maude, then addressed his men in a booming voice that still held a thick Scottish accent. "Check your gauges!" Pinkerton called out to his men and the soldiers. "Watch your accumulator levels! Too high and the whole thing will blow up on your backs! Our mission is to put a stop to these renegades and their creatures, at any cost!"

"We are to keep the town and her people safe," Kate added, giving Pinkerton a dirty look. "Get the civilians off the street; keep them away from the fighting. You see any buildings or homes being over-run, you make that a priority!"

There was disturbance near the rear of the mustered forces. Porter Rockwell strode down Main Street with a large, armed party of local Mormon citizens at his back. "Since 'The One Mighty and Strong' has apparently deserted his duties and his people, I will stand with my brothers in battle. I swear by the saints of the church," Rockwell said, "these Lamanites shall not shed one more drop of Mormon blood today and they will reap destruction themselves for the murders they have committed!" A cheer went up from the Mormon militia that he led, and it spread through the rest of the forces quickly. As much as Kate hated to admit it, even if the man was a cold-blooded killer and a zealot, he had a weird aura about him that made you think he could take on Satan himself, and win. They needed that right now, regardless of the source.

Maude and Constance sidled their mounts next to each other.

"Be careful," Maude said to Constance and hugged her.

"You be careful," Constance said. "See you home for supper."

"Last one back has to cook," Maude said. She paused for a second. The practiced bravado slid away and it was only a mother and daughter. "You haven't seen everything yet," she said. "Remember your lessons."

Shelly approached Auggie and Gillian, her dark cloak wrapped tight about her. "I'm sorry I'm not going with you," she said. "I just...know I'm needed here. I *have* to be here. It is...hard to explain." She embraced Gillian, her oldest and dearest friend. "I love you. You'll save him. I know you will." She turned to Auggie, her beloved, her husband in a different life. "I love you, Augustus. I always have, and I always shall." She hugged him tightly, and when she pulled away, her dark eyes were large, and tears streamed down her face. "Goodbye."

"Goodbye, Gerta," Auggie said, softly.

The two missions split up, Clay's wagon leading the rescue party toward Prosperity Road, Argent Mountain, and the mines. Jim, Kate, Rabb, and Pinkerton led the small army they had mustered toward the edges of town to meet the renegade spirits in the still-dark desert.

───────────

Third shift was making its way out of the Argent silver mine when Clay's wagon and the horses came to a stop near the gates. The security men Bick hired to guard the complex approached Clay and the others, rifles in hand. "You folks can't stop here," the head of the security detail, a man named Hough, said. He paused when he saw Auggie. "Mr. Shultz, that you?"

"*Ja*," Auggie said, climbing out of the wagon. "Hello, Mr. Hough."

"Sir, I had no idea you were coming up," Hough said. "Mr. Bick hadn't informed me..."

"It's all right," Auggie said. Haugh also saw Emily with the group now, too. "Mr. Bick's daughter and I need to check on a situation down in the old, closed-off shaft, near the bottom."

"Of course, sir," the guard said.

"We'll need lanterns and tools," Auggie said. "Also, I just spoke with the deputies down in the town. There's an Indian raiding party approaching Golgotha. Cancel the shifts till further notice and lock down the mine behind us. Tell the miners to stay home and arm themselves."

"Indians!" Hough said, looking to his fellow guards. "Yes, sir!"

"Get every man you have on duty and raise the alarm in the camp," Auggie said.

"Tell them Mr. Bick will pay twenty dollars to every man who defends the town and the camp," Emily added.

"Yes ma'am!" Hough said.

Auggie looked over to Gillian, who was climbing down from the buckboard with the help of Professor Mephisto. Clay was gathering a large canvas satchel from the back of the wagon's bed. "And please hurry," he said.

The descent down into the darkness was hampered by the piles of rocks and debris that clogged much of the old, original shaft. The official story was that about four years back, there had been an explosion caused by a vent of methane gas, but in reality, it had been a deliberate attempt to seal the shaft forever. Maude led the way with Emily and Professor Mephisto following close behind. Gillian and Auggie were next, and Clay brought up the rear, struggling a bit with his satchel. They paused at an intersection, and the professor studied the map Emily had received from her father, while she held the lantern. "This way," Mephisto said, pointing toward a partially blocked passage. He winced as if he had been stabbed.

Emily looked over, a pained look on her face, too. "I felt that. What is it?"

"Something is stirring," Mephisto said. "We need to hurry." The party rushed down the sloping passage. They came to a juncture of several shafts. Maude stopped and cocked her head.

"I hear voices," the Daughter of Lilith said, "chanting. That way."

The entrance to the silver room was nearly buried under tons of collapsed rock. Maude slid through the narrow opening, and the others followed. The chanting was loud enough now for the others to hear it, a trio of male voices:

Hail that which cannot die.
All grovel to he, who eternal lies, the true one, the all-seeing eye! Couched in
blessed darkness, bound in light and lies, the ending of all that thrives,
awaiting the time that ends all times.
The mindless dancer at the edge of mind, the bridegroom to the Black Mother
with a thousand bleating, hungry young...

A baby was screaming over the chant. "Auggie Junior!" Gillian shouted out and struggled to make her way through the tight space.

Auggie cried out, rushing to follow her. "Gillian, wait!"

Maude remembered the silver room, the vast circular chamber with a floor of dull, pure silver etched with tiny, spiraling, cramped script. The well was at the chamber's center and was entombed under rocks that had fallen down as the Greate Olde Wurm had shaken the world apart in its fitful awakening.

Most of the chamber was still buried, but a section remained intact off from the passage. Two of the Sons of Typhon stood outside a circle of greasy, sputtering candles that filled the chamber with the stench of rancid, roasting pork. Rory stood inside the circle; Augustus Junior was on top of a wooden crate, squirming, screaming, swaddled in dirty blankets before the Son of Typhon. The upturned skull of an animal—a dog, or perhaps, a coyote—rested in the nest of Auggie Junior's blankets. In one hand, Rory held a blood-soaked athame, a ritual knife. In his other hand was the limp, lifeless body of Joel Hamblin. Black blood trickled from the child's pale, motionless body into the skull chalice below.

"Ah, you made it," Rory said as his companions turned toward the group, still chanting, now in some burbling alien tongue that sounded like the ravings of a lunatic as he was drowned in blood. "A mum and da should be here for their little boy's first communion."

"Get away from my son!" Auggie bellowed, raising the revolver Jim had armed him with. He cocked the pistol and aimed it at Rory. Rory kept smiling as he lobbed the dead baby over his shoulder as if he were throwing away a crumpled bit of paper.

"You sure you want to do that?" he asked, tossing the bloody athame outside the circle. It clattered on the silver floor out in the darkness of the chamber. "Have you ever fired a gun in your life, shopkeeper? Ever willed the bullet to end a life as you pulled the trigger?" Rory picked up the blood-laden skull and scooped up Little Auggie, holding him close to his chest. The baby wheezed, then took up his wailing again. "What if you miss? What if you strike your little boy?" Auggie's hand didn't waver, but he also did not fire.

"You hurt my son, I'll kill you with my bare hands," Auggie said.

Maude was moving toward Rory and the circle, but the other two Sons, Tidbull and Kern, moved to block her. Both were armed with mining picks. Emily stood beside Maude, ready to fight. Gillian stood with Auggie, struggling to not rush to her child.

"What do you want?" she asked.

"Nothing I don't already have," Rory said. "I was sent here by our mother to give our god a way back into this world, since this bitch," he nodded to Maude, who stood only a few feet from Rory's men, waiting for an opening, "saw fit to imprison our father and stop his good works."

"Mother?" Maude said. "What are you talking about?"

"You'll see," Rory said. "In good time, but for now, consider this her way of introduction as to what's to come for you and the other Daughters of Lilith." He raised the skull and tipped it toward the baby's mouth.

"Don't let him do it!" Professor Mephisto shouted. "It completes the mystic circuit!" The scholar drew a long, thin, sharp blade from the hidden confines of his cane. He dropped the empty cane and moved toward the circle, raising his free hand and beginning a chant of his own. "*Ù anzillu ilu n'gha! Gigim Xul Barra!*" The chamber shook, and small bits of rock and dust poured down. Clay knelt near the entrance and rummaged in his bag.

"No!" Gillian charged the circle to reach her baby. Auggie barreled after her. Maude headed to intercept Tidbull before Gillian reached the giant. Maude managed to deflect most of Tidbull's backhand of Gillian and Auggie, but the sheer force of the attack sent Gillian, Auggie, and Maude falling back to crash and bounce along the floor.

Emily rushed toward Kern, and the Son raised his pick to strike the girl. Mephisto blocked Kern's downward swing with a parry *quarte* of his sword as he continued his chant. Mephisto twisted his blade, bound with the pick's, to pull the ax out of its attack line, wrenching it from Kern's hand and sending it flying across the room. Emily drove a fist into Kern's face. The angelic blood of her father made her stronger than a mortal. Kern staggered back a few steps, blood pouring from his crushed nose, but he didn't fall. The room convulsed again, rock and dirt raining down on the rescuers and the kidnappers alike.

Clay knelt near the entrance and rummaged in his bag. "I don't think the critter down here cares much for whatever it is you're saying, Professor," Clay said, as he removed a pair of metal orbs that looked like small cannonball shot.

The blood patted into the screaming baby's mouth—only a few drops—but Little Auggie began to sputter and cough. Auggie, pulling himself up from the floor, felt as if a hand of ice had taken hold of his heart. He looked over to his son as the baby's tiny body convulsed. The smell of rancid meat grew powerful, and there were voices coming from somewhere, an invisible choir singing sweet, sweet blasphemies on the stinking air.

"Oh, no," Professor Mephisto muttered, stopping his chant. "No!"

Gillian looked up, her lip bleeding from the force of the blow that had sent her flying across the filthy, silver floor. "Baby?" she whispered. "Darling?"

Augustus Clayton Shultz Junior raised his tiny head. He drifted out of Rory's grasp and floated, suspended, in the suddenly freezing air. His tiny, naked body was rapidly being covered by black veins, spreading like rushing, forking rivers under his pale flesh. His eyes were black mirrors, wet and pitiless. The baby looked over to Gillian, who lay paralyzed in horror. The child's small, toothless mouth opened, and a roar spilled out of it that rumbled through the chamber, seemingly, throughout the whole mountain. It made the very earth shudder.

"Our Lord is risen!" Rory shouted over the bestial moan. "Let Earth receive its king!"

Maude was up, trying to get to the baby. Tidbull lumbered toward her, eclipsing everything. She had to get to Little Auggie, had to make this right for Gillian.

"Maude, no! Everyone, out!" Mephisto called out over the thrashing pain of the world and the baby's monstrous howl. "We have to fall back. It's too powerful!"

The baby gestured with his diminutive hand. The whole chamber, the very air, curdled and erupted as if a bomb had exploded. The candles were ripped to pulp, their light extinguished. Everyone in the chamber, friend or foe, was scattered, pulverized by the force of the blast. The whole cavern was swallowed in darkness and destruction.

"What was that?" Pinkerton asked, turning his head back toward Golgotha and the rumbling sound. The sky had lightened, and they could see black smoke rising from Argent Mountain.

"The mines," Jim said. He glanced to Constance and back to Pinkerton. "We should go see if..."

"Whatever is happening there, your friends will have to deal with it themselves, Deputy," Pinkerton said, puffing on his cigar and adjusting the dials on the odd rifle he and his men were carrying. "We've got patrols on all incoming routes, but we're spread pretty thin. I'm sorry."

"You're right, sir," Jim said. "Just frettin'."

"I understand," Pinkerton said. "A man who doesn't worry about the people he cares for isn't much of a man." The detective glanced over to Kate. She had a spyglass to her eye and was scanning the horizon, unaware of Pinkerton's admiring gaze. He looked back to Jim. "We have a job to do, son. Stay alert."

Atop some of the ancient, crumbling ruins that stood at the edge of Golgotha, within sight of the valley between Rose and Methuselah Hills, Shelly perched on the remains of a roof and scanned the desert. She felt the terrible pall of death that had appeared under Argent, like the bloom of some hell-borne flower opening, but she remembered her dream, remembered the outcome that had plagued her nights for weeks now. She was where she was needed right now, even if her heart screamed to be elsewhere.

As morning came to the 40-Mile, she felt the energies aligning, the door between worlds swinging wide, and she knew, she felt them before she ever saw them. The dead were here, and they screamed for old evils to be revenged. Shelly stood, and all around her were her sisters. To eyes that could not see, they were huge turkey vultures, ready to glide across the wasteland and feast on the table of death the desert had laid out for them. To Shelly, they were beautiful and horrible—a fusion of woman and raptor—ready to claim the fallen in the battle about to begin. Shelly called out, her voice more bird than human.

"What in blazes was that?" Rockwell asked, cocking his rifle.

"It's Shelly," Kate said, "one of the lookouts." She pivoted her horse toward the eastern desert, where Shelly had been keeping watch, and held the spyglass back to her eye.

"What is it, Kate?" Pinkerton asked. "Anything?"

"It's them," Kate said. "A war party, looks maybe two hundred strong, all of them...dead."

"Mobilize the eastern defensive line," Pinkerton said to one of Caxton's soldiers and Jim. We'll not fully commit all the troops until we see if this is the tip of the spear or merely a feint. May the Lord go with you!"

Jim looked over to Constance, squeezed her hand briefly, then galloped off on Promise with the soldier to rally their meager troops. He wished Sheriff Highfather and Mutt were with them, hoped for the hundredth time today they were even still alive.

THE SUN (REVERSED)

Mutt saw the caravan on the horizon of the desert. His wounds still ached, but they had already started to heal. He could use a few years of sleep, but when he saw the riders, all thought of rest disappeared. He coaxed his weary horse forward, and they eventually met up with the advance scouts of the party. It was some of Caxton's troopers, looking more dead than alive. They leveled their rifles at Mutt, and he raised his hand to show he wasn't brandishing a weapon. "I'm a deputy from Golgotha," he said. "Put your guns down."

"Fuck you," the younger soldier snarled and sighted down his gun at Mutt. "Another goddamn bushwhacking, lying injun!"

"Private, you lower your weapon right now," the older soldier, who wore corporal stripes on his bloodied blue coat, said. The younger man's gun didn't waver. Mutt saw the anger and the fear in a face so young.

"Sir..." the kid said from behind his rifle. The corporal sighed.

"I'm too tired for this shit," he said, pointing his rifle at the younger soldier's head. "Put your damn gun down, Hal, or I'm going to have to shoot you."

"His kind murdered Tony, and Albert, and..."

"He isn't one of the Indians who ambushed us," the corporal said. "He didn't kill anybody. We're soldiers, not bandits, and I'll be goddamned if I'm going to let you run off and start shooting every civilian you get a wild hair to. Now put that fool rifle down." The young soldier lowered his gun. He turned his horse, gave the corporal a dirty look, and rode back toward the troop.

"Sorry," the corporal said, lowering his own gun. "We got hit hard. There's a lot of ugly feelings. What brings you out here, Deputy?"

Before Mutt could explain, a horse galloped up, its rider calling out, "Mutt!"

"Jonathan!" Mutt called out, laughing. He urged his horse to sidle up and meet the sheriff. Highfather's clothes were bloody and covered in desert dirt. His unshaven face was pale and gaunt, but he looked happy to see Mutt.

"You look awful," they both said at the same time.

"Rabb and I found Izusa," Mutt said. "I know it may come as a bit of a shock, but she's crazy. She's headed for Golgotha with a mess of ghosts."

"Of course," Jon said.

"She intends to steal Jim's jade eye and use it to mess with the *Uktena* and kill a lot of people."

"How does she even know anything about..."

"Wodziwob," Mutt said. "I trusted him, and he trusted her. We both got diddled."

The soldier rode past. "Corporal," Highfather said. "Could you fetch General Caxton? It's important." The trooper nodded and rode back toward the slowly advancing survivors.

"You okay?" Jon asked.

"I'm good. You? You look sick."

"They were ready for us," Jon said. "Snake-Man turned on Caxton as soon as the shooting started, tried to kill me." Jon pointed to his neck wound. "I gut-shot him for his trouble, but he got away. I took a hit from a rattler. My gun belt must've blocked a fang, but I still took a little juice. I could do with a little lie down, but it ain't going to kill me."

"I know, I know," Mutt said. "Not your time."

That odd something passed across Jon's face again. Mutt thought it might be he was fighting to stay upright with the venom coursing through his veins. "Not today, apparently."

Caxton rode up with a few of his surviving officers. They were all wounded, bloody, and exhausted. Caxton looked at Mutt as if he had just discovered another rattlesnake. "Well, Highfather, looks like your Indian finally turned up. Fortuitous for him he wasn't available to ride us into that canyon, eh?"

"It would've been 'fortuitous,'" Mutt said, "if you hadn't let Snake-Man lead you around by your pecker into what any fool could have told you was an ambush."

"Why you foul-mouthed savage, I'll..."

"General," Jon said, raising his voice, "Izusa's ghosts are headed for Golgotha. They may already be there. She's with them, and she intends to raze the town. We have to get back there, right now."

Caxton licked the dust off his lips and narrowed his eyes. "That little bitch," he said. "She won't get away from me this time. Is that lying bastard Snake-Man with her?" Jon looked over to Mutt.

"I doubt it," Mutt said. "Izusa said she was leading the Golgotha raid, and she told us Snake-Man was leading a force to Carson City to destroy the capital and kill everyone."

"The capital! The governor!" Caxton said, looking to his aides. "We must be underway at once!"

"She mentioned some secret third army," Mutt began, but Caxton was already shouting orders.

"We've got forty-seven troopers left. I want twenty-five headed for Carson, under your command, Sergeant Curtis. Be ready to leave in twenty minutes." Curtis glanced to Highfather and then kept whatever he wanted to say to Caxton to himself.

"Yes sir," Curtis said instead.

"Get your fastest rider," Caxton said. "Give him our best, most rested horse and have him ride like hell for Camp Nye to raise the alarm and get us reinforcements." Curtis nodded and rode back to muster his men and summon the rider.

"I'll go with them," Mutt said, "deal with Snake-Man myself."

"You will do no such thing," Caxton said. "I will never allow one of you red-skinned devils to ride with my command ever again, as long as I have breath in my body."

"We can do something about that," Mutt growled. "You are, without a doubt, the stupidest white man I've ever met, and I've met some beauties."

"General," Highfather said, "taking Mutt would give your men a damn-sight better chance of making it home from this mission."

"Sheriff, it has become clear to me that you are a man of exceedingly poor judgment in who you call friend," Caxton said. "The half-breed's not going with my men to Carson City, and he's not going with the rest of us to Golgotha. You're more than welcome to ride with him, alone, if you are that determined to die."

Jon's eyes darkened, and Mutt saw a storm building there that he had seldom seen. He placed a hand on Jon's shoulder. "A word, Jonathan." Highfather glared at Caxton and then rode over a few yards with Mutt to confer. "You were ready to shoot that sumbitch, weren't you?" Jon said nothing. "I'm touched, Jonathan, almost teary, but I think you need to head back to Golgotha with them. Jim and Kate, Rabb, if he made it, the whole town, they need you."

Highfather wrestled down the anger inside himself. He took a deep breath before he asked Mutt, "Where are you headed off to now, then?"

"Have a few words with Wodziwob and then fetch some help for Golgotha. I'll be back as soon as I can."

"Thanks for coming looking for me," Jon said.

"You would've done the same," Mutt said.

"True." Jon paused for a moment. "Teary?"

"Weepy," Mutt said, "practically verklempt."

"Let's ride, before we both need a hanky. I'll see you on the other side of this."

"That you will, Jonathan," Mutt said. "That you will."

While Highfather, Caxton, and twenty-odd US Cavalry troopers headed for Golgotha at full gallop, Mutt headed for Wodziwob's camp. He decided to take a roundabout way to get there, hoping to come across someone in the wasteland. He found a sickly little pool of water in a field of wild buckwheat and a smattering of tobacco sage and left Muha there next to it.

Mutt could already feel the eyes on him as he walked away from his horse, his guns, and his clothes. He walked naked toward the wasteland that surrounded the oasis, feeling the grass and the sun-warmed soil under his feet. The cool wind ran its hands over his body like a returning lover. He felt his perceptions widen and diffuse at the same time. He could sense more, experience more, but the associations, the meaning, became less and less concrete and less important. He wasn't experiencing this moment, codifying it, cataloging it, he *was* it. He was breath and wind and blood and the spinning rock beneath his four feet.

He had forgotten how much he missed this feeling. All the things that had seemed so important, so crucial, and imminent in his mind a moment ago drifted apart, islands of memory that only held importance in a human mind, a human body. He wiggled free of his numb human skin, a sack on the ground that made everything harder, duller. Mutt shook himself dry.

The sky looked different now, a slowly rotating dome, windows full of different colored skies, different worlds. Mutt trotted along out into the desert. The radiance of the suns reflected off the edges of the sky windows like the light from a prism. Ahead of him was a tall rock formation standing alone in the desolation. On boulders and rock ledges, dozens of coyotes lounged and regarded Mutt as he approached. Mutt recognized some of them from over the years. The big, scarred, one-eyed coyote padded toward Mutt, blocking his way.

"Squint," Mutt said. "You seem to have lost another piece every time I see you, and the parts you hang on to look like shit."

Squint snarled. "Look who decided to stop pretending to be an ape for a spell. What do you want, Mutt? You don't belong here."

"That would be the title of my song," Mutt said.

"Mutt, Mutt!" a young coyote hopped down from a ledge and scampered toward him and Squint. She was little more than a pup, and her golden fur caught the light. She jumped and yipped around the two older males.

"Sunfur," Mutt said, laughing. He joined her in yipping and jumping about, while Squint looked on, softly growling. Mutt nipped and bit her muzzle in greeting.

"Are you here to stay?" Sunfur asked, trying to stand still but still jumping up and down in front of Mutt. "Father's missed you. He's so proud of you! He talks about you all the time!"

"No, he doesn't," Squint said.

"Where is the old man?" Mutt asked. "I need to talk to him."

"Up there," Sunfur said, nodding toward the top of the rock formation, "of course." A large gray coyote lay on its belly enjoying the warmth of the rock. It looked down at Mutt and snorted before rolling over.

"Hey!" Mutt called up to Coyote. "I need to talk to you."

"Borrrrring," Coyote said. "You are the least fun of all my children. It's always running around doing...stuff, and then there is all the important talking, also boring."

Mutt jumped from rock to rock, slowly making his way closer to his father at the top of the free-standing rock. "You know what's been going on, don't you?"

"Check this out," Coyote said. He batted a small rock back and forth between his paws. "I stole it from Grandfather Sky, and when I'm done playing with it, I'm going to let it fall down to Earth and make a huge boom. Cool, huh?"

"How cool is the dead rising?" Mutt said, jumping from a rock ledge and landing next to Coyote. "They're running around killing people." Coyote sniffed Mutt as he landed.

"*That's* what I'm smelling on you," he said. "You've been mucking around in the land of the dead, haven't you, boy? Playing with dead things."

"They are riding for Golgotha right now," Mutt said. "They are going to kill everyone in the town."

"So?" Coyote said. "Dying is what people do. What's the big deal? You really need to get out more, Mutt. You sound like a man, and you're not."

Mutt looked around, looked down at Coyote's other children. "I care about some of the people in that town. They're my family, more kin to me than you've ever been."

"Yeah, yeah," Coyote said. "I figured you'd given up on me and your brothers and sisters. We haven't really talked since book one."

"What?" Mutt asked, cocking his head in confusion.

"Nothing," Coyote said, "just me being an asshole."

"I need you and the others to help me," Mutt said. "Most things in the living lands are like dreams to the dead. They're hard to hurt, and harder to send back for good. You and the others, you could..."

"You know," Coyote said, "as much fun as it sounds to stop playing with my space-rock and go chomp on some ghost meat, I think I'll pass."

Mutt began to say something, but then he shut up. He looked at Coyote for a moment silently. Coyote stopped playing with his space-rock. "What?" Coyote said.

"Nothing," Mutt said and began to descend the rocks the way he had climbed up. "I guess I'll deal with Snake myself. I can always depend on not depending on you."

"Snake?" Coyote stopped playing with the rock, stood, and looked over to Mutt. "Snake's mixed up in this?"

"Yep. One of his kids is, and he's helping him out."

"Is it the one that you kicked his ass twice already?" Coyote said, a little pride slipping into his voice.

"Yeah," Mutt said almost back to the desert floor. "He's working with a Goshute shaman this time, a powerful one, too."

"I thought I heard some loud clanging and banging over yonder," Coyote said. "Must have been her working her medicine. That is pretty powerful. She cute?" Mutt had reached the ground and was padding away. "Hold it, hold it, hold it!" Coyote called out. "Hey, what's your hurry?"

"Let him go," Squint said. "He's trying to trick you."

"I'm way too smart for anyone to trick me," Coyote said, looking around at his other kids. "Right?" The other coyotes muttered in agreement.

"Absolutely, Father!"

"No one is as sly as you are, Coyote!"

"Remember when you tricked Porcupine out of his buffalo meat?"

"Well, actually," Sunfur began, "sometimes, Papa..." Mutt placed a paw over her muzzle to quiet her. Coyote soaked in all the praise; his chest puffed out, and his head jutting skyward toward the suns. Mutt waited patiently. Squint glared at Mutt with his one good eye, and Mutt said nothing and smiled, his prominent, yellow incisors poking out.

"Now that I've had some time to ponder," Coyote said, leaping down from the big rock, "I think mucking up Snake's plan sounds like great fun!"

"Never mind," Mutt said. "There's too many ghost warriors. You and the kids wouldn't stand a chance."

"I cannot believe you are falling for this," Squint said, laying down and burying his head under his crossed paws.

"Quit your kickin'," Coyote said, ignoring Squint completely. "You'll see; we'll chase their bony asses all the way back to the land of the dead."

"Well..." Mutt paused and sighed as if he were conceding defeat. "I suppose you can give it a try. But you have to hurry. Golgotha ain't got much time left."

"Already gone," Coyote said. He winked and yipped and his children took out his cry.

Hawthorne Wodziwob felt the numerous forces stretching out across the land, across the worlds, aligning for whatever came next...a miraculous change or a conflict of cosmic proportions. The old man shuddered a little as he heard the *Uktena*'s hungry bellow shake the ground beneath his feet, felt it echo throughout all of creation. He knew the creature's awakening was partial his fault, and he had been warned. The spirits had told him that in the final days of the white man's defeat and banishment, the ground would shake and split. They hadn't mentioned Izusa or the *Uktena* in their prophecy.

The old medicine man reached out with his spirit. It pulled free of his physical shell and soared skyward in the form of an eagle. He saw many tribes across the land performing the round dances, lending their spirits to the power of the ghostly braves. He also felt the power of the gods of the whites, of the Chinese, of the Africans, and all the other immigrants who had carried their beliefs with them to this land. Armies of faith on both sides prepared to clash, and while the gods and spirits may struggle and storm, it was always the believers who did the bleeding and dying.

The weight of it all awaited him as he returned to his mortal form. He couldn't help thinking of the children in the camp outside. Children, all children, carried a grace inside them, a blissful immunity to the horror and the injustice of this world, far stronger than any god, any belief. To rip that state of grace away from them one day sooner than necessary was an evil, a sickness that could never be wiped away, never taken back. Wodziwob wished he could go to the mountain again, wished he could speak with the spirits and try to find some way, any way to resolve this that didn't end with so much suffering and death for anyone.

There was a rustle of the cloth over the doorway to the wickiup. Wodziwob was expecting his friend and disciple, Tavibo, bringing him his evening meal. "You can set it by the fire," he said, his eyes still closed, still lost in his thoughts.

"How about I set your goddamn brains next to the fire?" Mutt's voice said. The cold steel of a barrel settled against Wodziwob's temple.

"How did you get in here?" the medicine man asked.

"A little coyote brought me," Mutt said. "Where's all your braves? Camp's almost empty outside." He was a man again, clothed and armed.

"They rode with Snake-Man for Carson City," Wodziwob said. "Not quite a day ago."

Mutt knelt by Wodziwob but kept the gun to the old Paiute's head. "Can you think of a single reason I shouldn't splatter your skull all over these walls?"

"At the moment, no. I take it you found her and spoke with her?"

"Yeah. You didn't send those Black Feathers out after her to have a nice chat. You sent them to kill her, and she took them all out."

"It was not my intention," Wodziwob said. "It was only as a final option, if she could not be reasoned with. I...cared for her. I was only trying to teach her, guide her." Wodziwob turned his head to look at Mutt. The gun remained pressed to his skull.

"Oh, you taught her, you might as well have aimed her. You gave someone crazy and scary powerful nowhere to turn for acceptance, or understanding, or love." For a moment Mutt felt a powerful connection to the medicine woman. He saw his mother, her sad, tired, beautiful eyes. If not for her, he might have become Izusa himself.

"I told her of my visions from the mountain," the old man said. "She already knew them. She lived among the dead, and they were among the spirits that spoke to me. She interpreted them in a completely different way than I did."

"Yeah, prophecy's funny that way, ain't it? You told her the things I shared with you," Mutt said. "The secrets about my friend, Jim. Now she's going to tear apart Golgotha, try to kill Jim to get the *Ulun'suti*, use it to poke the *Uktena* and shake the world nearly to pieces."

"No," Wodziwob said softly. "She knows that if it becomes too aware, too awake, it will destroy all the worlds."

"She'd realize that," Mutt said, "if she wasn't out-of-her-mind-shit-house-crazy. She thinks she's got it all under control. You two have that much in common."

"Before you came in, I sensed the *Uktena*," Wodziwob said. "Something is giving it access, a tunnel through the land of the dead to the land of the living."

"Is it Izusa?" Mutt asked. Wodziwob shook his head.

"No. It is...a bridge...a bridge of blood. If Izusa tries to agitate the creature now, it will awaken."

"And that would piss on your whole glorious new world, wouldn't it?" Mutt said.

"Not mine, *ours*. I just listened to the spirits," Wodziwob said. "I listened to the suffering of our people that has become as the wind's voice in this world. I make no apologies for trying to ease that pain, that injustice. I see now that perhaps I was narrow in my interpretation of the spirit's vision. Where there is life, there is hope for change, for renewal. The *Uktena* is death. It must not awaken."

"I guess you better get off your ass and help us keep that from happening."

"I thought I could control her," Wodziwob said. "Direct all that power and passion to a good purpose—to my purpose. I was wrong. I made the mistake old men often make; I assumed she lived in the same world I did." He glanced down at Mutt's gun. Mutt moved it away from the old man's head. "I know we have to stop her, but it hurts my heart to do it. We will never have a better chance than now to make our stand, to save our way of life, our future." Mutt holstered his gun.

"I know," the deputy said, "but there's never been a war that ended clean. Everyone gets bloody, compromised, diminished. We've already had so much of what we were torn away. So much, for so long. I'm not sure how much of us would be left after. That's not even an option anymore. This is no longer about us or them winning. It's about all of us surviving."

"'Us,' 'we,'" Wodziwob said with a thin smile on his weathered face.

Mutt shrugged. "Don't git your hopes up," he said. "So, any ideas how we stop her?"

"I'll head for a camp in Crescent Valley," Wodziwob said. "Many of the *numa* are headed there to stay out of the way of the cavalry and Izusa's and Snake-Man's forces."

"I heard about that place on the way to find Izusa," Mutt said.

"Lots of people there. It occurs to me I should try to organize a different dance. Perhaps the warring dead are scheming. Perhaps calling out to other spirits might balance them," he said. Wodziwob picked up a smooth rock and removed a perfect black feather that had been resting under the stone. "Many of our people don't see war as the way to endure. I may be able to focus their energy, their spirit, to try to placate the dead, to soothe the *Uktena* to sleep. Perhaps to give the future some small hope." He regarded the feather and returned it back to the metal box he had originally taken it from. "I'll do what I can."

They were both silent and still for a moment. Mutt knelt to look into his still-strong eyes. "End of it all," he said, "that's all any of us can do."

———

Mutt rode out of the Black Feathers' nearly deserted camp, already hearing shouts from Wodziwob's right-hand man, Mahkah, to begin preparations to depart quickly. He thought of how Maude's lips had felt, how her hair smelled, the weight of her body, the way her skin felt, her smile, her voice. He trusted she was alive and fighting, probably in the thick of the fighting. He missed her, and her memory gave him the power to push past exhaustion, to ignore his aching wounds.

It was a long, hard ride back to Golgotha, and he had to get there fast. He stroked Muha's ear and petted his loyal horse. "Come on, my friend," he said to Muha, "let's go home." They galloped off into the wastes, thoughts of the woman he loved willing him to go faster.

THE ACE OF SWORDS (REVERSED)

T he dead rode into Golgotha, blood-curdling war cries upon their frozen lips. Izusa, her face masked in mud, led them. They came in from the east, from the 40-Mile, but once within sight of the town, Izusa ordered them to split. Three forces would surround the town, approaching from the east, north, and south. Argent Mountain would act as a wall to pin any opponents against and to slow the escape of anyone trying to flee.

Izusa had to admit it was better to be alone among the dead. Even among her own people, among her most ardent supporters, they raised doubts, hesitated when she told them of her plans for the *Uktena*, for remaking the world. The best thought her...unwise; the worst feared their own death. She had no use for either. But the braves she led now, they had proven themselves already, had faced the test of dying well and moved beyond it. They fought for the future of those they had left behind on the other side, for the righting of old wrongs. The spear felt good in her hand, and she had placed many charms upon it to aide her in battle. Even now, Snake-Man was falling upon Carson City with his warriors. Today, the world would change forever, and they would get their home back.

The defensive lines of the town were each made up of roughly twenty men composed of the few troops Caxton had left at camp and the handful of desperate, yawning volunteers the deputies had been able to muster. Most of the eager civilian warriors had ridden off with Caxton a few days ago and were now most likely dead in the ambush. As the defenders watched, the war party split and headed into Golgotha by different directions. The cold realization settled over them that they were still outnumbered a good three-to-one and that their attackers were ghosts, not flesh-and-blood enemies.

Corporal Owen Anderson wondered again, as he heard the blood-curdling cries of the angry Indian dead coming closer, how the hell he had ended up in charge of this line. He had been sick as a dog and left back at camp when the troop took off a few days ago. Now, still very ill, he was manning a post and giving orders and encouragement to his fellow soldiers and the terrified civilians armed with everything from old muskets to bows and arrows. "Hold until I tell you to fire," he shouted, keeping his own doubts and fears out of his booming voice. *Join the fucking army, see the fucking country...*

There was a commotion behind the line. A handful of Pinkerton's men, a few more troopers and the lady deputy, Kate Warne, rode up with the damnedest looking rifles he'd ever seen. "What the hell are those?" Owen asked. "Lightning rods?"

"New weaponry," one of the Pinkerton men said. "Fresh from Washington."

Kate looked over to the others armed with the same weapon she now carried on her back. "Special unit, activate the accumulators. Watch your gauges and prepare to fire on my command!"

"Well, hot damn!" Owen shouted. "Boys, I don't have a fucking clue what those things are, but I just got powerful excited! Stand your ground, lads!" There was mumbling along the line as the transparent enemy charged ever closer.

On the balcony of his office in the Paradise Falls, Malachi Bick felt the weight of his compulsion to remain inactive lift off of him. He saw the approaching army, saw them splitting, and knew he had less than moment to do something before the battle was joined.

He sensed the belief of the young woman leading the ghosts, sensed the earnest desire of the dead, and found no evil within them or their cause, only the angry fire of hatred that comes from fear, pain, and misunderstanding. He sensed the equally earnest prayers of the huddled townsfolk, hiding, clutching their children, begging their silent god to spare them, to save them. The frightened prayers of the men protecting the town were wrapped in the same hatred for the enemy as the enemies' own.

The dark angel nearly wept. This was the saddest part of the human drama, how much blood was shed, how many innocent lives destroyed in a crucible of churning, unreasoning fear. One ugly, unthinking event tumbling into another and another. How do you convince one hand not to break the other when neither perceives the whole of the body they are attached to? Bick, Biqa, suddenly understood why perhaps God was so often mute, so often seemed impotent. Sometimes, there simply was no good answer, no good solution, no right, only wrong. God can't cure what ills man; only man can do that.

There were a few bright, lonely sparks in the darkness. Prayers for mercy for all, wishes and hopes for no deaths on either side, for understanding, for forgiveness, for peace. In these few, brilliant, orphan motes, Biqa remembered why humans were worth fighting for, worth never giving up on.

Bick felt the Darkling's roar behind him, deep in the living rock of Argent. He remembered his commission and turned his back on the war for Golgotha—the eternal struggle of man's nature—and entered the fray in the battle to preserve all life from the hungry darkness.

J im saw the southern spur of the war party cutting across the desert road onto Main, plumes of black smoke behind them. The smoke was most likely Sarah Pratt's farm or one of her neighbors'. Jim hoped the riders had given the outlying farms enough warning to prepare. "Here they come," Jim called out. "Test the silver rounds, see if they do anything. If not, then fall back and use the rock salt in the shotguns. We need to try to keep as many as we can from getting into the town!" Jim glanced over to Pinkerton. "Your men ready to fire those...whatever they are?"

The spymaster nodded, chewing on the end of a cold cigar. "Aye. I guess we'll see if Edison was worth all the money we paid him." The braves were closer, detail coming into view in the morning light. They were of many tribes, painted and dressed for war. The ones with rifles and bows opened fire. Those with blades and tomahawks howled out their war cries and spurred their horses forward.

Jim saw one of the locals, Fassbinder Tate, turn and run back in the direction of town at the shrieks of the ghost warriors as bullets began to whine and snap all around the line. Several other men began to look back toward the safety of the town's interior. A gunshot thundered down the street, and Tate's neck exploded. He fell dead, his blood soaking into the earth.

"Next one of you I see acting the coward in this glorious moment of divine service to your fellow man," Porter Rockwell said, his short-barreled revolver smoking, "will get the same." A ghost bullet passed through the shoulder of his coat, but the Mormon gunslinger didn't seem to even notice the near-miss. "The Lamanite enemy is in front of you, not at your back. Today, we will sing together in the tabernacles of Heaven! For the glory of the Lord, fight, damn you!" The other men and troopers held their ground, more afraid of Rockwell than the ghosts as gunfire rained about them.

Jim looked over to Constance. She was focusing on him. He wanted to kiss her and tell her things he might not get a chance to later, but instead he remained silent and held aloft the Jade eye. He breathed and tried to clear his mind while he began to hear men getting hit by the ghost's attacks.

"Special unit, fire!" Pinkerton called out as he raised his own odd rifle, took aim, and fired. The handful of troopers and Pinkerton men with him did the same. The guns made a hissing sound as the lightning-rod-like barrels glowed with dancing blue fire. There was an angry crack like thunder that spooked the horses, as the barrels launched what looked like curving, undulating lightning at the front line of ghostly braves.

"A glorious miracle," Rockwell muttered, grinning as men died around him. "God is with us today against the Lamanites' witchcraft." The blasts hit several of the spirits, and each one hit screamed in pain as it seemed to be ripped apart into glowing motes by the beam. The motes faded into darkness, nothing remaining of the destroyed spirits.

The now-angry braves were almost on top of the line, and the fire intensified. Several of the men with the special rifles were hit and killed, falling from their horses. Men of the line also screamed and died under the wave of Indian fire. Constance spun the rifle in her hands about and blocked a bullet headed for Jim's face. Jim blinked at how quickly she had reacted.

"Th...thanks!" Jim said.

"Keep your head down. You need that," Constance said, as she swung the rifle around and aimed at the braves. She fired and also discharged a parlor gun that she seemed to have summoned from nowhere with her other hand.

Jim fired into the ghost warriors' swarming ranks, as did the other defenders, but silver seemed to do nothing. "Shotguns!" Jim called out, holstering his pa's pistol and drawing the scatter gun. "Fire, fire! Give us some room!"

The line of shotguns boomed, and part of the wave of spirits evaporated in the widening cloud of speeding rock salt. Pinkerton and his two surviving special unit men checked the gauges on the sides of their lightning rifles and fired again. A few more of the ghosts were seemingly shredded into nothingness by the bolts of man-made lightning. The other warriors, unmolested, kept coming, killing defenders as they pressed to break through the line.

A t Prosperity and Dry Well, Rabb and his small group of defenders were engaged with the northern spur of the invasion. The Pinkerton men with the effective but slow lightning guns had done some damage to the spirits, but the agents were all dead now, having become a focus of fire. A line defender had grabbed one of the complex guns from its dead user and had managed to get off a few more shots with it before it exploded, killing him and raining fire everywhere.

They were using the only thing that seemed to work now—rock salt rounds—which were only delaying the inevitable. They were going to be overrun. Already, flaming arrows tipped with pitch were sailing overhead, setting fire to several small homes and shops. Rabb tried to summon his power, but his concentration was smothered under a mantle of injuries and exhaustion. The rocks and wind were silent to him. He looked at his handful of surviving men and made a decision.

Rabb sprinted to the body of another of the dead Pinkerton men and hefted up the strange weapon. There were gauges on the side of the rifle; they both were currently in the black. "Cease fire," he shouted, "but be ready to fire on my command. Fall back to me!"

The defenders obeyed, scrambling back as the rapidly re-forming ghosts galloped forward, pressing the retreating defenders. He leveled the lightning rifle and looked at the tense, frightened faces of his men. "When I say, all of you give them both barrels, point blank, and then duck." The ghost warriors charged ahead, firing more flaming arrows as they came. Rabb looked down at the gauge on the gun; it remained in the black.

The line of braves was twenty-five yards away now, twenty, ten.

"Fire!" Rabb shouted. The shotguns roared as the cloud of rock salt enveloped the first two lines of the advancing ghosts. Rabb fired the lightning gun and held the trigger down as the blue bolt struck the expanding cloud of salt. The crackling cloud caught the first two lines fully and vaporized a good deal of the third line as well before the sizzling remains of the cloud exploded with a whoosh. Hot stinging rock salt fragments burned down like some punishing biblical rain, scarring Rabb and his men, but over half the advancing ghost braves were destroyed. The others circled about, trying to regroup, obviously surprised by Rabb's maneuver. The defenders cheered.

"Set up a new line here," Rabb said, hurling the sparking and sputtering gun and backpack toward the remaining ghosts. The pack tore itself apart in an explosion with a thunderous boom. "You and you, go get some civilians out here to fight the fires while we have a second to breathe. Rest of you, reload and get ready for more of the same."

A civilian rider, an arrow in his side, galloped up to Rabb. "Deputy! If you can spare any men, we're losing the eastern and the southern lines!"

———

Constance was a maelstrom. She tumbled and flipped, knocking aside arrows and tomahawks that were pouring down on Jim. She already had a bullet in her leg and side. She tumbled near a fallen trooper, grabbed his shotgun, and fired it, dispelling a group of advancing spirit warriors. "Jim, are you alright?"

Most of the southern defensive line was dead or wounded. The survivors had been forced to fall back up Main Street nearly to Shultz's General Store, which now burned, as did Professor Mephisto's Playhouse. Pinkerton, alone, still manned a lightning gun, and sniped at the diminished but still formidable war party from behind the cover of a burning hitching post.

"I...I can't get this thing to work," Jim said. "The eye, it's not..." Constance dropped down next to him. "You're hurt!" he said.

"It's fine," she said. She was trying to push the pain to the back of her mind like mother had taught her, but it kept seeping back into her awareness. She hurriedly loaded two shotguns with the last of the rock salt. "Jim, you told me that you have been learning how to relax, to focus to use the eye. You have to do that now."

"I'm trying," he said as another round buzzed past him. "I keep worrying about what happens if I can't. What happens to Lottie?"

"Jim?" Constance took his hand.

"Leeza," Jim said. "Leeza...and you." Jim leaned forward to Constance and kissed her. She kissed him back but only for a second and then gently pulled away.

"Try," she whispered. "Your try is better than most folk's do. You try, Jim Negrey." She stood and snapped the breaches shut on both scatter guns with the flick of her wrists. "I'm going to buy you a little more time." She stood and charged the galloping lines of the war party. Tumbling, bounding back up and to the side, she dropped in between the riders in the advance and fired one chamber from each shotgun into them; they scattered and vanished to reform elsewhere. She headed into the next rank, staying low, avoiding arrows and bullets as if she were a ghost herself, only to reload, reappear, and fire the guns again.

Jim looked at the jade eye, and it looked back at him. "Okay, come on," Jim said. He closed his eyes, became mindful of his breathing, and reached out, reached inside the icy cold orb, his perceptions passing through a door, swinging it wide. A bullet struck less than a foot from him, and Jim remained calm, kept his eyes closed. He reached out further and further until he felt the presence of the spirits and of the woman guiding them.

He was seeing through the eye now, navigating cold corridors of power and will. Rabb arriving from the holding northern line, and Izusa sensed Jim too.

"The boy," the Goshute shaman said, "the *Ulun'suti*." She spun her horse and brought it to a full gallop, heading toward Jim and the eye. Rabb stood, despite the gun and arrow fire. He sprinted to get a clean shot at Izusa as she rode off, leaving her ghost troops to continue their destructive advance. He fired round after round from the six-gun at her, but he could sense the bullets veering, sliding off the slippery mantle of a protective charm. Rabb pushed his will into his final bullet, and it struck true, hitting Izusa in the side. A second later, he caught a bullet in his side as well and stumbled back to cover, fighting to say conscious. Izusa groaned and coughed up blood but stayed upright in the saddle and headed for Jim.

The eastern defensive line fell. The ghost warriors spilled over the bodies of the dead guardians. The survivors fell back, firing their last rock salt rounds to buy them precious moments to seek cover. Kate, one of the lightning gun packs slung over her shoulder, two bullets and a tomahawk in her, kept firing, covering her men as they fell back. The trick was quick shots with the gun, then give it a second to cool down. It was slower than an old whore in a tub of molasses, but it got rid of the spirits permanently.

"Deputy!" Corporal Anderson called out, as he dragged two wounded soldiers out of harm's way. "What is that?"

Kate saw something dark moving out among the ghost braves. She heard their spectral horses scream and saw the rear lines turn to face something from behind. The braves cried out as well, as loudly, as madly as their horses. What could make ice-cold undead warriors scream? The black shape darted about quickly, almost flying from warrior to warrior. Kate caught a glimpse of pale skin and raven hair. It was Shelly; at least, she thought it was. Shelly seemed to be slashing the immaterial braves with her bare hands, dissipating them.

Then, great ugly birds, crooked beaks black with blood, swooped down and tore into the ghosts, rending them, wounding them as if they were flesh and blood. "Goddamned vultures?" Anderson said, watching as the black-cloaked woman and the birds tore into the remains of the advancing raiders.

Kate fired into the stragglers that Shelly and the birds were missing. It looked as if Shelly was crouching by the fallen dead, hiding them behind her wing-like cloak and...pecking something from their rapidly fading bodies. "Clay's got a girl weirder than he is," Kate muttered. She sighed and let some of the tension slip from her body.

For his part, Corporal Owen Anderson was thankful his chapter in this war was over, but he wondered what exactly had heard his and his troop's prayers and what things had it sent to answer them.

I n the field, feasting on the dead, Shelly could feel, sense the closing convergences of knotting destiny, like the tangle of unseen magnetic winds that flights of birds followed and that she could now perceive as they did. All the nightmares were coming true, all the endings were being locked into place. She could no more change it, undo it, than she could change the face of the moon.

Her sisters gurgled and croaked all around her as they fed on what would not be their last meal today. The darkening sky rumbled. Shelly could sense the storm building, sensed it was not natural in its coming. The human part of Shelly cried for her friends, her family, her town. The cold, taut part of her tasted the ashes of the spirits' souls and hungered for fresher meat.

THE ACE OF SWORDS

olgotha was on fire. Townsfolk were on the streets now, braving attacks to try to keep the whole town from going up like a tinderbox. Bucket lines were formed near the well pump. Others led frightened and confused crowds to anyplace that wasn't on fire or under attack. The ghosts rode down Prosperity Street and began to burn buildings on the north end of Main. Some townsfolk opened their windows and fired down on the braves, but their bullets did nothing, passing through them as if they were made of a hot, angry, desert wind. The Methodist church and Mormon meeting hall were devoured by flame.

Pinkerton kept firing the lightning gun, but the capacitor had been damaged by a gunshot. He was lucky it damn well didn't blow up on him. The recharge between shots was taking longer and longer, and the needle took seemingly forever to climb back to the green. Pinkerton had lost sight of Jim Negrey and the young Stapleton girl. He had no idea where that Mormon maniac, Rockwell, had gotten to, either.

The remaining defenders were falling back as they fired their last few precious rounds of rock salt. The braves spotted where he was pinned down and concentrated their fire. He already had taken an arrow and a gunshot wound. They were coming for him. Pinkerton wasn't afraid. Dying for a cause he believed in, dying defending his homeland, that was a fine end. He'd face it proudly.

His regrets were all of a personal nature. Things undone, things unsaid. He knew himself well enough to know he was never built for bouts of emotion. He was a cause-and-effect man. He believed in facts and the power of them. Fact's enemy was emotion. It led to sloppy intelligence, sloppy conclusions, and sloppy lives.

Now, at the end of things, as the experimental weapon built for him by that arrogant self-promoter, Edison, sputtered and then died, the needle dropping from the edge of green to the base of the gauge, Allan Pinkerton wished that perhaps he had allowed a little more emotion into his life. Pinkerton thought of Kate, then of his wife and children, and then he made his peace with his Lord.

Jim Negrey stepped beside the spymaster, the strange Chinese jade eye in his hand. A green light swarmed around the orb and Jim's whole body.

"Please," Jim said, in a voice not entirely his own, "stop. Go back." The spirit warriors stopped their attacks. They all looked at Jim, anger in their eyes.

"You have no right to stop us," one of the ghostly braves said. "Especially with medicine you stole. You are a thief, from a tribe of thieves."

Jim's head ached. He was the window the eye's cold power burned through. "This was given to my father by the people who guarded it. It was stolen from evil men who took his life. I took it back from them. I ain't no thief. I can't allow you to kill innocent people who never did you no harm. Please, go back to the other side. Please."

The warrior raised his pistol with a struggling hand. Jim felt him resisting the eye's command. Jim could see all the lines of power, of will, interconnecting the ghosts to each other and to far away people, living and dead, to holy places, to men and women, dancing. Jim wasn't fighting angry ghosts; he was fighting a whole race's cry for justice.

The young deputy fell to his knees, trying to let the eye's near-limitless power pour through him. It was getting hard to remember who he was, where he came from. His mind saw his sister, Lottie, his mom, then little Leeza. Leeza shifted, changed from huddling in terror as the fort was destroyed around her to transform into a little Goshute girl, not much older than Leeza was now, than Lottie had been last time Jim had seen her. The girl was hiding in tall grass, sobbing, her soul bleeding out of her as she saw her grandmother, her mother, her father, and her brothers cut down by the swords and the guns of the federal soldiers. Everything burned; everything died.

A hand clamped onto Jim's wrist. His eyes snapped open. It was the same little Goshute girl, but now she was a woman, with a face and body covered in dried mud and a rabbit fur cloak. She sank her nails into Jim's skin, trying to force him to release his grip on the glowing eye.

"This belongs to my people! To me!" Izusa said. Jim had never gone this far outside himself before. He couldn't be sure if the shaman was really grappling with him on the street or if they were both some-where between the land of the living and the dead. He glanced up to a clear, blue sky filled with an enormous moon, so large and so close he could see great palaces upon it, built into the sides of the craters. Jim held on though the eye's cold was burning him and Izusa's clawing made his flesh burn. His hand began to open.

Izusa gasped, and her grip on him was gone. Jim blinked. The moon was no longer filling the sky. He looked down at his wrist. It was clawed and bleeding. Izusa was on her back behind the unmoving ghost warriors. She groaned and slowly climbed to her feet. Constance had knocked her back, several feet away from Jim.

"You leave him alone," Constance said, glancing over to Jim for a second. She had launched from her mount to strike Izusa and knocked her to the street again.

"You have no idea what you've done," Izusa said, getting up again, the gunshot wound in her side covering half the rabbit fur cloak in fresh blood, "but you will." She hurled a handful of street dirt into Constance's eyes as she spit out a hex with a hiss. Constance stumbled backward, trying to clear her eyes of the blinding, stinging grit. Izusa lunged at Constance with a knife and was shocked when the blinded girl deflected the arm wielding the blade to one side and drove the heel of her palm cleanly into Izusa's chin, sending the shaman sprawling back onto the ground. Izusa lay unconscious.

Jim fought to hold all the ghosts in town still. He was losing the fight. A trumpet sounded off in the desert, a call to charge. At first Jim thought he might be hallucinating again, but then he saw Jon Highfather riding at the head of a column of federal troopers. Jon rode through the frozen, struggling ghost warriors, blasting rock salt from his shotgun as he thundered past. The troops behind him followed suit, raising a loud whoop and holler of their own as they rode through, heading up Main Street, blasting as they went. The ghostly braves were dispersed by the salt clouds temporarily. Highfather reined Bright back in front of Jim and Pinkerton, coming to a halt.

"I sure am glad to see you," Jim said. Highfather, pale, sweating, and covered in days of dirt and dried blood, mustered a smile.

"Glad to see you, too, Jim," Jon said. He looked over to Pinkerton, who was shrugging off the dead weapon and its pack as he struggled to stand. "It's even good to see you."

"Where's Caxton?" Pinkerton asked.

"Took the other men in by Old Stone Road," Jon said. "We managed to link up with a long patrol from Fort Churchill. They sent scouts to warn the capital and sent an extra thirty men with us." Highfather looked around at the smoke, the fires, the bodies in the street. "Where's Kate?"

"On the eastern line, near the foot of Rose Hill. We had word they got overrun, but I haven't been able to send them much help till now."

"Let's go," Jon said, reloading his shotgun. He tossed it to Pinkerton and drew another from a saddle sheath. "Jim, you and Constance coming? Jim?"

Jim had run to Constance, and she was holding onto his shoulder and shirt now.

"You okay? She didn't hurt you, did she?" Jim looked over to where Izusa had been lying prone. The Goshute medicine woman was gone.

"No, she didn't lay a finger on me," Constance said, her eyes as beautiful as when Jim had first seen them. "But I'm blind, Jim. I don't know how, but I can't see a thing."

R abb and Kate had met up and reconstituted their surviving forces in the open space between the Baptist church and Town Hall when Caxton's force, trumpet calling, came up behind the raiders and hit them with rock salt.

"General," Kate said. "Thank you."

"It won't hold the devils for long," Caxton said. "They'll be charging back in any moment now." Through the smoke, the town's defenders could see the braves already riding back in from the desert. "Prepare to fire again," he called out to his troops.

"Wait," Rabb said. "Something's coming. I can feel them."

There was a sound that rolled out from the wastes and fell upon the burning town. It was a chorus of howls rising and falling in pitch, punctuated with abrupt bursts of yips and yaps. Coyotes, big, small, red, black, gray, even golden, charged the spirit warrior's advance, sending the vultures nearby scattering, flying into the air. The coyotes jumped, barking, ducking, and running between the horses' legs. The spirit mounts reacted to the pack as living horses would, bucking and stumbling. The braves tossed from their mounts were attacked by several of the coyotes as they fell to the desert floor, their throats ripped and torn savagely.

"What the blazes are those scavengers doing?" Caxton said, watching in surprise alongside Kate and Rabb. "How are they able to even touch those damned haunts, let alone hurt them?"

"I don't know, exactly," Rabb said, "but I suggest not firing on them. I think someone sent them to help." There was another sound that echoed across the desert.

In a very short time, the remaining ghostly warriors attacking Golgotha were either torn apart by the coyote pack or had ridden off into the desert to melt into the horizon.

It took longer to get the fires under control. Some were still burning by the time night finally wrapped her sable cloak around the town. There were no celebrations; too much, too many had been lost. A heavy rainstorm rolled in with the night and helped the citizenry defeat the last of the fires.

Jon Highfather held his head skyward and let the storm kiss him. Kate saw how exhausted he was and how badly he needed to see Dr. Turlough. There simply hadn't been time. There was still no word from Mutt or from the rescue party up on Argent.

Jon rode over to her. "You look tired," he said. She laughed.

"I'll manage. You want to get some sleep or go see Caxton's physician over at the Imperial? Rabb, Jim, and I can handle it."

"All of you are as banged up as me," Jon said. "And I'm allergic to Army sawbones. No, with Izusa and Snake-Man still out there somewhere, sleep will keep."

"Caxton's mad as a hornet," she said. "Swears he's going to hunt them both down."

"They made him look stupid," Jon said. "It's his pride. He doesn't have much of an army left to do anything about it right this second, but that will change. We hear anything from Carson City?"

"We got a telegram through before the lines got cut, and those scouts you ran into on your way back here alerted Fort Churchill," she said. "Caxton had a rider report in to him while and you Rabb were dealing with the fire at City Hall.

"The rider said they were able to repel the attack. It was all flesh-and-blood Indians, close to four hundred, no ghosts."

"Well, it's good to know they can't just summon up as many ghosts as they need," Jon said. "They have limits. I'm betting Izusa wanted as many of the dead with her on this raid as she could gather."

"There's more where they came from," Kate said, "I'm sure. Snake-Man was sighted in Carson City, but he didn't fully engage, personally. He got away in the rout. His men fought a hell of a holding action for him before they retreated and then scattered."

"The army's going to be cracking down on Indian settlements all over the state," Jon said, the rain dripping off the brim of his hat in a stream. "This is exactly what Izusa and Snake-Man want. Caxton will have more troops here in a day or two and start hunting again."

Highfather winced.

"Will you at least get out the rain before you catch your death like President Harrison did?" Highfather laughed, and Kate caught some strange association, some connection move behind his weary eyes.

"After the last few days," Jon said, "I need this rain. I'll take my chances." He began to head slowly up Main. They passed the still-smoking, charred skeletons of buildings. Kate rode along beside him. "Besides, no one's put down a salt circle for the last few days, and I need to tend that grave before we have much bigger problems."

"Jim tended it," Kate said. "He always does when you're away."

"Boy's after my job. He okay? He was banged up pretty bad, too, and I know he was upset by what happened to Constance. It looked like he was having a harder time with it than she was."

"Tough girl. Considering her mother," Kate said, "that's not surprising." Jon looked over to her. "Don't tell Maude I said that."

"Your secret's safe," Jon said.

"Jim took Constance home," Kate said. "He said to come fetch him if we needed him. He's staying with her until Maude's back."

"Any word from Rabb up on Argent? Has he found Maude and the others?"

"Nothing yet," Kate said. "There was some kind of explosion up there just before the war party rode in." She looked around at the destruction. "What a mess."

"You all did a hell of a job, Kate," Jon said. "I'm proud of all of you." Jon looked at her. "I'm glad you're okay, Kate."

"I'm glad you are too," she said.

"Come on, let's go see if we can give Rabb a hand up there."

"Jon, you've been going non-stop for three or four days. You need to rest before you fall off your horse."

Highfather looked over to the boards of the sidewalk where the bodies of soldiers and townsfolk were laid out, uncovered, in the rain. There had been no time to transport the dead in the middle of fighting the fires.

For a moment, Jon was back at Gettysburg, in the aftermath—vast seas of bodies, twisted, hewn, and left where they fell. Over forty thousand dead, the number split eerily close on both sides. The concept of "victory" in the wake of such slaughter still made Highfather ill. There were nights when in his dreams, he experienced every single death, himself.

"When everyone's home," Highfather said, "safe and sound, then I'll rest." He headed up Argent, slumped in his saddle as the downpour continued. Kate watched him for a moment as he began to ascend the mountain road. Jon Highfather carried a burden on him that no man could long bear, it seemed. She wished she fully understood it, understood him. It had driven him to awful places, driven him to the crumbling edge of sanity, but he had managed to pull himself back from his self-imposed hell. Kate watched the sheriff begin to vanish behind the curtain of the pouring rain and then followed him up the mountain.

THE FIVE OF WANDS

Brogan didn't mind working in the rain. In fact, on this job, he preferred it. Rain destroyed tracks, it obscured faces, and rain washed away blood. It was the Lord's way of helping out the murderer, and Brogan was much obliged.

His men were a different matter altogether. They had been bitching and moaning about the downpour since they had ridden out of the mining camp up on Argent around sundown.

"Goddamn it!" Clearland Pope exclaimed. "It's pissing on us! I can't see three feet ahead o' me!"

"We ought to get paid extra for this shit," Gavin Mooney said. The short brim on his felt derby was keeping most of the storm off his face, but the brim was beginning to flop a bit from acting as a gutter of sorts for the constant stream of rain across it. "And they sure as fuck owe me a new hat, I tell you."

"I'll buy you one with my cut," John Spence grumbled, "if you will just shut the hell up."

"All of you shut up," Brogan said. "We're close, and the rain does strange things to noise. I don't want this dirt farmer getting any notion we're coming 'till we're kicking in his door." They rode on in silence for a few moments, only the storm making a sound.

"I'll take care of the kids," Pope said. "I ain't squeamish 'bout killing kids." Brogan lowered his head and for the hundredth time fought the urge to put a bullet in the back of Pope's head. He wanted a cigarette bad, but it wasn't possible in this weather.

"You stay away from the children," Brogan muttered. "This is work, not an exercise for you to get your degenerate jollies. I'm a businessman, not a goddamn pervert." Pope was sullen but silent.

Brogan usually liked to know the men he worked with, liked to pick them himself when he was running the job, but this was a rush, and the client had to work with whatever was laying around Golgotha. That meant dealing with crazy, sick bastards like Pope. The other two were solid men. Brogan had worked a range war with John Spence, and knew he was reliable and not prone to getting alloverish about dirty work.

He met the client's representative yesterday afternoon in the lobby of the Imperial hotel. To Brogan's surprise, the contact was a lady of means, beautiful with honey-blond hair, dressed fancy. She gave him an envelope of cash and told him what needed doing and how it needed to be done. She also told him where he could find Pope, Spence, and Mooney. She told him the job needed to be done soon. Brogan could sense the heat of anger coming off of this lady who lived in a fine mansion on Rose Hill, saw the glint of it in her eyes. This was a clean-up job. Someone had failed to act or had fucked things up good and proper for this lady and for the client she represented in Virginia City.

Brogan rode back up Argent, located his men, and gave them a taste of the money. The Indian attacks on the town came the following dawn. The ghosts of Indian braves were pouring into the town. It was a perfect example of why Brogan tried to avoid work in Golgotha. The place was fucking cursed and the people, fucking crazy.

He spent much of the day, along with many others, up on Argent watching the battle unfold, watching the town begin to burn. There had been some kind of an explosion or cave-in at the mine that morning, and the camp's occupants were divided among those helping out at the mines, those who grabbed a rifle or pistol and headed down the hill to help defend the town, and those who kept their powder dry and waited for any indication of an Indian attack up on Argent.

By evening, it was clear that the Indian ghosts had been repelled, but the cost was great. Brogan had worked out the particulars of his scheme and went and gathered his men. He found Spence playing and losing cards at the Halla Damhsa. Pope and Mooney, he found holed up with public girls from the camp. "Hitch up your britches, and put your peckers away," he told them. "It's time to go to work."

B acktrail Road was more like a creek now. The storm howled in anger. Lightning flashed, dancing across the desert sky. They had passed several farms and ranches before finding the washed-out, muddy road that led up to the Winterton Farm. The buttery light spilling through the farmhouse's windows appeared for a moment through the sheets of rain.

Brogan raised a hand for the men to stop. "Okay, just like I told you. No freelancing, no fucking around. Spence, you got the door." Spence, a freed slave who had come out west to work on the railroad, nodded. He slid the double-barreled shotgun out of its saddle sheath. It was loaded with solid slugs, more than capable of killing the farmer right through his door, once he heeded the knock.

"Pope, you stay in the yard. Anyone gets out, you kill them," Brogan said. Pope was obviously unhappy with his job. His long, rat-like face drooped even further.

"Mooney, you get to work on the barn. Light it up. Remember, all of you, this is supposed to look like an Injun attack. No survivors."

"Maybe we could scalp 'em," Pope offered. "Make it look more realistic."

"Shut up and do your job," Brogan said, "or I'll kill you myself. Come on." They headed farther up the road when Brogan curtly ordered another halt. There was an unmoving shadow in the middle of the road, a lone figure blocking their way.

"Who's there?" Brogan said, drawing his pistol. The others followed suit. "Who is that?" The lightning danced between the clouds, and for a second, the shadow was illuminated. It was a man, good-looking, his long hair plastered to his head, dripping. His handlebar mustache drooped in the pouring rain. His long coat and fine clothing were already drenched from his vigil on the road. The flash of the lightning seemed to be caught for a second longer, trapped in the silver blade of the sword he held at his side.

Harry Pratt said nothing. He moved like the lightning, grabbing at Brogan's horse's reins and using the leather bridal to swing upward and drive his knees into Brogan's side. The gunman grunted and was knocked from this saddle to fall with a splash onto the flooded road before he could even aim at Harry. "Kill the son of a bitch!" he sputtered, spitting muddy water out of his mouth and fumbling for his pistol.

Harry swung off the horse from the opposite side, blocking Spence's and Mooney's line of fire. Pope was bringing his pistol down to fire straight at Harry's skull, when the mayor flashed out with the Blade of Laban and sliced the metal ring of the rear rigging dee clean off without even nicking the skirt under the saddle or the horse's flesh. With his free hand, Harry swatted the horse's flank hard, and the horse began to gallop, speeding away, just as Pope opened fire. The bullets whined and bounced around Harry but missed him cleanly. The saddle, its flank cinch cut loose, slid off the horse's back and Pope with it, sending the killer crashing hard to the ground.

Harry turned right into Mooney's shotgun. Mooney fired, and the blast picked Harry up off his feet and hurled him back into a water-filled ditch.

"Who the fuck was he?" Pope called out as he struggled back to his feet. His skull was cracked and bleeding. Brogan was back up now, too.

"Doesn't matter now, does it?" Mooney said. "Let's get back to..." A dark form launched itself out of the rain with feral snarl that sounded more like a wild cat than a person. Black Rowan landed behind Mooney on his saddle, grabbed his head with both hands, and violently twisted, snapping his neck. Spence fired on her, but Rowan used the dead Mooney's body as a shield. She hurled a knife at Spence, but it missed its mark in the darkness and the fury of the storm.

Pope aimed his gun at the mysterious woman's back. "I'm sick of this shit," he said and squeezed the trigger. Harry ran him through from behind with his blade. Pope's round whined off into the darkness. The late Pope slid to the ground. Harry stood about twenty yards from Brogan, both bathed in the sky's fire for a moment. Blood ran down the side of Harry's face.

"How the hell are you still alive?" Brogan said, firing again as Pratt charged him, limping. Another round struck the silent mayor and then another and another. Harry staggered a few feet from Brogan and fell again.

Rowan slid off Mooney's horse a few seconds before his body did. She scanned around for Spence and caught the sound of his boot splashing behind her in the water an instant before his pickax whistled down. Rowan side-stepped the pick and drove an elbow back into his shoulder. Spence followed up with a solid left to the back of her head that sent her skittering across the muddy road.

Brogan flipped Harry over to put a few more bullets in him. That was when he saw the breastplate Harry was wearing, gold with inlaid silver and brilliant jewels the size of a man's thumbnail, in a myriad of colors. The breastplate was unmarred by dent or scratch.

"Well," Brogan muttered, "I don't know where all this came from, your majesty, but I'll be taking this as compensation for the trouble you caused." Harry's eyes popped open as Brogan fired his final bullets into him. The magical blade sliced Brogan in two from below his right armpit, exiting where his neck and left shoulder met. The breastplate caught the bullets Brogan had fired, except one that blew a bloody hole in Harry's left shoulder. Brogan fell into two pieces, and Harry struggled to his feet, almost passing out from his throbbing, bleeding wound.

He saw Rowan and Spence dueling, circling. The pirate queen flashed out with strikes and kicks, connecting several times with the hired killer's jaw and gut. Spence refused to go down and continued to swing his pick from his old railroad days at Rowan's constantly tumbling, dodging form. Between the blow to her head and the slippery mud, Rowan stumbled, and Spence's pick struck true, slashing her back open. Rowen fell on her stomach, and Spence moved in to finish her off. As he stood over her ready to sink the pick into her, Rowan managed to do a handstand kick, driving both of her feet into Spence's throat, crushing his windpipe before she slipped and fell face-first again. The last of the hired killers dropped his pick, clutched at his throat, and then fell dead in the flowing water.

Rowan struggled back to her feet. Harry stood over Brogan's body, glaring at her. "Good," she said. "You got my message. When my girls told me what their customers were up to, I knew I had to get word to you." Pratt walked closer, staggering, almost falling a few times, but keeping on his feet. "I wanted to come out here to lend you a hand." Her foot moved under the pick handle that was lying at her feet. Harry moved closer.

"He's dead," Harry said, his voice a hoarse croak, words straining out through a sieve of pain.

"I know," she said. "I'm sorry."

"He died to save me. He died over this goddamned railroad, over politics. Politics!"

"Harry," Rowan said, her voice choking. Pratt couldn't tell if tears were streaming down her face or if it was merely the rain. "Harry, you don't understand. You don't know."

"I know he's dead, and it's because of Cooper, and you and me. We're all damned, Rowan. He's dead so we could all do 'business,' fucking business." He was only a few feet away now. "Goddamn you, and goddamn me too."

Harry lunged at her, the Sword of Laban practically glowing in the flash of Heaven's wrath. Rowan flipped Spence's pickax up off her foot and into her hand, just in time to parry Harry's sword. Harry pressed his attack. Rowan could see now that he had taken some of the scattergun shot not stopped by the breastplate in his thigh. It was throwing him off his fencing. She retreated as Harry swung again, wildly, and advanced on her. The pain and rage on his bloodied face made her heart ache more than it already did.

Rowan blocked his next blow with the ax, binding the blade in the crook of the pick. She took the momentary reprieve from Harry's advance to drive her knee into his wounded thigh and angle the pick handle downward to smash it into Harry's bleeding shoulder. Harry gasped in pain and fell. Rowan dropped on top of him, tossing away the ax and grabbing him by the collar of his sack coat.

"You're right, Harry," she said. "Goddamn me! He was my brother! He was my baby brother, and I used him to get to you! He didn't want to hurt you; he begged me to let you go, to find some other way to appease Cooper!" She was sobbing, driving her fists impotently against the breastplate. "And damn you for not just going along, like I thought you would, for not being a selfish bastard for once in your life!"

"I'm sorry," Harry muttered as his whole body heaved and shook. "Oh God, I'm so sorry."

Rowan slumped down onto Harry's chest. Harry put his arms around her, and they both wept and raged. The heavens wept and raged with them.

JUSTICE

aude's eyes clawed desperately for any scrap of light to amplify, to let her see, but buried in the earth, there was no light, nothing, only endless, dizzying darkness. She wasn't sure how long she had been unconscious. The silent clock of her body's rhythms, which she could normally read, was confused. Maude ran her hands along the smooth surface of the silver floor and could feel each tiny symbol scratched into the surface. There was space and air above her, so the chamber's ceiling had not completely collapsed.

Maude climbed to her feet just as there was a hiss and flare of red light and then a golden glow. Clay Turlough was kneeling, a drunkard's match sputtering in his hand. One of Clay's arms hung limply at his side, and his bald head was covered in cuts and blood. Clay lit a small lantern he pulled from his pack with his damaged arm. "Everyone still breathing?" Clay asked. Once the lantern was lit, he crushed out the match and gathered up the two small cannon-ball-like spheres he had removed from his pack, examining them for damage.

Gillian and Auggie were huddled together in a corner. Both were cut and bruised. Auggie was sheltering her under his arm.

"*Ja*," Auggie muttered, "alive. I'm not sure how."

"I am," Emily said, looking up at the creaking ceiling, rocks jammed into each other, keeping the whole from collapse, shakily balanced. "Someone...interceded."

"Praise the Lord," Auggie muttered.

"Something like that," Emily said.

"The entrance is sealed tight," Professor Mephisto said, running his hands over the wall of rock and debris. "Emily is right. It is a miracle we're still alive."

"Auggie Junior?" Gillian said. "Those men? What happened to them?"

"Over that pile of rocks," Maude said, already clambering halfway up the tall pile that bisected the room. She climbed up, working to reach the top of the obstruction.

Auggie turned to Professor Mephisto, while he helped Gillian to her feet. "Professor, the way my boy changed after they made him drink that concoction. He was floating...he made the chamber's ceiling collapse. How?"

"It's a form of possession. The creature locked away deep under us is using him, Augustus, using his blood tie to you to magically control his body and mind, like a puppet. You live only through the properties of the Wurm's blood, and that gives it a connection to the boy. It cannot free itself, yet, but it can act in the world and do unspeakable evil, through your son."

"What can we do?" Gillian asked.

"I had hoped we could stop the Sons of Typhon from giving the baby the blood," Mephisto said, grimly, "but now...now, there are only two options left to us." Mephisto and Auggie held each other's stare. "Both are...appalling."

"I see them!" Maude called from the top of the debris pile. The Sons of Typhon and the small, floating form of Augustus Shultz Jr. were gathered about a section of wall the infant was gesturing toward.

The rock crumbled to dust seemingly at the mere regard of the child. "They're trying to tunnel out, meet up with the shaft that brought us here, get to the surface," Maude said.

Maude reached for a poisoned hairpin and then paused. What was she going to do? Kill her best friend's baby? Her trained instincts screamed at her to do just that: *You are the Mother's sword. You exist to protect all of humanity, all the world. Do it!* Maude paused, hesitated. Gillian had lost one child years ago, and Maude knew how much it still haunted her.

The immortal evil that lived behind the baby's eyes now turned and smiled a drooling, black-oil-smile at Maude. He gestured toward the wall of debris she was perched on, and the chamber exploded. The carefully balanced ceiling slipped and tumbled down. Maude felt like she was in the blast wave of a pile of dynamite, but she also realized that, in a second, they would all be dead. She ran her hand along the ceiling as she was thrown across the chamber, focusing her every nerve on searching the crumbling map of the room's roof. She found what she was looking for and drove two of her fingers into the spot. The ceiling fell—hundreds of thousands of tons of rock slipping free of its delicate perch—and then it rumbled to a stop.

The dust drifted all around the tightening stone womb the rescue party found themselves sealed in. Everyone was crouched low. Only about three feet remained between the trembling roof and the silver floor. Maude held the entire ceiling, a good portion of the mountain, up with two fingers. She had found the precise balance point of all those thousands of shifting stones, massive rocks, and tiny pebbles. She began to move both hands quickly from spot to spot, adjusting to maintain the equilibrium.

"Maude?" Mephisto said, coughing from the dust.

"I...can...hold...it," Maude said, "but...not...for...long."

Auggie pushed with all his might against the rocks that had sealed the entrance. Emily joined him in his efforts. The rock shifted and creaked a tiny bit but nothing more. "Still blocked," Auggie said. Clay scooted over next to his friend and Bick's daughter. He placed one of the cannon-ball-like spheres at the base of the rocks that blocked the passage.

"This will clear it," Clay said, twisting a dial on the top of the sphere until a red cone directed at the rocks appeared on the dial. "I made these nitrocellulose mining charges based off the phenomena of the Monroe Effect and the work of the German engineer, Von Baader. They will direct the force of the explosive so that..."

"Clay," Auggie said leaning close to his friend. "You're a genius. I love you like my brother. Now, please shut up and do it."

"Thank...you," Maude grunted.

"It won't bring the ceiling down?" Emily asked. Clay shook his head, as he turned an outer dial and the orb began to tick.

"Shouldn't," Clay said, "if'n I place the charge just so, but I do think everyone wants to scooch back a-ways." Everyone did, coming to reside near Maude's trembling legs. The bomb blast was a muted thump with a flash of brilliant light, like the flash tray of a camera. The ceiling shifted suddenly, dust spilling down. Maude caught it, but it took her to one knee. Now less than two feet remained, but the chamber's entrance was clear.

"If this is the sort of thing that the sheriff and some of you are typically involved in around this town," Gillian said as she crawled toward the entrance, "in the future, feel free to leave me out." One by one, the party crawled free, back out to the tunnel that led back to the main shaft. Auggie paused long enough to pluck something from the debris on the floor. Only Maude remained, holding the roof until everyone was clear.

"Maude," Gillian called back to her friend, "we're clear. Can you get out?"

"We'll...see," Maude grunted. Maude bent lower, coiling like a spring. Every nerve, every muscle ached, far past the point of exhaustion. She honestly wasn't sure she could clear it. She thought of Constance, and of Mutt, and she commanded herself to make it happen. She launched herself as her fingers slipped from the balance point. The roof fell, and the whole mountain groaned and shuddered.

Maude fell into the entrance tunnel just as the chamber was sealed behind her under an unfathomable mass of stone. She lay on the floor of the passageway and exhaled deeply. Gillian helped her friend up.

"I've never...I'll never understand how you do what you do," Gillian said. "You amaze me." Maude looked up at Gillian's cut and bruised face, so full of care for Maude and worry for her child, the child Maude had considered killing only a few moments ago. Gillian had no special training, no mystical blood in her veins, just the old-fashioned kind. Few people could have gone through what she had tonight and remained so unchanged.

"You amaze me," Maude said. Everything she was had been pushed to their limit. She felt as weak as a kitten. She squeezed Gillian's hand and looked up into the gloom of the ascending passage. "Let's go get your boy back."

The party made their way to the tunnel that would lead them back to the central shaft and began to head up toward the surface, Clay's small, sturdy lamp showing them the way. Within a few moments, they found the hole that the baby had somehow blasted through the living rock. It too was now sealed under thousands of tons of earth, but boot tracks led away from the portal, heading up. Auggie held his wife as they walked past it. Gillian could see something going on behind her husband's eyes. He kept glancing over to Professor Mephisto.

"If they hit the camp, there's little chance we'll be able to find them," Maude said. "Especially if the Indian attack is underway. We have to keep them from getting out of the mine."

"They have a head start," Clay said, limping along. "And we're not exactly in the best shape for a trot."

"I am," Emily said. "I'm pretty sure I could go ahead and..."

"And what, young lady? Kill our son, *ja*?" Auggie said. Everyone stopped. "That is what we have all been dancing around, *ja*? Tracking down our child and killing him before he spreads death and destruction across the world."

"Sadly, yes," Mephisto said. "That's exactly what we're talking about, Auggie. I'm sorry."

"You said it's his blood tie to me, to the substance that restored me to life that gives this evil thing access to my son. What if that bond is severed? What if I die?" Gillian grabbed his arm tightly.

"No!" she said. "Augustus, we will find another way! There's always another way!" Auggie held her tight. He looked to Mephisto.

"Is there?" Auggie asked. The professor looked as lost as any soul Auggie had ever seen. Finally, he shook his head.

"Either you or your son must die to end this madness," he said. "There is no other way." Auggie looked from face to face.

"Then we all know who needs to die," he said, showing the athame he had picked up off the floor of the silver room. He looked down to Gillian. Tears streaked her dirty, bloodied face, still so beautiful, even in fear and grief and ruin, still so strong.

"You can't," she said sniffling. "You're a good Catholic. It's a mortal sin." Auggie's broad, cut, and filthy face broke into a wide smile, and he laughed. It echoed, booming down the corridor of night.

"My darling, I am already a dead man. I was given the blessing of extra time by you," he looked over to Clay, "and by Clay. My soul is safe. We both know you'd do the same thing to save our son." Gillian broke. She sobbed against his broad chest. Auggie lifted her chin and looked at her with the same kind eyes that had made her fall in love with him. He cupped her face, so small in his hands, and kissed her. He tasted her tears on his lips. It made Auggie think of spring.

They parted, and Auggie looked at his friends. He recalled what Shelly had said to him last night in the street, and he silently wished her happiness and peace. "My friends, you must be about stopping these monstrous men and recovering Auggie Junior. I'll deal...with what must be done. I promise you that. Find him, bring him to his mother safely, please."

"Auggie, Gillian," Maude said, her eyes red and wet, "I...I can do it. Make it painless, instant." Maude was fighting not to break down. She was exhausted beyond being able to control her tears, even if she wanted to. Gillian hugged her fiercely and kissed her cheek.

"Thank you, Maude," Auggie said, "but you must be there to deal with the Sons of Typhon. We both know what they will do once the tie is cut. You have always been a good friend to Gillian and to me. Save my son, and look after Gillian, please."

Maude had no words. She kissed Gillian and Auggie on the cheek, and turned to be on her way up the shaft, after the Sons. "Emily, you're with me. Professor?"

"Yes," Mephisto said, groaning a bit from his injuries. "More than ready for the challenge."

"Here," Clay said to Emily, handing her a second lantern and the second bomb he'd prepared. "Inner dial—the red arc points the direction of the blast. Outer dial is the timer—anything from about two to thirty seconds. Might need it with those bruisers. It's inert until you set the timer." Clay looked over to Gillian and Auggie and back to Emily. "I...don't think I can...keep up."

"Thank you," Emily said. She was wiping her eyes, but the tears returned. She stopped for a second by Auggie and Gillian. "Bless you," the daughter of the angel said, sniffling, and then hurried to follow Maude. Mephisto looked back at Auggie as the trio headed up in pursuit.

"You saved the world today, Auggie," Mephisto said.

"Just go save *my* world," Auggie said.

"I give you my oath," Mephisto said and limped away to catch up to Maude and Emily. Soon the three pursuers were gone, and the three old friends stood together in a circle of light.

"I'm sorry I got you all into this, Auggie," Clay said, his voice cracking, his scrawny frame fighting not to begin shuddering in sobs. "You're the best friend a man could ever hope for, and I...messed it all up." Auggie looked to Gillian and then embraced the scientist in a bear hug, and Clay began to cry.

"Shhhh, you old buzzard," Auggie said, patting Clay's back. "You two gave me more time than I would have had. You gave Gerta a new life, and you love her, Clay. You're a good man and a good friend."

"I'll do it," Clay said. "I ain't Maude Stapleton, but I know the quickest, most painless place to..." He swallowed and sniffed. His face was red and his eyes bloodshot with tears. "I'll do it."

"Clay, do you have any drugs you could give him?" Gillian asked, refusing to let Auggie go.

"I did, but they all broke in my bag with all the blasting and crashing. I'm sorry."

"It's all right," Auggie said, kneeling and laying down on the dirt and rock floor of the shaft. "You will do fine, Clay. I trust you."

T he Sons of Typhon and their god made their way along the central shaft, killing miners trapped in the cave-in from the Greate Olde Wurm's thrashing about.

"Soon, Lord, you will be free of this accursed mountain prison," Rory said to the silent, floating child, drifting as if he were bobbing in water. "We will spirit you away to our mother, the mother of all monsters, and she will raise you, nurture you until your body has grown to match your infinite power."

Kern paused and looked back down into the yawning darkness. "You hear that?"

"The mountain's settling," Rory said. "Don't worry. Stapleton is dead, her friends with her." The party continued forward, coming closer to the lift that would take them up into the accursed light. A group of miners were gathered near the damaged remains of the lift. Several of them were crying or praying. Others just stood, mute, blank-faced, waiting to die. They saw the Sons' lamp and turned, expecting new survivors from the various collapses off of the central shaft. Then they saw Auggie Junior, and the horror spread across their countenances. They were trapped in the depths of the earth, and now the Devil had come up from Hell to take them.

315

"Easy, gents," Rory said, "easy. Nothing to be alarmed about. It's actually a great privilege to be sacrificed to the true god of this world." The men looked about, confused, frightened. A few hefted their picks, ready to fight. "Probably best thing to ever happen in your sad little lives."

The baby opened his mouth, and a terrible cry—hungry, alien, mad—filled the tunnel with frigid air and the stench of putrefaction. The baby raised a tiny arm, and the crowd of miners began to scream and fall to the ground. The blood in their body streamed out of them in great gouts through the very pores of their skin, shooting through the air in defiance of gravity and reason. The men died, writhing in pain, as the thing inside the baby laughed and let their blood rain down. The blood covered the Sons, and the baby, some of it soaked into the soil.

"The lift is broken," Kern said. "We can climb up, though."

"No," a woman's voice said from the darkness of the main shaft. "No more die. These are the last. I am the Mother's blade, the Mother's wrath. This is your graveyard."

"Shit," Rory said, turning and drawing his pistol. "Well, darling, you certainly cocked my hat, once again."

Maude, Emily, and Professor Mephisto stepped into the feeble lantern light. "We spend your ninth life tonight, Rory," Maude said, her eyes hooded in anger. "No more escaping, no more chaos, no more sacrifices because of you."

"No," Rory said, "one more sacrifice."

The infant floated toward the trio. Professor Mephisto's deep base voice began to mutter incantations in some unknown language. Maude thought it might be Tibetan. The professor's hands moved frantically, contorting into cramped and intricate patterns. Maude recalled from her own study, they were called mudras. Gran had taught her a few basic ones she had picked up during her time in India.

The professor continued the chant as he locked his gaze with the ink-filled wells of the baby's bleeding eyes. The infant raised his hand,

and Maude, Emily, and Mephisto began to feel as if the universe itself were trying to smother them.

"Die, already," Rory said. Maude tried to move, to attack, but the force crushing them was overwhelming. Mephisto was using some spell to diminish the force and keep them all alive, but he was already losing his mystic battle with the endless power of the Greate Olde Wurm.

———

F ar below, Auggie looked into Gillian's face. "It's time, love," he said. Gillian looked down at him, his kind, calm face.

"How can you be so...you right now," she asked. Her eyes were swollen. She had thought she had no more tears to give, but she was wrong.

"Because whatever waits for me on the other side, I've already found Heaven here. With you, with our boy." He looked over to Clay, who was ashen faced, his hands holding a scalpel, trembling. "Clay, are you ready?"

"I...no," Clay said. "I can't do this, Auggie. I...I just can't."

"Think of me as a raccoon or a possum," Auggie said with a twinkle in his eyes, "a fat possum." Clay began to sob.

"I can't do it," he said. "I can't keep my hand steady. I can't..." Auggie put his hand over Clay's.

"You must do this," Auggie said, "please, Clay." Gillian's hand now rested on top of Auggie's. Clay looked over to Gillian.

"We'll do it together," she said. "Just like everything else." Clay's hand moved beneath theirs, and Auggie gasped. His eyes opened wider for a moment, then began to droop.

"Thank you," he muttered. "Thank you, Clay. I'm very lucky to have a friend like you." Clay wept. His whole body trembled and shook. He was a child again in a house full of dead people.

Auggie slipped his hand out and let Gillian's and Clay's hands touch. He put his hand back on top of Gillian's. "I know why you study death, Clay. I know why you hate it so much, want to cure it. I promise you, you'll never be alone. We are never alone." He squeezed Gillian's hand. She was someplace past grief, past sadness, an awful dream from which there was no waking. She looked down at Auggie as his face grew pale, and he struggled to keep his eyes open.

"I love you," she said.

"Tell him about me," Auggie said. "Tell him every day how much I love him, and how much I love you." Augustus Shultz, "Auggie" to friends of whom he had more than he would ever know, closed his eyes and slipped away.

———

The awful pressure vanished, and Maude knew, she knew the cost of her life, of everyone's. She charged at Rory, her mind a fire that devoured reason. Auggie Junior, squalling like a perfectly normal baby again, stopped floating and fell. Maude launched herself through the air, even as Rory fired. She felt the bullet burn through her, and she didn't care. Nothing was going to stop her. Nothing.

Professor Mephisto dropped to his knees, exhausted from his psychic battle.

Emily, bomb in hand, charged toward Tidbull. The giant charged toward her, as Kern followed him, ready to cut Mephisto's throat. Emily twisted the dials just as he was on top of her, jammed the bomb into the waist of his pants, and dove to the left. The explosion, aimed at the large Son's chest, cut Tidbull in half, the jagged scraps of his bones ripping through Kern like shrapnel. The pustules over Kern's body popped and hissed as they were pierced. Both Sons lay dead on the blood-soaked ground.

Maude caught the baby before he hit the ground, pulled him close to her, and then landed in a crouch. Rory turned and aimed to fire again. Maude's leg shot out and crushed his ankle. The final Son groaned in pain and fell, dropping the pistol. Maude stood, handed the wailing baby, covered in blood, to Emily, and pulled Rory to his feet by his throat. He was smiling through the pain of his powdered ankle, his monstrous mind already formulating his next scheme, his next ploy.

"I can tell you where she is," Rory said, "the Mother of Monsters, Alexandria Poole, I can tell you, if you let me..." Maude, her eyes pitiless stone, crushed Rory's windpipe.

"Shut up," Maude said. There was a hollow snapping sound as Rory died. "Just...shut up." She drove her other fist through his face, exploding the Son's skull in a spray of blood, bone, and brain. "And stop smiling," she said to the corpse as she dropped it.

JUSTICE (REVERSED)

The rain departed the next day as suddenly as it had come. It was sunny and cold. Clay's men were able to gather up the dead from around the town and those who had died in the Argent mine cave-in, including Auggie Shultz. The town was quiet, almost in shock at the news of Auggie's passing. It felt like someone had cut the heart out of Golgotha.

Highfather and Kate awoke late. They had both stumbled into bed shortly after the entrance to the mine had been cleared and Maude and the surviving rescue party had come out, carrying Auggie. The baby was quiet as he slumbered, safe in Gillian's arms. Jon couldn't recall ever seeing Maude looking so grim.

Jon struggled out of bed and slipped on a clean pair of pants. Their waterlogged clothing from the night before lay in rings around the floor near the bed.

"I think we earned a day off," Kate mumbled, rolling over.

"I need to see where things are at," Jon said, as he started a fire in the wood stove to chase away the chill. He noticed a ream of blackened papers in the stove. "What's this?" Kate sat up in bed.

"Allan gave them to me," she said, "while you were riding with

Caxton. It was records, reports...on you, Jon, on your past. Before the war...during...and after."

"Oh," Highfather said. "So, you know..." Kate got out of bed. She didn't stop to grab clothes as she walked to him and wrapped her arms around his neck.

"I do," she said, "and I don't care," she said. "I told him that, too." She kissed him. "I'm from a very rough place, Jon. I did desperate things, awful things, before I met Allan, before I came here. You think I'm going to judge you?"

Jon kissed her back. "I always figured if people knew the truth, knew who I was before, they'd lose confidence in me doing my job."

"This job? Jon, none of them could do what you do."

"I can think of a few who might," he said and kissed her again, kept kissing her.

"Yeah," she murmured against his lips, "but they wouldn't be stupid enough to want it." The kiss grew in hunger, and they found their way back to the bed.

"I think you're right," he said. "We do deserve a day off."

Highfather rode through the field near his house, toward Drywell Road and the jail. There were signs of the fire everywhere. He also saw neighbors helping each other clean up and begin to rebuild. That was the part of Golgotha not everyone saw or heard about. This town brought out the best in its people as well as their worst. Several folks waved to Jon as he passed, and he returned the wave. He hitched Bright in front of the jail and began to enter.

"Highfather!" It was Pinkerton, walking up the street toward him. His arm was bandaged and in a sling, and he had bandages on his cheek. After his morning, after Kate told him Pinkerton had spread his life out on paper for her, to convince her he wasn't a good man, Jon wanted to punch his teeth down his throat, but he focused on Kate and tried to let it go. "You get checked out by the doctor yet?"

"More or less," Jon said. "I stitched up a few of the cuts. Made sure I didn't have any balls or bullets in me. The snake bite was bad, but I didn't catch enough venom to put me down. I'm fine."

"You did a hell of a job," Pinkerton said. "I talked to the men Caxton left behind, and they told me what you did during the ambush at Armageddon. You saved a lot of lives."

"What do you mean 'left behind'?" Jon asked. "Where's Caxton?"

"We've already secured some of Doctor Turlough's bio-restorative formula for the federal government," Pinkerton continued. "Do you think Turlough would build another of these magneto-field devices like you had on the cart at Armageddon for us?"

"Pinkerton," Jon said, raising his voice, "where is Caxton?"

"Pacification mission," the spymaster said. "He left this morning."

"Pacification?" Jon said. "What are you talking about?" Pinkerton looked annoyed.

"The general got word that another Indian force was mustering in Crescent Valley. He took about forty men with him and headed out to keep the peace."

"Keep the peace?" Jon said. "They aren't 'mustering.' They're hiding. It's a civilian camp, all the locals who wanted to stay the hell out of the fighting."

"And who told you that?" Pinkerton asked.

"Mutt," Jon said. "He and Rabb found out about it when they were tracking Izusa."

"Mutt," Pinkerton said. "Clearly, someone who couldn't possibly have an agenda to protect his fellow Indians."

"You clearly don't know him," Jon said. "I trust Mutt. Caxton is going out there to punish, to get his revenge. You know that. It's going to be a bloodbath! We have to stop him!"

"You will do no such thing," Pinkerton said, his face red, his eyes dark with anger. "Look around you, Sheriff. Your town, your people suffered because of these renegades. General Caxton and I are here to put a stop to that. Major raids on Carson City and Golgotha must be redressed. The general kept the peace out here during the war. A war,

I might add, that you fought on the wrong side in. He knows what he's doing, and he has the full confidence and support of the president and the military."

"He's going to kill a lot of innocent people," Jon said. "They're mostly unarmed, and they're not looking for a fight. He's going to stir the pot. You want this uprising over, then let me ride out and get him back here. You want war in these parts for decades, then you let him commit an atrocity the Indians won't forget."

"Ridiculous. You think Caxton and forty men, all armed for bear and looking to settle accounts, is going to listen to you? They'll cut you down. Besides," Pinkerton said, "the Indians started this, but, by God, we'll finish it."

"Go to hell," Jon said. "You got a damn peculiar way of figuring they started all this. I'm stopping him." He opened the jail door. "Get out."

"You take any action toward General Caxton or attempt to stop him from carrying out his legal duties," Pinkerton said, standing at the jail door, "and I'll have that star on your chest. I will have you charged with interfering with federal authorities and treason against the American people. You'll hang. I'll see that you do."

"Maybe fourth time will be the charm," Jon said and slammed the door in Pinkerton's face.

Highfather paced the jail and calmed his mind. He remembered what he had been told a few days ago, and his heart ached at the thought of it, especially after everything with Kate. Then he remembered Caxton had a lead on him, and it was widening. Best get to it. He sat down at his desk and composed some letters, quickly. He removed his silver star and placed it on top of one of the letters.

Jon left the letters arranged on his desk and turned to the gun cabinet. The pickings were pretty slim. They had gone through a lot of guns and bullets in the last few days. He loaded up as many guns as he could carry on horseback, took as much spare ammo as he could, and headed back out the door. He paused for a moment to look back at the jail, his desk, the chairs where Mutt and Jim and Kate had all sat. He could hear their laughter, remember the fights and the jokes, the desperate hours and the victories. He smiled. Sometimes haunted places felt the most like home. Jon closed the door on his way out.

Highfather headed south out of town on Main. He stopped at the blackened husk of town hall, which was still open for business in the aftermath of the attack and fires. He spoke briefly with Colton Higbee and left him a letter and one for Harry Pratt.

As he passed the Paradise Falls, Jon looked up and saw Malachi Bick standing on the balcony to his office upstairs, garbed as always in black, looking down at Jon. They locked eyes. Bick nodded slightly to Highfather, and the sheriff returned the nod. Highfather rode on.

"Safe journey, Jonathan," Bick said, but only the sky heard him.

M utt rode into town, exhausted, about an hour later. He thought about just going straight to bed, but then he saw all the damage from the fires and dismissed the motion. Rest would keep. He walked into the jail only to find Rabb standing alone, a letter in his hand.

"What happened?" Mutt asked. "Everyone all right?"

"It's Highfather," Rabb said. Mutt looked to the desk and saw Jon's star. He felt his stomach drop. "He's gone after Caxton, alone."

"What the hell? Where? Why?"

"He left us letters," Rabb said. "Caxton is hitting that Indian camp down at Crescent Valley. He's going to murder everyone there. Revenge for Armageddon. He left on Caxton's heels not long ago."

"Well come on, let's go back him up," Mutt said.

"He said his last official order as sheriff before resigning was for us to not go after him. Pinkerton threatened that anyone who tried to stop Caxton would be branded an outlaw and hang. Jon said the town needed us, now more than ever."

Mutt drove his fist into one of the wooden support posts for the ceiling. Some dust trickled down. "This. This is Izusa's 'secret third army' that she was going on about. She knew, win or lose, she and Snake-Man could count on that jackass Caxton to ride off and do something like this." He looked at the star on the desk and then back to Rabb. "Jonathan's right. You, Kate, and Jim stay put." He pulled the star off his shirt and looked at it for a moment. Then he tossed it to Rabb. "I'm going after him. He'll need help. Pinkerton be damned."

"Mutt," Rabb said, "you may not be able to help Jon. He may be beyond anyone's help."

"I need to know," Mutt said. "I need to know the message. The message for Jon from the dead man, the one that sent you across the country, across the desert. The one neither you nor Jonathan wants to tell anyone."

Rabb looked pained, a war inside himself. Mutt took a step closer.

"If we have to throw down about it, then we can do that, but I think you and I both have been through enough of that the last few days. I need to know, Rabb. He's my... Please."

Rabb sighed and looked at the star in his hand, then to Mutt. "The message was, 'It's your time.'"

JUDGEMENT

Wodziwob and his disciples arrived at the camp at Crescent Valley the evening of the attacks on Golgotha and Carson City. The old healer asked to speak with the elders and the medicine men of the various tribes, bands, and communities present. Many had come to the valley seeking refuge from the expanding conflict between Izusa, Snake-Man, and their followers and Caxton and his federal troops.

That evening, gathered around a fire with only the elders, the medicine men, and the few remaining members of the Black Feathers, he made a daring proposal to undertake a different dance than the circle dance as soon as preparations could be made.

"I think it is time for the renewal ceremony," he said to the gathered leaders and teachers. An uproar came from the assembled.

"It must be done at the solstice!" one medicine man of the Washoe exclaimed. "Those who have vowed to dance this year...many are not here; others are nowhere near prepared for the ordeal!"

"Early spring is fine. Don't be foolish!" a Goshute elder snapped. "But we have not been able to prepare. It takes close to a year to prepare! We can't just rush into this!"

"We each undertake the ceremony in our own traditional way!" one Northern Paiute said, rising. "We cannot sully our most sacred ritual by not doing it properly!"

"Meaning *our* way sullies the dance?" The tribal leader of the Western Shoshone glowered, also rising. "It is you who perverts..."

"Enough," Wodziwob said softly. A spear of flame from the camp-fire launched itself heavenward, higher than the tallest tree, with a roar, then flickered back down and returned to normal. The group grew silent and sat again. "This," the old man said, "is why we need the dance of sacrifice, of renewal, now more than ever. I have spent too many years listening only to spirits of death. I grew much as Izusa is now, bitter, locked into a cycle of violence with the whites. I forget to heed the call of the living earth, of the spirits of life, and of hope."

The elders around the fire looked from one to another as Wodziwob's words settled over them. Wodziwob saw at least the seed of understanding. "I know this is not of the traditional ways. I know, but the *numa* bleed, the *toha* bleed. The land weeps tears of blood."

"Let the white devils die," a Shoshone elder said, his voice cracking. "They took from me my only son five years ago. They call us 'snakes.'" The old man hunched, the weight of his grief and his hate on top of him. "Why should we care if they live or die?"

"The white men do not listen to the earth," Wodziwob said. "They do not hear the sky's voice, or the water's song. They're already like dead men. If we fight them with their guns, their hatred, then we will become a dead people too."

"They already kill us a day at a time," one of the medicine men, a young Modoc named Kintpuash, said. "They drive us from our homes; they force our children to learn their language, take white names, and pray to the white gods. They burn our history in the minds of our own sons and daughters. Even the dance you wish to do, what the whites call 'the sun dance,' they threaten to kill it, to make it illegal by their laws." A murmur of agreement went up around the circle. Kintpuash looked at Wodziwob. "With respect, elder, fighting them Izusa's way may be the only path that remains open to us."

327

"I understand why you would think that. I, myself, have thought that way for a very long time," Wodziwob said. "With every lie we are given as oath, with every compromise, every eviction from our lands, it seems we are being pushed to war or extinction. You may be right. We may be out of time, out of options. Look out at the camp, look out at all the innocents who only want to live in peace, to raise their children in peace, to grow up in peace." The Black Feathers' leader searched each somber face, bathed in fire and shadow. "I say for those too young to know, those generations yet to be, we must try to find a way, to find hope once again, one more time. The spirits have shown me the end of the world—it is coming to pass before us now. It will not end in our victory; it will end in defeat for all. We must do all we can with our medicine, with our knowledge, and our hearts, to end this. If I am wrong, if it is too late. Then at least we will end as the same people we began as—proud, true to ourselves. There are worse fates than ending in such a way."

The leaders looked from face to face as Wodziwob continued.

"We have always had our differences, our fights, yes, even our hatreds, but we must put these aside now if we are to survive, all of us. We must renew our commitments to the *numa*, to all the people, to one another, to the land and to life, or we will all fall into darkness and death. We must decide, we must choose." There was a long silence, only the crackling of the fire filled it.

"I will try," Kintpuash said to Wodziwob, "one more time to believe. I will take part in the dance."

It took most of the night to argue and talk out the details. Not all of the tribes and bands were happy with the compromises, but the decisions were made and the preparations begun for the ritual. A great tree, a cottonwood, was found by the scouts in the night to act as the pole for the ritual. It was cut down but not allowed to touch the ground and carried back to the camp. Within sight of the camp, a ring of sticks was arranged in a great circle. The pole would reside in the center, and the ground around it was prepared for the dance.

Wodziwob and the others who were to participate began to fast as the dawn arrived. All day and all night long, everyone did what they could in the short time before the ritual was to begin. Medicine men arranged buffalo skulls around the ritual circle, and many of the camp's women prepared the robes and cloaks and headdresses that were needed for the dance.

The children were sent to gather the sage needed and the cattail that would be used later to help speed recovery. Each group in the camp had the responsibility to create their own circle for their people to reside within, orbiting the ritual circle. Barriers were created to block the view of the ritual from the eyes of any outsider.

Wodziwob and many of the other elders and medicine men purified themselves, prayed, and fixed their minds on what was to come, what must come. For Wodziwob, there was still great conflict within himself, though he had kept his troubled feeling to his own council, alone. Now, kneeling upon a prayer blanket, Wodziwob debated if perhaps he was damning his people, not saving them.

The dead still possessed great power, thanks to Izusa. Perhaps enough power to prevail over the whites. But there had been so much bloodshed on both sides, and her instability made her final goals uncertain. He had started this, perhaps he should see it through? He tried to imagine the young faces of the generations to come. What world would he be leaving them?

There was a momentary distraction in the medicine man's thoughts. A tiny ant scuttled along the edges of his blanket. Instinctively, Wodziwob reached out to crush it. He stayed his hand at the last instant. He watched as the ant moved along its way, disappearing into the rocks and soil of the tent's floor. Wodziwob looked at his own hand for a time. He began his prayers once again, his mind clearer, his heart less filled with doubt.

E verything was being rushed, but Wodziwob had convinced the others that time was of the essence. Many doubted if the ritual would be received by the spirits due to its hasty preparation.

The ritual began the following morning at sunrise. The renewal ritual, what the Lakota called *Wiwanke Wachipi*, was known by many other names by the many tribes that performed it in their own fashion. It began slowly. There was song and chanting, from the assembled viewers.

The half dozen men who had volunteered to undertake this first dance, including Wodziwob, stood mute and stone-faced, crowns of sage on their heads, rings of sage on their wrists and ankles. A few had whistles made of the hollow bones of an eagle's wing about their necks. The sides of the men's chests were pierced by sharpened bone and then tied by rawhide cords to the central pole.

The dance began, slow at first, a shuffling orbit around the circle, around the pole. The song, the chanting, continued as the men fed their blood, their will, into the goal they had set for themselves: The protection and renewal of the spirit of the *numa*, so that it might not be obliterated by violence and death or washed away in a flood of hatred and fear. Wodziwob gathered all his *buha* about him. He reached out, calling to all the spirits under the great wheel of the sky for strength and for the wisdom to change his own heart as he struggled to change others'.

The assembled, mostly women, the elderly, and the children, sang with all their hearts. They sang for a world in which they did not have to hide, to run, to be afraid. They prayed for their loved ones to come home and to come home safe.

No one in the camp knew what was riding their way as the ritual unfolded. None of them knew that an assassin was already in their midst and that two powerful spirits were already in attendance.

General Aries Caxton's mind was flush with anger and an almost-sexual thrill of violent revenge. Everything had gone wrong since he had been given this assignment, from the interference of Allan Pinkerton and his secret schemes to the progressive whining of the sheriff and people of Golgotha. Caxton assured himself that after yesterday's massacre, they no longer bemoaned the plight of the poor Indian. He smiled a bit at that. It usually took someone getting smashed in the face, tasting their own blood, before they learned the futility of turning the other cheek.

The men who rode with him had all volunteered to come, even though most had suffered wounds from the ambush at Armageddon and at the battle in Golgotha. Even a few town locals, so angry by the attack on their homes and families by the Indians' demons, had agreed to come. It was a small band, but they were well-armed, and their cause was just. God rode with them.

It took them a while longer to reach the Indian's camp than he had wished, given the size and composition of his force. They had been forced to proceed at a less urgent pace for most of the day, due to injuries and the needs of their mounts. Still, it gave the general time to savor what was coming, to imagine every detail of his vengeance.

Caxton was surprised that the camp didn't appear to have any outlying scouts or sentries. If they did, his people hadn't detected them. A scout did mention seeing a dust cloud off to the north that he thought might be a rider paralleling them at great speed, but it was a solitary sign and had vanished over an hour ago. They were confident it wasn't a look-out.

Caxton swore that this time there would only be one surprise, and that would be his upon the Indians. The hooves of over forty horses shook the ground as they approached Crescent Valley at late morning. The sky was a heartbreaking blue, no clouds to be seen. The chill had burned off the morning air, but the wind that knifed along the vast open expanse of the plains kept it cold even as the bright eye of the sun rose higher.

Caxton swore he heard chanting carried on the battering wind. It made him spur his exhausted horse on even faster. They wouldn't escape this time. Even if that sorceress bitch Izusa wasn't here, or that traitorous dog Snake-Man, they would know what he had done here today. All the Indians, everywhere, would know, and they would all come to fear the name of Aries Caxton and the United States government. He had acquired something from the mines in Golgotha to ensure they would never forget.

Ahead were a few small hills and ditches dotting the scrub-covered prairie. Large rocks and boulders lay scattered as if some giant had tired of playing with them and tossed them carelessly aside. As they neared the final boundary between themselves and the camp, the report of a gunshot rolled across the tableland. Jon Highfather, rifle in one hand, six-gun in the other, stepped out from behind one of the boulders. "Caxton!" Jon called as the patrol came to a stop about fifty yards from him. "That's far enough," Jon called out.

"Highfather, what the hell are you doing here?" Caxton said. "You need to be home tending your flock, Sheriff, not out here doing a man's work."

"You call yourself a man?" Highfather said. "Murdering a bunch of civilians—women, children, old men? Most of them unarmed. Heroic."

Caxton shook his head in obvious disgust. "You're a damn fool, Highfather. They're Indians, they don't have 'civilians.' They're all thieves, all liars, all killers. How many men have to die around you before you acknowledge that?"

"These people have done no one any harm," Jon said, "but you and I both know we're not going to settle this talking." Caxton smiled a little.

"I do," the general said. "Where's your badge, Sheriff?"

"Not a sheriff anymore," Jon said, scanning the faces of the front line. He saw the troopers and the volunteers readying their guns. "Just a concerned citizen."

"Good," Caxton said. "That will make explaining you getting blown to hell a might easier."

Highfather felt the old peace settle over him once again as he looked past the guns and the gunmen, out at the plain, the sky. He had only known soul-deep peace a few times in his life, when he was farming his family's land, when he had gone into battle—be it a war or a gunfight—and in the arms of the two women he had loved in this life. Eden had died, and he had figured that was the end of that for him. But then Kate came along, out of nowhere, and reminded him how good it felt to be in love. It felt like watching a desert sky that took your breath away, like really being able to breathe.

"A damn sight better men than this rangy bunch have tried," Highfather said. "Here I am."

The heavens above him went on forever, endless, blustery, perfect, and the land chased after the sky, always reaching, aching, for a kiss. Jon lowered his rifle and his pistol, to his side; his gray eyes glinted in the sun.

"I've heard your hogwash," Caxton said, drawing his pistol free of its holster. "'The dead man,' 'the man who can't die because it's not his time.' Tell me, dead man, you ready to die? Are you?"

The first people who had looked upon this land so long ago, the ancestors of the people at his back, Jon thought, must have known that peace long ago, known that there was healing in this land. This land had healed him, made him whole again, after Larson, after the war, after Eden. It was a big place, beautiful and powerful, with more than enough room for everyone. He was ready.

"Last chance," Highfather said to the patrol of over forty men he faced alone. "Turn around and go home. Keep living. Otherwise...draw."

Highfather and Caxton searched each other's eyes for the second, for the instant. Jon saw the flicker in the general's eyes, saw the beginning of an order building in his throat. Jon began to move.

"Fire!" Caxton shouted.

Three of Caxton's troopers died in their saddles and fell to the desert floor. A cloud of dust swirled in the spot Highfather had been in a second before the storm of gunfire had filled it. Jon was behind the cover of a bolder, crouched low. The new bullet wound in his chest burned, felt like he had a hot iron under his skin.

He popped up and fired, rifle in one hand, pistol in the other. He rolled the lever on the rifle with a flip of his wrist and fired again. Three more men died. A bullet struck the rock just by his head, and hot chips of stone stung his cheek. He didn't see Caxton at the fore any longer, but he heard the rumble of the horses galloping toward him, moving to flank him and his cover. The first riders shot past him, firing as they came, one on the right, two on the left. Jon's left was his weaker arm, so he looked left as he fired both rifle and gun again and again. He hit all three, and they tumbled and fell from their still-galloping horses. A second later, he felt his side explode in wet agony. A bullet had taken a chunk out of his flank. Nothing vital had been hit, but it burned and ached.

If he stayed behind this rock, he was going to die. Jon ran as best he could with the wounds and dove behind another, larger rock. Bullets, like a swarm of angry bees, whined and buzzed around him.

"Flank him, damn you!" Caxton shouted to his men. Jon heard the general's voice off to the left. More riders rode around the rocks and began to turn. Jon fired the last bullet in the rifle and shot and killed another soldier. He dropped the rifle at his feet and drew another pistol from his belt, even as he was firing the last few bullets from the six-gun. Another trooper fell, but he missed the other two that rode by. Jon felt a nauseating pain nearly pull him into blackness as two bullets hit him, one in the gut, the other a little higher. He doubled over and dropped to one knee. The two riders that he had missed turned, and one gave up a whoop.

"We got the sumbitch!" the trooper cried out a second before Highfather stood and blasted him and his comrade with one of the shotguns he'd planted among the rocks in the few minutes before the patrol had reached him. Both men fell from their frightened horses and lay still on the ground.

"Sumbitch's still breathing," Highfather called out. The gut shot, the one he was the most concerned with, had miraculously passed through him, out his lower back. He ached and wanted to vomit and lay down, but he was still able to fight. He stayed low and tried to remain awake as he reloaded the shotgun and his pistols, then moved to another rock.

"He's *one* goddamned man!" Caxton shouted. "Wounded, hurt, exhausted, and on goddammed foot! Surround him, damn you! Overwhelm him, and kill him!" For a moment, the stories of Highfather's supernatural reputation rushed back into Caxton's mind. He shook his head to dismiss them.

Jon stood and fired both pistols, dropping three more men and blowing Caxton's hat off his head before he had to drop back down behind the rock, under the withering return fire. He still had the shotgun, and there were more weapons cached around here. He had sent Bright off, and he didn't want to call for his loyal horse for fear the troopers would shoot her, so he really didn't have a way out of this. They would swing around in great numbers, and they would nail him to the stone with their bullets. He just hoped that all the gunfire had given the refugee camp enough time to make a run for it. However, Highfather knew Caxton would ride them down. The thought made Jon cold with anger.

"All right, you bastard," Caxton called out, his voice hoarse with anger. "Done playing with you! You get a taste of what I have in store for the..." Before Caxton could utter his next word, there was a yipping bark, then a howl that came from behind the troop. It grew louder, and then a chorus of new gunfire began.

Mutt, speeding in on a frothing Muha, fired his rifle again and again into the troopers as they spun to confront the new threat from behind. Troopers fell as they were hit. Highfather pulled himself up as he heard the commotion. He began firing, too, putting the troops in a crossfire.

Mutt cut through the cavalry's ranks, dropping several more of the men. He cut tight, causing a few of Caxton's men to shoot each other, trying to hit him. As he reached the front line of the patrol, Mutt spotted Caxton and a subordinate pulling something from a saddle bag. He didn't have time to see much as another soldier shot him and another trooper hemmed him. The bullet went into Mutt's arm in a spray of blood and meat.

Mutt shot his attacker and swung onto the soldier's horse as the man fell. Muha galloped clear of the troopers and headed off across the plain. Mutt pulled his new mount in an arc and reached out his uninjured arm for Highfather. Jon grabbed the hand and was pulled up onto the back of Mutt's horse. Jon fired with both guns at the closing troops, giving them some breathing room.

"I came out here to tell you I quit," Mutt said, wincing from the bullet in his arm. "This is ridiculous. My bullet holes have bullet holes."

"After this," Jon said reloading a pistol, and handing it to Mutt, "we can have a nice, long rest until they hang us." Mutt brought the horse around again as bullets buzzed past them, charging into the fire of the soldiers. Jon and Mutt fired together into the maelstrom of death they hurtled headlong into.

"Caxton," Highfather said. "We need to take him out."

"He was messing with something," Mutt said, "but I couldn't..." A hissing stick of dynamite dropped on the ground before them. "That, I think," Mutt said. The two men grabbed each other and tumbled toward one of the ditches off to the left just as the dynamite exploded. The horse's scream was lost in the whoosh and roar of the blast.

"That is how you deal with that," Caxton said to the private next to him as the dirt and shattered rock tumbled back to Earth. "Shame— the bastards know we're coming now, thanks to those two." He slipped the fuse into a few more sticks and put them in his saddle bag. He handed the rest in a satchel to the soldier. "Lieutenant, take these and some men. Head up the northeast ridge to the camp. I'll take the remainder and take the northwest advance. You know what to do."

"Yes sir," the young trooper said. The remainder of Caxton's men rode past the site of the brief battle.

In the ditch, buried under dust and powdered rock, Mutt and Highfather groaned and opened their eyes, tangled together, their ears ringing. Their dirt-covered faces were very close, almost nose to nose.

"People gonna talk," Mutt said, hacking and trying to untangle himself.

"Let 'em," Jon said, pulling himself free and upright with a moan of pain.

"He blew up the horse," Mutt said. "I didn't think it was possible for me to hate him more than I already do, but I do."

"He must have grabbed some dynamite from the mining camp," Jon said.

The two struggled to their feet, leaning on one another. They saw the distant dust clouds of the greatly diminished troop as it divided and headed for the camp. "We got to stop this," Jon said. "He's going to blow those people up." Jon whistled.

"Wodziwob is in that camp too," Mutt said and whistled as well. "Caxton kills him, this thing ain't never going end."

"You take the right path up the ridge to the camp," Jon said. "I'll take the left." Muha and Bright whinnied and galloped up to their beloved owners. Mutt and Jon climbed up into their saddles. "Meet you in the middle."

"You better," Mutt said. Highfather looked at his former deputy and shook his head.

"Rabb told you," he said.

"After all we've rode into together," Mutt said, "no way you're going into this alone." The two men looked at each other for a long second. "Jonathan," Mutt began. The words all choked and failed him before they reached his lips. Jon tried too, with no more success.

Finally, Highfather nodded. "No one I'd rather have ride with me." The two men looked toward the valley, to the camp up on the tip of the ridge. "Come on, let's finish this."

The horses, more exhausted than the men, more battered and

weary of this war, found the heart to gallop across the plain, the wind against them, as so often it was. They rode side by side, as they always had. As they approached the slopes, they peeled away from one another, riding into bad odds to stop an evil and end a war. They parted ways, taking the final steps alone, but knowing, bone to blood, that they were never alone.

DEATH

The ritual dance went on even as the sounds of gunfire and then explosions grew closer. Wodziwob moved into the space beyond the pain, the ache that came with each breath. Time was spreading outward, slowing, smearing. The healer looked over into the blurry mosaic of faces watching the dance. Wavoka's face crystallized into focus. The boy—his follower, Tavibo's son—had his eyes fixed on Wodziwob as he danced. It felt to the old man the young man was looking into his very soul, drinking of his medicine, his *buha*, that they were in some primal way becoming as one across the bridge of time.

In that moment, Wodziwob knew that the round dance, the ghost dance, would go on, that Wovoka would keep it alive, keep it pure, and not allow the taint of Izusa's madness to destroy it. The spirit of the people would live and they hold to their ways, never allow themselves to fade away, to stop fighting. A promise passed from boy to elder and Wodziwob laughed in joy, even as his flesh tore free of the bone and rawhide lash. Wodziwob saw a future where the *numa* endured and remained strong and proud. The old healer stumbled and almost fell as he was loosed from the tether to the pole, but he kept his footing, maintained the dance of renewal.

Some of the medicine men took Wodziwob to a wikiup that had been prepared to minister to the participants of the dance. As they approached, gunshots rang out, and the holy men helping Wodziwob fell, dead. Struggling to stay on his feet, Wodziwob looked up to see the assassin. It was Snake-Man, a smoking rifle in his hand and the body of a dead federal soldier slung over his shoulder. He dropped the body at the edge of the circle of dead medicine men.

"Just to make sure the *toha* get the blame for your death," Snake-Man said. "In case that idiot Caxton doesn't pull this off." He cocked the lever on the rifle and took aim on the old man.

"Awan," Wodziwob said, "I am sorry for how I failed you. You came to us wounded in spirit, and I did not heal you. I only fed your hatred."

"How touching," Snake-Man said, "especially at the barrel of a gun. Don't flatter yourself, Hawthorne, or do you prefer 'Fish Lake Joe'? Not quite as distinguished, true, but perhaps closer to your true self."

"Awan, please."

"I have buried that name with my family," Snake-Man said. "And don't flatter yourself. You taught me a bit of medicine, but you know nothing of true power—true hate—old man. Your hate is tepid and less than useless. You don't hate the whites; you hate what they have done. You think it can be cured, like a sickness. They *are* the sickness." There were gunshots, screaming, and the sound of more explosions inside the camp. Still, the dance continued; the chanting, the singing went on unabated. Snake-Man smiled at the sounds. "The sun dance is about renewal," Snake-Man said, "visualizing a better tomorrow and sacrificing for it. The blood shed in this village today will be your sacrifice for the better tomorrow."

"A future built on hatred cannot stand," Wodziwob said. "It is like building a house that is on fire. You cannot build fast enough to outrun what devours you."

"Once it is known that you were found dead at the hands of a white soldier," Snake-Man said, taking a bead along the rifle's sights, "especially after your talk of healing and finding a peaceful way, it will draw many to our cause. We'll raise thousands of warriors to the fight by summoning your name alone." He cocked the rifle. The old man looked past the gun. He locked eyes with his former disciple.

"You can bury me but not the truth," Wodziwob said. "There is no hole deep enough, no cave dark enough the truth won't climb out of."

"You should thank me, Hawthorne. I'm going to make you into a legend, and legends never die." The gunshot thundered, and the rifle flew from Snake-Man's hands. The renegade looked over to see Mutt, pistol in hand, crouched on top of a boulder.

"You sure do like the sound of your own gums flappin', don't you?" Mutt said. Snake-Man turned to face him. Mutt was bloodied, wounded. He had taken out several more of Caxton's men before he had found Wodziwob. "Wodziwob, gather who you can and head for the other side of the ridge. Me and Highfather will keep them busy."

"You think that gun's going to stop me from killing you?" Snake-Man said, taking a step forward as he slipped on his thumb blade "fangs."

"Let's see," Mutt said and fired. The bullet hit Snake-Man dead center in the chest. He dropped to his knee and then slowly stood. Blood poured from his mouth and his chest, but his eyes were bright with anger.

"Mutt, I can't leave the ritual; we can't stop it," Wodziwob said.

"Y'all are going to die if you don't get moving," Mutt said as he fired again and put a second round into Snake-Man's chest. This time, he didn't fall, only staggered back a few steps.

"My father's spirit will sustain me until the end of you," Snake-Man said through a waterfall of blood.

"You spit in the face of everything your father represents," Mutt said. "You're a spoiled, angry child who Snake's indulged." He tossed the gun and drew his Bowie knife. "All right," he said, "let's get to it." Both men charged, their war cries louder than the chaos erupting all around them, louder than the healing chants and songs of the ritual. Their anger split the sky.

The majority of the camp was unarmed. A few had rifles or bows, but little experience with them. Those not engaged in the ceremony still rushed to defend the others. They didn't last long against the dynamite and the trained marksmanship of the federal troops, but they made their mark and it cost the ever-dwindling number of soldiers. Jon rode through the camp, around the sea of screaming, crying, shouting humanity that was looking for some new refuge now that their safe haven was being destroyed around them.

"Head farther up the ridge!" Jon shouted to a group of old women leading a bunch of children. His Paiute was pretty awful, but he thought they got the jist of it. Jon fired across the crowd and hit a trooper preparing to open fire at the edge of the crowd. The man fell, but two other mounted riflemen appeared behind him and fired on Jon.

"Goddamn if he ain't a dead man walking!" one of them shouted. Another bullet tore into Jon's body, and he felt the fringes of darkness try to take him again. He bit his cheek and tasted blood. His awareness pulled back into focus, anchored by the fresh pain. He fired on the two men, a gun in either hand. They died. He heard another explosion, in the direction of what looked like newly erected shelters, one of them pretty large. He rode toward the sound of the blast, staying low on Bright and trying to stay conscious. Pain was a steady, constant companion, now, and he welcomed it. It told him he was still alive.

A cluster of troopers, roughly a dozen men strong, were gathered. One of them had a satchel and was handing out sticks of dynamite to the others, while a circle of shooters faced outward ready to repel anyone getting too close. The refugees had already fled from this section of the camp. Dozens of native bodies were on the ground, most of them near the smoking craters created by the dynamite blasts.

Jon pulled Bright to a stop. Bullets from the outlying ring of troopers began to whiz and snap around him. Jon raised his pistol, took careful aim, ignoring the pain, the exhaustion, the death hissing past his ears. He heard the chanting, the songs. He fired a single round. The satchel exploded. The sticks of dynamite still in it went up in a massive fireball that enveloped the cluster of troopers and rose into the sky, a great fist of fire and black smoke. Bodies and parts of bodies rained down around the huge crater the explosion had created. The gunfire, at least in this section of the camp, was silent. There was only the crackling of the newly born fires and the humming in Highfather's ears.

Jon counted in his buzzing head and figured there were only a few stragglers remaining of Caxton's "pacification" force. Once they were found and Caxton himself... A staccato blast of gunfire hit Highfather multiple times. He slipped from Bright's back even as his loyal horse gave a whinny of surprise and concern. Highfather fell among the bodies of troopers and refugees, his lifeblood seeping into the thirsty soil. He fought to raise his head. His insides felt like they had been kicked by a team of mules. The new wounds burned, and it was hard to get a good breath. He tasted bright copper.

He looked up to see Caxton, an arrow in his side and back and several other bloody wounds. The mounted general lowered his smoking cavalry pistol, a grim smile on his bloody face. Caxton's gloved hand reached into his bag and removed a few sticks of dynamite. He turned his back on Highfather and began to ride toward the large shelter where the chanting and singing still came from. Jon tried to shoot him, but his fingers were numb, and he seemed to have lost his pistol somewhere. His head was too heavy to hold up any longer, and he fell back into blackness and silence.

I n his long life of seeking wisdom, Wodziwob had seen many miracles, many wondrous things that could not be explained, only appreciated. He had watched powers and medicines of awe-inspiring and terrible fury and felt his very soul shiver. He had never witnessed anything like what he saw before him now. Today, he saw two mighty spirits waging war. Both men, wounded, close to death, both burning with the blood of their fathers inside them, moved with the force of thunder, struck like lightning. Wodziwob knew that across all the worlds Snake and Coyote battled. Here, it was through their sons.

Snake-Man's curved finger blades sparked and flashed against Mutt's great knife, infused with his own spirit-powered blood. Mutt tumbled and danced as he fought, his arm cracking like a whip with each punch, each strike of the blade. Snake-Man was even faster, if that was possible. He slipped under Mutt's tight swing, flicked out with his steel "fangs," and drew blood, again and again, until Mutt would tumble his way free of the trap.

"I have no illusions about this," Snake-Man said as the two bloody, panting foes circled one another. "I'm already dead. How about you, Mutt, still ready to dive into oblivion with a laugh on your lips? Or have you found something to live for, maybe someone?"

Maude. She was there in his thoughts when his every instinct needed to be in this moment. She was there. "Keep your mind in the fight," she whispered, as sweet as a kiss. Mutt pivoted at her words, only instinct, only trust in her. The fangs should have sunk into his stomach, disemboweled him, finished him, but his last-second turn meant they only buried themselves in his flank. Snake-Man tore them free in a spray of Mutt's blood.

Mutt didn't let the pain slow him, pause him. He drove his knife into Snake-Man's neck up to the hilt with all the strength left in him. Snake-Man gurgled as he stumbled away and fell. Mutt staggered a few steps, and then he fell too. They both dragged themselves to sit, leaning their backs against rocks. Their blood mingled in a pool between them.

"I found something to live for, someone," Mutt said, coughing up some blood. "She's better than I deserve. Saves me every day." Mutt closed his eyes and was very still.

"I'm...I'm glad you found someone," Snake-Man said, his smile stained red. "Comes a point where you no longer fight for yourself, you fight for the future. I found someone, too. She's carrying my child, blood of my blood. That...that was her secret. My father *loves* secrets, did you know that? She whispered it to me when she saw I was entering the cave...saw my death was here. I fought for her...for them. I don't regret dying...for them. I died for something I believe in, Mutt, and I died taking you with me. So...this is all right. See you next life..."

They sat there for a time, both silent and unmoving. The life gone from Snake-Man's eyes. Mutt's chest was still. Wodziwob watched them and said a silent prayer to the Great Spirit to protect them both on their way.

There was a great explosion somewhere in the camp. The ground shook, and the sky darkened, but still the ritual did not cease, the chanting did not stop. Wodziwob looked off in the direction of the blast. When he looked back, Mutt's eyes were open, and he was struggling to his feet. The lower half of his body looked as if he had been dipped in blood. "Jonathan," he muttered.

"I thought you were dead," Wodziwob said, helping Mutt to his feet.

"Close," Mutt said. "They pulled me back, Maude and Jonathan. I got to find him."

Wodziwob, dizzy from pain and loss of blood, held onto Mutt, and Mutt did the same. They managed both to stay on their feet. "Come on," the old man said, "let's find your friend." Mutt gave one final look back at Snake-Man's corpse and then limped away with Wodziwob's help.

———

Caxton lit the sputtering fuses of the two sticks of dynamite he had remaining as he rode toward the shelter where the renewal dance was being performed. He'd shut the savages up, silence their damn yammering, and then he'd go home to parades and medals and a grateful nation. It was hard to keep thinking, hard to stay awake, but the singing, the voices, they drove him forward. These voices did not belong in his America, his land.

Jon felt a big cold nose and panting warm breath on his face and neck. It tickled. His eyes fluttered open, and he looked into the wet snout and huge, kind eyes of Bright. "Good girl," he muttered. He grabbed the leather strap of the reins and began to agonizingly pull himself to his feet. *I should be dead*, his mind screamed. *I should be dead*. He climbed up Bright, who helped him as much as she could. *Maybe I am.*

Jon looked around. He had no more guns. He saw Caxton riding toward the large shelter, toward the singing and the chanting that refused to be silenced. "Bright," Jon whispered in his horse's ear. "We have to give all we have left, girl; we've got to stop him." Bright snorted and nuzzled Jon's face for a moment. "Best horse a man could ask for," he said. "Yah!" Jon shouted and grasped the reins tight, hanging onto saddle with all he had left in him.

Bright whinnied and began to gallop like her life depended on it. This man, her man, had always been good to her, always. He had risked his own life to save her before. She felt his life fluttering, flickering in the cold wind, in the silent language of the world only her kind could understand. He needed her; he was counting on her. She wouldn't fail him now.

Highfather saw them gaining, saw the dynamite in Caxton's hand, the fuses creeping lower. The general was close, planning to toss the explosives over the shelter's high wall and then ride away. *No*, was all Jon could summon in his mind. *No.*

Caxton raised his hand and prepared to hurl the sputtering death. "No!" Jon shouted and jumped from Bright onto Caxton's horse. Caxton drove an elbow into Jon's bleeding side. Jon groaned and grabbed the arrow in Caxton's side and pushed it in, hard. The general roared, and Jon saw his chance. He grabbed Caxton's hand and locked his own around it. The wound in his arm stung and tried to disobey his command, but Jon wouldn't have it. The dynamite was going nowhere.

"No, you fool!" Caxton shouted. "You're going to kill us both!" He suddenly recognized Highfather. "That's...no! I killed you! I killed you twice! Let go of me!"

Jon tugged on the reins, fighting Caxton for control. The general released the reins to grab his pistol from his holster, Jon jerked the leather cord, and Caxton's horse galloped at full tilt toward the edge of the ridge, away from the camp and the ceremony. "This ain't right," Jon said, struggling with Caxton.

"You can't do this!" Caxton screamed as they reached the edge.

Highfather pulled the horse's head to the side, back toward the saddle, while applying pressure with his hips to the other side. "It's time," Jon said. The horse obeyed and came to a sudden and complete one-rein stop. Both men flew off the horse and over the cliff. They fell as the fuses reached their end.

The dynamite exploded in midair, the sound tearing the very air. The ridge shook, and sections crumbled, tumbling down to the plain below. Caxton's horse moved back to avoid falling down the slope. Bright let out a mournful cry and pawed the air.

Mutt and Wodziwob, struggling, reached the ridge a few moments later. Many of the survivors of the camp followed them. In the distance, the renewal ritual continued, as it would continue for many days to come. The chants and songs spoke of the renewal of life, of the return of the connection to the earth, and to the reawakening of the spirit of the people. Mutt shakily stepped away from Wodziwob and looked over the crumbling edge of the cliff. His heart was a jagged rock, cracking in his chest. He stood at the edge, alone. Only the wind heard his voice.

"Jonathan..."

THE STAR

Spring arrived proper the day of the funerals. The procession began down Main and led to Old Stone Road. It gathered black-clad mourners as it went.

The hearse had been delivered from Carson City at the direct orders of Governor Bradley. It had glass side windows and fine polished silver rails. It arrived with a massive, beautiful arrangement of desert wildflowers and a card that said simply, "From a grateful state."

Clay Turlough drove the hearse in his finest Sunday suit. He'd even shaved, though Shelly had to help him a few times to finish when he stopped and sobbed. She sat beside him on the hearse's bench in a black dress, a veil covering her face. Pain came off Clay in waves, and she took his hand when she could and held it. It was all she could do. That and protect the honored dead.

The procession grew into most of the town, walking slowly down Old Stone, toward Rose Road and then up Angel's Ascent to the new cemetery on Angel Hill. The mourners walked in-between all the wagons carrying the caskets of the dead soldiers and civilians from Izusa's raid, including the bodies of Zevon and Brighten

348

Hamblin. Joel's tiny body had not been recovered in the mine collapse, but a small casket had been made so that the family could be together in their rest. The coffins of the miners who died in the cave-in and had been found were carried on the shoulders of their fellow miners. The hearse Clay drove carried two coffins, Golgotha's dearest blood.

Thousands of miles to the east, General Aries Caxton's body was arriving in Washington by train. He was to lay in state with full military honors. The eastern newspapers hailed him as a hero of the Indian campaigns. "Lost to our young country far too soon, his work, unfulfilled."

Jim Negrey, in a suit as fine as anyone could ever recall him dressed, escorted Constance Stapleton. She wore a beautiful but somber dress and smoked glasses over her sightless eyes. She walked with a cane, her arm looped in Jim's. Leeza Turley walked with them in a simple spring dress and bonnet. A few steps behind them was Mutt, dressed in the suit he had borrowed from Jonathan to take Maude out the first time some years back. Mutt's eyes were glassy with pain. Maude walked behind her daughter and beside Mutt, her arm in his. Today, no one said anything; today, no one cared. To Maude's right was Gillian Shultz, wearing the veil of a widow for the second time in her life. Maude held Gillian's hand. Malachi Bick, as dark and resplendent as a Borgia prince, walked beside Gillian with his daughter, Emily, accompanying him. Bick and his entourage walked with the other town dignitaries, like Ora and Sarah Pratt. Porter Rockwell walked behind the mayor's wives, a silent, grim guardian.

Other dignitaries included Acting Mayor Colton Higbee and the surviving Mormon elders. Rony and Daaron Bevalier's services had happened earlier in the week, but the elders, along with all of Golgotha's religious leaders, came out for the services today.

Even Ch'eng Huang left his fortress in Johnny Town to attend, surrounded by a small contingent of Green Ribbon bodyguards. Allan Pinkerton accompanied Kate Warne, who wore a full mourning dress and veil. Pinkerton looked over to eye Mutt, and something ugly and silent passed between the two.

Professor Mephisto declined to attend, instead watching Auggie Junior and examining him for any lingering signs from his ordeal. Barabbas Hayes was not present at the service. He had volunteered to mind the jail since the town didn't stop, even for the funeral. Even there, alone among the empty cells, one of the first men to mark the world with his footprint offered up his prayers to the orishas for the safety and peace of the souls of the departed.

Black Rowan walked a-ways behind Bick, alone. She wore a conservative black gown and a lace veil hiding her face. Word had gotten out that the piano player, James Ringo, who had assassinated the Bevaliers, was in fact her brother. No one offered condolences to Rowan. She heard sharp whispers at her back, as she soaked in the pain of loss. Ringo's coffin was somewhere far behind the sheriff's and Mr. Shultz's in the procession, among the plain pine boxes of the soldiers, the nameless, and the poor. She had made quiet arrangement to have James's body secretly transported to San Francisco. He would be buried by the sea that they had played beside as children, a million years ago.

Rowan glanced over to her right and discovered, to her surprise, that the Scholar in a fine suit had slipped up and was now walking at her side. She raised her veil and looked at her agent with eyes near tears, rimmed in confusion. "You...you looked like you could use the company, madame," he said. Rowan squeezed his oaken forearm and lowered her veil.

They arrived at the grave sites on Angel Hill. It took some time for all the coffins to arrive and to be unloaded. The crowd gathered, and before them, row after row of coffins were laid out on the grass. Highfather's and Auggie's were at the fore. Ringo's was somewhere far behind theirs, among the plain pine boxes of the soldiers and the poor. The view from Angel Hill took in all of Golgotha and beyond, out into the 40-Mile to the east, and the sun beginning to rise above the cold shadow of Argent.

There was a murmur among the mourners as Higbee stepped out of the crowd and turned to address them. "I...uh...thank you all for attending," he said. "I'm not terribly good at this sort of thing. Speeches were more Mayor Pratt's bailiwick than mine." The mention of Harry's name sent a ripple through the crowd, but it quickly silenced as Higbee continued, raising his voice, slightly.

"If Mayor Pratt could be with us today, I know he would have words of inspiration and comfort for all of us. I am afraid all I can do is express my sincere condolences for everyone here today who has lost someone in the awful chaos that has befallen our town. I can promise you that we will rebuild and that Golgotha will be...stronger for having survived another tragedy." Higbee looked down. It was obvious each word was like a razor cut for him. He scanned the crowd and adjusted his glasses.

"In Mayor Pratt's absence, I asked Mr. Bick to say a few words. Mr. Bick?" Malachi stepped forward, the panorama of the view at his back.

"In my time here," Bick began, "I have found the concept of death to be one that has often confused and confounded me." He looked to his daughter, Emily, and then to the mural of faces of the townsfolk who stood before him. "Death is part of the cycle of being. Birds die, stars die, ants die, worlds die, people die. All things of this universe have an ending." Bick looked to Clay Turlough and saw the inventor fighting not to cry as he stared at Auggie's coffin. "Death is no different than sleep or requiring nourishment, and yet virtually every person's mind is filled with thoughts of the end of their life, of their death, for most of their time among the living.

"It has been my experience that a death seldom says more about the man than his life does. That extraordinary men often have very, very ordinary ends." Bick looked across the sea of coffins. "Death is common; it's cheap and inevitable. At the end of all things, it is what comes before that end that defines and distinguishes, that gives context. If one is truly fortunate, truly blessed, then death mirrors those things that mattered in life."

"This world, this place, it takes and it gives, but it is rare that there is a balance in that transaction. It is easy to feel yourself cheated by life, sold short, and unfairly treated. It wears us all down, like a millstone. It is easy to return that bitterness with an equal or greater measure and therein lies the state of the world, the state of man.

"There are few in this life that refuse to be ground down, to be diminished regardless of how harshly they are put against the wheel..." Bick's gaze fixed on Highfather's coffin, then Auggie's beside him, and his eyes darkened, the sky seemed to as well. "I can only speak to Mr. Shultz and Sheriff Highfather, personally, but I can tell you, both of them taught me lessons...I shall never forget. They died as they lived, uncompromising, unbowed. They represented the finest parts of humanity, the parts worth striving for, the parts you should be very, very proud to possess. They died in the service of others. There is no greater love; there is no finer death." Bick stood silent for a moment, regarding the caskets, then walked back to the crowd and joined Emily and Gillian.

There were prayers and hymns, concluding in "Now the Day is Over." The assembled slowly departed in groups. Some tarried by the graves, by their loved one's coffins, but slowly, one by one, they left the necropolis and walked back into the world of the living. Bick was the last.

He stood on the same hill on which he used to watch the little primates play and fight and huddle together against the terror of the night, so long ago. He watched the sun cross the sky while behind him the gravediggers did their work. Clay Turlough came back, still in his suit, and assisted in burying Auggie and Highfather himself. Clay looked to Bick, but neither said a word.

Eventually, their jobs done, Clay and the diggers left. The sun began to drown on the sanguine floor of the desert. Bick finally turned his back on the living art, the divine puzzle, he had watched all day, and regarded the mounds of the fresh graves, the new markers and crosses planted, a garden of memory, as beautiful in its own way as any other garden. If there was one gift he could give the little primates that scuttled across this world, playing at owning it, it would be to spend more time meditating on the sky and mountains, the sun and the stars, than upon the grave. The angel walked down his hill and headed for his home.

THE FOUR OF SWORDS

I f you have any reason to contact me, I'll be in Virginia City at our estate for at least two months," Ora Cooper Pratt said to Sarah Pratt as they walked through the grand foyer of Pratt Manor and out the main doors. Ora talked to Sarah as if she were a servant; in their few exchanges, she always did, but Sarah ignored it, as usual. She used to do it for Harry's sake. Now she did it to get this reprehensible creature away as soon as possible.

It was the afternoon after the funeral, and Ora was ready to get out of Golgotha. Her coach was packed, and her driver, one of her father's men, opened the door and lowered the step. "I've treasured every moment here, sweet Sarah, but most of all meeting you."

"I feel the same, Ora, dear," Sarah said. "I'm so sorry the railroad project has had to be delayed. I know it's a difficulty for your poor father, your whole family, really." Ora's mask slipped for a moment, but then she recovered her composure.

"Thank you." Ora practically spit out the words. "It will get done. Daddy says this is a setback, nothing more."

"It's really for the best, pet; this desert was playing havoc on your complexion," Sarah said with wide, earnest eyes that held not an ounce of malice. "You were beginning to look like the tanner's wares." Ora glared, touched her cheek, but said nothing. The coach door closed and sped away without Ora saying another word. "I'll write at Christmas, dear," Sarah added as the coach disappeared out of sight. "Have a nice trip...back to Hell." Sarah sighed and turned to get back to helping Lamarr and Judith pack Harry's things away.

That evening, Porter Rockwell came by to bid farewell. "I was sent to help the mayor address the problem with these Lamanites' raids, Miss Sarah," the Mormon gunslinger said. "It would seem that after a lot of caterwauling, things have been resolved, and I should get home and give President Young my report."

"Thank you for all you've done, Mr. Rockwell," Sarah said. "I felt better knowing Harry had you...protecting him."

"I must admit, I'm pretty disappointed in your husband, ma'am. For one with the claim laid upon him of being the One Mighty and Strong, I didn't expect him to just cut and run when things got tough."

"Harry suffered losses, terrible losses, in recent days. He needs time to heal from that, Mr. Rockwell," Sarah said. "Never confuse cowardice with knowing when you must retreat."

"I must confess that is a weakness I, myself, am afflicted with, madam," Rockwell said, taking his hat. "Still, I am pleased that I did not have to perform some of the tasks laid at my feet during my visit. I like this town, keeps you hoppin'. I think I might come back if my duties allow." He bowed to her and kissed her hand. "Goodbye, Miss Sarah. Please extend my good will to your husband if he turns up again."

"I will," Sarah said, "*when* he does."

Sarah Pratt descended into the cavern under the mansion for the first time later that night. Holding a hooded lantern to guide her way, she walked down the narrow passage into the cave, and the lantern's light was caught by the gleaming surfaces of the treasures of

Heaven. Sarah audibly gasped as the light seemed to be amplified by the mere presence of the artifacts of her faith. "Oh, Harry," she muttered. "I always half-thought you crazy, but it's true. It's all true."

Sarah sat the lamp on a ledge and wandered among the treasures, afraid even to touch anything. She gave the iron box, which held the skull Harry had warned her about, as great a distance as she could. She paused at the great metal plates that held prophecy within them, written in an angelic script, and she wondered where Harry had gone. Was he taking care of himself? Was he ever coming home to Golgotha again? Wherever Golgotha's lost mayor was, his wife said a prayer for his safety, his healing, and his return. Then Sarah noticed something that gave her pause and made a tiny smile come to her lips. The holy sword and breastplate that Harry had often carried and used over the past few years was not among the treasurers. *He must have taken them with him.* The thought gave her hope and hope for Harry, too. Sarah crossed her arms and looked around the cave.

"Oh, goodness, Harry," she said, "didn't you *ever* dust down here?"

The riverboat, *Lady of Saints,* chugged her way down the muddy-brown snake they called the Mississippi. She was out of Memphis and making her way leisurely toward New Orleans. Harry Pratt leaned against the rail and watched the ancient river flow around the big paddles of the showboat. Night was creeping its way in as the brilliant sun flashed and hid behind the cypress trees along the shore.

Harry worked hard to not think past the burning end of the hand-rolled cigarette between his fingers. He would smoke this one. Perhaps make another and smoke it too. Then there were cards to be played, money to be won or lost. Harry hadn't smoked or gambled much since his university days. When he had returned home after college, there were appearances to maintain, expectations from his father and the elders. However, both seemed like damn good ideas now. They filled up his brain and anchored him to here.

"I hear you are the man to beat on this boat, Pratt," a handsome blond man in a dark green velvet smoking jacket said, joining Harry at the rail.

"Am I?" Harry said, his eyes scanning the water and the banks. "I was not informed." The blond laughed and removed a cigarette from a silver case.

"Well, you have been, now. Justinian Oarr," the man extended his hand. Harry shook it, "at your service. I look forward to…"

A woman dressed in a beautiful yellow dress rushed onto the deck, sobbing loudly. Her face was swelling, and one of her eyes was already closed. Her nose and mouth bled. "Please, someone help me!" she gasped. "He's mad. He intends to kill me!" The half-dozen or so well-dressed men of leisure on the deck either turned away and ignored her or chuckled and muttered under their breath. No one approached the woman. "Please," the woman cried, her eyes full of panic and fear.

"An adventuress," Oarr said with a shrug. "They're like bedbugs, blood-sucking annoyances. For boasting such an exclusive clientele, it seems they let the worst class of folk on this ship." Harry grunted and kept his eyes on the water, watched his cigarette burn to his fingers. *Stay out of it.*

"There you are," a man's voice said at Harry's back. "Come along, m'dear. You have already bothered these gentlemen long enough with your childish prattling."

"No," the woman said, almost whispered it, like a prayer.

Keep out of it, Harry told himself. *Smoke. Drink, gamble. You're not responsible to anyone, anymore. You're not the One Mighty and Strong. You never were. Mind your own business.*

The gentlemen with the bloody knuckles reached out for the woman. A hand caught his wrist.

"The lady said no," Harry said.

The cave entrance in the side of the mountain at Izusa's old camp was buried under half the mountain's face. "Dynamite," one of Izusa's soldiers said. "Quite a bit too, *teniwaaten*. I'm sorry. The white man's army must have done it while we were away in battle. We can try to blast into it ourselves. Get some dynamite? I know we can find another way into the caves, Izusa."

"They would just be caves, now," Izusa said. "Leave me." The brave did as she asked and joined his companions in the field. Where once she led hundreds, thousands, now only a handful remained. So many had died in the battles, and now the cavalry hunted them relentlessly. Since the death of General Caxton, the whites had sent more soldiers, more men like Caxton and worse. And now, the lands of the dead were closed to her.

"Mutt," Izusa said as she looked at the wall of stone. She said the name like she was spitting poison out of your mouth. Word had come that Snake-Man was dead. The federals said he was killed by them. The renegades told the tale of him fighting till his last breath against the whites. Izusa knew, felt, the truth. Mutt and Wodziwob, they had killed him.

It was Mutt who had come here and sealed the cave. Wodziwob now preached that the paradise beyond his ghost dance was for all, not just the *numa*, but for the white men too. She wondered how long before the federal troopers would outlaw his dance, all dances, even the sun dance. By the time those fools realized their way led to death, it would be too late. She would spit on the dry stones if her mouth held the water to do it.

Izusa touched her belly. The blood of a great spirit resided within Snake-Man's and her child. The baby would grow and become a great leader, would lead the *numa* to victory. And Izusa, she would see to it that the son of Coyote was nothing but bleached bones in the desert before her child's ascent. She made a silent oath to her child that the baby would grow up in a far better world than this one, regardless of how many bodies she had to pile.

Izusa reached out to the voices of the dead, which had comforted her and taught her since she was a frightened child, running from the white troopers who slaughtered her band. She asked them for guidance, for wisdom and aid. The voices were so soft, so muted, she could hardly hear them now. Her door between worlds had been closed.

She called out to her followers. "Prepare to ride," she said. "The medicine in this place sleeps now. The dead sleep again."

"What will we do?" one of her braves asked.

"Survive," she said. "Grow strong again. Rise." They rode east, toward the Utah line, the mute dead at their backs.

<hr>

The day of Auggie Junior's confirmation was on the same day as the funeral. Mutt and Jim and Leeza joined Constance, Maude, and Gillian for dinner at Maude's home that evening after the services and ceremony. Little Auggie snored contentedly, wrapped in blankets in Constance's arms.

"I'm ashamed to confess," Gillian said, sipping her tea, "I was quite relieved when the priest rubbed the holy water on his forehead and it didn't burst into flames or anything." They laughed, but it was a little forced. "Thank all of you for coming today. It meant so much to me, and I know it would have to Auggie too."

"Where's Clay?" Maude asked. "He took off right off after the services."

"He wanted to see to the burials himself," Gillian said, "and then he was going to dispose of the rest of the bio-restorative formula," she said. "It's too dangerous, knowing what we know about it now."

"He's sold a mess of it to folks all over," Jim said. "Seems like the cow's already got out of the barn, if you get my meaning."

"Yes. Hopefully that horrid concoction won't cause any more trouble. Clay is blaming himself terribly for this whole situation. Shelly says he hasn't eaten or slept since Auggie passed." No one spoke for a few moments. The baby cooed as he woke, and Constance sniffed, wrinkled her nose, and smiled.

"Well, either some critter just expired nearby or our little gentleman just pooped himself." They laughed. Gillian began to rise. "Oh, may I change him?" Constance asked.

"Of course, dear," Gillian said. Constance stood and began to move away from the table.

"Mr. Negrey," Constance said, "since you are expert at being a stinker, you will assist me." Mutt chuckled. Jim looked little pale.

"Me? Uh, you sure?" Jim said, his voice holding more than a little apprehension. Constance snickered. Leeza laughed.

"Deputy Jim's skeered!" Leeza taunted.

"You've fought soul-drinking monsters and crazed desperadoes," Constance said, "and a little baby's bottom is giving you the shivers?"

"Blood-drinking monsters I know," Jim said. "Baby bottoms, not so much."

Jim looked to Mutt for help. What he got was the crooked grin that showed up whenever Jim was in discomfort. "Pinch your nose," Mutt said, "and aim for the middle. Good practice for you." Jim blushed. "Ah, those big old red ears!" Mutt said. "They could lead you home in the dark."

Jim stood and joined Constance. Though she didn't have her cane, she navigated easily, and the two teens went down the hall to the spare bedroom where Gillian and Auggie Junior had been staying since The Sons of Typhon had wrecked their house. The two young people whispered and laughed as they disappeared to attend to their smelly task.

"How's she getting along?" Gillian asked Maude. "Did Clay say anything?"

"Clay says her eyes are perfectly fine," Maude said. "There is no physical reason for her not to be able to see."

"It's witchcraft," Mutt said. "Izusa put a hex on her when they were scraping. Only a more powerful medicine worker or Izusa herself can remove the spell."

"I'm going to track her," Maude said, "and she's going to do right by my daughter, or I swear, she'll wish she had."

"I'm so sorry this happened, Maude," Gillian said, touching her friend's hand.

"I'm sorry for everything you've had to go through," Maude said. "Constance has her senses to help her in this, and she's strong."

"Just like her mother," Mutt said. A strange pain seemed to pass behind Maude's eyes. Only Mutt saw it.

Gillian looked over to Leeza, who was yawning. "I think, young lady, we need to fix you a nest to lay down, don't you?"

"We staying the night?" Leeza asked. Gillian looked to her hostess, and Maude smiled. "Okay-doke. Good night, Miss Maude, 'night, Mr. Mutt."

"Come here, kid," Mutt said. Leeza, rubbing her eyes, hesitantly walked over to Mutt. He took a slip of paper out of his pocket and handed it to her. "You give this to Jim from me?" The little girl nodded. "And this too." Mutt hugged her and kissed her on the forehead. Leeza giggled. "You take good care of Jim for me, okay?"

"Okay-doke," she said and kissed his scarred and pitted cheek. "Night, Mr. Mutt."

"Night, darlin'," Mutt said.

Gillian led Leeza toward the bedrooms. "I think I'm turning in, too," she said. "Goodnight." Mutt and Maude were alone now at the table.

"Want to get a breath of air?" he asked. They both stood from the table and walked outside. The warm spring day had fled, and there was a chill in the night air. Mutt slipped off Jon's suit coat and draped it over Maude's shoulders.

"You're leaving," Maude said. Mutt looked out into the darkness.

"That jackass, Pinkerton, he put out bounties on Jonathan and me for going after Caxton and his men," he said. "I'm a wanted man now, Maude. He let it slide at the funeral today, but by tomorrow morning, I'll be in irons, headed for the gallows."

"You could fight it," Maude said, taking his hand, "in court."

"Given your recent experiences with the open-mindedness of the American legal system," Mutt said, "how well you think that's going to play?" Maude sighed. Hands that had held up a mountain squeezed his gently.

"We never get a break," she said.

"Sure, we do," Mutt said. "We found each other." They kissed, fed each other the breath of their souls, and never, ever wanted to let go.

Mutt's rough hands caressed her smooth cheek. "That thing I've been meaning to tell you for a spell now?"

"Yes?" she said smiling and, bringing her face close to his.

"I love you, Maude." Maude entwined her arms in his. "I love you with everything I got in me."

"I love you," she said. They kissed again.

"I better go," he said, untangling them, hating himself for having to do it.

"You...going tonight?" She felt the heat in her eyes, her heart stuttering as if she were in mortal peril. She could control her breathing, her blood flow, her reaction to the cold. She could have stopped the tears, slowed her heart. She didn't want to.

"I reckon I better," Mutt said, beginning to walk toward the path that led down Rose Hill. He paused and turned back to her. "Say," he said, "once I get this whole wanted-outlaw-price-on-my-head thing taken care of...you fancy getting hitched?"

"That is one of the worst proposals I've ever heard in my entire life," Maude said smiling, tears running down her cheeks. "Yes. Yes, I do."

Mutt nodded. "Square deal." He wiped the tears from her cheeks, kissed her small hands. "I'm coming back. I'm coming back for you," he said.

"If you don't," Maude said, hugging him and then letting him go, "I'll come get you." Mutt walked out into the darkness. Maude listened to the sound of his breathing, the drum of his heart, until they were lost in the distance.

THE KING OF WANDS

D eputy Negrey, thank you for coming," Colton Higbee said.
Jim looked around the mayor's office and realized he had
never been in here before. Parts of town hall had been
destroyed by fire, but the building still stood, and its structure was
still sound. Jim could hear the pounding of hammers from the
workmen downstairs. "Please have a seat. Would you care for
anything to drink?"

"No, thank you, sir," Jim said. Higbee looked as awkward in his
seat as Jim was in his. While Higbee came off as a rather mild soul, Jim
had heard a story over the last few days that this quiet bureaucrat had
rushed in during the Indian raid and the fires and single-handily
saved the town's archives and records from going up in smoke. Jim
wasn't entirely sure what to think of a man who risked his own life to
save a bunch of government papers.

"As you know," Higbee said, "Mayor Pratt left me in charge as
acting mayor until his return. Sheriff Highfather, just before his death,
informed me he had to resign his position, and he recommend to me
that you take his place as sheriff of Golgotha."

"Me?" Jim said. "He left me a letter, but he didn't say anything about me being sheriff. Mr. Higbee, sir, I'm not the man for that job. Deputy Mutt did a great job as sheriff when Ray Zeal..."

"Deputy Mutt also resigned," Higbee said, interrupting. "In fact, he and Jon Highfather were both listed as fugitives from justice, wanted dead or alive for treason and the murder of federal soldiers."

"No, sir," Jim said. "The sheriff and Mutt were trying to keep General Caxton from hurting those people."

"That may be," Higbee said, dabbing his upper lip with his handkerchief, "but Mutt's fate is out of my hands. I'm sorry."

"Mr. Higbee, either Miss Warne or Mr. Hayes has a lot more experience than me. Either one would be a fine sheriff." Colton removed his glasses and began to clean the lenses, looking at them instead of Jim.

"Deputy Negrey, how can I say this as delicately as possible... I agree with you that either deputy would make a fine sheriff...but the people of this town...they won't follow the orders of a negro or a woman. I'm sorry, but you know it's true."

"Mr. Higbee," Jim said, "all of the other deputies have had to deal with that trough water since they put on the badge. They all handle it in their own ways, and they all command respect and authority, sir. You give them a chance, and they'll show you that." Higbee looked even more uncomfortable than he already did. "Besides," Jim added, "I heard tell over in Rock Ridge there's a black sheriff."

"I'm afraid Golgotha is just not that progressive," Higbee said. "I wish it were, truly. You are the most qualified candidate."

"Having eliminated all the others," Jim said. Higbee sighed and began to clean his glasses.

"If you turn the job down and remain a deputy," Higbee said, "I'll understand. We'll begin advertising for a new sheriff; though, given our reputation, that may take a while. Perhaps you'd accept the job on a temporary basis? See if it suits you? Jon Highfather spoke very highly of your ability and your character, I must say. He said Golgotha would be very fortunate to have you as her sheriff."

Jim looked over at the mayor's desk. Highfather's silver star sat on top of a pile of papers. "I know how you're feeling," Higbee said. "You're about the same age I was when I began working for Mayor Pratt. I don't feel qualified to sit in this chair, to do his job. However, life seldom prepares us for what's next or lays out a clear path for us to follow. I'll do the mayor's job until he returns or they find someone better, because I owe that to the man who believed in me."

Jim stood. "I'll take the job."

"Very good," Higbee said, smiling. He handed Jim the silver star.

"Same conditions as the town had with Sheriff Highfather. I do this job my way, with the people I trust. Place like this, you can't have a bunch of politicians second-guessing everything you do. People die if that happens." Jim paused for a moment, Highfather's words coming out of his mouth.

"Of course," Higbee said. "You have my full and unconditional support and confidence."

Jim removed his deputy's star. He looked at Highfather's badge in his hand for a long time. Not Highfather's badge, his. He pinned the sheriff's silver star to the lapel of his coat. They shook hands.

"Guess I better get to it," Jim said, walking to the door. "Mr. Acting Mayor, I won't let you down."

"I know you won't," Higbee said, "Sheriff Negrey."

K ate was on Bick Street, watching several crews working to repair some of the fire-damaged buildings near the corner. A buggy rolled toward her and then slowed and stopped. Allan Pinkerton was at the reins.

"Hello," he said. Kate smiled.

"Hello, Allan," she said. "I figured you had already taken off."

"On my way to Hazen to catch the train east. I didn't intend to leave without you," he said and looked about furtively. "I had hoped a few days might change your mind."

"I'm staying," she said. "This is a good place, with good people. They deserve protection from the things that come calling."

"You are one of my best operatives," Pinkerton said. "You and I both know you will save a lot more lives out in the field than being a deputy in a one-horse mining town." Kate said nothing. "This isn't about duty, is it? It's about him." The shade from the brim of Kate's hat hid the intent in her eyes.

"I know I came here on a mission," Kate said, "but this place...grows on you. It feels like home, Allan, and that's something I can't ever recall having." Pain crossed Pinkerton's face, but he mastered it quickly.

"I...had...hoped I had been able to be that for you," he said, his voice choking a bit in his throat. "You are...very precious to me, Kate." Kate leaned in to the buggy and took Pinkerton's cut and bandaged hand.

"And you to me," she said. "But I can't be one of your 'assets' anymore. You gave me purpose, and confidence, and comfort but all under your rules. I can't be at your feet anymore. I need this. I need to make my own rules, my own way. I need to build my own home." She kissed Pinkerton on the cheek and let go of his hand. Pinkerton held hers a second longer and then finally let her go.

"I've convinced Doctor Turlough to do some contract work for OSIRIS," he said. "I may be back through from time to time. I hope I may call upon you?"

Kate laughed. "Of course," she said. She felt like she should say more, but she kept her tongue. Pinkerton seemed to be dealing with the same conflict, but he quickly won his internal battle.

"Very good, then," he said as he always did at the conclusion of a meeting. He snapped the reins, and the buggy jerked forward. Kate watched it go and felt odd, both sad and renewed. She decided she liked the feeling. She missed Jon Highfather, but there was comfort in his memory more than pain, and strangely that made her think she had made the right choice to stay. The deputy walked down Prosperity Street, making sure all was well in the town, her town.

I tried to tell Mr. Higbee that either of you would be better suited to this," Jim said to Kate and Rabb. They were in the jail a little past noon, and all three were clustered around Jon's desk. Jim hadn't sat down in it. No one had since Jon.

Rabb and Kate looked at each other and laughed. "I'm sure that suggestion went over famously," Kate said. "No, Jim, Higbee's right. Rabb and I would spend half our time dealing with damn fools and not getting the job done. Even under Jonathan, it was only the fact we were 'subordinates' that kept the idiots mollified. It has to be you, now."

"It ain't right," Jim said, shaking his head.

"Very true," Rabb said. "But that don't change the world from being wrong. We'll fight, we'll bleed, and we will not accept defeat. It is nearly impossible to push the world with a lever. Nearly."

"I just wanted you both to know I thought you were better suited to this job than me. I'll need your help and your honesty every single day." Jim looked between the two deputies' faces. "Please, please let me know if I'm screwing up and point me true."

"So," Kate said smiling, "business as usual, then."

Jim laughed. "Yeah, exactly the same as he would do," he said. "I can work this job, but I can never replace him."

"He'd be proud to know you took up his star," Kate said. Her voice was tight with pain. "Very proud."

"Sun's low," Rabb said. "Shouldn't we get to work, Sheriff?"

Jim pushed his hat back on his head. The words echoed in his head, Mutt's words from what seemed a million years ago. "Gonna be dark soon. Time to earn our pay."

T he man from West Virginia knocked on the open door of Clay's clinic. The place had seen better days. While it had been spared the fires of Izusa's raid, the place had been overrun for days afterward as Clay, beaten and exhausted from the ordeal in the mines, worked non-stop to try to save as many lives as he could. Now, close to a week after the funeral, Clay sat on the bench in the outer office and stared out his window as the sun sank in the sky and the shadows grew.

"Doctor? Doctor?" It took a moment to pull himself out of his skull to hear the voice. Clay blinked and looked over at the man who had visited his practice before all the chaos and death had begun. "I'm sorry to bother you, but I heard you are no longer selling your bio-restorative formula?"

"That is correct," Clay said.

"May I ask you why?" the man, Clay recalled he said he was an attorney, said.

"No," Clay said and then just stared at the man with bleary eyes. Clay hadn't slept since Auggie's death, hadn't eaten or bathed. He looked more dead than alive.

"Well, I have been instructed by my client to purchase all your remaining stock as well as the formula and all rights therein."

"No," Clay said.

"I assure you the sum is very generous."

"I destroyed the rest of the formula," Clay said. Even talking, focusing on talking, was a painful chore. "I also burned the rare key ingredient so that no more of the substance can be made ever again."

"I see," the man from West Virginia said. "A tragic loss to the field of medicine, sir." Clay didn't reply, just stared. "A good evening, Dr. Turlough." And the man departed.

Some time passed, and Clay slid deeper into his bone home, letting broken thoughts and shattered emotions float about and bump into one another like debris bobbing in black water. Someone was near and trying to talk to him again. He blinked and focused. It was Gillian.

368

"I had considered bringing you a basket of food," she said. "I have so much 'sympathy food' cluttering up Maude's place, but then I decided I didn't want to put it in a basket and bring it to you. I'd prefer to drag you up there and let you graze at your leisure."

"I'm not hungry, Gillian," Clay said, his voice cracked from lack of use.

Gillian smiled and leaned in closer. "I don't think you understand the seriousness of this, Clayton. If I see another ham biscuit, I shall surely lose my mind. I've set Jim Negrey upon it twice now, and even he has been defeated by this mass." Clay's expression remained empty.

"How do you do that?" he asked after a few moments. "Stay cheerful, joke? I wish I knew the secret. People...I've never been able to understand them."

"I know," she said. "I just try to think how much the other person must be hurting and try to make it better for them."

"Who makes it better for you?" he asked, as earnest as a child. Gillian blinked and laid her head on his bony shoulder, put her arm around him. She sniffled, and the tears began.

"My friends, my family, my little boy, you, Clayton. You all make it bearable, just barely bearable." Clay looked at her as if he had just awoken.

"I reckon I could put back a ham biscuit or two," he said.

"Thank you, Clay," Gillian said. "I'll help you lock up."

They walked together down the street in the pink halo of the end of the day. "You mind if we fetch Shelly?" Clay asked. "She's been real sad, too."

"She'll probably beat us there," Gillian said, wiping her eyes.

"Gillian," Clay said as he paused in the street, fighting to form ideas, words that were so hard for him. "Thank you...for being my friend." Tears fell down his face, and Gillian wondered if he even was aware of them. "I don't even like ham biscuits," Clay said, looking at her earnestly. She choked back a sob tangled in a laugh and put her arm around him, guiding them both. They made their way in the fading glow of the twilight, two hollowed-out people, struggling to make a whole.

The man from West Virginia walked to the telegram office near the fire-gutted stagecoach depot on Main to report the bad news about Clay destroying the formula. He paused for a moment as he saw a young man with a sheriff's star on his coat lapel pause to talk to a passerby. The lawyer's eyes widened in recognition. He hurriedly entered the tiny office and discovered he was interrupting the telegraph operator's evening meal of beans and cornbread. He didn't bother to apologize. "I need to send a telegram to Albright, West Virginia, with haste." The operator pulled the pencil from behind his ear and prepared to transcribe the message.

"No further merchandise available from Dr. Turlough, stop," the man began as the operator scribbled. "Formula also unavailable, stop. Returning tomorrow by train, stop. Good news, stop." The man from West Virginia's face unfolded into a smile. "Tell Colonel Upton I have located Jim Negrey, stop."

Mutt sat on his horse at the crossroad of Rose Road and Angel's Ascent; a second horse, tied to Muha, waited patiently behind. The moon was high and bright, and he had been lucky to make it back to the edge of town again without being seen. He wasn't sure how much longer his luck was going to hold. Then he glanced up the hill of Angel's Ascent and saw a lone figure, a man, walking down the hill, silhouetted in the moonlight, dust swirling about him in a cloud with each step. Mutt's face spread into a wide grin.

"What took you so damn long?" Mutt asked.

"How long?" Jon Highfather said, sounding tired and confused. He pulled off the burial suit he had been draped in, slit up the back. A new pattern of ugly scar tissue covered his chest and stomach. Mutt recalled he and Clay, both ashen, gathering up what they could find of Highfather's ruptured and fragmented body.

"A week, give or take," Mutt said. "How are you, Jonathan?"

"Considering I just busted out of my coffin and crawled my way to the surface...no complaints," Jon said. "You could've installed one of those little tubes with the bell on it to let people know I was still alive."

"You have any idea how expensive those things are?" Mutt said. "Stop your bellyaching. I told Clay to use short nails on your box. That should have made it a little easier." Highfather looked at him incredulously. "And here, here's some pants." He tossed Highfather a pair of his denim work pants. Jon slid into them as he tried to shake the dirt out of his hair.

"What happened, Jonathan?" Mutt asked. "I mean...after."

"I don't remember much," Highfather said. "I met someone. The one who gave Rabb the message for me."

"The dead man?" Mutt asked. Jon nodded. Mutt tossed him a clean shirt and his boots.

"He needs me to find his real killers and bring them to justice," Jon said, struggling into the clothing. "He said he knows the reason why I can't seem to die proper. He said that's why it has to be me."

"This dead man have a name?" Mutt asked.

"Lincoln," Highfather said, "President Abraham Lincoln."

"Of course," Mutt said. "That should be easy. I guess we're heading east then."

"*We?*" Jon said, "Mutt, I have to do this alo..."

"Just shut up," Mutt said. "I was hoping a little time in the ground would improve your disposition. No such luck. Without me, you'd be running around the countryside naked and scaring folks. Hell, you wouldn't even have a horse." Mutt tugged on the reins of the second horse, and Bright trotted up to nuzzle her old master.

"Hey, girl," Jon said, petting her nose. "I'm so glad you're okay." He looked up to Mutt. "Thank you for looking after her."

"It's good to see you, Jonathan," Mutt said. "Let's get going. It sounds like we have a long ride ahead of us and a lot of country to cover. That ain't going to be easy."

Jon buckled on his gun belt and climbed into Bright's saddle. "How's that?"

"We're both outlaws now," Mutt said. "Wanted dead or alive."

"Which category do I fall under?" Highfather asked, slipping on his Stetson. They began to ride off the road, heading east into the fringes of the 40-Mile.

"You joke all you like," Mutt said. "Once they find your grave all opened up, it's going to be the start of the legend of the dead desperado."

"And his faithful Indian side-kick..."

"I will side-kick your bony white ass," Mutt said. Both men chuckled.

"What happened with Caxton? Wodziwob? Izusa?"

"I'll tell you on the way," Mutt said.

Their horses fell into a rhythm, and they galloped away from Golgotha, feeling her release them from her embrace. Jon didn't know if he'd ever return, could ever return. He thought of Kate, and his newly beating heart ached. He swore then to return. Mutt was committed to coming back to the only real home he'd ever known. He felt Maude at his back like a compass in his chest.

"Thanks," Jon said, "for waiting for me."

"Thanks," Mutt said, "for coming back."

They rode side-by-side, as they always had, as they always would, come what may.

EPILOGUE

THE WHEEL OF FORTUNE

August 23ʳᵈ 2020

That's how Jim Negrey became the sheriff of Golgotha," Bick said. Will Negrey sipped his ridiculously large soda, referred to on the plastic cup as an "Uber-Slurp," and pushed his paper plate away from him on the table. The plate held the remains of a lunch of greasy, over-cooked chicken tenders and potato wedges that were kept ready under a heat lamp for any would-be victims, behind glass at the squat counter near the island of tables.

"Hawthorne Wodziwob amended his prophecy in the later years of his life to include the white men as well as his own people coming together to create a new world, a new paradise. It...didn't work out that way, as you know. The young man, Wavoka, grew to adulthood and kept the circle dance and the prophecies and customs of his people alive through dark days even though the U.S. Government tried very hard to outlaw them, to erase them. The Ghost Dance Movement energized generations of young Native Americans to rediscover their cultures and continue to fight for a better world."

"What happened to Izusa? Harry Pratt, Clay? Maude Stapleton? Highfather and Mutt?"

"Legends," Bick said. "The west is full of legends. Tall tales and wild stories. History and myth all tumbled together, larger than life. I often think only the west is large enough to hold them all. Come back another time, young man, and I'll tell you some more. It helps me...pass the time."

"Thanks, Marcus," Will said, shaking his hand. "I'd like that." The "young man" comment struck Will as odd. Bick looked to be in his early thirties, not really the age you'd expect to hear millennial clichés from. The way he had told his tale had been odd, too. The detail was so rich, and it was clear that Bick had an emotional connection to the people and events he'd described. It went beyond passion for history, and it made the hair on Will's neck stand up. This innocuous, articulate store clerk suddenly seemed much more than he had when Will had walked in the door.

"Family history is kind of my thing," he said as he stood and took his trash to a kitchen can near the counter. "Maybe you can help me with a little piece of forgotten lore before I scoot."

"Certainly," Bick said, also standing.

"Jim was supposed to have had in his possession a family heirloom," Will said. "It belonged to William 'Billy' Negrey, Jim's dad, my great-great-great grandfather. I was actually named after Billy."

Bick's eyes narrowed, and his gaze grew more intense. Will felt like the whole universe was suddenly a very tight place. He felt held by Bick's regard, like a butterfly on a pin. "I see. What was this family heirloom?" Bick asked.

"A glass eye," Will said, shaking off the oppressive feeling. "Jade, actually. Jim kept it in his possession his whole life, but somehow there's no record in the family bible or any other accounts of what became of it after that."

"I've heard stories of it," Bick said. "Supposedly it was Asian in origin. Jim carried it as a kind of...good luck charm."

"Any idea where I might start looking for it?" Will asked.

Bick shook his head.

"I'm afraid not. I'm sorry. Any particular reason you're looking?"

"Just to bring it back into the family," Will said. Bick smiled.

"Of course. Good luck in your search, Agent Negrey. It's a pleasure to meet you."

Will gassed up the SUV and was glad he had a company credit card to afford the full tank. He drove off just as a pack of kids—Hispanic, white, black, and Native American—rode down the deserted street on off-road bicycles. The kids waved and said hi as they left a jumbled pile of bikes near the door to the convenience store and raced each other inside. Will imagined them making a beeline for Bick's comic books, Slim Jims, and slushie machine. He liked Golgotha in spite of himself. Will pulled over to the side of the road, not too far from the store.

He turned on his phone and managed to get a single bar of service by moving it around a bit. He called the proxy number that would go through a number of switches and eventually reach C&C.

"Control," a man's voice said flatly, "go."

"I'm here," he said, "but no sign of the asset yet."

"We don't have much time left," the man's voice said, the frustration and fatigue leaking over the horrible connection.

"I know, sir," Will said. "I will find it."

"Any indication Odom Sodd might have it?" the man on the phone asked.

"No," Will said. "And he hasn't been here yet. What's left of the town is still standing."

"Good," the voice said. "Then we're not done yet. You coming in?"

"Negative," Will said, looking in his side mirror, back at Bick's store. "Something I want to run down here first. OSIRIS doesn't need me there to pace and fret. I think there's more going on here. I want to chase it down."

"Do it, Will," the man said. "Do whatever you have to. The Eye of the Moon is our only hope."

"Yes, sir," Will said and hung up the phone.

In his store, Marcus Bick looked out his dirty window at Will Negrey's idling SUV as he dialed a number on an old phone with a rotary dial. The connection sounded like being underwater; after several hums and clicks, someone picked up the line.

"Hello?" It was a woman's voice, old, but still strong and clear.

"I just had a visit," Bick said, "from a man named Negrey."

"Malachi, is that you?"

"He was looking for the eye, Maude," Bick said. "I've felt something moving across the Earth, through it, for a time. The Darkling under the mountain is restless. That's no coincidence. Something as old as me is moving across the world. It wants the moon god's eye as does our Mr. Negrey and whoever sent him."

"What do we do?" Maude Stapleton asked.

"I think it may be time," Bick said, "to get the band back together."

ACKNOWLEDGMENTS

Thank you to my Agent, Lucienne Diver, of the Knight Agency, and John Hartness, the Publisher of Falstaff Books, for bringing everyone back to Golgotha. Thank you to Greg Cox and Stacey Hill for blazing that trail. Thank you to all of them for believing in me and my tiny little town.

To Melissa McArthur, Associate Publisher at Falstaff and a fantastic editor. Thank you so much for everything!

Thank you to all the patient and kind indigenous people who answered ignorant questions and explained their faiths to me unto the wee hours online. Your knowledge enriched and guided.

Thank you to my wonderful children, Jon, Emily, and Stephanie for every day with you.

ABOUT THE AUTHOR

R.S. (Rod) Belcher is an award-winning newspaper and magazine editor and journalist, as well as an author of short and long fiction in a number of genres.

Rod has been a private investigator, a DJ, a comic book store owner and has degrees in criminal law, psychology and justice and risk administration, from Virginia Commonwealth University. He's done Masters work in Forensic Science at The George Washington University and worked with the Occult Crime Taskforce for the Virginia General Assembly.

The Grand Prize winner of the Star Trek: Strange New Worlds Anthology contest, Rod's short story "Orphans" was published in Star Trek: Strange New Worlds 9 published by Simon and Schuster in 2006. It was his first professional fiction sale.

Rod's first novel, The Six-Gun Tarot, was published by Tor Books in 2013. The sequel, The Shotgun Arcana, was published in 2014 and the third book in the Golgotha series, The Queen of Swords was published in 2017. The fourth book in the series, The Ghost Dance Suite, will be published by Falstaff Publishing in June of 2020.

His novel, Nightwise, was released in August 2015, and was reissued with additional material in January of 2018. The sequel to Nightwise, The Night Dahlia was published in April of 2018. Rod hopes to begin work on the third Nightwise book, Mother of Night, in 2021.

Rod's novel, The Brotherhood of the Wheel was published by Tor in March of 2016. It was a Locus Awards finalist for Horror in 2017 and is currently in development as a television series. The sequel to Brotherhood, The King of the Road, was released by Tor in December 2018. He will begin work on the third Brotherhood novel, The Zodiac Lodge, in early 2021.

His novel adaptation of the film, MiB International was published by Titan Books in the Summer of 2019 and he is writing an original audiobook space opera series for Audible with the first novel, The Queen's Road, released in December of 2019.

Rod has spoken at numerous schools, colleges, and universities on the subject of being a full-time working writer and the craft of writing.

He is represented by Lucienne Diver of The Knight Agency.

He lives in Roanoke, Virginia with his children, Jonathan and Emily.

ALSO BY R.S. BELCHER

Other Books by R.S. Belcher

Golgotha Series

The Six-Gun Tarot

The Shotgun Arcana

The Queen of Swords

The Ghost Dance Judgement

The Hanged Man (coming soon)

Slap Leather with the Devil (coming soon)

Nightwise Series

Nightwise

The Night Dahlia

Mother of Night (coming soon)

The Brotherhood of the Wheel Series

The Brotherhood of the Wheel

King of the Road

Lot Lizard (short story available in the Predators in Petticoats Anthology)

The Zodiac Lodge (coming soon)

The Queen's Road Series

The Queen's Road

The Queen's War (coming soon)

MIB International (movie adaptation)

FRIENDS OF FALSTAFF

Thank You to All our Falstaff Books Patrons, who get extra digital content each month! To be featured here and see what other great rewards we offer, go to www.patreon.com/falstaffbooks.

PATRONS

Dino Hicks
John Hooks
John Kilgallon
Larissa Lichty
Travis & Casey Schilling
Staci-Leigh Santore
Sheryl R. Hayes
Scott Norris
Samuel Montgomery-Blinn
Junkle

Made in the USA
Las Vegas, NV
08 April 2021